JULIA STAGG

Last Chance in the Pyrenees

First published in Great Britain in 2015 by Hodder & Stoughton
An Hachette UK company

1

Map by Sandra Oakins

A CIP catalogue record for this title is available from the British Library

Trade Paperback ISBN 978 1 444 76448 2
Ebook ISBN 978 1 444 76450 5

Typeset in Plantin Light by Hewer Text UK Ltd, Edinburgh

Printed and bound by Clays Ltd, St Ives plc

Hodder & Stoughton policy is to use papers that are natural, renewable and recyclable products and made from wood grown in sustainable forests. The logging and manufacturing processes are expected to conform to the environmental regulations of the country of origin.

Hodder & Stoughton Ltd
Carmelite House
50 Victoria Embankment
London EC4Y 0DZ

www.hodder.co.uk

Pour Christian Guibert

Un raconteur extraordinaire
et un bon ami

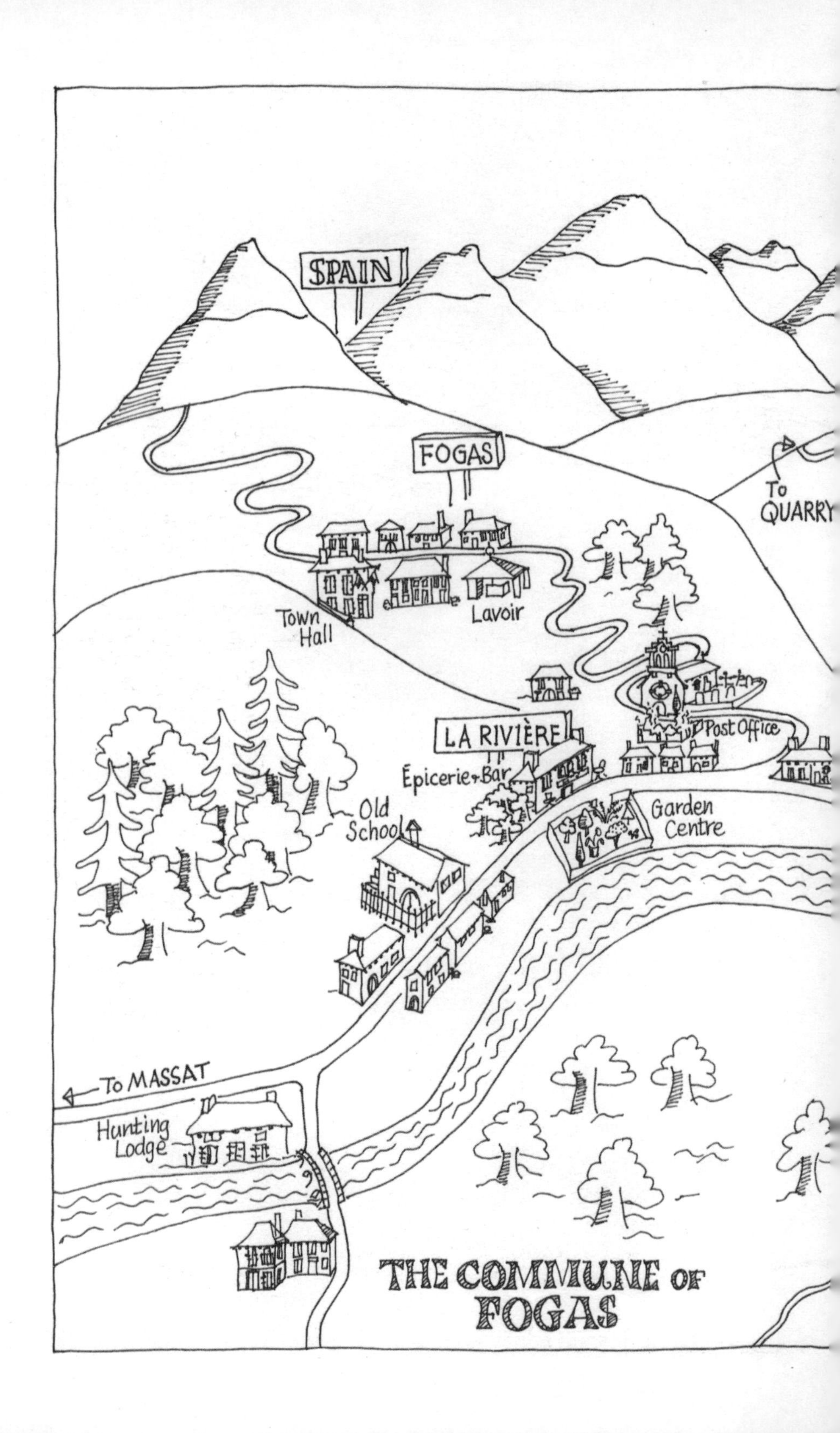
SPAIN
FOGAS
To QUARRY
Town Hall
Lavoir
LA RIVIÈRE
Post Office
Épicerie+Bar
Old School
Garden Centre
To MASSAT
Hunting Lodge
THE COMMUNE OF FOGAS

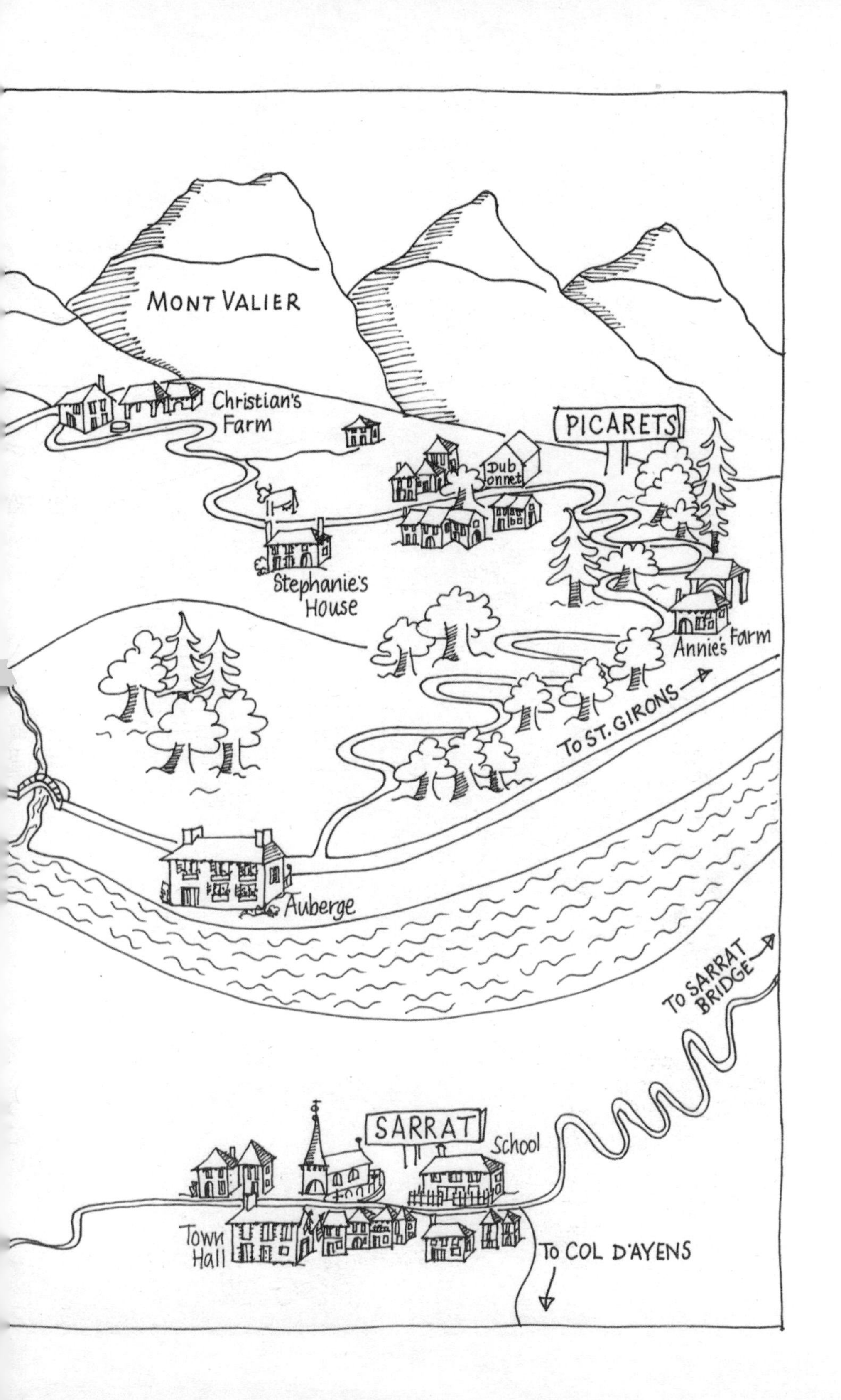

MONT VALIER
Christian's Farm
PICARETS
Dubonnet
Stephanie's House
Annie's Farm
To ST. GIRONS
Auberge
To SARRAT BRIDGE
SARRAT
School
Town Hall
To COL D'AYENS

I

Winter in the French Pyrenees can be a schizophrenic season. The furious storms that swoop down out of sullen skies to smother the peaks and valleys in thick snow, layering treacherous ice on sheltered stretches of tarmac and hanging icicle pennants on exposed rock, can give way overnight to sun-dimpled days, the heavens a broad expanse of blue cradling the brilliantly white mountains below. Serge Papon, Mayor of Fogas, loved the mercurial nature of this time of year, the switchback changes of mood as the weather vacillated, making the residents of the three small mountain villages over which he presided wary of even the brightest skies.

Today was such a day. After a few weeks, the snow, which had arrived on the sleigh of Père Noël, had departed, leaving behind a crystalline sky and a warmth that held a premature promise of spring. Even though he was well acquainted with the vagaries of the season, as he gazed out of the windows of the bar in La Rivière six days into January, Serge Papon couldn't help being filled with a sense of potential.

Life was good. His community had recently survived a direct challenge to its autonomy from the more affluent commune of Sarrat across the river. They had welcomed the first babies born in the area in a long time. Then on Christmas Eve there had been a wedding to celebrate, Serge officiating over the ceremony of Fabian and Stephanie, two young people who were fine examples of the good folk of Fogas. And, thought Serge with a roguish smile, who would help repopulate the ailing commune.

A burst of laughter took his attention across the narrow valley road to where a crowd of locals were clustered around the Christmas tree that dominated the space next to the garden centre. René Piquemal was protesting about something, the sound of the stout plumber's indignation carrying through the bar's open windows, while the others teased him good naturedly as they set about the task of dismantling the tree. Serge's eyes came to rest on the woman standing at the bottom of the ladder leaning against the fir, her right foot resting on the last rung. Véronique Estaque. His daughter. She was laughing, her face alight and cheeks dimpling, auburn hair held back in a clasp, and he could see his mother in her features – that way she had of tilting her head as though constantly analysing the world around her.

She was happy, sparkling as brightly as the tinsel in the morning sunshine. Serge felt his own lips curving in response, struck once again at how much joy he had found in knowing her, being privileged to call himself her father even if that fact had only recently been disclosed. That she had found happiness simply intensified his feelings for her.

René Piquemal made another comment, his words lost to Serge in the rumble of a tractor rolling past. But whatever he'd said caused Véronique to double up with laughter and in turn provoked a grumble of discontent from atop the ladder where a curly-haired giant of a man was gingerly balanced, clinging to the tree in an attempt to remove the star.

'Stop shaking the ladder!' he bellowed, causing Véronique to blush and everyone else to laugh even harder.

Christian Dupuy. Second deputy mayor of Fogas. Farmer. Sufferer of vertigo. And, Serge hoped, his soon-to-be son-in-law. Although judging by the fact that it had taken the farmer almost three years to ask Véronique out, Serge wasn't counting on performing the nuptials himself. In fact, he knew he wouldn't be presiding over the wedding of his daughter. Because this very day, after twenty-seven years of dutiful service, Serge Papon was resigning as mayor of Fogas.

'Sorry! But I did say you should let me go up there.' Véronique waited for Christian to come down the ladder in careful steps before rewarding his return to the safety of terra firma with a kiss. Colour flooded back into the wan cheeks of the famer whose head for heights was notoriously lacking.

'And what kind of a man would that make me? Allowing my . . .' Christian stalled, still not sure about the terminology for the new status Véronique occupied in his life. At forty-two, he was reluctant to use the juvenile-sounding 'girlfriend', 'lover' felt ridiculous and made him sweat, and 'sweetheart', 'babe' or 'woman' were liable to unleash the legendary Estaque wrath down on his head. Instead he fudged the issue. 'Allowing you to go up there in my place?'

'He's right!' interjected René from the other side of the tree where he was wrestling with a string of fairy lights. 'You women need to leave us some pride. It's bad enough that you're kicking us off career ladders without taking over the real thing as well!'

A series of groans met his outburst. It was all René had been able to talk about since opening his copy of the *Gazette Ariégeoise* over an espresso in the bar, a state of high dudgeon following the sharp shock of caffeine because the new appointment for the position of préfet for the department of Ariège, where the commune of Fogas was situated, had been announced. And it was a woman.

'Mock all you like,' he growled, his frustration at the day's news exacerbated by the fact that the Christmas lights were now tangled around him, binding him to the prickly branches of the enormous conifer. 'But I'm entitled to my opinion. This region can't be ruled by a female – it's too wild, too remote.' He cast a light-entwined hand up towards the mountains which towered in the distance, and the conjoined tree shook precariously over him, a shower of dead pine needles falling on his beret. 'How can the fragile female temperament be expected to govern that? Or the men who live here?'

'He's right,' said Stephanie Morvan, stepping across to the plumber's side from where she'd been winding up lengths of tinsel, her long, nimble fingers setting to work on the twisted cable that held René captive. 'We aren't a match for the brute strength of the men of these parts. And what would we know about hunting or fishing, which so dominate these valleys? In fact, I don't think any of us women would last a week in the wilds of this area if we didn't have men around to keep us safe . . . And rescue us from Christmas decorations.'

With a grin, she disentangled the last section of lights and held up the knotted flex in triumph to a burst of female applause, René glowering at his damsel in shining armour as he moved away from the tree.

'Don't fight it, René,' said Christian with a laugh. 'I, for one, am happy to be governed by a woman!' He glanced down at Véronique and slipped an arm around her waist, pulling her close to his side. And as Véronique Estaque, postmistress of Fogas and girlfriend/lover/sweetheart of the second deputy mayor, looked up at the large man next to her, she knew she could never be happier.

'They're taking their time getting that lot down,' said Josette Servat, surveying the commotion across the road from the doorway of the épicerie.

Annie Estaque nodded, an indulgent look in her eyes as she

saw her daughter laughing with Christian Dupuy. 'Therrre's no rrrush,' she said, her Ariégeois accent rolling across the words. 'Let them enjoy life.'

Josette turned her gaze on her friend. 'You're sounding very philosophical all of a sudden.'

'Old morrre like!'

'Not so old that you can't still waltz with the best of them . . .' Josette cast a mischievous glance towards the archway that led to the bar, beyond which the robust figure of Serge Papon could be seen sitting at a table, his focus on the group around the Christmas tree and a contented smile on his face.

It had been the talk of the commune – Annie Estaque and Serge Papon dancing on Christmas Eve. The story of the wedding waltz had twirled out of the bar in La Rivière on the valley floor, and swept up the mountains to Picarets and Fogas, the other two villages which made up the commune and which sat astride opposite ridges. Embellished, polished and retold again and again over the festive season, the tale had captivated the residents of these Pyrenean settlements who, normally in a state of perpetual discord, were united in their fascination at this possible rekindling of a romance. A romance thirty-seven years in the making, which had produced an illegitimate daughter along the way who had only found out less than a year ago the identity of her father.

It was the stuff novels were made of.

Annie snorted, knowing only too well that while little else grew in the mountains during the winter, gossip was sure to flourish. 'It was just a waltz.' But even as she said it, she gave a fond look across the épicerie at the mayor. 'He always was a good dancerrr.'

Josette raised an eyebrow and nudged her friend in the ribs. 'Seems like it's not just the youngsters who are enjoying life!'

⋆

Pastis in hand, Serge Papon was taking stock. It wasn't something he was prone to do, far more a man of action, caught up in the politics of this region which had held him enthralled for so long. But now, at the moment when he was taking a step back from it all, it seemed only apt to reflect on his tenure on the Conseil Municipal, the body that ruled the commune.

It had been eventful. Fresh out of the Tungsten mines up in Salau, he'd been fuelled by ambition in the early days, the more prestigious stages of departmental and regional governments his initial aim. But it hadn't taken long for him to be seduced by the needs of his community, to become convinced his talents were better spent here than in some modern office block on the banks of the Garonne in Toulouse, far from the mountains and the valleys that defined him.

So he'd concentrated on Fogas. Had seen off initial challenges to his position. Had cemented his place in the hearts of the locals by working diligently – and sometimes with a bit of cunning and low-level corruption – on their behalf. He'd won battles and lost some too – the Auberge des Deux Vallées at the end of La Rivière being the most recent. He smiled wryly as he watched the owners, Paul and Lorna Webster, helping to take down the decorations across the road, Lorna rocking a pram with one hand as she unhooked baubles from the tree with the other.

To think he'd tried to stop them moving in. What a mistake that would have been. For now, not only were they running a thriving business which brought tourists and valuable tax revenue into the commune, but they had increased the dangerously dwindling population with the birth of their twins in the autumn.

The skirmish two years ago surrounding their purchase of the Auberge had been a warning to him; a gentle reminder that he was getting old as he was successfully out-manoeuvred by one of his deputies. And that perhaps it was time he moved aside. But politics was never a smooth ocean and over the following twenty-four months, the small boat of Fogas which he captained had been faced with high seas, leaving him no option but to remain in command until things quietened down and he could hand over to the most suitable person; someone who had grown into the role just as Serge had felt his own abilities waning.

The problems besetting them had been two-fold. Firstly, the terrible trouble over the re-introduction of bears in the forests of Fogas, which had enraged the local population and concluded with the awful death of one of the creatures in what had been termed an accident. Had it been? Serge still wasn't convinced. A large presence of hunters in an area of the woods earmarked for agricultural burning just didn't make sense. The fact that a bear had been trapped in the resulting fire and then fell to its death . . . ?

Not surprisingly, the official report into the incident had been far from conclusive. But it had stated that two of the alleged attacks by bears on livestock in the region, which had helped fuel the unrest, had been staged. As for what purpose? The investigators had been at a loss to suggest a reason although inquiries were ongoing. So Serge, receiving the document last October during a second wave of political upheaval, and not wanting to add more fuel to the fire in the form of the inconclusive file, had taken a decisive step and kept the information to himself until the latest tempest had passed.

He took a long sip of his pastis and thought about the report that lay buried in his desk drawer up in the town hall in Fogas. It was time he shared it with his fellow councillors, now that they had reached a relatively peaceful period. He'd pass it on to Christian tomorrow, along with a copy of his resignation letter.

Which brought him to the most recent bout of rabble-rousing that had almost been the end of Fogas. Even thinking about it caused a burning sensation in Serge's chest akin to indigestion. He took another swig of pastis to ease the discomfort, and mulled over the turbulent summer before.

It had started with a letter. Sent from the mayor of Sarrat, the commune basking in the sunshine across the river, long winter shadows draped across the gentle slopes of its pastureland. No one looking at the pastoral picture this January morning could conceive of the chaos that had come out of it. A turmoil precipitated by greed and ambition. And a ruthless mayor who wanted to annex the much smaller, less-prosperous Fogas. But what the people of Serge's commune lacked in wealth, they made up for in passion, and after several months of acrimonious debate, the matter had been taken out of their hands when the former préfet had ruled that any talk of merging the two political districts should be shelved for a period of twelve months.

A year. That was all they had before the matter of the takeover – for that was what it would be – was raised again. But this time, there would be no last minute reprieve. It would go down to a council vote, possibly even a referendum, and the decision would be final. And if Serge and his supporters – who were against the proposal for so many reasons, not least a distrust of the man across the river orchestrating it all – were to win, they had to start preparing for battle now.

Which was why there was a letter on his desktop waiting to be delivered the following morning. Serge Papon was resigning as mayor. But he would keep his place on the council. And in doing so, the necessity of a by-election would be avoided, the councillors simply proceeding to vote in the new mayor at the next meeting of the Conseil Municipal. Having calculated his move with the precision of an old campaigner, Serge knew the person to take his place would have plenty of time to get his ammunition sorted before the issue of the merger raised its head again. More importantly, he also knew that in the current climate, Pascal Souquet, first deputy mayor, social climber and advocate of the amalgamation, would struggle to win a mayoral vote. Which should, if Serge was gambling correctly, leave the route clear for his preferred choice of successor – Christian Dupuy.

The man had shown over the last two years that he had the necessary accomplishments to make an excellent mayor. Loyal, passionate, genuinely interested in the lives of those around him, he was led by his moral convictions, which had proven infallible throughout the troubles that had befallen the commune in recent years. To Serge's relief, he had also revealed the cunning streak essential for any politician to survive in this region. Although it was a long way from the innate guile of the present incumbent, it would suffice.

Serge Papon took a final drink of pastis and decided he would walk across the road and tell Christian his news. It was the Epiphany. A time for kings. It was only fitting, therefore, that he was handing over his crown on this auspicious day.

He stood, glass in hand, reached to the back of his chair for his jacket and felt a sharp pain shoot down his left arm. Then he saw the glass fall, a chair tip over and the sound of a scream. When he looked around, he could see the sturdy shape of someone on the floor.

'Josette!' he shouted through to the épicerie. 'Josette, call an ambulance!'

But Josette was already hurrying towards him. And she was screaming.

2

It cut through the winter sunshine like a jagged knife through silk, tearing at the fabric of the day, renting holes in the perfection of the morning that could never be repaired. A scream. Primeval. Urgent. Impossible to ignore.

'What the hell—?' Christian spun round to face the bar where the wailing had been joined by a cry for help.

'Chrrristian! Vérrronique! Come quickly!' Annie's grey features were at the window.

They all ran.

'He's not breathing!'

'I've called an ambulance.'

'Loosen his collar.'

'Get those tables and chairs out of the way—'

Panic, thick and dark, bringing the chill of fear despite the fire blazing in the hearth. All of it focused on the crumpled figure lying across the floorboards.

Véronique fell to her knees, tugging at the paisley tie, her fingers numbly undoing the top two buttons of the crisply ironed shirt, feeling for a pulse. Beside her, Christian, kneeling, his large frame bent over, broad hands splayed across the prone chest. Pumping. Willing life to continue.

'Hail Mary, full of grace, blessed art thou . . .'

A soft murmur of prayer floated over the bodies clustered around them, providing rhythm as the farmer's arms flexed and extended, flexed and extended. Véronique tried to join in with the familiar words, one hand clutching the cross that lay in the hollow of her throat, the other stroking that proud forehead. But her tongue was tied, twisted into a desperate supplication.

'Don't leave me. Please don't leave me,' she whispered.

In the distance, the shrill sound of a siren echoed faintly down the valley.

Jacques Servat was ripped awake by the commotion. Torn from his mid-morning snooze in the inglenook that dominated one wall of the bar, his dreams of boyhood hikes across mountain meadows scattered on the screech of furniture being hastily moved, the mutterings of prayers and the wail of an approaching ambulance. He peered blearily at the cluster of stout figures pressing in on him, backs towards him, focus on something on the ground. Or someone. For Jacques could see a shoe, leather polished, sole worn, a strip of sock above it, and then his view was blocked by the anxious onlookers. Who was it?

He stood, joints creaking, and craned to see what held them all transfixed. Twisting to one side, through a mass of people he caught a glimpse of Christian, on his knees, his thick arms pumping up and down. And Véronique kneeling opposite him, the fresh track of tears on her cheeks, her face so close to the figure on the floor that she was shielding his identity from Jacques.

The siren blared ever closer and then stopped, a staccato of doors slammed and heavy feet hastened across the terrace.

'Move aside, let them in!'

More bustle, people shuffling to make way for the doctor and three volunteer firemen from the station up the valley and Jacques was pushed even further back.

*

Annie Estaque knew. From the colour of the skin to the blue tint on the lips. From the look in Christian's eyes as he yielded his place to one of the *pompiers*. From the shake of head the doctor gave as he reached for the defibrillator.

But more than that, she knew from the black despair that was welling up inside her, suffocating, sucking the oxygen out of the room and leaving her faint. She felt Josette's hand grip her and when she heard her daughter scream, Annie knew that she was right.

'No!' Véronique's cry filled the bar as she flung herself across the exposed chest, wires trailing from the equipment that had failed to work its usual miracle.

'I'm sorry . . .' The doctor, head bowed, hands gesturing futilely. 'There's nothing more—'

'No—' A sob tore at her throat and Christian bent down to fold her body into his, her cries discordant and anguished, shredding the stunned silence.

'Let me through! Let me through to her!'

Jacques Servat turned at the voice, his old friend Serge Papon bellowing from the back of the crowd, trying to force his way through to his distraught daughter.

'Let me through, I said!'

Serge pulled at the arm of Bernard Mirouze, the rotund *cantonnier* blocking his way. But Bernard didn't move. Didn't even acknowledge him. Just stood there, beret in hand, fat tears spilling onto chubby cheeks, his back hunched in pain at Véronique's distress.

'Christian,' Serge shouted, trying to call over the heads of the people in front of him. 'Christian, is she okay?'

The farmer didn't hear, kneeling beside Véronique, his arms cradling her to him, his broad shoulders shaking.

It was chaos. And Serge was more than a bit confused by it all. One moment he'd been putting on his jacket and the next, some poor sod had collapsed and triggered a meltdown. Josette and Annie had come racing through from the shop and before he could do anything to help the man on the floor, everyone from across the road had arrived, shouting, panicking. He'd been pushed to the back of the bar, up against the fireplace, and had struggled to see over those in front of him.

But when Véronique had started crying, it had torn his heart. He had to get to her.

'Bernard, René. Move. Let me through.'

As though in response, the crowd parted and Serge Papon was afforded his first proper glance into the heart of the maelstrom. Christian and Véronique, entwined, crying. Annie Estaque standing behind them, a hand on her daughter's head, face warped with grief as her old friend Josette supported her, tissue at her eyes. And radiating out from the splayed form on the floorboards, the people of Fogas, sombre, sobbing, shocked.

Who on earth was it?

Serge craned forwards to see the body. He let his eyes travel upwards, from the sharp-creased trousers to the jacket, open, the shirt, undone. Arms carelessly flung to the side. The tie – that tie! – loosened and draped around the neck in the manner of a lothario after a late night. He recognised it. Had worked his arthritic fingers hard tying it some hours ago. And above it, the chin, the fleshy jaw. He'd shaved them that morning.

'I don't understand,' he muttered, looking down at the dead man who had thrown Fogas into mourning. A man he knew better than anyone.

'Welcome to my world, Serge.'

He turned. Jacques Servat was standing next to him. His childhood friend. Husband of Josette. Jacques, who had been dead for more than two years.

3

Twenty-four hours later, the residents of Fogas were greeting the first day in this new era with sadness. And profound shock. That the robust figure of Serge Papon would no longer feature in their lives was something many of them couldn't contemplate. For the group gathered in the bar that morning, it was the only topic of their subdued conversation.

'The doctor reckons he was dead before he hit the floor.' René shook his head in disbelief. 'Cardiac arrest, he said. Gone. Just like that.' He snapped his fingers and stared at the spot where the mayor of Fogas had collapsed.

'It must have been the stress,' commented the man next to him. A councillor, like René, Alain Rougé was well acquainted with the political turbulence that had rocked the commune for the last year and a half, the mayor caught up in all of it.

'How's Véronique holding up?' Josette asked as she passed a coffee to Christian Dupuy, who was sitting on the other side of René.

Christian shrugged and wiped a hand across his weary features, as though he could erase the events of the day before. 'Not good. I stayed with her last night but she didn't sleep. She's not eating either . . .'

Josette pursed her lips, knowing the postmistress and her love of food. A lack of appetite in Véronique Estaque was unheard of. And alarming.

'It's hardly surprising,' said Stephanie Morvan, gathering up her things and preparing to cross the road to open her garden centre. 'She only discovered her connection to Serge last year and now . . .' She grimaced. 'She must be heartbroken.'

'She's not the only one. Annie won't answer my calls. How did she seem when you popped in, Fabian?' Josette cast a worried glance at her nephew, who was leaning on the far end of the bar.

'Old. Confused. She's really not taking it well. I brought Chloé with me,' Fabian said, referring to Stephanie's eleven-year-old daughter and his newly acquired step-daughter who was a favourite of Annie Estaque's. 'But even that didn't seem to cheer her. I think we're going to have to keep an eye on her.'

'I'll drive up there later,' said Josette. 'Take some of that new coffee we've just had delivered. Anyone willing to act as my co-driver?'

Over a year on from first getting behind the wheel, and despite hours spent driving the roads and valleys of the Couserans region in the company of Véronique, Josette had yet to get her licence. Anyone who'd had the dubious pleasure of accompanying this learner driver knew why. Slower than a tortoise in winter and unwilling to accept that gears three to six served any purpose, she was far from a natural. It was little wonder then that when she made her request, backs turned, eyes averted and there was a palpable sense of relief when the door opened and claimed her attention.

'Bonjour, Bernard,' said Josette.

The shambling form of the *cantonnier* entered, head hanging low, eyes red-rimmed, his vibrant orange hunting beret replaced with one in black. As if in sympathy, his normally exuberant beagle trailed after him, ears drooping, face forlorn, a black collar encircling his neck.

'Bonjour. Coffee please, Josette.'

'And a croissant?'

'No thanks. I'm not able to eat.'

His reply was met with surprised expressions. But in a mark of appreciation for the man's pain, René Piquemal bit back the glib retort that came to his lips. For everyone knew that Bernard Mirouze had idolised the mayor of Fogas, who had offered him the job of *cantonnier* when no one else would employ him. Given Bernard's frequent mishaps with the snowplough and his general incompetence in the position of caretaker for the commune, it was widely believed that Serge's initial benevolence and continued tolerance of the hapless Bernard could only be the result of a distant family connection between the two men on Serge's wife's side. Whatever the reason, the grateful *cantonnier* had focused all his devotion on the charismatic mayor. And given that Bernard was in his mid-forties and unmarried, he had a lot of devotion at his disposal. Granted, some of that affection had been transferred onto the beagle he had acquired two years ago but even then, in naming the dog after the man he adored, he'd merely consolidated the two great loves of his life.

Stephanie put an arm around the chubby *cantonnier* as he lowered himself onto a stool.

'How are you?' she asked.

He shook his head, fresh tears welling up in his eyes. 'I just can't believe it. Even Serge is affected.' He flicked a hand at the dog flopped on the floor in the very spot where his namesake had last lain. Head on paws, eyes sorrowful, the hound cast a further pall on the already sombre gathering.

'I've got a *galette des rois* for you, Bernard,' said Josette, trying to lighten the mood. 'Perhaps this time you'll get lucky!'

She placed a cake decorated with a paper crown on the counter and offered him a knife, but the *cantonnier* shook his head.

'I'm not in the mood.'

Which was when those gathered knew that Bernard Mirouze was upset indeed. Because for the last week, ever since the cakes which marked the Epiphany had gone on sale, the *cantonnier* had driven the populace of Fogas demented. Having discovered that this year the collectable porcelain figurines traditionally hidden in the *galette des rois* were shaped like miniature dogs, he'd been determined to find a replica beagle. So far he'd eaten a cake a day and although he'd accumulated a fine array of canines ranging from German shepherds to poodles, a tiny Serge had eluded him. Consequently, he'd taken to pestering everyone he knew to keep an eye out for the elusive *fève*. Yet even the prospect of finding such a treasure in the cake in front of him couldn't alleviate his present despair.

'Perhaps leave it until later, then?' said Josette, placing the *galette* in a box and pushing it across the counter to the dejected man.

'There's something we can't leave until later,' said René, straightening up and addressing Christian Dupuy solemnly. 'We need to talk about what happens next. On the council.'

'This is hardly the time for politics—'

René brushed aside Stephanie's interjection with a wave of his hand. 'It's always the time for politics. And Serge of all people would agree with me.' He pointed a finger in the direction of Fogas, which was situated up the mountain that towered over the bar. 'While we're down here moping, that conniving bastard Pascal Souquet will be up there in the town hall measuring for a new desk.'

'Give him some credit,' muttered Christian, defending his fellow deputy mayor. 'Even he wouldn't be so crass.'

'Pah!' René's moustache quivered with disbelief. 'How can you be so naive? He's already acting mayor thanks to Serge's death. You really think he won't be scheming how to turn that into a permanent position? Which means we need to start thinking right now about who we put forward for the by-election—'

'By-election?' asked Stephanie. 'Can't the council choose a new mayor without going through all that?'

'Not if we don't have a full complement of councillors. We have to fill Serge's place before we can proceed and we won't get long to do it. Which is why we need to get organised, because if we don't win that seat, we could well be attending the inauguration of that weasel Pascal as our next leader. I, for one, don't want that.'

'Neither do I!' snapped Christian, slamming his empty cup onto the counter. 'But at the moment, I'm more concerned about taking care of Véronique and Annie, and preparing a suitable send-off for a man I admired, than the machinations of local government.'

He threw a handful of coins on the bar. 'Thanks for the coffee, Josette. I'll let you know when we get the details of the funeral sorted.'

With a sullen nod at the room, he took a step towards the door just as it was thrust open by the sturdy arm of Agnès Rogalle, driver of the butcher's van that visited the area once a week.

'Christian Dupuy! I want a word with you.' She advanced into the room, hands on her ample hips, face puce, bosom shaking with anger, and the farmer found himself confronted by the indignant woman, a strong smell of raw meat assailing his nostrils from the smeared apron tied around her waist.

'That thieving bastard has stolen another rabbit!' she said, poking him in the chest with a sausage-like finger. 'Yesterday, while I was parked up in Fogas serving customers. I didn't report it straight away, out of respect for Serge Papon . . . may he rest in peace.' She broke off and flapped a podgy hand through the four points of a cross before accosting Christian once more. 'But I'm here now to register my complaint. Nine months this has been going on. Sausages, rabbits, a couple of steaks – all of it stolen off my van. I've complained to your council. I've called in the police. I even changed my visits here to Thursdays instead of Tuesdays, hoping to shake the felon off. And none of it has done any good. So I'm telling you this. Either you and the equally useless councillors who sit with you on the Conseil Municipal catch this bugger within a month, or I will stop calling in at Fogas. Let's see how your voters like being without their mobile butcher when it comes to the next elections!'

She let her glare encompass the room and then fall on the dejected dog.

'What's up with him?' she barked, striding across to lay a solid hand on his head, the beagle snuffling appreciatively at the gamey odour that made Agnès less welcome in human circles.

'He's depressed,' mumbled Bernard, as the dog made a half-hearted effort to expose his stomach for a rub. 'About Serge dying . . .'

Agnès nodded, gave the hound one last pat on his belly and headed for the bar.

'Here,' she said gruffly, reaching into a pocket before thrusting a fist in the direction of the *cantonnier*. 'I heard you were looking for this.'

Bernard held out his hand and felt something drop into it.

'As for you,' said Agnès, glowering at Christian once more. 'You've been warned. Catch the Butcher Burglar or there will be no more meat for Fogas!'

She strode across the floor, boards bouncing under her solid step, and was out of the door before anyone reacted.

'That wasn't fair . . .' protested Christian, rubbing his torso where the imprint of that firm digit remained.

'Fair?' René gave a dry laugh, his fingers playing impatiently with a packet of Gauloises. 'It's politics, Christian. And like I said, it doesn't stop just because we go into mourning. So I suggest we get our heads together and soon or it won't be just Agnès and her butcher's van that passes us by. It will be the next election too.'

'Okay!' Christian waved a hand in resignation. 'Let's meet tomorrow evening. Right now, I'm going to check on Véronique.'

'Hang on, Christian!' Josette was holding out the phone to him. 'It's Céline up at the town hall. She says she tried your mobile but it's turned off. As always!'

Christian gave a sheepish grin at the admonishment and took the phone.

'Bonjour, Céline—'

A tirade of squeaks could be heard issuing from the receiver, the town hall secretary clearly irate about something. The farmer listened intently, face grave.

'Right. I'll be straight up. Don't do anything rash!'

He hung up and ran a hand through his curls.

'Well?' René was watching him over the rim of his cup.

'You were right. When Céline got to work, Pascal was already there. She found him in Serge's office, sitting at the desk as though he was the incumbent. When she challenged him, he reminded her that, as interim mayor, it was his prerogative. And then made a veiled threat about her position.'

René slammed a fist down on the bar, startling the others and making the beagle bark. 'The bastard!' he fumed. 'I told you—'

The farmer raised a large hand, forestalling any further contribution. 'That's not all. Pascal was holding an envelope addressed to her. He'd opened it and was reading the contents.'

'And?'

'It was a resignation letter. Serge was resigning. Effective immediately.'

The news settled silently into the room, adding a poignancy to their already great loss. Then René jumped from his stool.

'We need to get up there,' he said. 'I don't trust Pascal one bit.'

'I agree,' said Christian, heading for the door once more. 'Although it's not Pascal I don't trust. It's Céline. Knowing her longstanding antipathy for him, I don't trust her not to kill him!'

Accompanied by Stephanie and Alain, the two men left, and as the door closed behind them, Josette and Fabian went through to the épicerie, leaving Bernard alone at the bar. They'd all forgotten about Agnès and her gift. The *cantonnier* hadn't. Bernard's hand was still clenched tightly around something small and hard.

Tucking his arm into his chest, he slowly opened his fist, and there, lying cute against the swell of his palm, was a tiny porcelain beagle. In a spasm of awareness, his fingers closed back over his prize and he felt the thud of his heart galloping within his chest. To a wounded soul, raw and vulnerable, Agnès Rogalle's twin acts of kindness were almost too much to bear. And in the months to come, Bernard Mirouze would never know whether his feelings originated from her concern for his downhearted dog, or the figurine dropped into his hand. The end result, however, was the same. In a fertile soil devoid of focus, the shoots of love had started to grow.

For the first time in twenty-four hours, the tears that trickled silently down Bernard's cheeks weren't generated by sorrow.

*

Véronique Estaque was alone in her flat on the first floor of the converted old school. Sitting in an armchair, knees tucked under her chin, she was staring out of the high arch of windows at the village of La Rivière. Down below, Agnès Rogalle was striding away from the bar; a cyclist was making his way painfully along the road, following the river up to the village of Massat; and from the church at the back of the épicerie came the toll of bells sounding the hour. Rising out of it all, the sharp sides of the valley which culminated in the white-capped mountains that ranged above them, a blue sky spanning their peaks. It was idyllic. A view to soothe even the most troubled soul.

She was oblivious to it all. Instead her gaze was concentrated on the Christmas tree, neglected strands of tinsel dangling forlornly from its branches, a string of lights left trailing on the ground. No one had had the enthusiasm to return to the task which had been so brutally interrupted the day before. So now the tree stood there ragged and abandoned, the best part of it stripped away. Véronique knew exactly how that felt.

Ten months. That was all she'd been given. After thirty-six years of not knowing, she'd been granted the briefest of intervals with her father – barely enough time to get used to saying 'Papa'. But time enough to make her affection for him grow, and the pain at his sudden passing seem unbearable.

She'd have laughed a year ago if anyone had told her that she'd be so affected by the death of Serge Papon. Back then, he was just the mayor. Roguish. Not always trustworthy. A figure of authority from her childhood, and sometimes one of political opposition in her adult life. Then Maman had made her revelations last spring and slowly, surely, Véronique had begun to see the man in another light. A strong bond had formed between the pair of them – Serge, newly widowed, clearly delighting in his sudden conversion to fatherhood, while her initial caution mellowed into love. Now that had been ripped from her and she was left with an aching heart and a regret for all the things that would never be said.

Her father was dead. And she didn't even have a photograph of him.

The phone rang but she didn't move. Just hugged her knees tighter and tried to stem the anger that was rising in her chest. But it was difficult. Because no matter how Véronique viewed the situation, she couldn't help thinking it was the political shenanigans which had plagued Fogas over the previous eighteen months that had killed Serge Papon, robbing her of any future with her father. And her mother, by withholding his identity for so long, had deprived her of any past.

Véronique Estaque wasn't sure that she would be able to forgive either culprit.

'Can I come out now?'

The tone was both imperious and irritated, because Serge Papon was a vexed ghost. Deciding not to wait for the all-clear, he eased himself out from his cramped quarters and flexed his tired knees, his shoulders and back protesting as he straightened up.

All morning he'd been bent double, squashed into the recess under the hinged flap on the bar that butted up to the wall. With the coffee machine situated on the flap, the access was never used and provided an ideal hiding place. But after spending several hours there with Bernard's fat feet dangling precariously close to his head and the coffee machine spluttering and gurgling above him, he'd had enough.

'What are you doing?' hissed Jacques Servat from the fireplace where he'd passed the morning pretending to snooze but with half an ear on proceedings and the odd glance at his new companion who was known not to take orders too well. 'She could come back in at any minute!'

Serge grunted. 'I don't care. And anyway, how do we know she'll be able to see me?'

'Because she can see me,' retaliated Jacques. 'So logic dictates—'

'Logic?' Serge's eyebrows shot up. 'You're talking of logic and here we are, both dead, yet both in the bar having a conversation. Logic has nothing to do with this.'

And it didn't. Serge Papon's new existence defied everything he'd ever learnt, either through science or religion. Seemingly, although he'd died, his consciousness hadn't, and as a result, he was capable of arguing with his old friend without Bernard Mirouze being aware of a thing. Despite sitting right next to them.

It was going to take some getting used to.

At first, he'd thought he was dreaming when he saw the shock of white hair and the scrawny frame of Jacques Servat beside him. It was hard to say who'd had the biggest surprise, both of them staring at the other in disbelief. Then Jacques had explained the situation and, in the hours that followed, Serge had tried to come to terms with what he'd been told. He'd watched numbly as his corporeal frame was taken away by the undertakers and the bar – which had become the focal point for the villagers in the aftermath of the tragedy – emptied, leaving only a few regulars behind. Which is when Jacques had made him take cover. To protect Josette, he'd said. Stop her having a coronary when she realised that she now had two ghosts to contend with.

Serge hadn't believed him. Couldn't conceive that all this time Josette had been living with a ghost in her hearth and had never said a word. But when the customers had left and

Josette started closing up for the night, Serge had seen it for himself. With the door locked and the shutters pulled to, she'd come over to the fireplace and started talking to her dead husband. Jacques hadn't been able to reply, of course – his voice inaudible to Josette. But they'd communicated with gestures and facial expressions, conversing with such ease that Serge, cooped up in his hiding place with the cold draught from under the cellar door chilling his back, had wished Josette would hurry off to bed so he could get closer to the fire.

Which was what he intended to do now. He stretched, joints creaking and popping, and Jacques winced.

'So run it past me again,' Serge said, sitting in the opposite side of the inglenook to Jacques. 'Who else can see you?'

'Chloé Morvan.' Jacques' face lit up at the mention of the young girl who was the closest thing he had to a grandchild. 'It must be something to do with her being half-gypsy on her mother's side.'

'And she hasn't told anyone?'

'Not a soul!'

Serge shook his head. It was impossible to comprehend. 'But not Stephanie? If Chloé can see you, why can't her mother?'

Jacques shrugged. 'Who knows? Although I think Stephanie suspects something now and then. Almost as though she can see me out of the corner of her eye.'

'And you can't go beyond these two rooms?' Serge nodded towards the épicerie in the background, visible through the arch that connected it to the bar. 'That's it?'

'It's enough,' said Jacques.

'Well it might be for you,' muttered Serge, already feeling trapped by the limitations of his new life. Or death. Whatever it was. 'Some of us are used to having a bit more power!'

'You're about to have even less,' muttered Jacques in response. 'Josette's coming. Get back under there!'

And with a firm hand on his back, Serge was propelled towards the counter to resume his position next to Bernard's feet. It was not, he fumed as he shuffled to get comfortable, befitting to someone of his stature. And he didn't know how long he would endure it, the frailty of Josette's heart notwithstanding.

Serge Papon wasn't the only one contemplating the weakness of that vital organ. As Annie Estaque reached the top of the mountain ridge that looked down over her farm, breath coming in short gasps, pains in her chest, she knew she'd overdone it. Less than a year on from her 'episode', as she liked to call the heart attack that had felled her last spring, she was feeling the effects of climbing the hillside. And of the last twenty-four hours.

Dead. That vibrant life force which had dominated the community for so long, gone. She'd known the minute she saw him lying there, his face in repose, arms cast out. Christian had insisted on trying to resuscitate him but Serge Papon had always been a stubborn bugger. Why would his heart be any different? If it had chosen to stop working, there wasn't anything they could do to change that.

She sat on a rock and took deep breaths, waiting for her pulse to drop to more normal levels, her two Pyrenean mountain dogs flopped next to her, their bodies warm and heavy against her legs. Above her the sky stretched cloudless, the sun yielding a heat akin to late spring, and in the distance she could just make out the cluster of buildings that formed the village of Picarets.

What now? Politically, the three villages that formed the commune of Fogas had been cast adrift by the sudden death of their redoubtable leader. And in the vacuum Serge's loss left behind, the issue of the merger with Sarrat was sure to raise its head once more. Perhaps this time it might meet with success.

Politics! Here she was, thinking about politics. That was the effect he had on you. He took hold of you, pulled you into his world and made everything vibrate with energy. When you were with him, you felt the intensity of his focus, overwhelming, discomposing. Then when it switched away from you, the loneliness, the loss. She hadn't stood a chance when he'd turned his attentions on her that day, up on a plateau above Picarets. A surprise encounter, a beautiful sunset and a man who had the ability to make you feel special. Loved even.

The result? Véronique. And thirty-six years of lying, depriving Annie's daughter of a father and Serge of his child in order to save the marriage of an innocent woman who couldn't have children.

Some might say it had been a noble sacrifice, others that it was pure selfishness. Annie didn't know what it was. It had been, in her view, the only option back then. Better than the alternative the wronged-wife, Thérèse Papon, had urged on her, which would have seen Véronique never born. So Annie had weathered the snide remarks and the gossip that came with being a single mother in a rural community. Had kept her head down and raised her child in the best way she knew how. But if she could do it all again . . . ?

Annie rested a hand on the solid head of one of her dogs, the animal pushing against the comfort of her palm. She'd made mistakes. Many of them. Falling for Serge Papon in the first place. Agreeing to keep a secret that should never have been. Now she was reaping the consequences. Because it turned out the biggest danger to her heart wasn't the physical weakness she'd discovered the year before. It was the loss of the only man she'd ever loved, and the potential loss of her daughter.

Véronique was refusing to answer her calls. She didn't want her mother anywhere near her. And Annie didn't blame her.

She tipped her head back, letting the sun pour over her face in a vain attempt to stop the tears in her eyes from spilling over.

He'd almost been caught. The thought brought a sheen of sweat to his brow that had nothing to do with the warm temperatures outside. A second earlier and she'd have seen it – the evidence in his hands.

In the village of Fogas, across the valley from the rock where Annie Estaque was sitting, interim mayor Pascal Souquet quickened his pace, heading down the hill from the town hall to the sanctuary of his home. He'd awoken that morning filled with a sense of well-being, an optimism that had been lacking from his life of late. For unlike the majority of the local population, Pascal saw only opportunity in the wake of Serge Papon's death. The permanent position of mayor was up for grabs and he was determined it would be his.

Knowing it was important to be seen as the steady hand on the tiller in this time of turmoil, Pascal had got to the town hall earlier than usual, before the secretary Céline Laffont had even arrived. He'd let himself in and headed up the stairs to the reception area where, as first deputy and only a part-time presence, he suffered the indignity of sharing a desk with Christian Dupuy. And while it could be said, thanks to Christian rarely spending time in the town hall, that Pascal had full possession of the lump of unappealing stainless steel squeezed into the corner by the photocopier like an afterthought, it was a constant annoyance to him that the other occupant of the office space, Céline Laffont, habitually used the flat surface as a dumping ground. Unwanted photocopies. Tubes of toner. Packs of paper. She'd even installed a recycling box on it. As if he and his workspace were of no account.

This morning had proved no exception. Several stacks of envelopes and letters were strewn across the grey metal, submerging the computer keyboard – a mailshot which, judging by the half-drunk lipstick-stained cup of coffee next to it, had been abandoned abruptly. And Pascal had found himself looking forward to the day when he would take his rightful place in the now vacant office next door. Which would also be the time when he could give the insolent Céline her marching orders.

Then it had dawned on him. He was acting mayor. He had every right to be in there. With confident strides, he'd crossed the room and opened the door to the mayor's office.

It was vast, allocated to the first elected mayor of the commune of Fogas just after the Revolution when the mountain villages of Picarets, La Rivière and Fogas, inspired by the ferment sweeping the land, had decided they too wanted self-rule. Tired of their demands being drowned out by the louder, more numerous inhabitants of the pastureland opposite, the three villages had broken away from the mighty commune of Sarrat and formed their own political district. And as if to compensate for decades of being deemed insignificant, they'd built a grandiose town hall high up on the ridge in Fogas so their former neighbours could no longer look down upon them. The room Pascal was standing in was the pinnacle of their achievements.

The interim mayor crossed the bare floorboards to the massive desk in front of the window and sat down, surveying the space with a critical eye. Rugs. He'd order in some Persian rugs to cover the scratches and dents in the old boards. And he'd decorate the dour panelled walls with modern art, purchased through his contacts in Paris. The hideous map of the commune, faded and torn, would have to go. So would that stupid aerial photograph Serge had persuaded the council to buy simply because it showed all three villages at once, something which the geography of the region normally made impossible. As for the desk . . .

He pushed himself back in the chair and regarded the solid mass of wood with distaste. Not a barley twist in sight. Not a hint of an ormolu mounting. It sat, broad and stout, the surface nicked and scratched in the process of governance; and while it was no doubt a fine example of the woodworking talents of some local peasant in the nineteenth century, it was not the work of a craftsman. It too would be making its way to the tip. And Pascal already knew what would be taking its place.

He'd seen it in a small antique shop in Courchevel a couple of weeks ago during the Souquets' traditional Christmas sojourn to a ski resort. Dating from the 1850s, it had a black hide writing surface and gilt edges, barley twist detailing down the side pedestals and, most impressive of all, a floor-length vanity panel on the front complete with ormolu florets. Greeted by the desk's grandeur, people walking through the door would know they were dealing with a man of influence, a person of rank. As opposed to someone prepared to while away his days sitting behind a woodworm-infested block of ugliness.

In his former life, when the boulevards of Paris had been his playground, Pascal Souquet would have bought the antique the moment he saw it. But since falling victim to a pyramid scheme, which had collapsed just after he'd entered it at the height of the financial boom, things had been different. He'd lost everything. The house. Their life savings. His job, too, thanks to stress. Now he was the poor relation – the

Souquets' home in Fogas inherited from his wife's mother, the majority of their income from his wife's wages, and rare indulgences like skiing trips only possible because they stayed in a luxurious chalet owned by his wife's wealthy brother-in-law. When it came to shopping for antiques, Pascal was reduced to looking longingly through the window.

But that was about to change. Soon he would be elected mayor and from there, the national stage beckoned. It wouldn't be long before he was moving upwards, taking steps to the Conseil Général in the departmental capital of Foix and then on to the regional government up in Toulouse. And with that heady rise back to where he belonged, his financial situation would revert to what it should be.

It was a goal that made his exile amongst the yokels of Fogas just about bearable. In the meantime, like the Persian rugs and the modern art, the desk he'd seen in exclusive Courchevel could be bought on expenses. Fogas and its inhabitants could foot the bill.

Pascal reached into his pocket and pulled out a scrap of paper. The dimensions for his new desk. Eager to get started on what was promising to be a bright future, he'd begun rummaging for a tape measure in the drawers next to him. Which was how he'd found it. In the bottom drawer, wedged down below the files hanging neatly from metal railings. He wouldn't have seen it but for the fact that he noticed the files at the front were higher than those at the back. Curious, he'd parted them and seen the dull green folder lying beneath.

He'd lifted it out. Opened it. And knew that he had just saved his own career. Possibly even sidestepped a stint in prison. He'd been staring aghast at the flimsy pages when he'd heard a creak of floorboards on the other side of the open door. Acting on instinct, he'd shoved the papers down the back of his trousers, dropped the folder back into its hiding place, kicked the drawer shut and spun towards the desk. Flustered, he'd picked up the first thing he'd seen. An envelope, addressed to Céline. Without thinking, he'd flicked a finger underneath the flap, pulled out a letter, and by the time the footsteps had crossed the threshold into his room, he was apparently engrossed.

'What are you doing in here?' Céline had spat at him. 'And what's that?'

Sweat on his brow, he'd resorted to authority, reminding the impudent secretary of his new status. And of the vulnerability of her position. She'd reacted by snatching the letter out of his hands and telling him the day he was made mayor he'd have her resignation. She'd embellished her statement with her colourful opinions on his abilities as a community leader but he'd withstood her onslaught and her accusations of snooping with a forced calm, aware all the time of the danger he was in. When she'd stormed back into reception and reached for the phone, he'd stood up and headed for home. Because he didn't want to be in the town hall when Christian Dupuy came haring up from La Rivière. He couldn't risk being caught with the papers that were scratching at his back as he walked down the hill.

Reaching his house, he opened the door, threw a quick bonjour in the direction of his wife and, without answering her startled query about his hasty return, headed for his office. There he placed the papers in the small safe he'd bought before Christmas, justifying the odd purchase to his wife by alluding to the growing number of break-ins in rural areas. He closed the door, turned the dial on the front and slumped onto a seat, staring at the grey box that now held enough to finish him forever.

When he got the chance, he'd have to burn them. Every last one of those incriminating pages. It was the only way. Because if his wife found them, Pascal Souquet could no longer guarantee she wouldn't use them against him.

The three villages that make up the commune of Fogas are tucked into the steep sides of the Pyrenees, down where France nestles up to its neighbours of Spain and Andorra. Hence, if you walk due south from the little commune, traversing the difficult terrain and the numerous peaks, you arrive surprisingly quickly in the Catalan province of Lleida. There, high up in the mountains, is a remote village, consisting of little more than a church, a bar and a clutch of houses. With the sun shining as brightly that day as it was across the Pyrenees in France, the terrace of the small bar was the perfect place for lunch.

'There you are!' Maria Dolores, the bar owner's wife, placed a heaped plate in front of the massive man who was her only customer that day. And most days at this time of year. Too secluded to benefit from the ski business that brought people flocking from Barcelona and Madrid, the village survived on a mixture of summer tourism and agriculture. It was the latter that had brought this French Adonis to their community, the big man walking down from the border one day last summer to declare himself, in his limited Spanish, available for work. His offer had been snapped up and he'd lived amongst them for six months, working hard, saying little, but impossible to ignore. Especially if you were a woman with any sense of romance left in your bones.

And Maria Dolores, despite being married for thirty years, having raised five children and being a grandmother, had plenty. So between serving beers, preparing meals and keeping the two small guest rooms clean, she spent her idle hours thinking about the Frenchman, Arnaud Petit. Maria Dolores didn't speak much French, the lip-numbing contortions required for pronunciation having put her off a long time ago at school. But she knew enough to spot the irony of the man's name. For there was nothing 'petit' about him.

Large, strong hands, capable of handling sheep with ease yet nimble enough to skip across a laptop keyboard, a stern jaw that occasionally softened into a smile, a mane of long black hair like midnight on a new moon, and those eyes! Burning with intensity, they made you feel as though you were the only other person in his universe. All that and then there was the way he moved. An economy of motion, like a panther, full of coiled energy straining to be unleashed.

Maria Dolores shivered delightfully, and with one last look to make sure he was enjoying his food – because ultimately appreciation of her cooking was how to win her heart and keep it – she left him to his meal.

Arnaud Petit, aware of the pride his hostess took in her culinary skills, was always careful to show his delight in her offerings. Luckily, he never had to feign his pleasure. And today was no exception. Talking a mouthful from the plate before him, he groaned with satisfaction. Succulent chicken covered in herbs alongside the piquant flavour of chorizo, her *Arroz con Pollo y Chorizo* was one of his favourites. He leaned forward in his chair and prepared to savour it. After all, he doubted he would ever taste it again. For tomorrow he would be leaving. Heading back across the mountains into France.

It was early. Much earlier than he had planned. But the moment he'd seen the obituary in the digital version of the *Gazette Ariégeoise* that morning, he'd known he had no option. He owed it to Serge Papon. Out of respect, he would attend the great man's funeral. Then he would wreak his revenge.

Revenge. It was perhaps his only motivator. Henri Dedieu, mayor of Sarrat, cleaned the last of the grease off the pistol in his hand and held it up to the light. Not bad, considering the condition the gun had been in when it had been unearthed last September. After sixty-six years buried in a biscuit tin in the abandoned orchard next to the épicerie in La Rivière, it had been found by accident, rusted and seized up.

How had it got there? It was a mystery the mayor might never be able to solve. Last seen in the possession of his grandfather as the Germans began their hasty retreat at the end of the war, the gun had then disappeared. The body of his grandfather, the legendary Resistance leader, had been easier to find. Shot from behind, he'd been left to die by some traitor in the melee that overtook France in the final days of occupation. The tragic loss for the Dedieu family had been made more distressing by the theft of the gun, his grandfather's favourite weapon, which he'd personalised with the engraving of a boar's head on the grip.

Henri Dedieu stroked his fingers across the image, the unofficial emblem of his family. It was good to have such a valued possession back. And all due to an extraordinary turn of events: a haphazard marriage proposal in the form of a treasure hunt, which went awry and exhumed the pistol instead. It was an omen, he was sure, leading him to believe that the equally unexpected death of Serge Papon would prove to be as fruitful. Because the passing of the old man had opened up the distinct possibility of Henri Dedieu bringing yet another lost family heirloom back into the fold.

He looked out of the window across the broad expanse of rolling pasture that dropped down to the river. On the other side, trees rose up the steep sides of the mountain, shielding the three villages of Fogas from view. But they were there. And if everything went to plan, soon they would be merged under the banner of Sarrat. For that is where they belonged. Where they had resided for centuries before the Revolution tore everything apart.

It had been another ancestor, Louis Dedieu, who'd been mayor of the much larger pre-Revolutionary Sarrat and had suffered the ignominy of seeing his neighbours across the water vote to leave his stewardship in order to establish their own domain. Now it was Henri's turn to right that particular wrong by reuniting the two communes.

He gave the gun a final wipe, running an affectionate finger the length of the barrel, and then placed it back in the gun cabinet. Things were about to be set in motion. And this time they would go to plan. Henri Dedieu was determined. Even if it meant using one heirloom to secure the other.

4

'I'm sorry, Christian, but it's the only solution. We need someone with charisma. A political background. These are mighty big shoes to fill.'

Christian grimaced. 'I understand, René. I just don't think she'll say yes.'

The plumber grunted and shook his head, toying with his packet of cigarettes in frustration. Saturday evening, with the dark of winter settled outside, the two men were seated at the table nearest the fire in the bar in La Rivière, where so much of the administration of Fogas was carried out. Over the years, the locals had become accustomed to seeing a hard core of their Conseil Municipal gathered in front of the inglenook at least one evening a week, a practice that had originated during the Second World War when the town hall wasn't always the safest place to talk. It was a custom Serge Papon had encouraged to continue, ostensibly to provide the community with easy access to their representatives but, in reality, just as fuelled by his enjoyment of pastis and the opportunity to gather valuable intelligence in what was the hub of the commune.

This time, however, the solid shape of Serge Papon was missing from the chair opposite. And it was the problem of finding someone to take his place that was consuming those present.

'Have you asked her?' Josette paused at the table long

enough to add her thoughts, a tray of dirty glasses in her hands. 'It might be what she needs. Something to take her mind off everything.'

'I haven't dared! She's taken it all so badly. And she's placing the blame for Serge's death entirely on politics.' Christian sighed. 'Even if I were brave enough to broach the subject, I can't see Véronique agreeing to stand.'

'Christ!' muttered René, tugging fiercely at his moustache, his fingers fidgety in the absence of a cigarette. 'It's not like we have a lot of time for changing her mind either. That bastard Pascal will already have a letter on the way to the préfet in Foix. The election could be as soon as the end of the month.'

'They'd give us more leeway than that, wouldn't they?'

René shrugged. 'The official timescale is two weeks but it's rarely enforced. However, I can't imagine Pascal is begging for an extension, seeing as this unexpected situation is playing into his hands. And given that the new préfet is a *woman* . . .' He threw up his hands in contempt.

'So,' said Josette, refusing to rise to the bait of René's sexism, 'whichever way you look at it, we need to get a move on and choose a candidate.'

'What about Annie?' René asked. 'Would she be able to talk Véronique round?'

Christian and Josette shared a concerned glance.

'You haven't heard?' Josette asked the plumber.

'What?'

'Véronique won't have anything to do with her. Won't answer her calls. Won't go up to the farm. It's two days since Serge Papon passed away and they haven't seen each other since they were in here looking at his dead body.'

Placing the tray on the table as though suddenly overcome by its weight, Josette took a seat.

'I'm worried about both of them. Their relationship has

always been fragile but now . . .' She pushed her glasses up her nose and shook her head. 'No, it wouldn't be fair to ask Annie to help. The last thing she needs is for Véronique to have another excuse to exclude her.'

But René wasn't about to be put off. 'Annie wouldn't be willing to stand? She used to be on the council. Perhaps now's the right moment for her to rejoin it?'

Josette gave a wry laugh. 'Not a chance. She walked away from it after all the gossip surrounding Véronique's birth and vowed she wouldn't return. Knowing Annie, I don't think she'll have changed her mind, do you?'

'But that's ancient history,' said Christian. 'Who cares about that now?'

'Hmph! Not so ancient,' retorted Josette with affront. 'And you know well enough that memories last longer than lives around here.'

'So where does that leave us?' asked René with exasperation.

'How about Stephanie?' mused Christian.

René snorted. 'With her temper? She wouldn't last a minute in one of the meetings without killing someone.'

'Well, Fabian then?'

It was Josette's turn to cast doubt. 'I'm not sure politics are his thing,' she said, lowering her voice so her nephew wouldn't hear her aspersions in the épicerie where he was serving the final customers of the day. 'He's not . . .' She chose her words carefully, trying to fairly describe the characteristics of her relative whose oddities made him both endearing and infuriating. 'He's not a people person.'

'Plus he's a Parisian,' said René with the solemnity of a mountain man who knew birthplace was enough to terminate a political career in this region before it had even started. Especially when that birthplace was the capital. No matter how charming the young man was, or how much the community had grown to love him in the two years since he came to live amongst them, the fact of the matter was, Fabian was, and always would be, a Parisian.

'So I suppose that rules Paul Webster out too?' Christian asked.

'Why? Because he's English?' Josette responded with bite. 'Isn't that racist?'

Christian shrugged helplessly. 'No more than barring Fabian because he's Parisian!'

But René was nodding his head in contemplation. 'Paul Webster,' he muttered, twisting to look out of the darkened window in the direction of the Auberge des Deux Vallées, the Englishman's hotel visible in the weak light of a streetlamp down the road. 'He's a businessman. He employs local people. And he and his wife have just helped safeguard the commune by having twins. It might be enough for people to overlook his heritage. But,' the plumber paused and turned back to face his audience, 'is he up to it?'

'How do you mean?' asked Christian.

'He's an Anglo-Saxon.'

'And?'

René gave a scornful look. 'How would he survive in the politics of this place?'

'You mean he won't be corrupt enough?' said Josette dryly.

René spread his hands and moved his shoulders in the Gallic fashion that the Auberge owner would never be able to emulate.

'Well,' said Josette, taking off her glasses and rubbing her tired eyes. 'I can't think of anyone else for the job.'

'Perhaps we're coming at this the wrong way?' Christian leaned forward with sudden zeal. 'Instead of trying to find the perfect candidate, all we have to do is find one capable of—'

'Beating the opposition!' René thumped the table, face

alight. 'You're right. We simply need someone who can garner more votes than whoever Pascal puts up for the seat. So we start with that. Who is likely to be Pascal's nominee?'

'Do we know?' asked Josette.

'No. But we can have a good guess,' said Christian. 'His power has always rested on the same base. It will have to be one of his faction, another second-home owner.'

René growled, his antipathy typical in a region that held an uneasy truce between those born and living in the locality and those who merely spent their long summer vacations in homes they had inherited. Led by Pascal Souquet, who had himself been a second-home owner before bankruptcy had forced him to settle in Fogas permanently, these infrequent visitors had little time for the grittier aspects of local politics such as schooling provision and public transport, preferring instead to focus their energies on trivialities like the annual summer fête. As such, a natural schism had developed between the two groups who shared equal voting rights but held such differing standpoints on the future of the commune. René Piquemal, however, while despairing of the deep divide, knew it was ripe for exploitation.

'That's our angle, right there,' he stated, hands rubbing together as he began to relish the idea of the forthcoming battle. 'I'm not the only one fed up with people living in Toulouse and elsewhere having such a say over how this place is run. I don't think there'll be much stomach for another absentee councillor with a non-Fogas postcode.'

Christian sat back in his chair, smiling. 'We agree then? We choose someone who appeals to the local community. A direct contrast to the likes of Geneviève Souquet and Lucien Biros. And we make that the focus of our campaign.'

The mention of the two councillors from Toulouse, staunch supporters of the interim mayor, drew a look of disdain from

René. 'It shouldn't be hard. I reckon we could nominate Sarko the bull on that platform and he'd win!'

'If only we could!' said Josette with a laugh. 'The miniature Sarko toys sell really well in the shop. And he has the right name for politics . . .'

Christian shook his head, never failing to be amazed that his temperamental Limousin bull was now an internet sensation thanks to his role in the protests that had erupted in the area the summer before. And to the local tourist initiative which beamed live images of the Pyrenees from a webcam around his thick bovine neck.

'Somehow I don't think the authorities would allow it,' he said. 'So we still need a candidate. Preferably a human one.'

'Paul,' said Josette, her eyes brightening behind her glasses. 'Paul the Englishman.'

The two men looked confused at her returning to a name they'd already rejected.

'Don't you see?' she asked with renewed energy. 'He lives here. Works here. But he isn't so local that we can be accused of being parochial for nominating him. And he may just appeal to those second-home owners who aren't completely in Pascal's thrall. He's a progressive choice. Especially if he's incorruptible.'

René tugged at his moustache again, a grin forming beneath the bristles. 'You know, Josette, I think you may be right.'

'A drink,' declared Christian, agreeing with the plumber. 'To celebrate.'

And Josette stood to fetch the bottle of pastis that hadn't been touched since Thursday.

'It's only fitting . . .' she said as she poured out generous measures, adding water to turn the liquid opaque.

'To Serge!' said René, clinking glasses with the others. 'And his successor.'

'To Serge,' the other two concurred. Then they drank up, René with relish for the liquorice apéritif, Josette and Christian with forbearance.

'Do you know who they're going to put forward?'

'Not yet . . . I mean, I haven't—'

'Find out.' High on a mountainside lit only by a sliver of moon, a long draw on a cigarette revealed eyes like shards of ice, fixing Pascal Souquet over the orange glow. The interim mayor of Fogas shivered, the plummeting temperature and the biting wind slicing through his coat only partly to blame for his sudden chill.

It was ridiculous. Meeting up here in the middle of the night in winter. Pascal had been nervous enough at the summons without the tense drive up the isolated mountain track, the headlights of his Range Rover smothered by the unrelenting dark and the wheels bouncing through ruts so deep that he feared for the car's undercarriage. But it was his co-conspirator's preferred meeting place, a forgotten forestry road which ended in a small clearing that looked out across the valley to the village of Picarets. Tonight, flickering pinpricks of light breaking up the solid mass of black on the opposite hillside were the only indication of habitation.

The piercing screech of an owl from the forest behind made Pascal start, the man next to him laughing derisively at his nerves.

'It's the endgame, Pascal. No time to be jumping at shadows.' Henri Dedieu, Mayor of Sarrat, threw his cigarette butt to the ground, the soft crunch of gravel accompanying the dousing of its feeble illumination. 'And no time for mercy.'

Pascal swallowed. He'd been collaborating with the mayor long enough to know the very real threat held behind those casual words. Already Henri Dedieu had blood on his hands in his relentless pursuit of his political goals; blood which had spattered onto Pascal and shackled him to the man, leaving him with no choice but to comply with Dedieu's schemes or risk being sent to prison. He knew this ruthless hunter wouldn't flinch if more brutality was called for. Especially now that their prize was so close.

'I don't need to tell you how important this election is.' Dedieu turned to trap Pascal in his gaze again, his eyes now no more than glimmers of white under the inadequate moon. It was still enough to leave the interim mayor shifting uncomfortably.

But for once, Pascal didn't need telling. He knew the fortuitous death of Serge Papon had given them a second chance at reuniting their two communes. For with the cornerstone of the opposition gone in Fogas, resistance to the merger with Sarrat would disappear like a cloud on a summer's day. Before any of that could happen, however, Pascal had to be elected mayor. And that was where the problem lay.

Out of the remaining ten members of the Conseil Municipal in Fogas – the people who would be responsible for choosing the next leader – Pascal could only count on the support of three. His cousin and second-home owner, Geneviève, would condescend to visit from Toulouse to provide him with her vote. Likewise living in the large metropolis to the north, Lucien Biros, a dull academic, would throw his weight behind the interim mayor, in the mistaken perception that because they shared a tenuous familial connection to Fogas, they were somehow equal. Once the new commune was formed, the man would be cast out into the wilderness and left in no doubt as to the error of his beliefs. For now, he was vital.

The person who made up the final part of Pascal's power base was the beekeeper, Philippe Galy. Brought into Pascal's fold by the bungling of the previous administration after the dreadful attack on his hives by a bear, Philippe had proven an admirable addition to the team. But the beekeeper would cease to be such a willing ally if he ever discovered the truth behind those attacks – a truth alluded to in the papers Pascal had stolen from the town hall and secreted at his home.

Four votes, then, including Pascal's own. It wasn't enough. He would need an outright majority to attain the red, white and blue sash of office. So he needed to ensure that his candidate won the by-election to grant him a fifth. And then he needed to work on the wavering Monique Sentenac to secure that vital sixth vote.

Only then could he begin to look to the future. To the promises he'd been made. With the Fogas council in hand, the merger could be brought back to the table. This time however, it wouldn't be the Préfet of Ariège suggesting such a move. It would be the leaders of the two communities, in harmony. No need for a referendum. A simple vote in the closed confines of the town hall would condemn Fogas to history.

In return for this treacherous act, Pascal would finally taste real power – deputy mayor of the new, much larger and more influential commune. And within five years, on the word of the man himself, Henri Dedieu would step aside and the mayorship would be Pascal's. After that, he would be on his way. Moving up to the Conseil Général in the departmental capital of Foix. To the Conseil Régional in Toulouse. And finally, if all went well, back to Paris where he belonged.

Time, however, was running out. Proposals to abolish the middle tier of local government were gaining support with the cost-cutting President and his circle. If pushed through, the scrapping of the Conseil Général would leave any rural mayor wishing to make it to the national stage an even bigger gap to leap. It would be almost impossible, even from the enlarged commune of Sarrat. Much better to have climbed the political ladder prior to those changes being implemented.

So Pascal Souquet was well aware of how important the forthcoming by-election would be.

'You're planning on nominating a second-home owner?' Dedieu continued.

Pascal frowned, sensing an ambush. 'Of course. I've already asked—'

A contemptuous snort cut him short.

'No one. You've asked no one. Because I'm going to tell you who your candidate is.' The mayor paused long enough to slip a cigarette between his lips, hands cupped around his face as his lighter flared, the boar's head on his signet ring seeming alive in the flames. He inhaled deeply, and on an exhalation of acrid smoke, he spoke again.

'Vincent Fauré.'

Pascal looked blank.

'That's your nominee.'

'I've . . . never heard of him.'

Another scornful laugh. 'That's because you don't really belong here. He's my nephew.'

'But he doesn't live—'

'In Fogas? No, but he's going to. In the old shepherd's cottage up on the ridge.'

'You mean Gaston's place . . . ?' Pascal's nostrils twitched at the memory of the malodourous *berger* who had dropped dead at the fête the previous autumn.

'The very same. He was Vincent's great-uncle. Vincent was his only surviving relative. And now my nephew is returning from Toulouse to make the cottage his home.'

'But why would . . . I mean, who would . . . ?' Pascal stuttered, realising the danger of offense.

'Vote for him?' Another long draw on the cigarette and an exasperated sigh. 'You really don't get it, do you, Pascal? He's a Fauré. In Fogas, that name alone is sufficient. Add in the fact that he's the great-grandson of Fauré the Resistance hero and he's coming back here to raise a family of his own, and we have a winner. And if that isn't enough, he's a lawyer.' A dry laugh followed. 'The ill-educated peasants of Fogas will be queuing up to elect him onto the council.'

With a swift turn of the head, Henri Dedieu had Pascal caught in his fierce regard once more.

'That slow-witted farmer, Dupuy, and his faction will be expecting you to name a second-home owner. An outsider. And in doing so, you'll give them all the ammunition they need. Whereas with Vincent . . . they won't know what's hit them. Even you shouldn't be able to foul this up.'

With a decisive flick, the spent cigarette was sent spinning into the void below, Pascal watching the faint spark plummet and then disappear. It was ingenious. A Trojan horse, looking to all appearances like a local boy. A Fogas peasant made good. Yet related to Henri Dedieu. It could work.

Why then, was Pascal filled with apprehension?

'It won't work,' muttered Jacques Servat from his seat by the fire while Josette placed the dirty glasses on the bar and walked through to the épicerie to close up. He scowled over at his companion in the hiding place who had dozed off during the meeting, knees folded awkwardly under his chin, that large head tilted back against the bar, guttural vibrations issuing from the tipped back fleshy throat.

'I said it won't work,' Jacques repeated with increased volume. This time he was rewarded with the opening of a bleary eye. 'Christian and René are taking things for granted.'

'Huh? What?' Serge yawned, stretched and promptly smacked an arm against the underside of the counter. 'For God's sake!' he shouted, twisting to one side and wriggling out from his hideout. And Jacques was reminded of the adage about sleeping dogs.

'No, no,' he said, jumping from his seat to shoo the old mayor back out of sight. 'Not just yet. Give it another five minutes and she'll be gone.'

But Serge wasn't having any of it. Still on his hands and knees, he pushed against the scrawny legs now barring his exit, determined to escape. So Jacques, just as unwavering, pushed back. They quickly reached stalemate, the heavier Serge handicapped by his position and the lighter Jacques unable to capitalise on his advantage, leaving them locked in a wrestling hold that would have been unorthodox in most leagues. With the mayor's head thrust against Jacques' thighs and Jacques' hands on the mayor's forehead, neither of them saw Josette approach. And when the former mayor sank his teeth into the bony leg in front of him, Jacques' scream prevented them from hearing her.

Luckily for both of them, Josette was so concerned by the image of her ghostly husband staggering back from the bar, hobbling, that she didn't notice the head and shoulders disappear turtle-like into the recess below the counter.

'Jacques?' she said, shocked. 'What's the matter?'

Jacques froze, one hand rubbing the patch of skin that had suffered the attack, the other screwed into his curly white hair in pain. With a supreme effort, he nonchalantly lowered his injured leg to the floor and limped to his seat next to the fireplace, drawing his wife's attention away from the ghost under the bar.

'Are you okay?' she asked again, looking worried.

He nodded, clenching his fist and pointing at his calf.

'Cramp? You're a ghost but you still get cramp?' Josette chuckled and Jacques' already injured pride suffered another dent. 'Sorry, I shouldn't laugh but . . . well . . .'

Josette noticed the bottom lip beginning to protrude and knew she had pushed her husband into a sulk.

'Anyway,' she continued, before she could do any more damage. 'I'm going up to bed. All that plotting has left me tired.' She cast a weary hand at the three dirty glasses on the bar. 'I'll clear those away in the morning.'

Jacques nodded, blowing her a kiss and waving goodnight. It was only as she was getting under the bedclothes, the cotton sheets chilly in the unheated room, that Josette thought to consider the unusual alacrity with which her husband had accepted her decision to retire. Normally, after a meeting of that sort, he would have insisted she stay up and talk things over with him. Not that they talked in the traditional sense. But still, he was always keen to communicate his opinions. Especially when it came to local government.

Tonight however, he'd gladly waved her off. Thinking nothing more of it, she drifted off to sleep, unaware that her husband had found someone else to talk to.

'You bit me!' Jacques declared the minute the door to the hallway closed.

'Nothing more than you deserved,' huffed Serge Papon, extricating himself once more from his prison, this time unopposed. 'Perhaps you'll think twice before blocking my path in future.'

'It hardly merited sinking your teeth into me!' Jacques rubbed his leg, the track of the mayor's bite still painfully fresh.

Foregoing a warm seat by the fire due to Jacques' proximity to it, Serge lowered himself onto a bar stool. Since childhood, Jacques had been slow to rile but once his temper was raised, it didn't pay to treat him lightly. He'd once threatened Serge with an axe when he'd caught him embracing Josette behind the counter in the épicerie. With his womanising reputation already damning him, Serge hadn't waited around to explain that the situation was innocent, his actions prompted by Josette's unexpected tears. He'd run, leaving behind his shopping which had taken some explaining to his wife, Thérèse, when he'd arrived home empty handed.

Judging by the ferocious gleam in Jacques' eyes right now, he was best kept at a distance. Besides which, Serge wasn't in the mood for his relentless chatter. Particularly not on the topic of the by-election.

Although he'd been half asleep throughout Christian and René's huddled meeting, he'd heard them discussing their options. Had vaguely been aware that they'd settled on Paul Webster as their candidate. But unlike during his life when politics had been his first passion, in death, Serge Papon, former mayor of Fogas, was indifferent.

They could all cross the river and run straight into the arms of those bastards in Sarrat for all he cared.

'Like I said before you decided to start chewing on my leg,' grumbled Jacques, not in the mood to let the subject drop, 'nominating Paul Webster is a big mistake.'

Serge grunted, shoulders hunched, back resolutely towards his old friend. But Jacques ploughed on.

'Christian needs six votes out of the eleven when the council sits to elect the new mayor. At the moment, he can only guarantee five.' Jacques began to tick the names of councillors off on his fingers, ignoring the fact that Serge had started humming tunelessly. 'René, Josette, Alain, Bernard and of course, his own vote. He can't rely on Monique Sentenac anymore, not as she seems to be in favour of the merger.'

The look of disgust that accompanied Jacques pronouncement on the hairdresser's possible defection was wasted on the broad back of his friend, who was now tapping the bar in time to his dissonant crooning.

'So,' continued Jacques undaunted, 'he's going to need the support of the new councillor. Which means he has to pick someone capable of winning the election. And we both know that means Véronique's name has to be on the ballot paper. She's astute. Popular. And with her connection to you . . .'

The warbling had increased in volume, Serge's large head now bobbing along.

'Serge!' shouted Jacques, his temper flaring once again. 'This is important. We have to make Véronique change her mind and agree to stand.'

It was enough to turn Serge around, an eyebrow raised high. 'And how, fellow ghost, are you going to do that?'

Jacques folded his arms across his chest. 'I have ways.'

'Really?'

'You'd be surprised,' muttered Jacques.

Serge's laugh was filled with sarcasm. 'You're invisible apart from to two people. You can't leave the confines of the rooms you spent the majority of your life in. And apart from me, no one can hear a word you utter. I'd say you're about as powerless as it gets. A bit like you were in life, really.'

It took a heartbeat for Jacques to understand, the silence filled with the lazy pop of a pine log on the fire.

'Is that it, then?' he finally asked. 'You've decided to waste this second chance because it doesn't come with the sash of elected office?'

'Second chance?' Serge growled. 'You call this a chance?' He shook an arm at the darkened space of the bar, its walls crowding them in the firelight. 'What kind of existence is this? We're useless. Ineffectual. There is no point to this whatsoever. There is no point to us. We might as well be dead.'

He swung back, away from the fire, staring at the unwashed pastis glasses on the counter in front of him and wishing with all his might that he was buried next to his wife in the damp earth behind the church. He didn't even move when headlights flitted across the room as a car came up the road from the direction of the Auberge.

'Pascal!' breathed Jacques, hurrying over to the window and catching sight of the unmistakable giant box of a car that the interim mayor drove as it passed under a streetlight. He watched it turn up the hill towards Fogas. 'Out late again. What is he up to?'

Serge ignored him.

'I've seen him skulking round at night lots of times,' continued Jacques. 'I'm sure it's connected to the trouble we've been having. Even more reason why we need Véronique on the council.'

Serge started drumming his fingers on the bar once more.

'Fine!' snapped his friend, taking a seat in the inglenook. 'You can choose to sit there like Sartre and brood over your existence. I, however, am going to come up with a way of changing your daughter's mind.'

Five minutes later Serge looked around to see Jacques deep in thought. So deep that soft snores were echoing around the fireplace. He turned morosely back to stare longingly at the abandoned glasses.

Jacques had, as always, hit the nail on the head. Serge couldn't cope with this afterlife that he had found himself in. Couldn't bear the thought that this futile condition might be endless – and in the bar, of all places.

God, he could do with a drink.

He reached out to stroke the nearest glass, fully expecting to feel nothing as usual. In this second chance, as Jacques liked to call it, Serge had discovered that although he was capable of smacking his arm into the bar, or sitting on a stool, he couldn't hold anything. The physics of this existence didn't come equipped with the ability to pick things up. If he tried, his hand just went straight through the object, like fingers through a damp cobweb.

But as his touch met the glass, he felt a residual warmth. It wasn't solid, like it would have been before he died. But still, there was definitely resistance there. Concentrating on the sensation, he put the fingertips of his right hand together and focused on them. Then he began to push.

Nothing. The glass didn't budge. But Serge wasn't one to give up. He placed his two hands on the glass and tried again, his brow crumpled with the effort. Arms straining, back bent over, he put everything into it. And when the glass finally squeaked across the bar, Serge lurched forward and hit his chin on the counter.

It had moved! He stared at the smudged circle of wet that showed the extent of his achievements. A centimetre. No more. But it had moved.

For the rest of the night, he sat there, honing his skills. And in the early hours of the morning, when most of Fogas was snoring along with Jacques, the pastis glass finally reached the edge of the bar and crashed to the floor.

The noise wasn't enough to wake the sleeping ghost in the fireplace. But it was plenty to tell Serge Papon that he had power. All he had to do now was work out how to use it.

While Jacques was trying to revive Serge's flagging interest in politics, a perturbed Pascal Souquet was making the drive home from his meeting with Henri Dedieu. It seemed so straightforward; a simple demand to name Vincent Fauré as the candidate for the by-election. For any other man in Pascal's position, it wouldn't have required a second thought. After all, Henri Dedieu had him dancing to his bidding thanks to the testimony the vindictive mayor of Sarrat could level against him if cornered. It would be all too easy for Pascal to be linked to Dedieu's illicit scheming and, more alarmingly, to the killing of a bear, a criminal offence. Surely, a reasoned man would argue, Pascal had no choice but to comply with his orders or risk being sent to prison.

But as always, life wasn't that simple. For Pascal Souquet was serving two masters, both powerful and both with his future in their hands. He wasn't sure which one he feared the most – the sadistic hunter, or the political virtuoso who had come to light in the furore over the merger last September. Violently opposed to the unification owing to her strong sense of heritage, this woman had managed to brilliantly deconstruct the best of Henri Dedieu's plans and all without revealing her identity to any but Pascal. Having crossed swords with her already, he knew she was a formidable opponent. She also happened to be his wife.

Which placed the interim mayor of Fogas in an unenviable position. Because Fatima Souquet had given her husband an ultimatum. Prevent the merger from happening or she would divorce him. Of itself, it didn't sound much. But since his bankruptcy, he was reliant on his wife. From the house they lived in to the wages she earned. And if all else failed with Henri Dedieu, it was Fatima Souquet who could get Pascal to where he needed to be. He knew that now.

Which one did he follow?

Still pondering that question, Pascal crossed the small bridge in La Rivière, the river to his left nothing more than a black ribbon as it tumbled over the weir, and just before the épicerie, he turned up the mountain road that led to Fogas. His headlights raked over the burnt-out ruins of the post office, a permanent reminder of the tragedy that struck two years ago. And another of his failures.

It was hard not to dwell on the many ways he'd been thwarted. The post office was a prime example. Burnt down in an accident, it had provided a perfect opportunity to strip Fogas of a vital amenity and hence make the commune more amenable to a merger. But no. His plan to resituate the facility across the river in Sarrat had been overcome by the postmistress, Véronique Estaque, and her stubborn refusal to accept change. A new office had subsequently been opened in the épicerie.

Likewise, the attempt to oust Serge Papon from office had resulted in nothing but trouble. In cahoots with Henri Dedieu, Pascal had used the unrest arising from the reintroduction of bears to the area to agitate for Serge's demotion. The outcome? A dead bear, a police investigation which could yet lead to prosecutions, and a leader who'd been more popular than ever.

Perhaps the frustrated interim mayor shouldn't have been surprised when the attempt to merge the two communes last autumn had met with similar defeat. It had started so well, the people of Fogas wooed by the charm of Henri Dedieu. By his promises of equality, which only Pascal knew were empty. Nevertheless, Serge had triumphed again, pulling rabbits out of hats and securing the future of his precious commune. For twelve months.

It was a litany of disaster that would have sunk another man. Yet Pascal had somehow survived each episode, with no one suspecting his part in the trouble that had beset Fogas or his allegiance to the leader across the river. But as he drove up the winding road to his home, the interim mayor knew his luck couldn't hold. This would be his last chance.

Vincent Fauré.

There was nothing in the name to give it away. Perhaps Fatima wouldn't suspect. And if the young man was elected onto the council and Pascal was duly elected mayor, things would move quickly. The merger would be fast-tracked, the paperwork signed before the electorate even registered what was happening. And Pascal Souquet would be secure in his position as deputy mayor of the new commune, with fingers able to reach far more lucrative pies and thus no longer dependent on his wife.

Besides, he knew what women were like. Once the salary was coming in and the status was conferred, she would acquiesce, happy to bask in his reflected glory.

Yes, he decided, as he finally arrived outside the small terraced house up in Fogas. He would go ahead with Henri Dedieu's plans. Because it was the quickest guarantee of getting him out of this backwater where he had been stagnating for far too long.

With a briskness to his step, he walked up the path and opened the front door. He paused in the darkened corridor, the lights off as always in an attempt to save money, and cocked his ear. Nothing. Just the languid creak of floorboards letting the warmth of the day escape from them. He hung up his coat, wincing at the repulsive odour of cigarettes, and crept down the hallway, heading for the lounge and the drinks cabinet. After the evening he'd had, a brandy was just what was needed.

He had his hand on the doorknob when suddenly it was whisked away from him and there she was, ferret-like face even fiercer in the backlit lounge. It was enough to make him jump.

'You're home,' she announced. 'Good. We need to talk.'

'Can't it wait?' Placing a dry kiss on both bony cheeks, Pascal slipped past his wife into the room, hoping she didn't catch the stale smoke smell and guess where he'd been. As far as she was concerned, he'd been up at Philippe Galy's debating the coming election. Reaching for the decanter and a glass, he poured himself a large nightcap. 'It's late and I'm rather tired. We've been hammering out the nomination.'

'It's about that.' Fatima was facing him, a familiar secretive smile on her lips. It was how she'd been since the autumn when, shielding her identity under the name of SOS Fogas, she'd launched a ridiculously effective internet campaign which had helped scupper the merger. It was only by chance that Pascal had unmasked her as the authoress of the successful blog and discovered the extent to which she'd covertly undermined everything he'd planned for. She'd made him look like a fool, all because she had some sentimental tie to the commune. What she didn't know was that he knew about every single betrayal. And when the time was right, he would be showing her the door. For now, she had him over a barrel.

'I've come up with the perfect candidate,' she said. 'Someone local. Someone who can win this for you.'

Raising the brandy to his lips, Pascal raised an enquiring eyebrow, trying to ignore the thudding in his ribcage. 'Go on.'

'Me. I'm going to stand in the election. And I expect your full support.'

5

The morning of Serge Papon's funeral dawned in La Rivière with wide ribbons of mist strung across the valley. In the half-light, streaks of frost edged the roadside, a brittle coating covered the fields, and floating in the clouds rising off the river, the trees were sculpted in white. Even the abandoned Christmas tree had regained some of its lost glory, layers iced in a festive patina.

Josette thrust open the shutters and let the sharp air flood into her bedroom, knowing it brought promise. For any local could tell you that within a couple of hours, when the sun finally rose over the ridge behind them, the mist would disperse and the day would be glorious. Nodding her head at the appropriateness of such a beautiful morning for what lay ahead, she made her way down the stairs. And as had become habit of late, when her hand reached out to push open the door that led to the bar, she felt a jitter of nerves.

What would it be this morning? More broken glasses? A picture frame left askew? A bag of coffee on the floor?

It had begun on Sunday. She'd descended early, knowing the bar would be busy with churchgoers seeking a coffee and croissant to reward themselves for their piety, and had taken no more than three steps into the room when she saw it. A glass, smashed on the floorboards behind the bar. One of the pastis glasses that she'd been too tired to stack in the dish-washer the night before.

Puzzled, she'd stared at it a while. Then she'd glanced over to the inglenook where the blurred lines of her husband rested against the soot-stained wall, head back, eyes closed. He was still asleep. Deciding it was simply an accident, a case of her leaving it too close to the edge, she got the dustpan and broom and swept up the shards.

The next morning had been harder to explain. A bag of coffee, burst open on the floor after falling from the shelf next to the coffee machine. By Tuesday, when Josette had opened the door to find every picture on the walls in the bar tilted to different angles, she'd begun to worry. And when she'd discovered several lengths of saucisson coiled on the épicerie counter instead of being draped over the pole above, she'd started to panic.

How to account for them, these isolated little episodes which occurred when the premises were closed up for the night, Josette the only occupant? Apart from Jacques, and he didn't exactly count. She'd come to the only conclusion she could.

It was the beginning of dementia. She was rising from her bed, coming downstairs to carry out the various acts of vandalism and returning to sleep soundly until the alarm woke her.

What else could it be?

Taking a deep breath, she opened the door, flicked on the lights and stepped into the bar.

Nothing. The photos of Fogas in bygone times were hanging correctly. The coffee hadn't jumped off the shelf. And not a single glass was out of place. With Jacques stirring dreamily by the embers of the fire, she hurried across to the épicerie and walked up and down the two aisles, bending down to check underneath the display racks.

Everything was at it should be.

Allowing herself a relieved smile, particularly upon noticing that the cabinet containing knives behind the till had remained untouched, she unlocked the front door, flipped the sign to *Ouvert*, and returned to the bar to turn on the coffee machine. When the church bells began to sound the Angelus, she decided to give Annie a quick call, the farmer still an early riser despite having entered partial retirement. Turning to the shelf behind the bar where she left her mobile recharging every night – still not convinced it was safe enough to sleep in the same room with it despite Fabian's exasperated protestations that the radiation levels it gave off were miniscule – Josette paused.

No phone, just the dangling cord of the recharger.

'That's funny . . .' she muttered, patting her pockets to make sure she hadn't already picked it up. When a quick search of the vicinity failed to retrieve it, with a resigned shrug, she reached for the landline.

If Josette had been born later, into the generation that had adopted such technology faster and as such, worked with it better, she might have thought to call her own number to track the mobile down. But she didn't. Instead she called Annie Estaque. Which was perhaps just as well. Because if she'd heard the sound of 'Non, Je Ne Regrette Rien' ringing out from the pile of dirty tea towels on the floor down by the coffee machine, she'd have been even more perturbed about her sanity. As it was, she was to remain blissfully unaware of the truth of the matter for at least a little while longer.

Spiders' webs etched in white, branches of trees brilliant with crystals, the boulders protruding from the river capped with ice. A hoar frost. Véronique leaned out of her window and took a deep breath, savouring the needle-sharp sensation of the cold air hitting her throat. She loved mornings like this, the mist already beginning to lift as the sun crept ever higher and the sky grew lighter. They were a reminder that winter didn't have to be all dark days and ashen clouds. Normally she'd throw on a coat and head out for a walk before breakfast, following the river along the valley, feet slipping on the frozen path, breath puffing softly in front of her. Today there would be no such treat. Because today she would be burying her father.

Yanking the window closed with a bang, she turned to the empty flat. What a difference it made when Christian was here, his large frame dwarfing the lounge, his bulky body ridiculous in the tiny kitchen. And the bed. They really had to get a bigger bed. Now, without him, rather than regaining a sense of spaciousness in his absence, the flat was forlorn. A vacuum in which everything hung in suspended animation, awaiting his return. Including her.

She hadn't let him stay the night, despite his protestations. Somehow, it just didn't feel right, having him here on the eve of the funeral. Like a wedding, perhaps . . . She gave a dry laugh at the stupidity of her own superstition. How much better to have woken this morning in his arms. To know that the day would be bearable because he was there. And to have the gravity of the occasion alleviated by his inability to negotiate the route from bedroom to bathroom without tripping over something.

But she'd turned him away. Some perverse gene in her, probably from the Estaque side. The same perversity that had enabled her to have minimum contact with her mother for the last week. A couple of calls, that was all. Because that was all she'd felt capable of. She had a tight hold on her temper and she didn't think it would survive seeing her mother in the flesh right now.

Which was a problem. Since in precisely three hours' time,

she would be standing next to Maman in the church as they said farewell to Serge. Véronique Estaque only hoped she'd be able to control herself.

While La Rivière languished in the mists of the morning, up in Picarets, where the tips of the sun's slender fingers were beginning to stretch over the serrated ridges that surrounded the village, the sky was clear and streaked with pink. Annie Estaque had risen long before Josette telephoned, her sleep fragmented, her resting hours nothing more than a series of tormenting images of Véronique and herself arguing. For the last week, she'd woken in her bed, the dawn still a way off, and she'd wished that the misery of her dreams could come true. Because surely the heated exchanges with her daughter that she fabricated while asleep were a million times better than the painful silence she'd had to endure in her conscious hours.

Coffee in hand, she sat at the kitchen table, choosing the chair closest to the fire burning in the hearth. She was ready way too early. Now she had time to kill and that was never a good thing for an Estaque. Spurred on by nervous energy, she'd already seen to the handful of cows she'd retained after Christian took over her farm the summer before. Needing something to occupy her mornings, she'd insisted on keeping a small herd. Too small. This morning she'd had them milked and fed in record time. Likewise, the dogs had been dragged up the hill at the back, Annie's restless energy pushing the pace as they made their way to the ridge. She hadn't taken time to watch the sky slowly changing colour, to marvel at the wreaths of mist down below or to analyse the coming weather from the wisps of cloud scattered behind Mont Valier.

With a fire searing along her veins, she'd been back in the farmhouse and eating breakfast before it had got fully light. Then she'd hurried upstairs, put on her black suit that had seen service at too many funerals, and returned to the kitchen to leave her shoes, polished the night before, by the back door.

She glanced over at the longcase clock marking time in the corner. Two hours. She had at least two hours before Christian called in to pick her up. It was a long time for an Estaque to be sitting idle. Forcing herself to be still, she sipped her coffee, watching the pink give way to blue beyond the windows.

It was going to be a stunning day. Typical of Serge to have such luck. He was already guaranteed a big turnout, the small church in La Rivière expecting its largest congregation in decades. And with the weather as it was, even those souls who didn't normally venture forth in winter would brave the roads and make their way to the funeral.

Annie just wondered if the bright sunshine would be enough to thaw her daughter's heart.

In the six days since Serge's death, Annie had been cast into the wilderness. One moment she'd been holding her grieving daughter in the bar, the next, Véronique wanted nothing to do with her. Not that she'd said as much. But it was apparent in the unanswered calls, the ignored text messages that had taken Annie an age to compose, mobile technology not her forte. Frustrated and saddened, Annie had got as far as paying Véronique a visit. Well, almost as far. She'd laced up her boots, donned her winter coat and strode out of the farm, but when she'd reached the bend in the road where the path to the village starts to descend, she'd had a change of heart.

Fear. As she stared into the dark tunnel of bare branches that lined the track to La Rivière, Annie Estaque had been paralysed with apprehension. It wasn't the route she was afraid of, the twisting footpath as familiar to her as the age-dappled skin that stretched across the broad expanse of her hand. It was the reception at the other end. Annie knew her daughter. Knew the temper and the stubbornness that came from both sides. She also knew that, pushed too far, this delicate situation would be tipped beyond salvation. So while Annie's instinct was to barge down to her daughter's flat to sort out this mess in her typically blunt manner, she was terrified that this would prove disastrous. Especially as Véronique's distress was justified.

Less than a year. That was all the time she'd been granted with her father, thanks to Annie and her insistence on observing a promise made to a distraught wife. How could Véronique be anything but angry? Unforgiving?

Annie shivered, despite the fire blazing beside her. Salvaging her relationship with her daughter was going to be difficult. But she'd done it before. She would do it again. Because without Véronique in her life, the future was too bleak to contemplate.

The longcase clock sounded the half hour and Annie lifted her gaze from the burning logs, her eyes coming to rest on the photographs on the dresser. An infant held by a proud mother, a gap-toothed young girl with a shy, dimpled smile, and a group of three people, Annie in the middle, grinning into the sun. They were all she had of her past. But at least she had that. Poor Véronique had nothing. Not even . . .

Being an Estaque, Annie was out of her chair and heading for the stairs before the thought had fully materialised. She was in the spare bedroom, rummaging in the wardrobe, before she had time to consider the pros and cons. And once she found what she was looking for, she dusted it off, wrapped it in tissue paper that had come with the teapot and china mugs Lorna Webster had bought her for Christmas, and laid it next to her shoes before she could change her mind. When Christian pulled up at the farm some time later, she emerged, chin jutting forward, a small parcel clutched in her hands.

Being well acquainted with the Estaques, having become

custodian of Annie's farm and sharer of Véronique's bed, Christian recognised that look. He also knew better than to get involved. Whatever Annie was up to, he only hoped it resolved the awful tension between daughter and mother because, caught in the middle between two people he cared for, the big farmer couldn't bear it much longer. He was only glad Serge wasn't around to witness it.

'Hurry up, Chloé!' Stephanie's voice called from the front door of the small cottage situated on the far side of Picarets. She was rewarded by the sound of feet galloping down the stairs.

'I'm coming! I just wanted to get these.' Chloé brandished an unopened pack of tissues. 'Just in case Annie or Véronique get upset.'

Black curls bouncing, the young girl raced out of the door to the blue van, leaving Stephanie and Fabian to exchange looks.

'When did she get so wise?' murmured Stephanie, as she locked up and followed her eleven-year-old daughter down the path.

Fabian grinned, putting an arm around his wife. 'She's always been wise. I think you're only just noticing it.'

'That's probably true! But do you think we're doing the right thing? Letting her come to the funeral?'

Fabian's face turned sombre. 'Definitely. She's a part of the community and Serge was a large part of her life. Plus, Annie will be glad to have her there. Especially with how things are between her and Véronique at the moment.'

Stephanie grimaced. 'God, yes. It's awful. I popped in to see Annie yesterday and she looks terrible. She's aged a decade in a week. I think Véronique will get a shock when she sees her.'

'Maybe that's what Véronique needs,' said Fabian as they got in the van. 'Something to take her mind off things. Get her back to normality.'

'Normality?' Stephanie gave a laugh as she turned the key in the ignition and the van juddered into life. 'As if anything is ever normal in Fogas!'

With a crunch of gears, she swung out onto the narrow mountain road and headed towards the handful of houses that constituted Picarets. They'd reached the majestic lime tree, which marked the closest thing the village had to a centre, when their progress was halted by two adults and two children dressed for church running around the road chasing hens.

'Can we help, Maman?' asked Chloé, eager to join the Rogalle twins, Max and Nicolas, as they darted here and there after their wayward chickens.

'If we don't, we'll be here all day,' muttered Stephanie, opening her door. 'But make sure you stay clean!'

Chloé was already out of the van and scrambling after the nearest hen, Madame Rogalle greeting her as she ran past after another escapee, her formal attire hindering her progress.

'Chicken catching,' said Fabian, bending and straightening his legs as though preparing for earnest sporting endeavour. 'It never was my speciality.'

Stephanie laughed. 'Just look as though you're trying,' she said as she swooped on the nearest bird and caught it with a confident hand. 'And no one will know the difference.'

Fabian took her at her word. Targeting the smallest of the hens in the hopes it would be slower, he ran after it, his ungainly gait only succeeding in scaring the frightened creature off the road and into the garden of the nearest house. Fabian didn't think twice. He followed through the broken gate and across the tangle of weeds and briars, the thorns snagging at his good trousers, until he rounded the corner to the back of the building and spotted his prey cowering beneath a rotten bench below a windowsill.

'Got you!' he shouted, stretching his arms under the broken slats of the seat to pluck the subdued chicken from its hiding place. 'Ha! Not so fast now, are you?' he crowed, as he straightened up, the bird held at arm's length from his suit.

It was only then he took in his surroundings. A vegetable patch long abandoned and smothered in brambles. A shed, the bare branches of a young tree pushing out of a hole in its roof and the door forced open by thick, woody tendrils of dead ivy. An overturned wheelbarrow next to it, rusted and covered in moss. Ash saplings pushing up through what had once been a patio. And several huge fir trees towering over it all, blocking out the light and casting the entirety into perpetual dark.

He was in the back garden of Old Widow Loubet's derelict cottage and it was more than a bit unnerving.

For Fabian Servat, a Parisian whose long schoolboy summers had been spent in Fogas with Tante Josette and Oncle Jacques, the house had held a certain fascination. Granted free rein by his summer guardians during daylight hours, he'd roamed the commune, often in the company of Véronique, and had passed many idle days under the broad lime tree in front of the well-kept cottage. The product of a turbulent and spiteful marriage, Fabian had grown up in a house without love, a building that wasn't a home. So he'd been drawn to this property which was so obviously cherished, and to the rake thin widow who'd lived there, always out sweeping the paths or washing her windows.

She'd passed away in the years he now referred to as his exile – the long period from late adolescence to his early thirties, when Fogas and its charms had seemed puerile to a man making his way in the capital and the world of finance. So when he'd returned two years ago, Fabian had been saddened to see the sagging roof timbers, the slipped and missing slates, and the glass that Widow Loubet had cleaned so assiduously now shattered and scattered upon the gravel path. The house was a breath away from being beyond repair, and just as sinister as the garden.

Bird still in hand, Fabian cautiously approached the nearest window, jagged bits of glass lodged in the frame, peeling shutters hanging drunkenly from broken hinges and entwined with uncurbed wisteria which reached as high as the gable. Curiosity getting the better of him, he pressed closer, taking in the stale smell of damp, his eyes struggling to adjust to the gloomy interior.

He could never be sure afterwards what he saw. He just knew he saw something. A movement perhaps? A glint of light? It was enough to make him jerk backwards. And enough to make the trapped chicken squawk, sending Fabian's already fraught nerves jangling.

He was out of there as fast as his incredibly long legs could carry him. When he emerged back into the sunshine bathing the road, he had the hen clutched tight to his chest like a talisman and his face was drained of colour.

'You caught the last one!' cheered Stephanie. Then she noticed his pallor. 'What's the matter?'

'In there . . . Old Widow Loubet's place . . .' he stammered. 'I thought I saw . . .'

'A ghost?' joked Madame Rogalle as she disentangled the protesting chicken from Fabian's scared clutches. 'Because that's the only thing that could live in there with the state it's in.'

'Didn't someone say it was sold?' Stephanie was herding the three wide-eyed children and her spooked husband away from the house and towards Monsieur Rogalle who was waiting by his car.

'Last autumn, supposedly,' said Monsieur Rogalle. 'I don't know who bought it. But there's been no sign of anyone moving in.' He gave a slight shudder as he passed an appraising eye over the dilapidated structure. 'Rather them than me.'

'Can we have a look around it, Maman?' asked Chloé, reluctantly getting back into the van, her focus still on the house.

'No,' said Stephanie, taking her seat behind the wheel and starting the engine as a pale-faced Fabian got in beside her. 'We can't. That would be trespassing.'

'Even if we don't know who owns it?' Chloé's eleven-year-old logic raised a smile on her mother's face.

'Especially if we don't know who owns it. But as they'll be neighbours, we ought to find out who they are. I'll ask Serge for the details when I see him—'

She broke off, realising her mistake, Fabian and Chloé staring at her as the three of them were suddenly reminded of what the morning held in store. And what the years to come would be missing.

'Lord,' muttered Stephanie, tears springing to her eyes and a tissue being proffered from the back. 'This is going to be a difficult day.'

'It was a ghost, I swear!' René's eyes were huge, moustache trembling with remembered fright. 'I was up there last night and I saw it. A strange glow that crossed in front of the windows. It wasn't natural.'

'You didn't think to knock on the door? Perhaps the new owners have moved in?' suggested Josette as she served coffees to the people crowding the bar. She couldn't remember when she'd last been this busy and sent a silent thanks to Serge for providing such custom; and a curse to her nephew Fabian for not getting down sooner to help out.

'Moved in to Widow Loubet's? Are you mad?' René cast a dismissive hand in the general direction of Picarets. 'When did you last see the place? It's a wreck. No one could live in it without substantial work being carried out. No, I'm telling you, it's haunted.'

Bernard Mirouze shifted uneasily on his bar stool, Serge the beagle cowering under him. Neither was in any rush to visit Picarets after hearing René's news.

'Don't be ridiculous, René!' interjected the sane voice of Alain Rougé, former policeman and sceptic. 'There's no such thing as ghosts. Anyway, who bought it? Do we know?'

'Last I heard from Serge, it was being bought through some company,' said Josette. 'I don't know any more than that.'

'Mark my word, after what I saw last night, they won't hold on to it for long. The place gives me the creeps.' René tipped his cup and drained the last of his coffee. 'Give me another one, Josette. My nerves need it.'

'Bonjour!' The door to the bar opened, admitting Fabian, Stephanie and Chloé and another cluster of mourners looking to start the day with caffeine.

'Thank God you're here!' Josette stretched to kiss her nephew as he hurried behind the bar. 'I need all the help I can get.'

'Sorry we're late. We got held up by the Rogalles. Long story!'

'And Fabian saw a ghost,' teased Stephanie, making Fabian blush.

'Where?' René was leaning across the bar, face intent.

'It was nothing,' said Fabian. 'Just a trick of the light up at Old Widow Loubet's—'

'See!' René thumped the bar in triumph, making the Parisian jump. 'What did I say?'

'Oh for God's sake,' said Alain, as those around him started muttering anxiously. 'That's all we need. You convincing everyone that we have a haunted house in the commune.'

'A haunted house?' Christian Dupuy had arrived in the doorway, a wry smile on his face. 'I know what Serge would have made of that.'

'Yeah,' muttered René. 'He'd have told me there was no such thing as ghosts and then charged people to visit it anyway!'

A rumble of laughter rocked the bar and Chloé Morvan, who had taken her usual seat close to the inglenook and was sipping at the hot chocolate Josette had placed in front of her, smiled at the person opposite. Jacques Servat smiled back. The pair of them sharing a private joke.

Annie wasn't sure if she was doing the right thing. Christian had tried to talk her out of it. He'd diplomatically tried to tell her that she wouldn't be welcome. But there was enough stubbornness in the Estaque family to ensure each member got an equal portion. So, parcel held tight to her chest like armour, Annie pressed the doorbell and took a step back.

'Come in, Christian. It's open,' Véronique called out from beyond the door.

Straightening her back, Annie turned the handle and entered the small flat before her courage could fail her.

'I won't be long,' came the same voice, this time closer, steps approaching across a tiled floor. 'I've just got to—'

'Bonjourrr, Vérrronique.' Annie pushed the words past her dry lips as her daughter stopped at the doorway to the kitchen, her face expressionless as she regarded her mother.

'Maman,' she finally said, dipping her head to pass a perfunctory peck in the vicinity of Annie's cheeks without actually touching her. 'I thought we were meeting at the bar?'

'I wanted to give you this.' Annie held out the oblong parcel, the tissue paper crinkling in her trembling hands.

Véronique took the present without a word, walked through to the living room and placed it on the table.

'Arrren't you going to open it?'

Véronique twisted her wrist and consulted her watch. 'We don't have time. We should be going.' She put on her coat, collected her bag from the couch and headed back out to the hall. As she passed, Annie couldn't help herself.

'Vérrronique!' she said to her daughter's back. 'We need to talk.'

Véronique halted, a deep breath lifting her shoulder blades, and Annie could visualise her pulling hard on the tethers that held her temper in check. Then she turned, a polite mask smoothing out any signs of irritation.

'It's all a bit late for that, Maman. Right now we need to bury the man I barely knew was my father.'

In strained silence, they left the flat and made their way down the stairs and out into the brilliant sunshine that had chased the last vestiges of mist away. It was a glorious day. But as Annie accompanied her tight-lipped daughter up the road to the large crowd gathered outside the bar, she wished she could swap places with Serge Papon. Being dead had to be preferable to what she was currently enduring.

6

'"For you shall go out with joy, and be led out with peace; the mountains and the hills shall break forth into singing before you, and all the trees of the field shall clap their hands . . ."'

Christian lifted his gaze from the gaping hole in the earth and let his eyes roam up the mountainside that rose from the back of the small cemetery in La Rivière. A light breeze was sighing through the bare branches of the oaks and ashes that lined the slopes and from across the road came the mellifluous rush of the swollen winter river. Having followed his wife's example in forgoing the option of being interred in the Papon family vault, its grey marble mass squatting broodingly by the church door, the mayor of Fogas had left strict instructions in his will that he be laid to rest alongside his faithful Thérèse. Standing at the plot bathed in sunshine, a fine view over the village and to the Pyrenean peaks beyond, Christian had to acknowledge that if you had to be buried somewhere, it was hard to beat a setting like this.

And while he wasn't a man of God, far from it with his political beliefs, Christian appreciated the words being spoken over the coffin as it was lowered into the ground. Appropriate for a mountain dweller like Serge. The new curé had done well. If only he'd thought to put the heating on in the Lord's house a bit sooner, the funeral would have been perfect. Although to be fair, it would have to have been on at least twenty-four hours in advance to make any indent on the tomb-like cold that lingered inside the thick stone walls of the Romanesque church, winter or summer. Veteran of many a chilblain-inducing service, Véronique had warned him to put on extra layers. But his benumbed state today was caused by more than just frigid temperatures.

He couldn't believe it. In the casket before him, the same casket that he'd carried into the church with René, Bernard, Alain, Paul Webster and Philippe Galy, lay Serge Papon. It didn't look big enough. How could those narrow wooden sides contain such charisma? How could the flimsy lid hold in that sheer force of personality? How could the person that held the commune together be gone?

His eyes blurred and the hand holding his squeezed tighter. Véronique, by his side, shoulders hunched forward, a tissue to her face. Next to her, young Chloé, being comforted by, or comforting, Annie Estaque, rare tears tracking down the old lady's face as she hugged the girl close.

The curé stepped back from the grave, closed his bible and bowed his head. Then he nodded at Véronique who took a red rose from the basket Stephanie was holding out and, features taut with pain, dropped the flower down onto the coffin. It landed softly, a splash of colour in the dark below. She stifled a cry with her gloved hand and Christian pulled her to him, burying his face in her hair as one by one, roses fell from the hands of the mourners until a layer of vibrant scarlet concealed the sombre casket.

When the last flower had been thrown, the curé said a final blessing before approaching Serge's sister who had made the journey down from Toulouse; a shorter, softer version of the mayor, she was clinging to her husband's arm and crying openly. Behind her, some of the crowd began to disperse, trickling slowly across the graveyard, through the gate and down the back lane to the Auberge. But the majority remained, waiting to say a few words to the bereaved family. One after the other they came forward, eyes sad, faces mournful, and Véronique straightened her back, lifted her chin, and accepted their commiserations with a fortitude she'd inherited from her father.

It was only then, standing next to her and shaking hands as he greeted them, that Christian had a chance to marvel at the number of people who had turned out to say goodbye to Serge Papon.

There were hundreds, stretching right across the cemetery – locals, second-home owners, dignitaries from nearby villages and towns – all of them here because the man resting in the ground beside them had touched their lives in some way. Major Gaillard, a high-ranking official from the Ariège Fire Service, was one of the first to draw near, expression grave as he spoke to Véronique. He was closely followed by several civil servants from the offices of the Préfecture in Foix and a group of older men Christian recognised as various mayors from the region; all of them allies of Serge, they had helped him, and been helped by him, in numerous – if not always strictly legitimate – ways over the decades of his incumbency. Even Jérôme Ulrich, the former Préfet of Ariège who had only left for his new post in the Charante at the beginning of the year, was there. His pregnant wife, Karine, put her arms around Véronique, while Pascal Souquet, to Christian's disgust, tried to monopolise the high-flying civil servant. So typical of the man, using a funeral to network.

There was also a healthy contingent from across the river. Henri Dedieu was expressing his condolences to Serge's sister as more neighbours from Sarrat waited patiently to have a quiet word with the grieving relatives. And then, of course, there were the people who really knew Serge: the people of

Fogas. Young and old, men and women . . . so many women, all of them profoundly upset at the passing of the old rogue who'd more than merited his reputation.

Before long, as the congregation filed past, Christian's hand began to tire, clasped in relentless succession by the strong grasp of farmers, old colleagues of Serge's from his mining days and working men who, like Christian, spent all their days in the mountains.

'Christ,' said René as the queue finally dwindled and only a small core of family and close friends were left standing at the graveside. He shook Christian by the hand and leaned forward to kiss Véronique. 'Serge would have loved to see this. I always knew the bugger had charm but I never thought . . .'

The plumber gestured towards the multitude heading out of the cemetery then he turned back to Véronique, his usual levity replaced with a sorrowful smile. 'You should be proud to have had him as a father.'

Véronique nodded, unable to speak, and as René walked slowly away, she began to cry in earnest.

'It's okay,' Christian murmured uselessly, gathering her into his arms as her shoulders heaved and the raw sound of grief tore from her throat. 'It's okay.'

Annie stood next to them, face pale, an unsure hand patting Véronique's back while Josette led the rest of the mourners away from the grave.

'I just can't . . .' sobbed Véronique, face buried in Christian's broad chest. '. . . I just can't bear the thought of leaving him here.'

'I know.' He stroked a rough hand through her hair, trying his best to offer comfort in a situation that was beyond his experience. What must it feel like to be her? To have known her father so briefly . . . ? He caught Annie's eye, a pained expression on the old lady's pallid face, as though she shared his thoughts.

'I'm sorry.' Véronique leaned back, tissue dabbing at her damp cheeks. 'You must think I'm stupid. I mean . . . our relationship was only just beginning . . .'

Annie shuffled uncomfortably, focus on her shoes, while Christian wiped the remaining tears from Véronique's face with a broad thumb.

'Not stupid. No one would think that,' he muttered as Véronique moved away from him to stare down at the flower-covered casket, bottom lip caught between her teeth.

She stood there in silent contemplation, then she reached to the back of her neck, fumbled under the collar of her coat and brought forth the silver chain and cross that Christian had never seen her without. She raised it to her lips, kissed it, and let it fall onto the bed of roses.

'Adieu Papa. This is to keep me close to you until we next meet.'

And with a resolute set to her shoulders, she brushed the back of her hand across her eyes and walked out of the cemetery, leaving Christian and Annie stunned in her wake.

From high on the hillside, on the path that runs between Picarets and La Rivière, he'd witnessed it all. The solemn procession into the church, the muted singing, the sad faces by the graveside. So many people! He'd recognised a few. Others, he'd recognised the type – hard mountain men, made uncomfortable by their emotions and the starched collars around their necks. Then he'd spotted his target, moving through the crowd with assurance and gravity, masquerading his real disposition under the guise of a politician. A bolt of fury had blazed through him at the sight of the man. But he'd held back. It wasn't the time. Nor the place.

He'd forced his gaze back onto her, bringing his anger under control by marking the brave tilt of her chin, the steadfast hold of her shoulders. And her hair, the sun striking fire from the depths of auburn. She looked beautiful despite her distress. He wasn't the only one to think so, the farmer's arm familiar around her shoulder, his touch a caress. Things had changed while he'd been away.

With the patience of a hunter, he'd waited until they had all left before he stepped out from his cover. Now, moving like a creature of the forest, he descended stealthily to the cemetery and made his way to the open grave.

Flowers, red roses scattered over the coffin, and across the top of them, the silver strand of her cross and chain. He stared down at it, thoughts on the man that lay beneath it all and the trouble that was around the corner. And he made a promise to the mayor whom he'd grown fond of in his short time in the commune.

'I'll keep Fogas safe,' he muttered. 'No matter what it takes.'

He threw the single snowdrop he'd plucked from the hillside into the gaping hole, a white droplet in the sea of red, and as quietly as he'd arrived, he was gone.

'Look how many people there are!'

Jacques Servat was shifting excitedly from one leg to the other, his spectral form pressed against the window of the bar, his breath misting up the glass as he stared out at the crowds heading down the road to the Auberge.

'Major Gaillard . . . and all the mayors from this valley and the next and . . . Céline from the town hall crying her eyes out and . . . why, that's Jérôme Ulrich! Serge, come and look. The former préfet is at your funeral!'

But the entreaty fell on deaf ears, the hunch of Serge's back visible under the counter in the same position he'd held all morning. He'd made no attempt to emerge from hiding when the bar had thronged with customers – a fact for which Jacques had been grateful, the mass of legs and bodies preventing sharp-eyed Chloé Morvan from spying him. Nor, when the room emptied out, everyone heading to the church to meet the coffin, had Jacques had to plead with him to stay concealed while Josette locked up. Even when Jacques had called him to the window to see Annie and Véronique approach, sad but dignified as they greeted the mourners, the old mayor had shown no inclination to abandon his cramped confines.

Depression. That's what Jacques had concluded after his many attempts to entice his friend forth had met with the same surly rejection. Serge Papon was upset at missing his own send-off.

And who could blame him?

With nothing left to see as the last of the mourners crossed the bridge, Christian, Véronique and Annie bringing up the rear, Jacques moved away from the window, concerned about his friend's low spirits. Serge had been quiet for days. Moping in his hiding place during opening hours and then sitting on a stool late into the night when Jacques was already falling asleep. Once or twice Jacques had stirred out of a dream to find Serge flitting aimlessly through the archway to the darkened épicerie or standing admiring the photos on the wall in the bar.

He was a restless soul. And Jacques, being an Ariégeois male, wasn't sure he was equipped with the tools needed to sort him out. Being a Servat, he thought he'd have a go anyway.

Talk to him. That's what Josette would advise. But there was no way he was going to try having a conversation with the hump of a turtleback that was all he could see of his friend from this side of the room. So he moved, noiselessly of course, to the far end of the bar, slipped around the counter and thus managed to creep up on the former mayor without him noticing.

At first he didn't understand. The strange glow reflecting off Serge's intent face. The concentration knotting that heavy brow. Then he saw a finger stretch out and touch something lying on a pile of tea towels. And Jacques Servat realised that, as in life, in death Serge Papon had acquired power.

What he was doing with it was another thing.

'What a crowd,' Josette said, helping herself to a chicken and tarragon *gougère* from a passing plate. And she gave thanks that she wasn't hosting the wake. She'd been reluctant to agree to the Auberge as the venue, knowing how much Serge Papon had enjoyed his time in her bar, but pragmatism had finally won her over. There were far too many people at the funeral to fit in her smaller premises. Looking around the large room that served as the Auberge restaurant, tables pushed to one side, chairs lined up along the wainscotted walls, Josette was glad she was the spectator for once. The place was packed, Lorna, Paul, Stephanie and Alain Rougé's wife, Francine, working hard distributing food and drinks to the hungry mourners.

'And what stories,' said Stephanie, pausing with a tray of smoked duck breast and goat's cheese canapés which Christian and René immediately helped themselves to. René took three – one in each hand and one straight in his mouth.

'Mmm . . .' he mumbled, eyes rolling in delight. 'Delicious.'

'As I was saying,' continued Stephanie, as she switched the tray to her other hand and out of the plumber's short-armed reach. 'Everyone seems to have an anecdote or two about Serge. It's brilliant to hear them all reminiscing.'

'Well, he was the sort of person people talked about. And remembered,' said Josette, equally unable to resist the canapés which were now under her nose.

'Hmph! You could say that again.' Annie Estaque had joined them, another morsel of duck and cheese disappearing from the tray.

'Talking of stories . . .' René leaned in, beckoning for them to imitate him, his voice lowered to conspiratorial levels. 'I just heard from a well-informed source that a certain person in our commune is standing in the by-election.'

'One of the second-home owners?' Christian nodded towards the cluster of people gathered around Pascal Souquet and his wife.

René shook his head. 'Much cleverer than that. And more worrying.'

'Who then?'

'None other than Madame Souquet.'

'Fatima?' Christian's surprise turned his normally deep tones into a falsetto, sharp enough to make the woman herself glare over at the clandestine group. 'Merde!'

'Indeed!' pronounced René, using Stephanie's huddled proximity to snaffle another canapé. 'We might need to rethink our strategy.'

'Which was?' asked Annie.

'To ask Paul to stand.'

'Paul? Why not Vérronique?'

René, Christian and Josette looked at each other, the farmer finally opting to be spokesman. 'We didn't think . . . or rather, I didn't think she'd say yes. The way she is at the moment… She doesn't want to talk about anything to do with politics.'

'She thinks it helped lead Serge to an early grave,' explained Josette. 'And deprived her of longer with her father.'

Annie blinked, knowing that the other factor Véronique was blaming for her lack of time with her Papa was being left unsaid.

'Do you think we should have asked her?' Josette continued.

'Like I'd know. She's barrrely talking to me. But it might do herrr good. Give herrr something else to think about.'

'Am I interrupting?' Alain Rougé had approached the group, an uneasy expression on his normally sanguine face. 'I wonder if I could have a word, Christian.'

'Sure,' said the farmer, using the distraction to steal another portion of the sublime duck appetiser. 'Fire away.'

'I'm resigning.'

Christian gasped, the canapé flying to the back of his throat and almost choking him.

'Resigning? From the Conseil Municipal?' hissed René, taking no notice of his spluttering friend whose back was now being thumped robustly by Annie Estaque. 'Are you trying to throw us to the wolves?'

Alain shrugged helplessly and tapped his chest. 'It's my heart. The doctor said I'm to start taking it easy. So after what happened to Serge . . . You all know how stressful the last few years have been.'

'Stressful? That's nothing compared to what's coming if we don't get a majority on the council. And of all the days to announce it—'

Christian, his breath finally regained, put out a hand to hold back the enraged plumber before turning to Alain. 'I don't suppose we can change your mind?'

'Sorry, but I've been thinking about it for a while. And I know today isn't ideal timing but, as interim mayor, Pascal will get my formal letter tomorrow so I thought I'd give you a heads up. No hard feelings, I hope?'

Christian smiled, grasping the ex-policeman in a firm handshake. 'None whatsoever. But you could help us choose a second candidate.'

'Véronique,' Alain replied without hesitation, his attention going to the postmistress who was listening intently to Major

Gaillard as he related a tale about Serge. 'And possibly Fabian or Paul as the other. But you have to have Véronique on there. She's all the good bits of her father with the benefit of her mother's wisdom.'

Annie sniffed at Alain's compliment and then belied her gruff reaction by passing him a canapé.

'See!' said René, arms held wide in exasperation. 'I said this right at the beginning. We have to get her to stand. It was bad enough when we were fielding just the one candidate. But now we need two and they're up against Fatima Souquet and God knows who else . . .'

'He's right,' said Josette. 'No disrespect to Fabian and Paul but this news throws everything out of balance. We've lost two supporters in Alain and Serge and I can't see anyone beating Fatima. Which means we *have* to win that second seat or we will lose control of the council.'

'And if Pascal has his way, we'll lose Fogas shorrrtly afterrr,' muttered Annie darkly.

Christian ran a hand through his curls. 'Okay, okay. We all agree. Véronique has to be persuaded. But how?'

They all looked over at the pale postmistress, still engrossed in her conversation with the fireman, apart from Stephanie, whose disbelieving focus was on the empty tray in her hand.

'What are you up to, you sly old bugger?'

'Less of the old!' snapped Serge from under the counter as he tried to cover up the object lying on the floor next to him. But it was impossible.

'How did you get hold of that?' Jacques pointed an accusatory finger at the glowing screen visible through Serge's translucent hands.

Serge sighed, accepting that his secret was out and partly pleased that it was. He'd been dying to share his discovery for days but hadn't known how Jacques would respond to it. He was about to find out.

'I got it last night,' he said, crawling out from his hiding place, his knees groaning as Jacques helped him to his feet. 'Josette left it recharging behind the bar.'

'But how . . .' Jacques looked at the shelf where an orphaned cable hung down from a plug and then over at the mobile phone nestled in the dirty tea towels. 'You *moved* it?'

Serge couldn't stop the smug smile from tweaking his lips.

'But . . . but . . .' Jacques shook his head, nonplussed. 'That's not possible.'

In reply, Serge stretched out an arthritic finger, bent and swollen with age, and gently pressed against the side of an empty espresso cup on the bar. Focusing intently, forehead creased with effort, he started to push. And to Jacques amazement, the cup started to move, jerking in tiny increments across the surface.

'You . . . you . . . oh!' An expression of delight suffused with guilt and trepidation floated across Jacques' face, making him look like the young boy all those years ago who'd spent a childhood being both awed and alarmed by the actions of his much more daring best friend. His fluctuating features settled on consternation when, with a final push, the espresso cup tipped off the edge of the bar.

Jacques instinctively reached out to catch it. And had to watch in horror as it passed right through his out-stretched hand and shattered on the floorboards.

'You broke a cup!' Jacques admonished. 'Josette will go mad.'

Serge shrugged and Jacques was reminded of his infuriating disregard for authority that had got them into so many scrapes as children. Like the time just after the war when he'd persuaded Jacques that it would be fun to teach the grocer,

Monsieur Pons, a lesson. A man who thought he was of superior stature to his neighbours – being a person of business as opposed to a farmer – Monsieur Pons had invited very few of them to the wedding of his oldest daughter. It was a decision which had caused much grumbling across the three villages of the commune and a boycott of his shop up in Fogas, the Servat épicerie in La Rivière benefitting temporarily from the resentment until people got tired of walking all the way down the mountain for their morning baguette. Fired up by the complaints of the adults around him, and from a sense of indignation at being deemed unsuitable company for the nuptials, young Serge had hatched a plan.

It involved climbing onto the roof of the Pons house. In winter.

While the wedding party was at the church, the two lads had scrambled up behind the property, its walls tucked into the hillside, thus allowing them to crawl easily onto the slippery slates of the roof. Making slow progress with trembling hands, Jacques had tried to quell his nerves as the more confident Serge clambered onto the ridge and laid a wet sack across the top of the chimney.

Slithering quickly back to the ground, they'd hidden in the woodshed, waiting for Monsieur Pons to lead the newlyweds and their guests home for the feast which was already prepared inside. It had been the longest fifteen minutes of Jacques' short life. Palms sweating, mouth dry, he'd tried several times to suggest they should abort – before there was any chance of real trouble. But every time, the words had got stuck in his throat. Because he feared Serge's derision far more than he did the consequences of getting caught.

Finally the last of the celebrants had entered the small house and closed the door. Serge sneaked out from behind the stacks of wood, gesturing impatiently for the terrified

Jacques to follow, and together they'd rolled the large water butt that normally stood under the downpipe across to the front door. Using all their youthful might, they'd heaved the full butt onto an edge, until it was resting precariously against the door, water sloshing over them in the process.

And then they were both running, keeping below window height across the yard so they wouldn't be seen. When they reached the cover of the woods at the edge of Fogas, they stopped, turning back to watch.

It didn't take long. The fire, lit as soon as the guests entered the house, started to smoke, inciting the complaining tones of Monsieur Pons as he castigated his wife for being incapable of getting the fire to draw. Amidst the spluttering and coughing and streaming eyes, a wise person suggested the only possible solution.

Open the front door.

Jacques would never forget the sight of Monsieur Pons in his finery, the door opening wide and the rush of water cascading over him and into the house as the barrel clattered to the floor. He stood there, mouth gaping, clothes soaked, while the screams and shrieks of the drenched local elite came from behind him.

The two boys had got away with it. The episode entered Fogas folklore with no names attached. Although Old Monsieur Papon, Serge's gruff father who only paid attention to kids when they needed a clip round the ear, bought them both a new fishing rod at the market the following Saturday.

'Perhaps they'll keep you out of trouble,' he'd said with a twinkle.

The present-day Jacques, staring at the shards of china on the floor of the bar, didn't think a fishing rod would be enough anymore. His friend of old had found real power.

'What else can you do?' he demanded, thrilled and scared by what the answer might be.

'Thought you'd never ask,' said Serge with a broad smile.

Pascal couldn't stop smiling. Which was unfortunate, bearing in mind he was at a wake and was supposed to be grieving. But every time he tried to pull the corners of his thin lips down into a respectful position, they curved back up again.

It had been a hellish week. The tension of walking a tightrope between his two masters had left him drained and in despair. For he had been at a loss as to how he could appease both Fatima and Henri Dedieu when it came to the council elections. It had seemed like an impossible task. But now . . .

His lips surged upwards once more.

'Pascal! For God's sake show some respect!' hissed Fatima, appearing at his elbow from nowhere and scaring any trace of a smirk off his face.

'Sorry . . . I . . . er . . .'

'Have you heard?' she continued, not waiting for his stuttering apology as her sharp cheekbones pressed close to his face. 'Alain Rougé is resigning from the Conseil Municipal.'

He did his best to look surprised. 'Oh?'

'Oh, indeed. That means two seats up for the taking. You'd best get thinking about who the second person is going to be.'

He managed a nod before she turned to speak to one of the interminable second-home owners who always seemed to be attached to her elbow. When her attention was fully diverted, he moved across to the table of food, helped himself to another *gougère* – which he had to admit were exceptional – and allowed the smile to develop once more.

Because he already knew. He'd heard Alain's announcement from Philippe Galy who had overheard that fool René Piquemal ranting. And the news had saved his life. Two places available on the council. Two spaces on the nomination papers that would be filed in the coming weeks. Which meant he no longer had to make the impossible choice between the two candidates he'd been told must stand.

Savouring the taste of the *gougère* and the taste of certain success in the crucial mayoral vote that lay beyond the by-election – for Christian Dupuy's majority was dwindling by the day – he raised his eyes and was caught in the steely trap of Henri Dedieu's gaze. And for the second time in mere minutes, Pascal Souquet's inappropriate smile fell from his lips.

'What a long affair!' exclaimed Josette as she walked back up the road in the early afternoon sunshine, Chloé Morvan keeping her company on an errand to collect a baguette for her mother. 'Never thought we'd get away.'

'But you didn't try to,' said Chloé with the perspicacity of youth. 'You kept stopping to talk to people.'

Josette was stumped for an answer. So she changed the subject. 'How's school going?'

Chloé pulled a face, her days spent in the classroom a torture depriving her of time in the mountains. 'I still hate it. But at least I've made friends with other kids who hate it too.'

Josette laughed. 'Well, there's a logic there all right. Just make sure you stay top of the class and you can hate it all you like.'

Still chuckling, she reached into her handbag for the key to the épicerie, opened the door and entered. When she glanced through to the bar, it took an awful lot of control not to scream.

'You cheated!' insisted Jacques. 'You pressed the wrong answer!'

'No I didn't. I pressed C. That was what you said.'

'I said B!'

Serge shrugged, eyes on the screen of the mobile phone

which now lay in the middle of the floor in the bar, the two of them kneeling over it, trying to read the text with aged eyesight that couldn't be corrected by glasses anymore. 'Sorry. My mistake. Feel free to enter your own answer next time . . .'

'That's not fair. I don't—'

'You don't have any power? I know!' Serge laughed, dragging a taunting finger across the screen, the image dimpling and flickering in response.

Josette's smart phone. They'd spent hours playing on it, Serge able to access the internet with a swipe of a digit. Considering that neither man had had much time for the new technology when alive, they were making up for missed opportunities. Sports news. Politics. Blogs. They'd not so much surfed the web as trawled it, looking at everything and anything on the way. And then they'd found the general knowledge quiz. Playable in two teams, they'd taken it in turns to answer, their abilities finely matched until Jacques got on a roll, answering several questions back to back correctly. He'd started to pull slightly ahead. Which was when Serge started to cheat.

'I do have power,' said an enraged Jacques, miffed that Serge had only just entered his world and seemed to have conquered it already. 'Look.'

He threw a fist at the mayor, connecting with his shoulder and causing him to jump up in pain.

'God you haven't changed. You're still a sore loser.'

'And you're still a cheat!' shouted Jacques, getting to his feet.

'Loser!'

'Cheat!'

Then Serge lunged at Jacques, Jacques leaned back and trapped the mayor's head under his arm, the former mayor threw his weight to the side to break free, Jacques countered by wrapping a thin arm around the mayor's leg, and the front door opened revealing Josette and Chloé on the threshold.

All Josette saw was a contortion of limbs cavorting around the bar. She thought it was Jacques in the throes of some bizarre seizure but then she noticed the second set of legs . . . the second sizeable bottom . . . and the forehead! That forehead which should be in a box in the cemetery up the road.

'Serge!' squealed Chloé, clapping her hands in delight, her gypsy roots leaving her completely unfazed by this unexpected development. The two ghosts froze, guilt stealing over their pale countenances.

'Josette!' exclaimed Jacques, releasing his hold on Serge who promptly staggered and fell on his backside. 'I can explain . . .'

Josette saw his lips moving soundlessly. But she made no effort to understand. Because the woman who had coped with having her phantom husband dwelling in her hearth for two and a half years, couldn't cope with this latest addition.

She sank to the floor in a dead faint.

7

'It's up! It's up!'

René burst into the épicerie, setting the bell on the door jingling furiously and nearly colliding with Fabian, who was stooped over, rearranging the soft-toy versions of Sarko the bull which for some reason had all been herded to the end of one shelf. It wasn't the first time the Parisian had arrived at work in the morning only to spend a large part of his day reorganising the shop, the past five days since the funeral having seen packets of biscuits moved, oranges rolled off their rack and the blasted strings of saucisson left draped over the till. Fabian didn't know what was going on but suspected that Tante Josette was having some sort of crisis that led to her mislaying things. Like her mobile phone which she never seemed to have to hand lately. Possibly this affliction was precipitated by the sudden death of Serge Papon. Whatever the cause, he was getting tired of the constant meddling with the stock and was on the brink of asking her outright what she was up to. It was opportune then, for Josette, that the end of Fabian's tether coincided with René's dramatic entrance and forestalled the inquisition. As she wouldn't have been able to give him the answer if she'd tried.

'What are you talking about?' she asked from behind the till where she was handing over change to Madame Rogalle, a worried eye on her nephew and his patient tidying.

'The notice for the election. It's up.' René pointed excitedly in the direction of the noticeboard, which was on the side of the épicerie closest to the church.

'And?' asked Fabian, his attention diverted from the wayward bulls. 'When is it?'

'The sixth of March.'

Josette's eyebrows rose in surprise. 'That's plenty of time.'

'Hopefully.' The plumber nodded towards the figure languishing behind the post office counter at the far end of the shop and dropped his voice. 'All we need now is to find a way to change her mind.'

'Here's just the person,' said Josette, watching a blue Panda judder to a halt in front of the épicerie window, steam hissing out from under the bonnet.

'That doesn't look good,' observed Fabian as Christian extricated himself from the confines of the small car in a blast of curses and profanities. He gave it a kick on his way to the épicerie and was still growling when he opened the door.

'Bonjour, Christian,' said Josette with a smile. 'Car problems?'

He grunted and bent down to kiss her cheek before shaking hands with the men.

'Blasted thing. The radiator is leaking again. But this time I don't think a bottle of Anti-fuite will fix it. I'm going to have to replace it.'

'Can't you get the garage to look at it?' asked Fabian, his mechanical expertise not stretching beyond two-wheeled, non-motorised vehicles.

Christian shook his head wearily. 'It's not worth it. I'd buy a new car for what they charge. I might as well have a go myself. When I find the time to get down to the scrapyard for the parts, that is.'

'Never mind all that.' René waved an impatient hand at the farmer. 'The date for the election has been announced.'

'And?'

'The first Sunday in March.'

'So how long does that give us before the nominations have to be in?'

'The closing date is the third Thursday before the vote. Which makes it . . .'

Josette patted her pockets for her errant mobile but Fabian beat her to it, his long fingers already skimming through the calendar on his phone.

'February seventeenth,' he said.

'A month from today, then,' murmured Christian. And he turned to look at the forlorn features of the woman in the post office. 'Let's hope it's long enough.'

'A year from today wouldn't be long enough at the rate you're going,' grumbled René. 'We already know we're up against formidable opposition in Fatima. If Pascal pulls another candidate like that out of the bag, we're doomed. We have to have Véronique on that nomination paper.'

'All right!' Christian snapped. 'I'll ask her again. But don't say I didn't warn you.'

And with that he took long strides down the length of the shop towards the woman with the sad face; the woman who was breaking his heart.

She'd kept her head down all morning, eyes fixed on La Poste's huge folder detailing overseas parcel tariffs. First class, second class, recorded, tracked, insured . . . She'd slowly leafed through the pages, careful not to look up even when René burst in making such a racket. Because if she looked up, someone would ask her how she was. Or try to get her talking. And she'd have to make an effort to be normal. To be the woman she'd been before. A person so alien to her now, it was like acting a part in which she kept fluffing her lines.

Eleven days. Less time than it took for an economy parcel to get to Saint-Pierre-et-Miquelon. But enough to turn her world on its head and leave her in a confused heap, dazed and disorientated in this new reality where she could no longer anticipate that stout figure barging through the door; where everything seemed fragile, the bonds that tied her to people, which had appeared so robust, so solid, now no more than wisps of gossamer, threatened by the mildest of breezes.

That made her think of Maman, up the hill on the farm with only the dogs for company. She hadn't seen her since the day of the funeral when she'd appeared at the door, so old. So worried. A spasm of guilt came out of nowhere but Véronique brushed it aside with an impatient turn of a page. What did Maman expect? Keeping that stupid secret all those years. Did she really think it would all turn out fine in the end? As for her peace-keeping present – Véronique hadn't even opened it. She'd got back from the wake late in the afternoon with Christian and had shoved it in a drawer in the dresser. He hadn't commented. Hadn't dared with the mood she'd been in. And she hadn't been near it since. Whatever it was, it could never make amends for what had happened.

The bell above the épicerie door trilled again and she heard his voice, heard him cursing about his car and greeting the others. And she knew that all the time, his anxious gaze would be on her.

She didn't deserve him. Not with the way she was behaving. One minute crying her eyes out, the next, snapping and snarling at anyone within reach. Which unfortunately happened to be Christian more often than not. But she was incapable of controlling her oscillating emotions and found herself simultaneously craving his presence yet longing to be alone. All of which resulted in the farmer being banished back to his farm most nights, rather than spending his sleeping hours at her apartment as had been the case before grief had torn her life apart. Christian had borne it all like a saint. But how much longer would he tolerate it? Tolerate her?

She heard his measured steps approaching, the heavy set to his walk, the smell of cold air and mountains.

Smile. For him. No matter how much it takes.

Véronique tried, pulling her lips into a curve as the big farmer came towards her. But her eyes remained doleful, not a spark to be seen.

'Morning!' Christian leaned in across the counter to kiss her, his lips cool against hers from his journey down from Picarets in the unheated Panda. 'Busy as always I see.'

She gave an attempt at a laugh. 'You missed the rush.'

He smiled, eyes warm but wary, and she knew he was assessing her. Testing her mood. After the last few weeks, who could blame him?

Reaching out a hand, she ran it down the side of his face, fingers grazing over his cheek.

'I'm sorry,' she said, her palm lingering on the rough bristle of his unshaven jaw. He turned and kissed it.

'What for?'

'You know . . .' She shrugged. 'I'm not exactly good company lately.'

He lifted a hand and enclosed hers in his, his grip strong, real, enough to cut through her lethargy.

Only it wasn't. Nothing was. Immersed in a grey world where the only flashes of colour came from bursts of sorrow or anger, Véronique felt like she was slowly drowning. She marked her days with morning stints in the post office, the routine of her job making no inroads on her concentration. And her afternoons she spent sitting in her flat, watching clouds scud across the mountains. Thinking of nothing.

Josette had tried to persuade her to take up her hours in the shop again, working odd afternoons when Fabian was busy, like she used to. But it was clear that with Francine Rougé helping out more and more at the Auberge, thus allowing Stephanie to run her garden centre pretty much full time and freeing up Fabian in the process, Véronique's assistance in the épicerie was no longer as vital. That was her excuse. The real reason, the one she hadn't explained? She could no longer be bothered. With anything.

'Considering the company I used to keep, you've nothing to apologise for,' Christian said.

Véronique felt the energy of his smile and tried to meet him halfway. 'Considering you're referring to a cantankerous old bull and René, that's not saying much.'

That provoked a grin, a flash of white in his weathered face shot through with relief.

'That's my girl,' he murmured, raising her still trapped hand and brushing his lips across her knuckles. 'It'll be okay.'

She lowered her gaze before he could see the truth. She was a long way from okay. And she didn't know if he would have the patience to wait while she found her way back there. If she ever did.

It was a beautiful day. Sure, the Monday morning air had a chill to it. You wouldn't want to linger too long in the shade. But out in the sunshine, it felt like spring was just around the corner. Up in Fogas, it was enough to bring the locals outside, the usual group of old men clustered around the disused *lavoir* at the entrance to the village and a gaggle of women gathered around the butcher's van parked opposite it. Normally only present in Fogas on a Thursday, today was an exception, Agnès Rogalle fitting in an extra visit to compensate for having missed the village the week before, the funeral having thrown her schedule. It was no hardship, however, and with the side hatch of the van propped open, Agnès was busy serving her customers meat and gossip, all parcelled up with the care of a true professional.

'Her cross. She threw it in the grave. I mean . . . that shows doesn't it . . . ?' she said as she swung her knife down and severed the head off a chicken which she threw into the bin at her feet while her audience digested the news.

'Oh my! I didn't see that—'

'Her cross? The silver one—?'

'The one the curé gave her—'

'The curé? What, the new one—?'

'—years ago when she was a kid. She was being bullied—'

'It's such a shame—'

'Is that everything?' Agnès asked, placing the headless chicken in the bag along with the other purchases.

'I'll take some of those Toulouse sausages too. Yves has taken a real fancy to them.' Madame Degeilh turned to the woman next to her. 'At his age, it's a miracle he has the energy to fancy anything!'

Ribald laughter burst from the group causing the men leaning against the *lavoir* wall to glance over.

'You causing trouble, Agnès?' called out Pierre Mené, his eyes squinting against the sun and the smoke of his cigarette.

'It's not her,' replied Widow Aubert. 'It's her sausages!'

And another peal of laughter rang out from the women, floating up into the blue sky and bringing forth delighted smiles on the creased faces of the old men. It truly was a wonderful day.

It was a perfect day. The sun was warm on his back. The air was filled with intoxicating scents. And the butcher's van was in town.

He crouched there, in the alleyway between two houses,

hunkered down. The van was in front of him, rear door propped partially open. Through the gap he could see the stocky figure of the woman as she sliced and chopped, her broad arms moving quickly. He watched intently. Gauged his moment. And when a loud shout of laughter came from the women at the serving hatch, he made his move.

Silently. Across the short distance to the open door, keeping his body low, hugging the walls as far as he could. Then a quick burst across the open space to the back door. He waited there, peering inside. This was the dangerous bit – that knife, the thick blade flashing in the sunlight. If she caught him . . .

But he was good – a hunter by instinct. She twisted away from him, reaching across to a tray of sausages. And he seized his chance.

By the time she turned back to serve the next customer, he was gone, slinking down the alley carrying his precious prize. Heading for home.

He'd chickened out. Christian slapped the steering wheel on the Panda and cursed out loud. It was impossible, he decided, as the car twisted and turned on the steep road up to Fogas. There was never going to be a right time to broach the subject of politics with Véronique. Not with the way she was at the moment.

So brittle. As though she would splinter into a million pieces at the slightest touch.

It wasn't the Véronique he knew. A tough woman, able to deal with anything, even the shocking truth about her father. But that robust façade had been fractured and he felt awkward around her. Like he did handling his great-grandmother's porcelain serving plates, which his mother insisted on using every Christmas and New Year. One slip with his clumsy hands and the delicately-patterned china would shatter on the kitchen tiles.

That's how it was with Véronique. And he was damned if he was going to go storming in, asking her to reconsider her stance on becoming a candidate, and risk rupturing what little control she had left. Even if he knew, possibly more than René, how important the forthcoming election was. For Fogas, it was the last chance.

Grim faced, he turned the final corner on the mountain road and emerged from the trees, the full span of the Pyrenees laid out before him, glistening in their snow-clad brilliance. And yet again, he understood – kind of – why his ancestors had insisted on building the town hall up here in out-of-the-way Fogas when they had picked up the courage to break away from the more powerful Sarrat across the river. One look at that view, and any qualms they'd had about stepping out on their own would have been quashed.

It was a view to kill for. And it was what defined this commune. But if he was to keep it within these borders, he would have to risk losing the woman he loved. For only Véronique's name on that ballot paper would extricate Fogas from the predicament it was facing. Even then, it would take a lot of work. Perhaps even a miracle.

Without her participation, however, there was no chance.

Facing the unsavoury prospect of a no-win situation, he swung the car left into the village and slammed on the brakes. The place was in chaos.

'One at a time, please!' shouted Christian, a large hand held up to stop the riot of voices that had accosted him the minute he got out of his car. 'Or we won't get anywhere.'

He was standing in front of the *lavoir*, opposite the butcher's van, and was surrounded by a group of men and women, all locals apart from Agnès Rogalle. But it was her voice that emerged from the chaos. Possibly because she was the loudest. Or perhaps because she was still wielding a tool of her profession, the knife glinting in the morning sunshine as she brandished it at Christian.

'That bastard . . . !' she fumed, face purple above her white apron. 'He's been here again.'

'The thief? Was something stolen?'

She threw up her arms in disgust, making those around her duck at the proximity of the blade. 'You have to ask?'

'What was it this time?'

'My dinner,' grumbled one of the men towards the back, beret sloped over an ill-humoured face.

'If you could be more precise?' sighed Christian.

'A rabbit. He took the last bloody rabbit.' Agnès shook her head. 'A really plump one it was too. I hope the bastard chokes on it!'

'When was this?'

'Not more than ten minutes ago,' said Yves Degeilh. 'Any sooner and it could have been my sausages!'

And just like that, the mood changed and laughter flashed around the group. But Agnès wasn't laughing.

'Tell me how it happened,' said Christian.

Agnès grunted. 'It just did. One minute I had a rabbit. The next, I had an empty shelf.'

Christian looked over at the van, back door open, side hatch propped up. Then he looked at the villagers gathered around him, most of the women clutching plastic bags bearing the butcher's name.

'Hang on,' he said. 'Are you telling me you were all out here when it happened?'

Nods all round.

'And you were in the van, Agnès?'

'Yes. Why?'

He scratched his head. 'None of you saw anything?'

They looked at each other and over at the van as though they could recall the moment and see the perpetrator in the act.

'Not a thing,' offered Yves Degeilh.

'Which just shows how cunning this bugger is.' Agnès gestured at the village with the knife, making people cower again. 'Next thing you know, he'll be breaking into houses and you'll all have to start locking your back doors at night. You won't be safe in your beds!'

A murmur of disquiet rumbled around the group.

'So, what are you going to do?' Hands now resting on her hips, she stared at Christian.

He shrugged, helplessly. 'What can I do, Agnès? I'll have a quick look around the area, see if anything is out of place. Then I'm heading to the town hall, so I'll make sure the secretary makes a note of it and I'll see if Pascal has any ideas. Other than that . . .'

'What about the gendarmes?' asked Widow Aubert. 'Can't you call them?'

'Don't be daft, woman,' said Yves Degeilh. 'They've got more important things to be doing than chasing someone who steals rabbits.'

'You wouldn't be saying that if it had been your sausages!' quipped Widow Aubert and another gust of laughter broke from the group.

Seizing his chance to escape, Christian abandoned his Panda and walked up the hill to the town hall, making sure to take the back route past the butcher's van and down the alley towards the orchards, eyes alert for any sign of criminal activity. When he arrived at the front of the majestic building that housed the Conseil Municipal for Fogas, he had seen nothing more suspect than a few pieces of litter, several discarded cigarette butts and Bernard Mirouze playing with his dog in his back garden. He climbed the steps with a weary tread and entered the tiled hallway. Placing a hand on the worn wood of the newel post, he heard a string of curses coming from the offices up above. His day wasn't about to get any better.

'How can you have deleted it? The entire bloody electoral register?' Céline Laffont, secretary of Fogas Town Hall, slammed her chair back from her desk and stood, hands balled into fists at her side as she glowered at the interim mayor across the room. 'What kind of a blundering incompetent are you?'

'I must remind you to whom you are talking—'

'I know exactly *to whom* I'm talking! You're the worst thing that ever happened to this place.'

'You can't speak to me like that! I'm the interim mayor—'

'*Don't*!' The icy anger in Céline's tone brought Pascal up short. 'Don't you dare use that title in my presence. You're not fit to even mention Serge Papon's name, let alone take his post.'

Christian stood in the doorway, debating whether to intervene, enjoying the sight of Pascal squirming under Céline's onslaught. Then she spotted him and whatever pleasure he'd been taking in the scene quickly evaporated under her withering glare.

'And as for you, Monsieur Dupuy! It's about bloody time you showed up. There's a mountain of paperwork that needs organising for the election and none of it has been processed yet. And you haven't replied to any of the emails I've forwarded that need your attention.'

'Sorry, I've been so busy—'

Céline didn't give him time to finish. '*Busy*? When are you going to realise that *nothing* is more important than this? Because without this, the commune ceases to exist. Serge knew that. And I thought you, Christian, of all people, understood it too. Now if you don't mind, I have to try to retrieve the electoral register which your idiot colleague seems to have deleted.'

She gave one last wrathful look at the pair of them and sat back down, her fingers thumping away at the keyboard, face still dark with anger.

Pascal turned on his heel and took refuge in the mayor's office, leaving Christian to endure the tense atmosphere. He had only just crossed the room to stare dejectedly at the pile of files on his desk that required his attention when ponderous steps could be heard approaching up the stairs.

'Bonjour!' exclaimed Bernard, his beagle close on his heels. 'Have you sorted out the clock yet, Christian?'

Christian looked up. 'Bonjour, Bernard. What clock?'

The thump of keys got noticeably louder.

Bernard frowned. 'Céline said she emailed you.' He glanced at the secretary but her face was pure granite. He shrugged, and turned back to Christian. 'The one out front. It's not working.'

'Really? I came in just now and didn't notice.'

The sharp noise from behind Céline's computer screen was as good as an entire harangue about Christian's worthlessness.

He scratched his head. 'When did it stop?'

'The day after Serge . . .' Bernard faltered, still not at a point where he could talk about the great man's demise without distress.

'That long? And no one's done anything?' Christian shot a look through the doorway into the mayor's office where Pascal's haughty features protruded above what looked like an auction catalogue. The staccato of typing had got even louder.

Bernard shuffled awkwardly. 'I tried. But it's so high up. I couldn't do it.'

Christian nodded. It wasn't an easy job. The clock was on the façade of the town hall, a precarious climb up a ladder and such an unenviable prospect that it had been decided long ago, long before Christian joined the council, that it was too onerous to change the time every spring and every autumn. Consequently, the people of Fogas had become accustomed to the town hall timepiece galloping ahead in the winter months, an hour faster than real time as though impatient to get to summer.

'Pascal?' Christian called out. 'Have you sorted out someone to look at the clock?'

'I've delegated it to you,' came the snippy reply. 'Didn't you get my email?'

'Email. Email. Always bloody email,' muttered Christian. 'When did we all stop talking to each other?' He sat down at his desk, quickly logged on to his account and flinched at the quantity of mail demanding his attention, most of them from Céline and Pascal. Skimming through his inbox, ignoring a circular from L'Association des Maires Ruraux de France decrying the latest government calls for the merging of small communes and a complaint from a second-home owner about the fact that the Christmas tree in La Rivière was still standing, he found the relevant one and opened it to read a brusque instruction that he fix the clock.

Fix the clock? There was no way he could climb all the way up there. Not with his vertigo. Not even if it was Véronique doing the asking.

'Right. We'd best call someone in then,' said Christian, looking hopefully over at Céline. His silent entreaty was met with a deafening rattle of keys. There would be no help from that quarter. 'Don't suppose you know of anyone, Bernard?'

The *cantonnier* shook his head. 'Nope. We've never had need to repair it since I've been here. All the while Serge was in power it kept time perfectly. And then the minute he . . .' He paused and wiped a hand across his eyes.

'Like everything else around here,' came a loud mutter from the corner. 'Falling to pieces now he's gone.'

'Leave it with me,' said Christian, ignoring Céline's running commentary and reaching for the telephone directory. 'I'll see what I can—'

The door smacked open, cutting him off and revealing a panting, red-faced Agnès Rogalle on the threshold, something dangling from her left hand.

'Where is he?' she demanded as Serge the beagle went trotting over to investigate what she was carrying.

'Who?' asked Christian.

'Your *interim* mayor.'

Christian tipped his head towards the office next door and then scrambled round his desk to get a better view as Agnès stormed towards an already apprehensive Pascal.

'There!' she said, thrusting something down in front of him which made the refined man jump to his feet with what could only be called a shriek, while the dog started barking. 'I know you Parisians can't tell a rabbit from a squirrel, so that's what you're looking for. Now find the bloody culprit who's stealing my stock. And when you do, let me know and I'll resume my deliveries. In the meantime, Fogas will have to go elsewhere for its meat.'

She turned, Bernard and Christian both leaping away from the doorway where they'd been straining to see what Pascal was staring at, and, scooping the beagle up with one hand, she marched back in to the outer office.

'Here,' she said, placing the dog into Bernard's arms, her voice noticeably softer as Serge nuzzled her palm. 'I take it you've heard about the traps in the forests round here?'

Bernard shook his head and she glared at Christian.

'What kind of half-baked Conseil Municipal is this? Why haven't you posted the warnings?'

'What warnings?' asked Christian.

'From the forestry department! They sent out a notice to all communes in this district last week. Someone has been setting illegal traps in the woods. Louis Claustre's dog got caught in one above Picarets three days ago. Had to be put down. But you're acting first deputy mayor, you should know all this.'

Christian shook his head, glancing over at Céline who was now hammering at her keyboard. 'No. It's the first I've heard. I'm not that good with email—'

'Email?' Agnès snorted. 'That's not how Serge did things. He talked to people. He listened to people. If he was still here, he would have known this was going on before the relevant department had to tell him.'

She gave Christian a searing look, jerking her thumb at Pascal who'd been turned to stone by whatever was on his desk. 'This place has no chance with him in charge, but I thought you were capable of a bit more. Seems I was wrong. Looks like Sarrat will be expanding over the river after all. Ah well. Makes no difference to me.'

With a final pat for the appreciative beagle, she nodded over at Céline, who actually smiled in return, and took her leave.

'Céline,' came a pitiful cry from the mayor's office. 'Céline, get this off my desk. Please!'

Whether it was an inability to resist such a plaintive call for help or an insatiable desire to know what the offending item was, Céline stood up and headed into the mayor's office, closely followed by Christian and Bernard.

'It's revolting. Please, Céline. Take it away.'

But Céline did no such thing. She was too busy laughing at the severed rabbit's head that was bleeding all over the Parisian auction catalogue. And standing there, in that immense room, with the secretary's derisive laughter echoing off the bare walls, Christian got a sense of just how much work was needed to begin filling even a fraction of the gap Serge had left in the life of Fogas.

They weren't ready. The man behind the desk clearly didn't have the ability to lead. Under the stewardship of Pascal Souquet, there would be no need for a merger, as he would single-handedly run Fogas into the ground. But after today, Christian wasn't even sure that he could successfully run the commune. Certainly not alone. If he had help, however . . .

And the farmer knew more than ever just how important it was that Véronique be persuaded to pick up her political baton once more. The only problem was convincing her.

8

By mid-February, in what was proving to be one of the mildest winters in living memory, Fogas was beginning to show signs of spring. Snowdrops had left the riverbanks and the ground beneath the trees splattered in large patches of white, and mistletoe provided a vibrant green in the still bare branches. The fields were beginning to shake off the hues of winter and, down at the Auberge, the tender shoots of daffodils were already poking through the soil.

It was most unusual. And it made the bedraggled Christmas tree, left forgotten on the patch of land outside Stephanie's garden centre, look even more incongruous.

'We must take that down,' mused Josette to no one in particular as she stood at the épicerie window, her gaze fixed on the forlorn relic of the festive season which had remained half-stripped of its decorations since the day Serge died. The bows and baubles that had been so admired were now bedraggled, offering no splendour amidst the brown and withered branches of the once majestic tree.

It was like a metaphor for the commune, she thought, frozen in time at the point of the mayor's death, unable to move forward and starting to die.

Over a month since the fateful day and nothing had happened in Fogas. Nothing at all. The tree hadn't been cleared away. The council hadn't met. Applications for permits and planning permission weren't being processed. The Butcher Burglar hadn't been apprehended and Agnès Rogalle no longer visited with her van. Christian hadn't plucked up the nerve to ask Véronique about standing for the election. And even the clock on the town hall had entered a period of stasis, with no one yet booked in to fix it.

The three villages were paralysed.

A movement down the road drew Josette's attention away from the miserable Christmas tree. Véronique, head down, black coat tucked tight around her despite the morning sunshine as she made her way to church. She was losing weight, the fabric drooping from her shoulders, her cheekbones more pronounced. Someone else who'd been paralysed by Serge's death. Her relationship with her mother turned more than frosty too.

Annie had made a rare excursion to the shop last week and had yielded to Josette's insistence that she stay for a cup of coffee. They'd taken their drinks outside in the back garden, away from the prying ears and eyes of Fogas, and over a pain au chocolat or two Annie had poured her heart out. She was in despair. Véronique wouldn't answer her calls and had visited the farm only twice since the Epiphany. Both times she'd brought Christian Dupuy with her, preventing Annie from addressing the poisoned atmosphere between them. Annie was at her wits' end and Josette hadn't been able to help, other than listening and plying her friend with coffee.

Paralysed. It really did reflect the situation in the commune. Apart from in here, in the épicerie and bar, where there was altogether too much going on . . .

A distinct tut from behind made Josette turn. Fabian, fussing over the shelves, rearranging the tins and pieces of fruit that had repositioned themselves overnight. She could tell from the tension across his shoulders that he wasn't happy. The low murmuring that was accompanying his work was another clue.

'Everything okay, Fabian?' she asked, a thrill of devilment taking her. He glanced up, an orange in one hand, apple in the other, and he blushed.

'Fine. Why wouldn't it be?' he replied before resuming his Sisyphean labour.

It wasn't, of course. Yet he was reluctant to say anything. Instead he subjected Josette to the same routine of tutting and reorganising every morning he was there, which was pretty much daily now that Stephanie had taken the brave step of giving up her job at the Auberge to concentrate fully on her garden centre. With Fabian no longer needed across the road to provide cover, he was free to work more hours at the épicerie; a fact Josette had been glad of until the 'incidents' started.

The incidents. It was the only way she knew how to describe them. Saucisson falling off the rack, oranges rolled across the floor, pictures askew . . . And her mobile phone never where it should be. After four weeks, Josette was still none the wiser as to the cause of the nocturnal happenings. She was, however, a lot more tired. Convinced that she was stumbling her way downstairs every night to create somnambulant havoc, she'd tried staying awake, determined to catch herself out. A double espresso followed by a slice of spicy saucisson had been her bedtime routine for the last week. The result? A couple of hours wide awake with stomach cramps and adrenalin, followed by a comatose sleep that couldn't be penetrated by the alarm. After two mornings of complaints from customers when she was late opening, she'd abandoned her scheme. Especially as it hadn't made any difference – she'd still been greeted by mayhem in the shop when she finally made it down there.

She turned a weary glance to the bar where two ghostly figures were sitting either side of the fire, bickering away. She could just ask them, of course. See if Jacques or Serge had spotted her wandering around in her nightdress when she should be asleep. But her sense of dignity wouldn't let her. If she was losing her mind, she didn't want anyone else to know about it. Not yet.

So tonight she was going to try something different. Something that would tell her once and for all whether she was leaving the confines of her bedroom during the small hours and behaving in a way that could only be the onset of dementia.

And if she wasn't?

In the room beyond, Jacques had leapt to his feet and was wagging an irate finger in Serge's face, the two of them shouting at each other but making no noise. Was it possible that they were behind the mischief-making? Had Serge's arrival changed something? Josette knew little about the physics of her own world and couldn't begin to fathom theirs. But the timing fitted.

She shook her head, not knowing which proposition scared her more: losing control of her faculties or sharing a living space with poltergeists. Poltergeists that never stopped squabbling. It was unnerving. And tiring. Like living with teenagers. She wanted nothing more than to bang their heads together. If only she could catch hold of them!

With a loud sigh that made her nephew glance sharply at her, Josette picked up a bag of flour and, crossing through the bar without so much as a glance at the arguing ghosts, started up the stairs. Tonight. She would get her answer tonight, whether she liked it or not.

'You're abusing your power,' admonished Jacques. 'And making extra work for others.' He pointed at his nephew, skinny body doubled over as he picked apples up off the floor.

Serge shrugged and turned an indifferent face towards the window of the bar, beyond which he could see the figure of

Véronique slowly making her way to the church for Sunday mass. Shoulders hunched, head angled downwards as though battling against a strong wind despite the balmy weather, she was the personification of grief.

'She'd be ashamed of you!' said Jacques, noting the direction of Serge's attention. 'To think of all you could be doing with what you've been granted. And instead you choose to squander it on senseless shenanigans.'

Serge had heard enough. 'All I've been granted?' He threw an arm at the world beyond the open shutters. 'I've had everything I loved ripped from me and instead of resting in eternal peace in the graveyard, I get dumped in here with you, condemned to goodness knows how long of listening to your pious ranting, your jealous reproval. Who could blame me for having a bit of fun?'

'I'm not jealous!' snapped Jacques. 'And you can hardly call what you're doing fun.'

It hadn't taken long for Jacques to realise what his friend was up to during his night-time wanderings. The morning after the funeral, he'd woken early and had seen the pictures all tilted to one side. Going through to the épicerie, he'd spied the tins of boeuf bourguignon pushed to the far end of the shelf. The oranges rolling on the floor. In light of what he'd learned the day before, it all made sense.

On hearing the tread of feet on the stairs, he'd rushed back to the hearth where Serge was snoring soundly, and had pretended to do likewise. Through half-opened eyes, he'd watched his wife enter the room, trepidation on her face. When she'd noticed the pictures, her hand had flown to her mouth. She'd quickly righted them and then moved into the épicerie where she'd bent to retrieve the oranges.

'How am I doing this?' he'd heard her mutter as she placed the fruit back in the basket.

It had been the same every day since. Serge tormenting her with his mischief, and Josette becoming more and more nervous when she entered the bar in the morning. By the second week, she'd stopped tidying it all up, leaving it for Fabian who was clearly worried about the mental state of his aunt.

Why hadn't Jacques told her? Got up in the morning and greeted her. Pointed at Serge as she surveyed the changes wrought overnight and placed the blame where it belonged.

Jacques wasn't sure, himself. He had a vague notion that he could correct Serge's wayward behaviour and channel the talents the old mayor had to a better use. Persuading Véronique to stand for the council, for instance – although the exact details of how that could be achieved evaded him at present. But still, he'd felt the urge to conceal his friend's abilities, even if that meant duping his beloved wife. Which hardly made him the moral authority around here.

Serge gave a wicked grin. 'Really? You're not having fun?' He rose from his seat and moved silently to the archway through to the épicerie where Fabian was now restocking the shelves with the delivery from that morning. From above, the soft creak of floorboards revealed that Josette was still upstairs. He turned back to Jacques and tipped his head towards the bar.

'Come on. Enough of this arguing.' He pointed at the mobile phone hidden between two bottles of pastis. 'Let's text someone.'

And Jacques was transported back to his youth, that invisible thread pulling him after his wayward friend. That thrill of the illicit.

They'd sent the first text two days ago to Alain Rougé. Huddled over the mobile while Josette was in the shop, they'd agonised for ages over what to say and had decided on a simple sentence: I love you. With a quickening of the pulse,

Jacques had watched his friend's stubby finger press the send button and then it was done and the pair of them collapsed in laughter. It had been even more hilarious when Alain had popped in for his morning baguette an hour later. He hadn't said a word to Josette but had watched her carefully as she chatted away, ignorant of the declaration she had made.

The next day they hadn't found an opportunity to indulge, Josette keeping the mobile on her all the time. But now, with her upstairs . . .

'Who?' Jacques asked, trying to keep his features stern.

'Your choice,' said Serge, the mobile already on the bar before him, the screen lighting up his face. 'Whoever you like! But we need to be quick before Josette comes down.'

Scampering over, heart thudding, Jacques leaned over his friend's shoulder.

'René,' he urged. 'Text René.'

'And tell him what?'

Jacques' smile was impish. 'Tell him his secret mushroom patch is a secret no more!'

Serge's thick fingers flew over the screen and by the time Josette returned downstairs, the two men were sitting peacefully by the fire, the mobile nowhere to be seen.

'That's more like it,' she whispered in passing. 'Acting your age for once!'

She was through into the épicerie when they broke down in a fit of giggles.

'Did you say one for me?'

Véronique looked up as she exited the church to see Christian Dupuy lounging against the graveyard wall, a big grin on his face. She felt her lips lift in response.

'Seeing as you are both an atheist and a communist, I'm not sure my prayers would be of any use,' she retorted.

His grin grew wider and he pushed himself off the wall to walk towards her, curls riotous in the sunshine, shoulders wide. All she wanted to do was bury herself in that large frame, feel those strong arms wrap around her and never let her go.

But today she had something to do that she had to do alone.

'Thought I'd come and offer one last time,' he said, suddenly serious as he put his arms around her, making her tilt her head right back to see him. 'Are you sure you won't let me help you?'

She shook her head, determined to remain strong. 'No. It's fine. I need to do this myself.'

'You won't even consider asking Annie . . . ?' he faltered as her mood shifted, a frown chasing away the smile of moments before. 'Sorry!' he said. 'None of my business.'

She looked away, over the monuments and crosses that marked centuries of life, her gaze catching on the abundance of flowers that set apart the newest grave.

'I know you don't understand,' she said quietly. 'But I can't cope with her just yet.'

Christian cursed himself as he noticed the trembling hand reach for the silver cross that no longer resided at the base of her throat. She remembered once her fingers touched bare skin and he caught her hand as she let it drop.

'Then at least let me give you a lift up there?' he said, trying to make amends.

Véronique laughed, the sound rare these days. 'In the Panda? Why would I risk my life in that when I'm perfectly capable of driving up to Fogas myself?'

Christian smiled wryly, willing to allow his car to be ridiculed if it brought the sunshine back to Véronique's face. 'Fair point. So how about I meet you in the bar about five? I might even treat you to a meal at the Auberge later if you're good.'

And just like that, the shutters came down and she retreated back into the shadows. 'We'll see,' she said, stretching up to kiss him before turning to leave.

He watched her walk away down the alley that led to the épicerie and her apartment, not envying her the day she had ahead of her.

She stood on the roadside in Fogas, taking in the closed shutters, the pansies dying in a pot by the front door, the post sticking out of the post box. It was a house waiting for someone to come home. It was a house that now belonged to Véronique.

By French standards, the settlement of Serge Papon's worldly goods hadn't taken long. The *notaire* handling the will had sent for Véronique at the end of January and, accompanied by Christian, she'd gone down to St Girons and sat across from the hawk-faced lawyer, listening with disbelief as her life was changed forever. An hour later she'd stumbled out onto the pavement and Christian had guided her to Café Galopin on the bridge that spans the swirling waters of the Salat. He'd ordered two coffees and a couple of cognacs and having tipped the liquor into the espressos, waited until she'd drained her cup to the last before speaking.

'Christ,' he'd said, as stunned as she was. 'I wasn't expecting that.'

She shook her head numbly, watching the sunlight dance on the river below them.

'I thought maybe his sister . . . but no . . . the old rogue!' He gave a nervous laugh and ran a hand through his hair. 'The world is your oyster now, Véronique. Nothing to keep you in Fogas anymore. You're a woman of property. Two properties!'

Which she was. Being the sole issue of the deceased, as the *notaire* had stated in dry legalese, she was the recipient of

Serge Papon's entire estate as was mandated under French law. Serge hadn't sought to exploit any of the loopholes that could have enabled him to divert his assets elsewhere. In fact, his *notaire* explained, he'd taken the trouble to visit the lawyer before Christmas to enquire about Véronique's legal status, anxious that she should be his recognised heir. So Véronique inherited the old Papon house up in Picarets. And, as Thérèse Papon had died before Serge and left him everything in her will, Véronique also became the owner of the home up in Fogas that had belonged to Thérèse's mother; the home Serge had lived in all his married life. Added to that, a substantial amount in a bank account in St Girons was now in her name. Even after the *notaire* had been paid, funeral costs met, and death duties settled, Véronique was suddenly a very well-to-do young woman.

Fogas, of course, was abuzz over the developments. Speculation was already running high as to what she would do with her new-found fortune. Some had her buying a house in Collioure on the Mediterranean and living on anchovies and red wine for the rest of her life. Others had her investing all the money into stocks and shares and moving to Toulouse. Or even Paris. Still more were betting that she would give everything to the church and retire to a convent. None of this wild conjecturing suggested for one moment that she might stay in Fogas, with Christian and her mother. Why would she, when she could now do whatever she pleased?

But while the commune was busy planning her life for her, for Véronique, once the initial shock had worn off, her unexpected legacy changed nothing. If anything, it only made her depression deepen. The thought of Serge making sure that she was cared for in his will; it was enough to send her spiralling back down into the depths of grief.

So on this premature spring morning, with the sun gentle

on her back, Véronique faced the house she had been bequeathed and felt her heart break anew. How was she going to be able to sort through the minutiae of his life when she had only just begun to accept he was dead?

Wishing she hadn't been quite so resolute in her decision to face this alone, with trembling fingers she turned the key in the front door. She stepped inside and got the first waft of that familiar aftershave, a heady scent so evocative that she half expected to hear his booming laugh coming from the kitchen. Two minutes into what was going to be a long day and she was already in pieces.

After lighting a fire in both the lounge and the kitchen to dispel the damp that had built up in Serge's absence, she started upstairs, in the room Serge had shared with Thérèse. She hesitated at the threshold, held back by a daughter's sense of intrusion, and stared at the tidy bed, cover pulled up, sheet folded over it, pillows left neatly. He'd been expecting to return home. Expecting to go to bed as usual.

The wardrobe, she told herself firmly, suppressing the tidal wave of emotion that was threatening to engulf her. Start with the wardrobe.

She opened the doors of the huge piece of furniture, releasing yet more of Serge's distinctive cologne into the room, and surveyed the meagre contents. A couple of suits, several pairs of trousers, a dozen shirts and a rack of ties, and four pairs of polished shoes neatly lined up beneath.

She shook out a bin liner and placed it on the floor, taking a deep breath before reaching for the nearest suit. It was his best one, the shoulders still dusted with flakes of confetti from Stephanie and Fabian's wedding on Christmas Eve. How distinguished Serge had looked that day as he officiated, addressing the guests gathered in the town hall, the tricolour sash draped across his chest. No one would have predicted it would be his last wedding.

The thought hit her out of nowhere. His last wedding. If she ever made it that far, there would be no Serge Papon standing at the front of the town hall, not as mayor nor as father of the bride. She clutched the suit to her face and broke down in tears.

While Véronique Estaque was crying helplessly in Serge Papon's empty home, Bernard Mirouze was across the river from La Rivière, taking in the views from the Col d'Ayens. Little more than a dirt road in places, the mountain pass cut up through the commune of Sarrat, sliced through the pine forest at the top and then dropped down the northern slope towards the departmental capital of Foix. And this Sunday lunchtime, with the sun pouring down on the clearing at the summit, it provided a fine panorama of the Pyrenees, the peaks crowding the skyline.

It was beautiful, Bernard had to admit, as he shaded his eyes with his hand and gazed down at the pastureland, the smattering of houses, the smoke spiralling from chimneys, the tall tower of the church. Sarrat looked picture-perfect. Whereas across the ribbon of water way down below, the three villages of Fogas were barely visible: La Rivière a mere cluster of slate roofs, Fogas and Picarets obscured by the geographical twists and turns of the two valleys that led up to them.

The *cantonnier* didn't normally come over this side for his midday walk. Especially not since the dispute over the bears the year before, which had torn the two communities of Fogas and Sarrat apart. And then there was the whole mess over the merger . . .

Simply placing his foot on Sarrat soil was enough to make

Bernard feel disloyal. But, when it came to his dog, he would do anything. Even if it meant visiting enemy territory.

He turned to check on the beagle snuffling along the track that led to the forest, tail wagging. Until a month ago, Bernard's habitual walk was taken in the woods above Picarets or Fogas, depending on where he was working that morning. He would park up the tractor, eat his lunch and then stroll with Serge the beagle for about an hour. It was the highlight of their day. But when Agnès Rogalle had told him about the illegal traps in the forests of Fogas, the *cantonnier* had taken her advice and stopped going up there.

Faced with the choice of giving up the post-luncheon walk or crossing to the Col d'Ayens, which Agnès Rogalle had assured him was safe, Bernard had set aside his animosity for the neighbouring commune in favour of indulging himself and his dog in their favourite activity. Plus he was trying to lose a bit of weight and the daily routine was having a positive impact on his figure.

Patting his waist with a grin, Bernard picked up his lunch box and crossed the small parking area to a picnic bench where he took a seat with a commanding vista. Serge the beagle came running over, knowing that the odd slice of saucisson, or even cheese, would be thrown his way.

'It's not safe over there for you, is it boy?' Bernard patted the robust body and felt the rough lick of tongue caress his palm. 'Not until Christian's sorted it out.'

The dog barked, the echo carrying back from the hills across the river. And behind the *cantonnier* and his beagle, towering above them, pine trees circled the clearing, their high branches festooned in clumps of white.

Little did Bernard know, they were every bit as dangerous as any man-made traps.

*

Véronique had no appetite for lunch. Once she'd regained her composure, she'd spent the remainder of the morning sorting through Serge's clothes, deciding what to keep, what could go to the Croix-Rouge jumble sale and what needed to be thrown out, her ability to make these decisions impaired by her desire to hold on to everything that could be connected to her father. In the end she'd settled on putting aside a couple of ties, one of which she would give to Christian, and Serge's winter boots, which were virtually new and would fit Bernard Mirouze. She'd also held on to a beautiful walking stick, the carved stag's head adorning it a work of art. She had no real use for it but it was too gorgeous to give away.

With the town hall clock rendered silent by its malfunction and her focus far from food, she'd not noticed the hours slipping past, so it was late when she checked her watch and decided she ought to eat. She made her way down the stairs, her movements carrying the echo of an empty house, and entered the kitchen where she'd put the bowl of couscous and roasted vegetables she'd had left over from the night before. Not wanting to take a solitary seat at a table made for a family, she wandered the room while she ate, bowl in hand.

Despite the most recent occupant being a widower, the kitchen was surprisingly homely. Along one wall an oak dresser provided storage for glasses, plates and cutlery, the tall cupboard tucked in under the stairs next to it revealing jars of homemade jam neatly labelled in Thérèse's handwriting, bottles of preserved vegetables, pickles and apple compote. Running perpendicular to this was an ornate sideboard with an old TV propped on its surface. Opposite the dresser was the fireplace, two cosy chairs pulled up to the hearth where a small fire was now burning, and the back wall was taken up with the cooker, the sink – a huge metal affair that could accommodate a dozen pans – and a window looking out onto the garden and the hills beyond. Uniting all of this was the long table that spanned the middle of the floor, a bright yellow oilcloth covering its surface.

There was no dishwasher, a drying rack next to the sink as modern as Thérèse had got. But as she surveyed the room with its view of the hills and the forest that surrounded the village, Véronique imagined herself living there. For the first time since her meeting with the *notaire*, she began to consider her options.

Feeling more at home in this room, Véronique decided to concentrate the rest of her day on the sideboard, having ascertained that it was Serge's domain, the drawers crammed with paperwork relating to his position as mayor. Figuring that there would be little amongst all that administration that could chafe her already raw emotions, she pulled out the contents of the first drawer and placed it on the table. Copies of correspondence, a notepad containing a shopping list in Thérèse's handwriting, notices from the Conseil Général in Foix, circulars from L'Association des Maires Ruraux de France… Soon her eyes were glazing over, her hands on autopilot as she rifled through the stack of papers, most of it going straight into a bin bag.

The second drawer yielded much the same. And by the third, Véronique really wasn't concentrating anymore. Which was why she missed it initially. It had slipped between the pages of the winter issue of the Chambre de Commerce's magazine. Not interested in the proposed development of a new road network linking Toulouse with Barcelona, she'd discarded the journal without a second glance. It was only as it fell into the bag of rubbish that she noticed the corner of white sticking out at an angle.

An A4 envelope. She retrieved it and found herself looking at the name of a man she hadn't thought about in a while.

'Arnaud Petit,' she announced to the empty kitchen, a smile tracing her lips as she recalled the big tracker, his hair pulled back in a ponytail, the slash of white against his dark skin as he laughed. He'd left Fogas seven months ago; no one knew his whereabouts. Yet Papa had something for him in his sideboard.

Curious, she ran her fingers over the envelope, trying to guess the contents. Papers – not that many judging by the weight. Obviously intended for Arnaud but with no way of getting them to him.

'Oh what the hell,' she muttered, intrigued. She slipped a nail under the edge of the envelope, ripped it open and pulled out a thin sheaf of papers.

A report. From a government department, the official seal at the top of each page. She let her eyes skim across the front page and before she'd even reached the bottom she knew she'd stumbled on something important.

Christian, she thought. She needed to show this to Christian as soon as possible. Because in the wrong hands, it could be the downfall of Fogas.

9

'Christ! This is dynamite.' Christian ran a hand through his curls which were already wild from his distracted grooming, his focus entirely on the papers in his hands. 'And it was in his sideboard?'

Véronique nodded, the pair of them crouched furtively over a table in the bar, their reflections cast back from the windows that looked out onto the encroaching dark. 'It was in an envelope addressed to Arnaud Petit.'

'Arnaud . . .' The tracker's name brought a frown to Christian's forehead. 'Why would Serge be willing to pass this on to Arnaud yet he kept it from the Conseil Municipal?'

'You didn't know about it?'

'Not a thing. Believe me, I'd remember if Serge had raised this in a council meeting.'

'So, apart from us two, no one else knows about it. What are you going to do?'

Christian looked up from the folder, his face pale. Six flimsy pages of neat typing and it held the power to bring down the commune.

It was the official report into the attacks by bears that had occurred around Fogas the summer before. With the reintroduction of the beasts into the forests of the region already an incendiary issue – shepherds, farmers and hunters vehemently opposed to the government-backed initiative – the slaughter of a couple of sheep and the destruction of Philippe Galy's beehives by one of this protected species had been the catalyst to spark violent protests; protests which had brought Fogas to its knees and culminated in the death of one of the bears in a forest fire. Of course, doubts remained as to how accidental the unfortunate animal's demise had been, given that there had been a group of hunters in the same area at the time. But until now, no one had questioned the authenticity of the smashed beehives and the mutilated sheep.

Eight months on, the report made uncomfortable reading, suggesting that these two so-called ursine attacks had been staged and were subject to a police inquiry.

'I don't know,' the farmer said. 'I can't get my head around the fact that someone might have faked those attacks. I mean, that sheep up in Sarrat . . .'

Véronique shuddered. She'd seen the photos Arnaud Petit had taken as part of the initial investigation – the torn carcass, the blood, the sheer savagery of it. 'Who could do such a thing?' she whispered.

'And why?' Christian rubbed a hand over his face, feeling the weight of an office he wasn't even mandated to hold and yet seemed to have had thrust upon him. Not for the first time in the past five weeks, he missed Serge Papon.

'Whatever the answer,' he continued, 'I'm going to have to tread carefully because the last thing we need is another storm. Fogas is like a rudderless ship and the commotion this would bring would be enough to capsize us completely. Which would play exactly into the hands of the Sarrat camp.'

'But you can't sit on it . . .'

'Why not? Serge obviously did.' Christian pointed at the date on the first page. The report had been published in late October. 'And if he chose not to make it public knowledge, then he would have had a bloody good reason.'

'But it proves that someone was trying to undermine

Fogas! You can't keep that secret. Philippe has a right to know at the very least.'

'And he will. Once the by-election is over and the new council in place. By then the police investigations will be further along and it might all be taken out of our hands. For now, we keep it between ourselves. Agreed?'

'If that's what you wish. But you're possibly too late. Look.' Véronique took the report from him and pointed at the dark smudge along the left side of each page. 'That's from the photocopier up in the town hall which means—'

'Merde!' Christian thumped the table causing Josette to glance over from the épicerie. 'The original must still be up there! We need to find it before Pascal does. If he gets holds of this, God knows what damage he'll do.'

Véronique grimaced. 'He'll use it to smear Serge's memory and everyone associated with him – you, Josette, René . . . The by-election and the vote for mayor would be Pascal's to lose.'

'Exactly,' said Christian, pulling out his mobile. 'I'll give Céline a call, see if she's still at work. If anyone knows where the original report is, it's her.'

Véronique leaned back in her chair while he made the call, reading through the incriminating pages once more. And her thoughts kept coming back to one thing: whoever had staged these attacks had gone to incredible lengths to achieve their means. They were ruthless. And extremely violent.

A shiver ran the length of her spine. Perhaps Christian was right to keep the whole thing under wraps after all.

Céline Laffont's day had been awful. As had every day since the tragic loss of Mayor Serge Papon. Working alongside a man she couldn't stand, a man who was incapable of doing his job, she was finding the hours she spent at Fogas town hall a torment.

'Quit,' had been her husband's advice as she returned home bemoaning her situation once again. But Céline wasn't a quitter. Oh, don't misunderstand, she would have her letter of resignation slapped on the desk the minute Pascal Souquet was elected mayor, if such an unfortunate situation came to pass. But while there was a glimmer of hope that her new boss would be someone other – Christian Dupuy, for instance – she would endure the dreadful state she found herself in.

She owed it to Mayor Serge Papon to hold the place together, she told herself several times a day when the urge to inflict corporeal violence on the first deputy – even in her thoughts she refused to give Pascal the title of interim mayor – almost overwhelmed her.

'Don't forget to lock up, Céline.' The man in question, briefcase in hand, was closing his office door.

'Thanks for reminding me. I would never have thought of it,' she replied, straight-faced.

He paused, sensing the sarcasm but unsure how to handle it. Then, with a prim nod, he was gone. And Céline had her desk drawer open and her hands on the small bundle of cloth that made her day bearable.

'Take that!' she hissed, sticking a pin into the left leg of a six-inch doll fashioned out of old tights and rags, Pascal's face sneering back at her from the photo glued across its head. 'And that!' She stabbed another pin into the general area of his heart, which already had a cluster of skewers sticking out of it. None of which seemed to be having any effect. She was just musing on the necessity for a live sacrifice to intensify the magic, perhaps one of Madame Rogalle's chickens that always seemed to be escaping, when the phone rang.

It was Christian Dupuy and he was in a state.

'Slow down, Christian. I can't understand a word you're saying.' She listened to the farmer and frowned. 'No, I don't know of any such report. But I'll double check for you. When was it published?'

She stood, crossing to the old metal filing cabinet, the phone tucked between her ear and chin as she rifled through the relevant section.

'Nope. Nothing' she said, struggling to close the overstuffed drawer. 'Are you sure you're holding a copy?'

She was halfway back to her desk when she thought of something. An overstuffed drawer . . .

'Hang on. Are you suggesting Serge might have wanted to keep it a secret?' The famer's affirmative had her striding into the mayor's office. 'Well in that case, give me a minute and I'll call you back.'

She hung up, placed the phone on the desk and edged towards the window. Down below, she could see the effete figure of Pascal Souquet heading away from the building. It was safe.

Moving quickly back to the desk, she reached for the bottom drawer. Serge's hiding place. She'd known about it from the first week she'd started working here when, perplexed that the drawer never really closed properly, she tried to sort it out for him while he wasn't there. Lifting out the files suspended from the sides, she'd discovered the problem. On that particular day, it had been a box of aftershave and a birthday card smothered in lipstick kisses from some female admirer which were pushing up the files above and jamming the drawer. She'd put everything back, closed the drawer and never mentioned it. But periodically, she checked the space and had come across a lot of Serge's secrets over the years. And had never told a soul.

Today, however, she didn't think she was going to be in luck. The drawer was closed properly and when she opened it, all the files were hanging perfectly. But she parted them anyway. And beneath them, her hand closed around something. She lifted it out, opened it and then called Christian straight back.

'Thanks, Céline. And remember, not a word to anyone.'

Christian hung up and turned to Véronique who was placing two coffees on the table.

'Any joy?' she asked.

'Yes and no,' he said, frowning. 'There's no trace of the report.'

'But?'

'Céline found the folder it came in, complete with the official crest for the department responsible. It was hidden away in the bottom of Serge's desk where he used to stash all his secrets.'

'Just the folder? Nothing inside?'

Christian nodded. 'Exactly.' He stared at the report that lay between them. 'So either this isn't a copy and we're worrying about nothing. Or—'

'This is a copy and the original has been found!'

'Which begs the question, why hasn't Pascal gone public with it? Because it can only be Pascal who found it.'

Véronique shrugged. 'Maybe he's saving it up for the eve of the by-election. You know, hitting you with all the ammunition at the last minute.'

A groan escaped Christian's lips. 'I'm not cut out for this,' he muttered, head in his hands. 'I'm just a farmer. I'm not made for subterfuge.'

Véronique reached across and placed a hand on his cheek. 'You are,' she said. 'You're the leader Fogas needs.'

But Christian wasn't in the mood to be pacified. He raised his head and fixed her with a pleading look. 'Véronique,' he began, 'please. After today, can't you see we need you to stand for the council?'

She pulled her hand back sharply as though burnt. 'You agreed, Christian. No political pressure. Not from you.'

He swallowed, knowing that he had to continue; that without her support, Fogas was lost. 'I know. We agreed. But that was then. Now . . .' He pointed at the report. 'This is just the start of it. In a few days' time the nominations will be announced and then we'll have three weeks of bickering and recriminations leading up to the election. And without your name on that ballot paper, Pascal won't even need to use this report to beat us. Please, Véronique, if you won't do it for me, at least do it for Serge.'

Véronique stood, face white with anger. 'Don't you dare!' she said. 'I will not be badgered into something by the invocation of my father. Especially when that something is the very thing that killed him.'

'I'm sorry, Véronique—'

But she was gone, the door slamming behind her, bringing Josette rushing in from the épicerie to see what was happening.

'Everything okay?' she asked, before adding with a laugh, 'Or are you two having a lovers' tiff?'

Christian shook his head, gathered up the report and made for the door. 'Something like that,' he said enigmatically as he walked out into the dark. Seconds later the sound of a car engine struggling into life presaged his departure down the road, the Panda's rear lights soon disappearing up the hill to Picarets.

'What was all that about?' Josette wondered aloud as she watched the lights fade. She turned to regard the ghostly outlines of the two men sitting either side of the inglenook. Hands folded on laps, eyes closed, there would be no reply from that quarter as Jacques and Serge were both fast asleep.

'Well at least it makes a change, with you two not arguing

for once,' she muttered before crossing back to the épicerie to finish her stocktake.

'All clear,' whispered Jacques, focusing on the retreating back of his wife through half-opened eyes.

Serge's eyelids flicked up, an intensity in his gaze that hadn't been there in a while, and a thrill of anticipation went through the man next to him.

They'd been engaged in their usual activity of late, Jacques berating Serge yet again for his abuse of the powers he'd discovered and Serge refusing to see the error of his ways. The debate was just descending into personal insults when Christian and Véronique had arrived. The couple had taken seats close to the inglenook where the two old men were sitting and were so clandestine in their behaviour that the old friends were distracted from their habitual squabbling. Calling a momentary truce, they'd leaned in and listened intently. And when Véronique had stormed out and precipitated the arrival of Josette, Serge had thrown his head back against the chimney and played possum, Jacques following suit. In truth, after what they'd heard, they couldn't be further from sleep.

'Pascal,' Serge hissed. 'Always bloody Pascal.'

'You think he took the report?'

Serge snorted. 'Who else? The bastard was probably in my office and at my desk within minutes of hearing I was dead.'

'But what would he want with it? Is it really that inflammatory?'

'It has the potential to split the commune all over again. People will be pointing fingers, the anti-bear faction will be claiming it's a government whitewash, and it will provide a perfect weapon for vilifying my administration and anyone who was part of it. I'll be painted as an incompetent fool and my supporters along with me. As Christian said, it's the last thing

Fogas needs.' A long sigh issued from between Serge's pursed lips. 'So yes, the report could pose a problem in the wrong hands. And I'd say Pascal's are the wrong hands, wouldn't you?'

'None worse. The odious creep must be laughing at his good fortune and plotting how to use it.'

'Mon Dieu!' Serge ran a hand over a weary face. 'Even in death I don't escape his machinations. And to think I placed this within his grasp.'

'You weren't to know you were going to drop dead,' offered Jacques.

Serge grunted, not mollified in the least.

'So did the report say how the attacks were staged?'

'Not in great detail, no,' said Serge, trying to recollect the contents. 'It mentioned the evidence was inconsistent. Something about the DNA of the fur they found at both sites not matching the prints. But it offered no theories as to who or how. I think that's being left to the police to find out.'

Jacques scratched his chin and stared into the fire, watching the flames lick and curl along a length of ash. There was something nagging him. Something about that intense period last summer.

'Arnaud Petit tried to tell me,' continued Serge, recalling the unease of the tracker who'd helped with the investigation into the dead sheep and the smashed beehives. 'Right from the beginning he was suspicious. The two attacks in one night, kilometres apart and in opposite valleys. The pristine prints when the ground was dry. But when the initial report was published, his concerns never made it to the page. Instead, he was left to shoulder the blame, accused of misconduct and suspended. And that was when all hell broke loose.'

It had been a traumatic time. Tensions spiralling in a June heatwave, violent protests, the national media hanging around La Rivière. And then that awful day when the fire had started in the forest. Deliberately, that was for sure, a farmer burning off pastureland. But maliciously? With the intent to kill? Arnaud Petit had thought so. Heavily armed hunters, none other than the mayor of Sarrat amongst them, who just happened to be in the area when the fire was set. Perhaps Arnaud had reason to be sceptical. But no one had been able to prove anything and the bear had paid the ultimate price.

Things had settled down after that. Arnaud Petit had left the commune, no one knew where to. The bear cubs he'd been protecting had survived and were now monitored by the reintroduction programme. And Fogas had returned to normal. Until this latest report, the result of a fresh inquiry based on new evidence, had landed in Serge's lap in October.

It had been instinctive, the urge to bury it until the merger had been decided one way or the other. Now it looked as though Serge's actions would place Fogas in trouble all over again.

'I should have burned the bloody thing,' muttered Serge ruefully, 'instead of hiding it and keeping a copy for Arnaud.'

'Arnaud,' murmured Jacques, his memory going back to the big man. He'd been in here, in the bar, the day of the fire. He'd been sitting at a table, huddled over a laptop, watching a video. And Jacques had been standing right behind him. Then Chloé had come running in, screaming about smoke on the mountainside, and the rest had been pandemonium.

But Jacques remembered what he'd seen. He'd been puzzling over it for the best part of eight months. That frozen image on a computer screen of a man caught in the torchlight in the middle of a forest, a place that man in particular would never normally be. And now, the pieces had fallen into place.

'The bastard!' he shouted, leaping from his seat and nearly throwing Serge into the fire in fright.

'Christ!' Serge had a hand over his heart, which was pummelling his chest. 'Calm down before you kill me!'

'You don't understand!' Jacques turned to him, eyes wild with excitement. 'The video. The day of the fire, Arnaud came in here asking you for his laptop. Remember?'

Serge nodded, the day being one that would never be forgotten. The huge tracker had been living wild up in the forests, suspended from duty but refusing to relinquish his protection of the bear cubs that were at threat. He'd called in to the bar unannounced that day and he'd asked Serge to fetch his laptop, which he'd left with the mayor for safekeeping. He'd spent the next thirty minutes searching through his computer files and then the fire had been spotted and everything had gone crazy.

'He didn't find what he was looking for, I seem to recall,' said Serge.

'That's what he told you. But he found something all right. He was watching a video from one of the concealed cameras they had in the forest to track bears.'

'And?'

'He found footage of someone up there in the middle of the night.'

Jacques had Serge's complete attention. 'Why would anyone be up there at night?'

'Well, if you wanted to incriminate a bear in a fake attack, what would you need?'

'Bear prints . . .' Serge shrugged. 'Fur . . .'

Jacques raised an eyebrow and Serge's eyes widened.

'Fur,' he breathed, remembering the day Arnaud had taken him up into the forest to show him one of the ways his department monitored the bears. It was ingenious. A small enclosure of barbed wire encircled a tree from which hung a bag of corn. In reaching for the rare treat, the bears had to negotiate the barbed wire and invariably left behind a tuft of fur, a precious source of DNA. It was the perfect place for anyone requiring ursine souvenirs.

Serge shook his head, amazed at the audacity. 'The evidence against the bear came from one of the traps!'

A sharp nod from Jacques.

'And you're telling me you saw who was on the footage from the camera monitoring that trap?' Serge was standing now, adrenalin flowing through him at the thought of discovering who had been trying to sabotage Fogas.

'Yes,' said Jacques. 'I saw it. Although I didn't understand the meaning of it at the time.'

'Bloody hell, man. Tell me who it was.'

'Pascal,' he said. 'Pascal Souquet.'

Serge snapped his gaze from his ghostly companion, staring out of the dark window at the pinpricks of light across the river. And all the while his politically fine-tuned brain was whirring, making connections, putting it all together.

The unrest over the bears. The attempts to overthrow him. The threat of the merger. All of it orchestrated with the assistance of the first deputy mayor of Fogas, who was most likely going to be the next leader of the commune.

A grim look of determination settled across the former mayor's face and when he turned back to Jacques he was pulsing with life.

'Véronique,' he said to his old friend, guiding him back to a seat next to the fire. 'We need her on the council or Fogas is finished. There must be some way of using my powers to make sure that happens.'

When Josette checked in on the two old men before retiring to bed that night, she was relieved to see them both sitting by the dying flames, heads bent towards each other, earnestly discussing something. At last, she thought as she closed the door and started up the stairs, a bit of peace around here.

She couldn't have been further from the truth.

10

Flour. A wide line of it just outside her bedroom and as pristine as the night before, when she'd carefully shaken it across the threshold. No footprint. No slipper print. Just white flour that would need to be brushed up before Fabian arrived and concluded that, as he'd come to suspect, his aunt had indeed gone insane.

But did it prove it wasn't her?

Josette went downstairs slowly, not sure what she wanted to find on the other side of the door. If the bar and épicerie were unchanged, then she would have to conduct the experiment again. But if they weren't . . . ?

She really didn't want to face that prospect. Because the untouched band of flour told her that she hadn't left her bedroom last night. So any rearrangements inflicted on the premises downstairs would be the work of another. Which didn't bear thinking about. Unless, of course, she was levitating her way down there . . .

With a grim face, she entered the bar.

All fine. Two ghosts, awake early for once, deep in discussion by the hearth. Tables, chairs, pictures, glasses, all as they should be. She hurried across to the épicerie, spying Fabian freewheeling down the Picarets road in the distance and knowing he'd be at the door in minutes. She poked her head through the archway. Oranges and apples segregated; saucisson dangling above the till; miniature Sarkos corralled on their shelf; and the knife cabinet closed with all knives present.

'Thank God,' she muttered, a hand on her heart. Although it didn't prove anything.

She turned with a sigh to open the door to her nephew. It was only when she saw him thread a single red rose through the gate of the garden centre opposite that she realised it was Valentine's Day. She was far too preoccupied with her mental state to worry about romance.

Véronique hadn't slept well. Too disturbed by the argument with Christian, she'd spent the night assessing her behaviour, trying to understand why his simple request had brought about such a response.

Filled with remorse but too stubborn to do anything about it, she'd got up long before dawn and sat at the table nursing a hot chocolate, chiding herself for her quick temper. When she heard the bells of the Angelus, closely followed by the slap of the shutters opening on the épicerie door, she was tired and irritable – a perfect combination for serving customers behind the counter of the post office.

On a weary sigh she rose from the table and saw the lurid red love heart drawn around the day's date on the wall calendar. Christian. He'd given her the calendar as a Christmas present, a selection of twelve photographs of Sarko the bull, and had flagged all the important dates: his birthday, her birthday, the night they got together and today, Valentine's Day.

Their first Valentine's as a couple. And they were starting it in the aftermath of a quarrel.

With her heart heavy, she turned towards the bedroom to get ready for the day ahead.

⋆

Driving down from Picarets, Christian was in a foul mood. He'd messed up yesterday. Allowed infernal politics to come between him and Véronique; allowed it into his personal life. But living in a place like Fogas, it was impossible to separate the two. Everything you did was political. Because everything you did impacted on everyone else. So, he consoled himself as he turned right onto the main road and up towards the épicerie, he'd done what he had to. After all, he was supposed to do what was best for Fogas. And there was no denying it; Véronique's name on that ballot paper was what was needed for this commune that was teetering on the edge of extinction.

That bloody report. No wonder he'd felt cornered into pressurising Véronique. The chances of retaining control of the Conseil Municipal had been slim before, with two seats up for grabs – both vacated by his allies – and Fatima Souquet standing for one of them. But now, with the contents of that document possibly in Pascal's possession, things were looking grim.

He drummed his fingers on the steering wheel, trying to ignore the tight band across his chest. The deadline for nominations for the forthcoming election was six o'clock Thursday evening. It was now Monday morning. Across the intervening hours, Christian Dupuy could see no way to make Véronique change her mind.

As he stepped out of the car at the épicerie, he couldn't see a way to save Fogas either.

'It definitely came from you! And you of all people should know not to mess with a man's mushrooms,' huffed René in the épicerie, holding his morning provisions in one hand while he fished out his mobile with the other. 'Look! It arrived yesterday.'

He shoved the phone under Josette's nose where she couldn't help but see the screen and the text that had got him so irate.

Stephanie leaned over to have a look and burst out laughing but Josette paled, shaking her head defiantly. 'I didn't send it,' she said. 'I think I'd remember if I did.'

René glowered. 'Huh. You're telling me someone else sent it? From your phone?'

'Or it's a glitch of some sort.' Josette's adamant denial was undermined by the beseeching glance she sent her nephew who had wandered over to the counter and was now inspecting René's mobile. 'That's feasible, isn't it, Fabian?'

'Not really,' her nephew responded with typical bluntness and René's glower turned to a smug smile. 'Have you got your phone, Tante Josette?'

She reached into her pocket and pulled out her mobile, a cold dread seizing her as she handed it over. She'd thought it was all okay. So reassured by the unmarked flour this morning. So encouraged by everything being in its place, including her itinerant phone. And now this!

Fabian took the mobile, long fingers flicking across the surface as he examined the contents. Then an eyebrow flew up and he looked at his aunt, alarm on his face.

'What?' she asked.

He turned the phone so she could see. And there, on the screen, was a text from her to Alain Rougé telling him she loved him.

'I never sent that!' she declared, while Stephanie collapsed in laughter, even René's indignant moustache starting to twitch. 'When was it sent?'

'Friday morning.'

'Were you getting in early for Valentine's?' jibed René.

Josette cast her mind back. Three days ago. Did she have

her phone that day or had it been missing? But it was no use. She couldn't remember. So she took refuge in indignation.

'As if I would do such a thing!' she stated. 'The idea is ridiculous. Clearly someone else is behind it.'

Fabian was staring at her and she knew he was thinking about the tins of boeuf bourguignon that had a habit of shuffling around on the shelves, and the strings of saucisson that kept leaping off their rack. He was questioning her sanity. And he wasn't the only one.

'If you think someone's behind it, lock your screen,' suggested Stephanie, wiping tears of laughter from her eyes.

'You can do that?' asked Josette.

Fabian nodded, fingers flicking once more. 'Here,' he said, handing her back the phone. 'Put a password in there and don't tell anyone. If you're right, that should put an end to it.'

'And if she's wrong . . . ?' asked René, spiralling a finger at his temple.

Josette glared at him and then stared at the screen. She needed to think carefully and choose something no one would guess. But equally something she wouldn't forget. Seeking inspiration, she looked around the shop and her eye was caught by the display cabinet behind the till. Perfect. With shaking fingers she pressed the keys.

'There,' said Fabian, making sure she'd done it properly. 'Your phone can't be used now by anyone but you. So there should be no more rogue texts!'

Josette didn't miss the lack of conviction in her nephew's voice as he ambled back to the basket of bread he'd been stocking, leaving Josette to face René's amusement.

'Anything else?' she asked pointedly.

The plumber, a Gauloise already clamped between his lips, shook his head and made for the door with a final chuckle, pausing outside to light his cigarette.

'Don't worry about it,' said Stephanie, patting Josette's arm as the door closed. 'We all have senior moments.'

'Huh!' Far from consoled, Josette shot a glance through into the bar where the two banes of her life were sitting either side of the fireplace, looking like butter wouldn't melt. She pointedly stuffed her mobile back in her pocket and turned back to the épicerie window beyond which Christian's Panda had just pulled up.

'Christian!'

The big farmer levered himself out of the car to see René Piquemal hurrying towards him, a Gauloise hanging from his bottom lip.

'Just the man I wanted to see,' said the plumber, taking a draw on his cigarette. 'Have you had any joy persuading Véronique?'

Christian grimaced, shook his head and entered the shop where Josette was chatting to Stephanie by the counter and Fabian was busy putting out stock.

'Bonjour,' he grunted, heading for the basket of baguettes.

'No? She said no?' pestered René, reluctantly discarding his cigarette at the door before dogging the farmer's footsteps. 'Does she realise how important this is?'

'Leave it, René,' said Christian, brow darkening.

But the plumber persisted. 'How could she say no? We're mere days from having to declare the candidates. We have to have her name on that list. Especially as we don't know who else Pascal is putting forward.'

Christian growled as he bent to the bread basket, but even that didn't deter René.

'You can't have asked properly,' he insisted. 'Or did you even ask her at all?'

'Yes, I bloody asked her!' snapped Christian, whipping round to brandish a loaf at the plumber. 'And she said no.

Then she stormed off and I haven't heard from her since. It's Valentine's Day and for the first time in years I'm in a relationship, but thanks to Fogas, I'll probably be spending it on my own. Are you happy now?'

He'd backed René up against a shelf of cassoulet, the plumber's beret askew as he peered down at the baguette that was pressing into his throat.

'Everything alright, Christian?' asked Fabian, putting a hand out to restrain the farmer and relieve the pressure on the spluttering plumber's windpipe.

'Sorry.' Christian lowered his arm and René took a deep breath, eyes wide. 'It's just this blasted election. It's tainting everything.'

'That's politics for you,' wheezed the plumber, a wary eye still on the weapon in Christian's hand.

'So is that what you two were arguing over yesterday?' asked Josette, having broken off her conversation with Stephanie at the outburst between the two men.

Christian nodded glumly. 'I asked her to reconsider standing and she walked out.'

'Did you use those words, exactly?'

'Well, not precisely. I said something about the council needing her—'

'The *council*?' Josette tutted. 'You didn't say anything about you needing her?'

A streak of red flared across the farmer's cheeks. 'No . . . well . . . I mean . . .'

'Typical!' snorted René, now that he had regained command of his faculties. 'You went in all heavy handed, not a hint of diplomacy.'

'They might have a point, Christian,' offered Stephanie. 'Véronique is in a dark place right now and perhaps if you'd made her feel valued . . .'

'Pah! Trust a man to put his foot in it,' said Josette, causing the plumber to puff up with indignation.

'Now hang on a minute,' he said. 'Don't go tarring us all with the same brush. I'd have handled it completely differently. Taken her out for a meal. Got her defences down—'

'Oh God!' Stephanie rolled her eyes. 'Spare me the Ariégeois wooing manual! All he had to do was talk to her—'

'Enough!' Christian threw up his hands in exasperation. 'That's all I need. Advice from you lot.' He turned to the silent Parisian standing behind him. 'Don't you want to add anything, Fabian? Feel free, seeing as everyone else knows where I went wrong.'

The sarcasm was wasted on Fabian, who simply took the offer that had been extended to him at face value. 'It's simple, really,' he said, with the rare insight that made him so special, if occasionally exasperating. 'Véronique is wallowing in the past, which is understandable. You need to get her focused on her future.'

'And how are we supposed to do that?' asked Christian.

But René was already staring at Stephanie, who was in turn regarding her husband with a mixture of love and pride.

'What if we could show Véronique the future?' asked the plumber, twisting his moustache in that familiar gesture which usually heralded mischief.

'I don't understand,' said Christian.

'Who do we know who can read fortunes?'

One by one, they all turned to the tall, redheaded woman of gypsy descent standing next to the counter.

'What, you mean—?'

'We couldn't—'

'That's brilliant—'

'I'm not sure—'

'What?' asked Stephanie, disconcerted to find the group regarding her speculatively. 'Why are you all looking at me?'

'How do you fancy a bit of fortune telling?' asked René, his grin now broad. And Stephanie didn't need any of her preternatural talents to know that yet another Fogas plan was being hatched.

'She knows!' hissed Jacques, a nervous eye on Josette in the shop. 'I'm telling you, she knows what you're up to.'

Serge let a smile curve his lips at Jacques' easy reallocation of the blame for the mischievous texts. But he wasn't worried. He was too busy listening to René detailing his plan for making Véronique change her mind. It was masterful. And if Serge could only get them to alter a couple of details, it would be a success. He would make sure it was.

He stood and started walking towards the shop.

'What are you doing?' whispered Jacques frantically. 'Don't go in there. She's not in the mood for more of your games.'

Serge ignored his friend. It was time to get involved. And this was just the beginning.

'A tarot night?' Christian was shaking his head. 'She won't go for it.'

'Why not?' asked Josette. 'She's always reading the horoscopes out of the paper.'

'Yes but this is a bit different. I mean, no disrespect Stephanie, but it's . . . the occult.'

Stephanie laughed. 'You couldn't be further from the truth. But you have a point. It's not as simple as you think and I can't guarantee that she'd get the future you want her to.'

René stared at the redhead as though she were insane. 'Of course you can. You simply tell her what we want her to hear.'

A shake of Stephanie's curls met his words. 'I'm not willing to do that. If you want me to be a part of this then it has to be done properly. We have to let the future find Véronique.'

'Let the future . . . ?' René rolled his eyes. 'Mon Dieu. It's not like we're asking you to commit a crime or anything. Just mutter some hocus-pocus and steer her towards politics. And standing in the by-election.'

Stephanie's eyes flashed dangerously and the plumber took a step back. 'No hocus-pocus,' she said. 'A genuine tarot reading or nothing else.'

'Okay,' said Christian, raising his hands to separate the two of them. 'On the premise that we can get Véronique to accept an invitation to the tarot reading, Stephanie will only conduct the real thing. Who knows, it might work. And it's our last chance.'

'So where shall we hold it?' asked René.

'Up at mine?' suggested Stephanie.

'It's as good as anywhere,' said Christian, René and Fabian nodding agreement. Only Josette was looking sceptical. 'What do you think, Josette?'

'Huh?' The older woman turned her gaze to Christian, her mind racing. 'Sorry. What did you say?'

'The tarot night. We'll hold it up in Picarets.'

But Josette was shaking her head, her eyes drifting over Christian's shoulder, enough to make the big farmer check there was no one standing behind him.

'No . . . perhaps not . . .' Josette stammered. 'Perhaps . . . we should have it . . . in there?' She pointed through the archway.

'What, in the bar?' Christian regarded the others who were shrugging, unable to think of a reason why not.

'We'd have to close early, Tante Josette,' warned Fabian.

'That's fine,' replied his aunt. 'It's a one-off.'

'So, that's sorted then,' said René. 'Wednesday night, a tarot reading for Véronique in the bar.'

'Just Véronique?' asked Fabian.

'Yes, why?'

'Won't it look a bit strange if she's the only one getting a reading? She'll suspect something is up.'

'So what are you suggesting?'

Fabian surveyed the group. 'You should all have a reading. Make it seem more natural.'

'Oh no!' René shook a finger at the Parisian. 'No way. I'm not getting involved in this.'

Stephanie folded her arms, a smile on her lips. 'Fabian's right, René. It's all or nothing, I'm afraid. In fact, we should open it up to the entire commune. Make it a fund-raising event.'

'For what?' asked René.

Christian gestured up towards Fogas. 'Fixing the clock on the town hall. We've had a couple of quotes in and it's going to cost a lot more than we thought.'

'That's a brilliant idea,' said Josette. 'Let's charge a small fee, provide drinks and snacks and make a proper evening of it. And we'll all get a reading.'

René looked to Christian for support, clearly not convinced, but Christian merely shrugged. 'What's the harm?' he asked.

'You said it yourself. It's the occult!' The plumber's face had paled significantly. 'You can't go messing with that.'

'But it was your suggestion in the first place! So count yourself part of it. Now all I have to do is get Véronique to come. I might be able to bribe her with these.'

As Christian leaned over to add a couple of pains au chocolat to his purchases, Stephanie gave the squirming plumber a mischievous wink. 'Don't worry, René. I'll go easy on you.'

'Shush!' Fabian pointed at the hunched figure heading down the road. 'It's Véronique. Act natural.'

The group splintered, Fabian returning to his restocking, Stephanie and René taking their leave while Christian stood at the counter, Josette serving him. When the postmistress walked in minutes later, she would never have known the plot that was afoot. Any reserve on Christian's part she put down to the argument of the night before. And as for Josette, well she'd been a bit distracted in the mornings for a while now. Reaching up to kiss Christian, Véronique didn't suspect a thing.

Perhaps if she could have seen Serge Papon standing to one side, she might have been more wary. The look on his face was one that many a Fogas resident would have recognised; he was back in the game and he was confident of winning. All he needed to do now was become an expert on tarot cards. And he knew exactly how to do that.

Bernard Mirouze had changed his routine. It wasn't something he normally did, finding solace in the predictability of his life. But he was propelled to do so by a force larger than himself. With his heart aflutter and his mind preoccupied, he was compelled to comply with what his soul was demanding.

He was in love. And Agnès Rogalle, the object of this worthy affection, was visiting La Rivière at midday. Which meant Bernard had to be there. Which also meant his ritual walk with Serge the beagle had to be moved to late morning.

'You understand, don't you boy?' he murmured as he slipped the lead off the dog's neck.

Serge reached up to snuffle his hand and then trotted off across the clearing on Col d'Ayens, heading for the pine trees that encircled it.

Satisfied that his hound held no lasting resentment for the slight change in schedule, Bernard walked over to a bench and sat down to enjoy the view. But his attention couldn't settle. It was as though he'd had four espressos in a row, his brain skipping and jumping, an unfamiliar patter in his chest.

It had been weeks since he'd seen her. Four long weeks without a visit from the butcher's van up in Fogas. Not that he'd ever had the courage to go up to her and buy something. But he'd lingered in the background, watching her from afar as she chatted with the women, chopping meat with a dexterity that made him swoon.

Thanks to the Butcher Burglar, however, those sweet delights, which had made his life bearable after the loss of Serge Papon, had been abruptly terminated. True to her word, Agnès had withdrawn her services and was refusing to reinstate Fogas on her delivery route until the culprit was apprehended.

Bernard had tried to catch him. He'd utilised every skill and tactic the tracker Arnaud Petit had taught him last summer, skills he'd been honing ever since with regular sessions on his own in the forest. But the soil was hard thanks to the lack of snow and rain and despite a painstaking search of the ground around the scene of the crime, he'd failed to find any prints after the last theft in mid-January. Even Serge the beagle had drawn a blank, the dog doing nothing more than turn in circles when Bernard endeavoured to get him on the trail.

So with the burglar still at large and Agnès refusing to relent, Bernard had no choice but to be down in La Rivière at lunchtime when the butcher's van would be stopping. She was meeting Christian Dupuy in the bar to discuss the progress the Conseil Municipal had made in identifying the felon. And to discuss her boycott of the commune. Bernard, lovelorn on Valentine's Day, would be there.

He checked his watch. Another couple of minutes and then it would be time to leave. He wanted to arrive after her but not be so late as to miss her. He rose, scanned the area and spotted his dog walking out of the forest.

'Serge, come on boy. Time to go.'

The beagle didn't pick up the pace, his movements lethargic, almost drunken.

'Serge, here boy.' Bernard whistled, but the dog didn't respond. Instead he staggered to one side and collapsed, ears flopped on the ground.

All thoughts of Agnès flew out of the window; Bernard started running.

'So, have you caught him?' Agnès Rogalle had her sleeves rolled up, meaty forearms bared as she sat at a table in the bar, coffee in front of her.

Christian shook his head. 'No. Not a trace. But we are trying. We've put posters up. We've sent out emails. We're doing all we can. So please, Agnès, can you resume your round?'

'Not until you catch him.'

Christian's shoulders drooped. 'But we need you, Agnès. The majority of the population up in Fogas is over sixty-five. Many of them can't drive. Without your deliveries they can't get their weekly rations of meat.'

Agnès shrugged. 'I'm sorry, Christian. I really am. But I warned you. Find out who's stealing from me and I'll reinstate Fogas on my round. Until then . . .'

The famer ran a hand through his hair, trying not to think about the stream of complaints he'd had from the disgruntled residents of the village up the mountain. Madame Degeilh had confronted him a couple of days ago, actually hitting him on the chest with her fists, she'd been so frustrated at the butcher-van strike. And the old men who hung out at the disused washbasins, the Lavoir Gang as they were affectionately known, had taken to booing him whenever he passed by. It was becoming so that he didn't want to venture into the village at all.

'Are you sure you won't reconsider?' he pleaded, looking out at Agnès from under a furrowed brow.

Agnès Rogalle wouldn't have been female if she hadn't felt

a twinge of remorse when faced by those angelic curls framing such an anguished expression. But she also wouldn't have been the saleswoman she was if she hadn't known how to drive a hard bargain.

She tore her gaze away from Christian's begging eyes. 'I'm sticking by what I said. You catch him, and I'll be back.'

Before he could offer any further argument, she stood to go, holding out a hand to the farmer, her grip as strong as any man's.

'I'll call you if we have any developments,' said Christian, walking her to the door. 'And if you change—'

He came to a standstill, cursing quietly as he surveyed the small car park next to the épicerie where Agnès had parked her van. It was packed with a rowdy crowd, shopping bags in arms, defiant faces turned towards the épicerie.

'Open up, Agnès!' called out one voice.

'Yves has been missing his sausages,' called out another, prompting good-natured laughter.

Agnès glared at them and then turned on Christian. 'You orchestrated this, didn't you!'

The farmer's hands shot into the air in a gesture of innocence. 'Not at all. I had nothing to do with it.'

'Come on, Agnès. It's Valentine's Day. I'll give you a kiss if you open up!' Yves Degeilh accompanied his promise with a saucy wink, earning himself an elbow in the ribs from his wife.

'Humph!' Agnès marched towards the van, the crowd parting before her. 'Just this once, she said, opening the back door and climbing inside. When the side hatch flew upwards, a roar of delight rose up from her appreciative customers.

'Who's first?' she said, tying on her apron and reaching for a knife.

*

'Don't die,' Bernard muttered as he threw the car around the bend, haring down towards La Rivière with his dog on the passenger seat next to him. 'Please don't die.'

But it didn't look good. Serge was lying with his head lolling to one side, white foam issuing from his mouth, his eyes unfocused. Bernard didn't know what to do. The vet was all the way down the valley in St Girons. He didn't think his little friend would make it that far.

So when he crossed the small bridge by the hunting lodge and turned right onto the main road to see a big crowd at the épicerie, he acted on impulse. In a squeal of brakes, he pulled up and leapt from the car.

Agnès was in her element. Serving customers, catching up on gossip. She wasn't about to admit to Christian Dupuy, who was lounging on the épicerie terrace with a smile, that she had missed visiting Fogas as much as the people up there had missed her. She loved the banter of the place, the robust humour and the good hearts, so much more down-to-earth than some of the folk across the river in Sarrat who scorned her as a mere purveyor of meat.

'Next,' she called out as she passed a full bag across to Widow Aubert.

'Two steaks please, and not from a runt like you'd get in Carrefour!'

'No runts on here,' quipped Agnès, catching hold of her generous backside to much laughter. 'Now, how thick—?'

'Help! Please someone help!' Bernard's cry cut through the banter as his portly frame could be seen running towards the crowd, something in his arms. 'He's dying!

Agnès, being that bit higher up, could see what he was carrying. And she could see it was serious. She jumped down from the van and ran to the *cantonnier*.

'Let me take him,' she said, lifting the dog from his arms and laying him on one of the terrace tables where she began a gentle inspection.

'What happened?' asked Christian, also leaning over the prostrate beagle.

'I don't know,' sobbed Bernard. 'We were up at Col d'Ayens and he went for a walk and the next thing . . .' He waved a hand at the inert form.

'Did he eat something?'

Bernard shook his head, tears marking his chubby cheeks. 'I don't think so. He was snuffling around under the pine trees, that was all.'

'Pine trees? Merde!' Agnès slapped her forehead. 'Someone fetch some warm water! Now!' she yelled and Josette went hurrying to the bar.

'What?' demanded Bernard. 'What have pine trees got to do with it?'

'Processionary caterpillars,' Agnès said gravely and several sharp intakes of breath met her pronouncement.

'Already?' Christian looked up to the hillside above Sarrat that was covered in conifers. 'Isn't it a bit early?'

'Not with the weather we've been having,' said Agnès, reaching for the jug in Josette's shaking hand.

'She's right. A nest fell out of the pine behind us yesterday morning,' Yves Degeilh informed the worried onlookers as Agnès rinsed the dog's mouth with the warm water, the beagle barely responding. 'Saw the little buggers crossing the road in a long line. I kept well away from them.'

'I didn't know they could harm dogs,' said Josette.

Christian nodded. 'The nest falls when the days get warmer, the caterpillars emerge and that's when the trouble starts. Their hairs are highly toxic. Especially for canines.'

'Come on, Bernard!' Agnès was scooping up the beagle in

her arms. 'Let's get him to the vet. I'll drive, you pour water in his mouth. We might be able to save him.'

They ran back to the van, Christian slamming the side hatch shut and gesturing for people to move aside, and in a swirl of dust, Agnès turned onto the road and roared away, a sobbing Bernard beside her, his beloved hound held tight in his lap.

'Will he survive?' Josette asked Christian, tears in her eyes.

The farmer shook his head. 'I doubt it. At the very least, he might lose his tongue.'

'Poor Bernard.'

They stood in silent contemplation as the van disappeared down the valley.

'How's he doing?' demanded Agnès as she threw the van around the last bend before St Girons, the knives she hadn't taken time to put away clattering around in the back.

'Not good. He's losing consciousness.'

'Just keep rinsing his mouth. We're nearly there.'

She roared through the town, breaking speed limits and drawing reproving horn blasts from other drivers. She didn't care. She crossed the river Salat and pulled up outside a building marked with a blue cross on Avenue René Plaisant. Before Bernard had even got out of the van carrying the ailing beagle, Agnès was through the door of the vet's and in reception, shouting for help.

'In there,' said the receptionist, pointing at a treatment room, the vet rushing out of another door at the noise.

Bernard let Agnès explain, words beyond him as a nurse tenderly took Serge the beagle and laid him on a table. It was clear this was an emergency, tension creeping into the room as the vet hurriedly set up an intravenous drip while the nurse bathed the dog's mouth.

'Will he be okay?' Bernard managed.

The vet looked up, expression sombre. 'It's too early to say. The quick thinking with the warm water has given him a chance but we'll just have to wait now for the cortisone to take effect. We'll have to keep him in overnight.'

And that was the final straw for the *cantonnier*. He stared at the small shape on the table, so helpless with ears flopping to one side, lips swollen, eyes closed, and he felt his shoulders start to shake. A strong arm encircled him and he let himself be drawn into the warm embrace of Agnès Rogalle.

It's a strange thing, love. Sometimes it broadsides its victims in an explosion of emotion, leaving them reeling and disorientated. On others, it creeps up, like ivy on a wall, growing silently until every inch is covered. With Agnès it was a combination of the two. She'd known Bernard for years, her affection for him springing from a desire to protect him as he bumbled his way through life. As she held him in the stuffy confines of the vet's treatment room, feeling the tremors of fear rippling through his rotund body and moved by the depth of his despair for poor Serge the beagle, she was aware that she didn't want to let him go. Which surprised her.

Persuaded by the vet that they should leave the dog in his hands overnight, Agnès insisted on driving Bernard home, further insisting on arrival at his house in Fogas that he take a seat and allow her to cook him a decent meal, Agnès of the firm opinion that the only comfort in times of trouble was food. Bernard, being a bachelor, tended to have erratic shopping habits and thus, after a thorough investigation of the kitchen cupboards, all Agnès had to hand was a couple of onions, a head of garlic and a jar of mustard. The fridge yielded little more. When she questioned Bernard about the meagre rations, he gestured towards the cellar and muttered that, thanks to the prowess of his hunting hound, the freezer was full of meat.

Which is why Agnès Rogalle's bolt of love came down in the cellar of Bernard Mirouze's house as she lifted the lid on the chest freezer.

It struck her like a steam train. A cold one, mind. With her head thrust into the icy chest, feet barely on the ground, she felt the burst of shock, followed by a delicious feeling of warmth flowing through her limbs, counteracting the icy chill that was rising up from below her. And the cause of this?

Rabbits. A freezer full of rabbits.

She knew what it meant. Her Butcher Burglar had been identified. But instead of anger she experienced only admiration for the sick beagle lying down in the vets in St Girons. And an explosion of love for his naive master who had blithely accepted that his dog was catching their dinner on a regular basis. Even if he didn't have a clue how to cook that catch.

She felt tears then laughter, which she had to stifle, and then a happiness so intense she knew her life had been turned upside down. All of it, of course, tempered by the knowledge that the dog, her former nemesis, was fighting for his life. She picked up one of her rabbits, noting with a chuckle that Serge the beagle had been canny enough not to bring home the steak and sausages he'd stolen, wiped the smile off her face and returned to the kitchen to make Bernard's dinner. The first of what she knew would be many.

The evening of Valentine's Day was a curious affair that year for the Pyrenean commune. While Serge the beagle was fighting the shadowy form of death down in St Girons, up in the mountaintop village of Fogas, a subdued Bernard was sharing a meal of *lapin à la moutarde* with Agnès, their hands interlocked on the tabletop, their thoughts with the hound. Down the road, Pascal Souquet had passed a silent meal with his wife, the accoutrements of a day marking love something they had long forgone in their ambition to be successful.

Meanwhile, down in La Rivière, Josette retired early to bed, her husband having failed to mark the day with a single love heart. Instead, his focus had been entirely on Serge Papon, the two of them huddled over in the inglenook, whispering and plotting all afternoon. So Josette scattered another layer of flour outside her bedroom door and lay down to sleep. As soon as her snores drifted below to the bar, Serge reached for her mobile. When he saw the locked screen demanding a password, he turned to his ghostly companion, hoping a lifetime and more living with the same woman might enable Jacques to provide the answer. Half an hour and three incorrect attempts later, Serge's faith in the power of love was rewarded when Jacques, standing where his wife had been earlier that day while composing the password, lifted his head and saw his prized collection of knives in the display cabinet behind the till. Grinning, he confidently uttered the word 'Laguiole'. Under Serge's prodding fingers the mobile sprang to life and the two men spent Valentine's night on the internet learning everything they could about tarot.

On the other side of the abandoned orchard that was next to the épicerie, lights were still on in the old school, spilling out into the dark from Véronique's flat. Inside, the postmistress was sitting at the table, hot chocolate to hand. Sleep had abandoned her once more so she sat there mulling over the evening. A meal with Christian at the auberge – a peacemaking of sorts. And then that strange invitation to a tarot reading session to raise funds to fix the clock on the town hall. She'd been intrigued, surprised – especially that Christian, a hardened cynic when it came to psychics and soothsayers, was championing it – and had told him she'd think it over. Then she'd asked for his understanding as she sent him home yet again, wanting to be alone and immediately regretting her decision when she was.

So that evening, the night that should be marked by *amour*, out of the entire commune of Fogas there was perhaps only one house where cupid's arrows flew straight and true. In the small cottage on the outskirts of Picarets, shutters wide open to the starlit sky, two figures lay entwined on the bed, heart rates slowing, skin flushed, a gentle lethargy descending over them. In nine months' time, Fogas would be celebrating the birth of another baby.

11

'A glass table?' Two nights on from Valentine's Day, Stephanie put her bag on the bar, stared at the table in question and then looked at Josette. 'Why glass?'

Josette shrugged, her eyes shifting away from Stephanie's scrutiny, unable to tell her the real reason. Or describe the contortions and mimes it had taken for Serge Papon to get the message across. 'I thought it might add to the atmosphere.'

Stephanie glanced around the room and held in a smile. There was plenty of atmosphere, for the bar had been transformed in readiness for the evening ahead. The archway to the shop had been cordoned off with an old folding screen; the lighting was muted, scarves draped over the wall lamps casting eerie shadows and candles ranged along the counter; and around the area where Stephanie would be doing the readings, long velvet curtains hung to the ground, encasing the glass table and the two chairs against the fireplace.

It was a textbook mystic's habitat.

'It looks fantastic, Josette. And the food . . .' Stephanie crossed to the table inside the door that was laden with canapés and delicious looking morsels.

'It's from the Auberge,' said Josette, pointing to the small business cards dotted around between the plates. 'Lorna and Francine Rougé have set up a catering business. We're their first customers so they've given us excellent rates in the hope of drumming up support.'

Stephanie bit into a small tart of tarragon and mushroom and groaned in delight. 'They'll be besieged with orders,' she said, making her first prediction of the evening. 'And we'll be besieged with guests very soon so I'd better get ready.'

Josette waited until the tall redhead had disappeared behind the curtains and then she turned to the empty room; empty apart from the two ghosts standing by the window, an air of excitement about them.

'Whatever it is you're up to,' she whispered, a finger held sternly up to them, 'make sure you behave.'

They nodded solemnly in unison. But the devilment was dancing in their eyes. And Josette was left to wonder just what she'd let herself in for.

'A struggle, perhaps? Are you fighting anything at the moment?'

René stared down at the brightly coloured cards on the table, his forehead beaded with perspiration.

'Nothing,' he muttered, running a finger around the collar of his shirt, which had grown tight the moment he stepped behind the velvet curtain and saw Stephanie sitting there, the tarot deck in front of her. 'I can't think of anything.'

Stephanie tapped her lip, brow creased in concentration as she looked at the pictures before her. 'The meaning will come to you,' she said. 'But whatever it is, from the cards you've chosen, you're facing quite a battle.'

'Am I going to win?' The words came out in a squeak of apprehension.

'I'm afraid I can't tell that from this reading.' Stephanie raised her eyes to those of the plumber, who found himself caught in the green depths of a gaze which seemed to see right to the core of him. 'I think that's entirely up to you.'

He gulped, leapt up from his chair, unsure whether to shake

hands, bow or genuflect before this woman who was so unlike the neighbour he met on a daily basis, and made a hasty exit.

'Will he make a full recovery?' Véronique asked, standing close to Christian in the crowded bar with what seemed like the entire community of Fogas around her.

'Apparently so. I bumped into Bernard this morning when he was down for supplies and he said the vet is happy with the way it's going.'

'He was lucky,' observed Annie. 'Those caterrrpillarrrs arrre a buggerrr forrr dogs and the Col d'Ayens is rrriddled with them.'

'So did Serge the beagle eat one then?' asked Véronique.

'He didn't have to. It's theirrr hairrrs that triggerrr the rrreaction. Lost a dog to them yearrrs ago, beforrre you werrre borrrn. It was a terrrrible thing to endurrre.'

'Well, at least Serge is going to make it. But what was he doing up on Col d'Ayens if the place is notorious for processionary caterpillars?'

Christian hung his head. 'It's sort of my fault. Someone's been laying illegal traps up in the forests around here and we haven't managed to catch them. So Bernard decided to walk Serge where it was safer. Or at least, he thought it was safer.'

'Illegal traps? I haven't heard about that.'

Christian and Annie shared a glance. There was a lot the postmistress of Fogas, normally the first source of news, hadn't heard lately.

'The main thing is, the dog is on the mend,' said Annie, diplomatically filling the silence. 'Berrrnarrrd must be overrrjoyed to have him home.'

Her remark sparked a grin on Christian's face. 'Between you and me,' he murmured, bending down to the Estaque women, 'it's not the only thing making Bernard happy. He was buying a lot of food in here this morning for one man and his dog, if you get my drift . . .'

'What? Bernard has a girlfriend?' asked Véronique. 'Who?'

Annie cackled. 'Put it this way. Agnès Rrrogalle has starrrted deliverrring to Fogas again. In fact, accorrrding to Widow Auberrrt, the butcherrr's van has been parrrked outside Berrrnarrrd's house forrr the last two days!'

Véronique burst out laughing and Christian, delighting in the sound, decided that no matter the outcome of this masquerade of an evening, something good had come of it.

'Christ!' came a rasp from behind them and they turned to see a pale-faced René gulping down a beer.

'How'd it go?' asked Christian, throwing an arm around his friend.

René took another long swig, wiping his moustache before he spoke. 'I think I'm going to die.'

'What rrrubbish!' announced Annie. 'Stephanie would neverrr have said that.'

But René was nodding his head furiously, his cheeks drained of colour as he patted his pockets, searching for his Gauloises. Which was when he remembered that he'd gone cold turkey. Again.

'Merde,' he muttered, gesturing to Josette behind the bar for a packet of cigarettes, before turning back to Annie. 'She said I was facing a battle. One I might not win.' The plumber broke off to glare up at the big farmer standing next to him. 'I told you this tarot lark was a bad idea.'

'A battle? But that could mean anything!' protested Christian.

'I know exactly what it means. It means I'm going to be struck down by a terminal illness. My days are numbered. So if you don't mind, I'm going outside to have a cigarette.' He swiped the packet of Gauloises off the bar and stormed onto the terrace, the door rattling behind him.

'I thought he was trying to give up,' Véronique said, as they watched the plumber puffing frantically on a cigarette the other side of the door.

'He was.' Christian laughed and waved a hand towards the heavy curtains which hid Stephanie from view. 'Amazing to think people take this stuff so seriously.'

'Christian!' Josette was calling from the bar, tapping the clipboard she had in front of her. 'Your turn.'

The farmer handed his beer to Véronique. 'Feel free to drink it. If it's anything like René's reading, I'll need something stronger when I come out!' And with another laugh he sauntered towards the velvet enclosure.

It was exhausting. Josette could tell that from her vantage point behind the bar. She was the only living person in the room who could see Stephanie behind the curtains, her role as bartender placing her across from the young woman as she leaned in over the tarot cards. Far enough away and surrounded by the chatter of those waiting their turn, Josette couldn't hear a word that was being said. But she could see the strain on Stephanie's face as she told fortune after fortune. And raised a substantial amount of money to go towards the town clock repairs.

Josette's position also allowed her to keep an eye on Serge and Jacques. So far, they hadn't strayed from the inglenook, although they'd taken great delight in René's discomfort and had rocked with mirth when the plumber had staggered dramatically from the booth to declare his imminent death. Clearly, despite having insisted on the readings taking place in the bar and on the glass table, which Josette was still none the wiser about, the two ghosts weren't believers when it came to tarot.

Unlike Josette, who had a healthy respect for Stephanie's

talents and could see the effort she was putting into the readings. Whatever you believed, you couldn't deny that the young woman had an uncanny ability to sense things way before the rest of them. Which is why, when Christian pulled out several cards from the tarot pack and Stephanie snapped back in her chair, Josette moved slightly further down the bar to get a better view.

Stephanie was saying something, shaking her head, hands flitting over the upturned cards, the chime of her bracelets audible even though her words were lost in the din of the bar. Whatever she was saying, it didn't look good.

Christian shifted in his chair, the back suddenly hard against his spine, the seat uncomfortable. He'd entered Stephanie's lair with a laugh and a joke, shuffling the cards and spreading them out on the table face down before choosing five with nonchalance, taking none of it seriously; he was a sceptic, after all. But then Stephanie had leaned forward, her red hair falling across her face as she contemplated the cards, and the temperature in their snug enclosure had dropped. Despite the roaring fire. He'd shivered, pulled his jumper closer around his large body, and waited for her to speak.

She didn't. Not at first. She studied the cards and then sat back with a jerk, the blood drained from her face. And Christian's heart had stuttered.

'What?' he asked. 'What is it?'

She shook her head, lips moving, face blank. But said nothing.

'Is it something bad?'

She lifted her gaze then, green eyes bewildered, focus distant. 'I don't know . . . I can't . . .' She gestured at the cards, her hands quivering. 'I'm sorry, Christian. I can't read them. They're too . . . confusing.'

He stared down at the table, the innocent looking line of

colourful pictures displayed atop it. He couldn't make head nor tail of them. A man on a horse with a sword; another man strung up from a tree, which admittedly didn't look good; a tower tumbling down; and two other cards, one with five swords on it, the other with ten. None of it meant a thing to him. But he couldn't deny the sense of foreboding that was filling the space behind the thick curtains, turning the air heavy and constricting his throat.

He stood, awkwardly, and held out his hand to the pale woman opposite.

'Well,' he said with a nervous laugh, trying to lighten the atmosphere. 'I think I should ask for my money back.'

Stephanie slipped her hand in his and then covered them both with her left one, her grip tight as she gazed up at him. 'Be careful, Christian. Be very careful.'

He nodded. Not sure what to say. And then he brushed the curtains aside and returned to the bar.

Inside the alcove by the fire, Stephanie released the breath she'd been holding and with trembling fingers, picked up the cards Christian had chosen and hurriedly replaced them in the pack.

She'd been able to read them all right. She simply hadn't wanted to. For his cards pointed to one thing only.

Danger.

The young knight, heading for battle but unprepared. The hanging man, a symbol of sacrifice. And the tower, a bolt of lightning destroying it: a revelation of some sort that would change everything. It was a powerful reading, made darker by the five and ten of swords: betrayal and violence.

She shuffled the pack, running her hands up and down the cards, as though wiping blood from their surfaces. Should she have told him? Warned him? She shivered, the cold of dread sweeping across her skin.

'Here,' Josette was placing a coffee in front of her. 'You look like you could do with this. Everything all right?' The older woman tipped her head in the direction the farmer had taken.

'Yes,' Stephanie lied, reaching gratefully for the hot drink. 'Fine. Send Véronique in when you get a moment.'

Josette regarded her over the edge of her glasses but Stephanie merely smiled. So, with a frown of concern, Josette disappeared behind the curtain and Stephanie tried to settle her nerves. She needed to be calm to do a reading. Even a reading that was meant to be a charade.

She took a deep breath to dispel the lingering miasma of tragedy that had arisen from Christian's session and caught a definite scent of sandalwood. And something else. Something deeper, spicier. Like a familiar aftershave.

She glanced at the fire, a pine log spitting noisily as the flames devoured it. Thinking that was the source, she concentrated once more on the cards, unaware of the robust outline of a ghost standing to her right. Or of the more delicate spectral frame that was scrunched up under the table and complaining bitterly to his accomplice.

Véronique was about to have a reading. And Serge Papon was going to make sure it was the right one.

'I'm not sure I believe in all this. Just thought I should tell you up front.'

Stephanie smiled and held out the tarot deck to the postmistress. 'Believing isn't obligatory,' she said.

Véronique took the pack, holding them gingerly as though they could burn. 'So I just shuffle them? And then what?'

'We're keeping it simple tonight,' said Stephanie. 'Simply fan them face down across the table and then choose five.'

The postmistress did as she was told, shuffling the cards

with ease and then spreading them in a wide arc across the glass surface.

'I can't see them all,' came a panicked voice from below.

'Can you see the ones we need?' asked Serge.

'Not without getting closer . . . damn eyesight . . . *ouch*!'

Serge glared down through the glass at Jacques who was rubbing his forehead, which had just come into contact with the table thanks to his myopia. 'Christ, Jacques, she's about ready to start. Pull yourself together.'

'Easy for you to say,' grumbled Jacques, peering up at the cards once more. 'I'd like to see you squeeze your fat backside in down here.'

'Quick. Give me an idea of where I'm going!' snapped Serge as Véronique's hand started to reach for the line of cards.

'There! That one.'

Serge looked down through the glass to where a skinny finger was pointing and summoning all his strength, he laid his hand on Véronique's right wrist.

'Oh!' Véronique blinked as her finger landed on a card. Not the card she'd been intending to choose. One further to the right. Much further. It was as though her hand had travelled to it of its own volition. Which was silly. 'This one.'

She turned over her choice, a childlike representation of an angel blowing a trumpet to three figures below, and saw a smile dance across Stephanie's lips.

'Is that good?' asked the postmistress, rubbing her wrist which felt unusually warm.

But Stephanie refused to be drawn. 'Let's get all the cards before I start the reading. Four more please, two either side of that one.'

Véronique stretched out her hand again.

*

'Right a bit . . . More . . . A bit more . . . There, that's it.'

Following the directions issued from under the table, Serge pushed down as hard as he could on his daughter's arm, feeling the tingle of heat where he was touching her.

'Mon Dieu,' he muttered, as he felt resistance, her hand sliding back towards the centre of the pack. 'She's stubborn!'

'Huh! With her pedigree what would you expect?' came a retort from below the glass.

But Serge was too preoccupied to rise to the bait, all of his energy centred on moving Véronique's arm back to where he wanted it. When he finally forced it onto the target, he stood back and mopped his brow. Three more to go and his heart was rattling in his chest. He wasn't sure he had the stamina to do it.

Stephanie was watching closely. She could see the battle being played out – Véronique fighting fate, trying to dictate where she chose the cards from rather than allowing the cards to find her. Her broad hand was wavering, pausing at the centre of the deck and then shifting out to the side. And her face – she was surprised, clearly not sure what was happening.

'This one,' the postmistress finally said, turning over the card to reveal an elderly man sitting on a throne.

The Emperor. A perfect card for the reading that was supposed to be given. If she didn't believe in the power of tarot already, Stephanie would have been converted, because tonight the cards would be telling Véronique exactly what everyone wanted her to hear. And without any intervention.

It was clever and diabolical at the same time.

All pretence of tending bar abandoned, Josette was transfixed by the hunched-up ghostly form of her husband picking out the cards that would reveal the future Fogas needed Véronique to have. And by the former mayor guiding his daughter's hand to where Jacques was pointing.

Guiding her! Serge was moving her arm. His face contorted with the effort, veins protruding on his temples. It wasn't easy for him, but somehow he was doing it.

The glass table Serge Papon had insisted upon now making sense, Josette watched as Véronique twisted over a third card, confusion on her face, bewildered by the lack of influence she had over her choices. And Stephanie, her eyebrows flicking up as each picture was revealed, a small smile on her lips. Judging by her expression, Serge and Jacques were not only managing to control objects in the real world, they clearly knew a thing or two about tarot cards.

How? That's what was bothering Josette. How did Serge have the power to move things? And how had her husband, who'd had no time for the horoscope let alone mystical decks of cards, suddenly become an expert on tarot?

It was all there, of course. The answers to both questions contained in the experiences Josette had been having. And as Serge Papon inhaled deeply to begin his manipulations all over again, the penny dropped.

The broken coffee cup; the twisted pictures; the moving saucisson. And her phone, her smart phone, which had an internet connection. A connection accessed with a simple swipe of the hand that even a baby could manage. Or a ghost with limited kinetic powers.

Serge had had her thinking she was losing her mind with his trickery. And Jacques, that slight figure twisted under the table, he'd been complicit. Happy to stay silent while his wife convinced herself she was deranged.

'The bastards,' muttered Josette, a woman rarely given to profanity.

Her nephew, Fabian, on hearing the words, did a double take as he placed some dirty glasses on the bar.

'Everything all right, Tante Josette?'

She glared at him. 'So much for locking my phone,' she said, before swinging her gaze back onto the velvet folds of curtain to the left of Stephanie. Fabian made a mental note to ask his wife that night whether she thought that perhaps his aunt was going ever so slightly mad.

'This . . . one!' said Véronique with surprise as her hand slapped down on a card half a pack away from where she'd been trying to choose.

She turned it over and then rubbed her wrist. It was hot to the touch, like she'd been given a gentle Chinese burn. It was happening every time she went to pick a card, an immense force bearing down on her hand and moving it. She'd tried to fight it. Wouldn't be an Estaque if she hadn't. But on each occasion, the pressure had proven too much and she'd ended up yielding. It was inexplicable.

'One more,' said Stephanie.

'Thank goodness,' muttered Véronique as she tentatively reached towards the pack.

Left. She was going to go to the far left. She began to move, waiting for the force. And then she felt it. Only it was different this time, more subtle, a tingle along her skin as opposed to a solid weight against her. She let the pleasant feeling ripple along her arm, down her hand and into her fingers, shifting across the surface of the cards until it felt strongest. There. Not at the left at all, but in the very centre. That was her final card.

'This one,' she said, and she flipped it over with a smile.

'What are you doing, you idiot? That's not the one I was pointing at!' From his undignified position beneath the table,

Jacques waved an irate fist in the direction of Serge, who had deserted his post for a seat in the inglenook. 'What's the use of giving me a list of the cards we need to shape destiny, if you're going to sit over there and ignore me when I point them out to you?'

Serge sighed, flicking a hand of dismissal at the peeved ghost. After two successive nights spent trawling the internet learning about tarot and trying to school Jacques in the five cards they required, he was too tired. Way too tired to muster his energies and dictate Véronique's movements again. So he'd sat down and let Véronique have her way for the final card. They had four good ones. If Stephanie couldn't tell the future Fogas was crying out for from that, then she was no clairvoyant at all.

'Relax, Jacques,' he said. 'Come and have a rest. We've done all we can.'

And Jacques, taking one look at his friend whose face was pink, breathing rapid and shoulders slumped, grudgingly crawled out from under the table and sat next to the fire.

'Stephanie had better get it right after all that,' he muttered, as the red-haired fortune teller leaned in and began to study the cards.

'Let's see,' said Stephanie, pushing red curls behind her ears as she stared down at the table, a long finger trailing over each card in turn as though she were drawing inspiration from them.

'Well?' asked Véronique with more than a touch of excitement despite her initial scepticism. 'What do they tell you?'

Stephanie glanced up. 'They won't tell me anything. You chose them. You have to interpret them. I'm merely here as a guide.'

'Oh . . .' Véronique looked at the pictures afresh in the order Stephanie had directed her to lie them down. There was a white-bearded old man on what could be a throne; a large wheel with three animals scampering around it; the angel with the trumpet in the centre; a woman prying open the jaws of what could be a lion; and finally, an older woman, also on a throne. To the postmistress, they were merely a collection of archaic drawings.

'But I don't have a clue what they mean,' she said.

'Okay. So, let's start with this one.' Stephanie tapped the angel in the centre of the five cards. 'This is Judgement. It's in the position that represents the present and typically it suggests a calling. Usually to some higher cause . . .'

Véronique's head snapped up and her eyes narrowed. 'Like what?'

Stephanie shrugged, doing her best to look innocent. After all, she was only reading what was in the cards. 'That's for you to say.'

'And this one?' As though changing the subject, Véronique pointed to the far left, the old man with the beard.

'The Emperor. He's in the position of your past and usually represents a figure of authority. A father figure if you like . . .'

'Serge . . . ?' Again the postmistress lifted her gaze onto the woman opposite, this time tears forming.

Stephanie nodded. 'I'd say so. The Emperor is a powerful man. I think we could say that was true of Serge.'

'Mon Dieu,' muttered Jacques in the fireplace while Serge grinned beside him. 'You couldn't resist including that one could you?'

'So what does this signify?' Véronique pointed at the next card along while she wiped her eyes with a tissue.

'The Wheel of Fortune? Change. That's what it usually suggests. And as this is in your near past, I'd say that was pretty accurate to describe what you've been through in the last month or so.'

Véronique raised a trembling hand to her throat, fumbling for the cross that was no longer there. 'Damn,' she whispered, as she dabbed once again at the tears on her cheeks. 'I didn't expect this.'

Stephanie reached out and took Véronique's fluttering fingers in her own. 'We can stop if you'd prefer?'

At which point Jacques jumped up in alarm. 'Stop? You can't stop now. Not after all my hard work!'

'Sit down!' Serge yanked him back into his seat. 'Véronique's made from stern stuff. She won't quit.'

And he was right. His daughter shook her head, wiped her eyes one final time and gestured for Stephanie to continue.

'So, in the centre, as I said, we have Judgement,' said Stephanie. 'The call to action. And then here, in your near future, this young woman with the lion is Strength. Which suggests to me that whatever course you choose to take, you will find the inner courage to see it though, no matter how difficult or painful.'

'Huh!' said Véronique with a small laugh. 'Now you're sounding like Maman.'

'Funny you should say that . . .' Stephanie rested a finger on the last card, the older woman sitting on a throne. 'This is the card you chose last.'

'The one she wasn't supposed to choose,' hissed Jacques at Serge. 'This had better not ruin things!'

Oblivious to the ghostly wrath being displayed in the corner, Véronique gave a slight hunch of the shoulders. 'Actually, it was more like it chose me,' she admitted.

Stephanie smiled, no stranger to the power of the cards. 'Perhaps it did. This is the Empress. Just as the Emperor in your past is associated with your father, so the Empress—'

'Maman . . .' Véronique stared at the card afresh, her skin tingling, emotions haywire, guilt and love and regret chasing through her.

'Possibly,' continued Stephanie. 'She's often seen as a source of familial strength. Some say she's a suggestion to connect with and nurture others around you.'

'Are you saying this is linked somehow to my relationship with Maman?' A slight defensive edge crept into Véronique's tone.

'I've said before, Véronique, it's not for me to tell you what to think. I can only offer ideas.'

Véronique crossed her arms over her chest and glared at the final picture. 'So let me get this right. My father has appeared in the past along with a great change. In the present, I'm being called to action of some sort and I will find the strength to follow this call. And to round it all off, Maman is my future?'

She raised her head and glowered at the fortune teller. 'How much did Christian pay you to fix this?'

Stephanie laughed, throwing back her hair, red curls dancing in the candlelight. 'Fix it? I watched you, Véronique. It wasn't you or me choosing those cards tonight. And this is a powerful reading. You should ignore it at your peril.'

Véronique stared again at the cards. 'Maman,' she muttered. 'Bloody Maman. Trust her to turn up.'

'Well, there is another interpretation for that card,' said Stephanie with an impish glint in her eye.

'What?'

'Fertility. Perhaps you're going to get pregnant?'

Véronique sat bolt upright in her chair as Serge jumped to his feet in the inglenook. And Jacques, watching on, collapsed in a fit of laughter. Those two stunned Papon faces, foreheads thrust forward, jaws slack in shock. It had been worth the night's contortions just to witness it.

No witnesses. Nothing to disturb the dense night that closed around him on the mountainside above Picarets. Satisfied he was alone amongst the trees, he hunched once more over the patch of disturbed earth, his torch muted by the curve of his hand and the shield of his body, which gathered the feeble rays into the folds of his clothing. He directed the light downwards onto the primed trap, the jaws stretched wide, the teeth throwing up a sharp reflection. And his satisfied smile in the torchlight was a grim mirror of his handiwork.

Reaching down, he deftly covered the open jaws with a loose layer of soil. Another one ready. It was early. Only mid-February. But better to have the traps laid and waiting than miss the prey. Hibernation would soon be over. And this year, when the bears emerged to roam the mountains in search of food, their young cubs wouldn't find the hills of Fogas quite so welcoming.

Brushing the dirt from his gloved hands, he picked up his rucksack and began to make his way home. For Henri Dedieu, the future was looking rosy.

12

He found it at dawn. The telltale smear of soil newly turned. He hunkered down, careful where he placed his feet, and with a small branch, scraped the dirt away.

'Bastards!' he fumed, the glint of deadly teeth winking in the weak sunlight. Scraping ever more cautiously, aware of the damage those jaws could do to a man, he exposed the trap. It was large, and highly illegal.

Boars. That's what people would say when they heard. They were set to catch boars. But he had a feeling there was more to it than that. Boars were prevalent right across the commune and even across the river above Sarrat. Why then were these blasted traps only appearing here, in the forests above Picarets and Fogas, the exact area where the bears were?

He didn't believe in coincidences. Nor did he believe in fate. But as he stood there in the morning sun, the disarmed trap in his hands, he knew that this was his destiny. To catch the man threatening Fogas. And to catch the man threatening the bears.

More and more he was convinced they were one and the same. But until he had the evidence he needed to prove his suspicions, all he could do was keep vigil. Over the people down below and the sleeping beasts above.

He slung the trap into his rucksack and, eyes to the ground like a beagle on a trail, scouted the area, hoping to find something that would help him on his quest. Broken branches. Disturbed rocks. He could see where the man had arrived from, and where he went, but beyond that, nothing. He was tracking a hunter, someone skilled in bushcraft.

Fine. It would make it difficult. But not impossible. For he had never failed to catch his prey before and he didn't see why it should be any different this time.

With the sun beginning to warm his back, he wearily made his way home.

'Did Christian go home last night?'

'I don't know.'

'Is his car down there?'

'Why don't you go and look?'

'Did the fortune telling work, do you think?'

'For God's sake, René!' Josette's sharp voice jerked the plumber back from the épicerie window where he was staring down the road at the old school building. 'Stop pestering me. It's hard enough making the books balance without you wittering on.'

She had no sooner refocused on the accounts spread out on the counter in front of her than the door crashed open and Fabian came hurtling in, Stephanie close behind him.

'Any news?' he asked.

'Did she agree to stand?' echoed Stephanie.

'Nothing,' replied René with a grimace while Josette muttered something about peace and quiet as she jabbed a finger at the calculator in front of her. 'Here's Annie, though. She might have news.'

The door chimes sounded again, Annie striding in on a blast of fresh air.

'Well,' she demanded before she'd even closed the door. 'Is she standing?'

René sighed. 'We were hoping you'd know. Haven't you heard anything?'

Annie gave a sardonic smile. 'Me? Think I'll be the last to hearrr. What about Chrrristian? Hasn't he contacted you?'

'Not a word,' said René, glancing over his shoulder as Alain Rougé entered the shop. 'I don't even know if he's at her flat or not.'

'Who, Christian?' asked Alain, as he reached towards the basket of baguettes. 'He's down at Véronique's. I've just walked past and the Panda is parked outside. Why, have you got news?'

'He's at her flat—?'

'Did he stay the night—?'

'Prrrobably just means it's brrroken down again—'

'You'd have thought we'd have heard by now—'

'Quiet!' Josette threw up her hands in despair. 'Honestly. How am I supposed to be able to think with you lot making that racket?'

She threw a glare over the small group and included in it the two ghostly figures loitering anxiously in the archway. She let her smouldering focus linger on them, her bad temper that morning arising in no small part from the way Serge and Jacques had fooled her. They'd had her – and Fabian – doubting her sanity and that wasn't something she'd forget in a hurry. Or forgive.

'If you're so eager to know how it went,' she continued tartly, returning her attention to the living, 'why doesn't one of you go down there and knock on her door? It's only eight o'clock. I'm sure she won't mind!'

No volunteers stepped forward.

'But it must have worked,' persisted René after a heartbeat of silence. 'What do you think, Stephanie? I mean, what did you say to her exactly?'

Stephanie wagged a finger at the plumber. 'Oh no you don't. I told you last night that I won't divulge the content of anyone's reading.'

'Huh! No wonder, when you go around telling people they're going to die. Not exactly a good advertisement for the business!'

The plumber's indignation was met with a roll of green eyes.

'I never said you were going to die, René.'

'Might as well have done. Here, Josette, give me another packet of Gauloises. No point forsaking my only pleasure when the Grim Reaper is on his way.'

Alain Rougé laughed, his delight quickly smothered by a look worthy of Death himself from the glowering plumber.

'It's no joke,' said René, sticking an unlit cigarette in his mouth as though he drew comfort just from its presence. 'This is the last day for submitting candidates. And if we don't have Véronique's name on that list, Fogas won't have a future.'

It was enough to draw a sombre curtain across the entire shop.

'So, like I said. Do you think it might have worked, Stephanie?'

The redhead turned to look out of the window at the old school. 'I don't know,' she mused. 'All I can say is that it was a powerful reading. Maybe too powerful. Sometimes people can't cope with the truth when it comes in such a form.'

She gave a delicate hunch of her shoulders and faced the others again. 'All we can hope for is that Véronique proves herself the child of her parents.'

'Stubborrrn and contrrrarrry?' asked Annie with a wry cackle.

Stephanie put an arm around the older woman. 'No. Principled and courageous. She saw what the tarot cards were suggesting. Whether she'll be brave enough to accept it is another thing.'

'Bonjour!' The door opened once more, this time Fatima Souquet walking in, basket on her thin arm. 'My, you're busy very early for a Thursday morning, Josette.'

'Tell me about it,' the shopkeeper muttered as she closed her account books with resignation.

'Is something up?'

'Nothing,' retorted the plumber, striking what should have been a carefree pose, which, given his desperate need for both news and nicotine, merely made him look even more strained.

'Isn't it the last day for nominations?' continued the interim mayor's wife, not even making a pretence to shop. 'I presume Christian has submitted his?'

'I couldn't say,' said René, left foot tapping impatiently, arms folded over his chest.

Fatima twisted a bony wrist and consulted her watch. 'Well, if he hasn't, he only has until the close of business today so he'd better get a move on. I'd hate to win a place on the council without a contest!'

And with a sharp smile for the gathering by the till, she retreated to the back of the shop.

'Mon Dieu!' René cursed quietly as Fatima moved further away. 'Those bloody cards were right. If Christian doesn't call soon, I'm going to die of a heart attack.'

The cards. Véronique had been so thrown by them that when the evening was over, she'd asked Christian to stay with her, a rare occurrence since the death of Serge. He'd been somewhat subdued once they left the bar, responding briefly when she'd asked how he'd got on behind the velvet curtain and not pressing to hear the details of her reading. Which she'd been glad of, as she hadn't had time to rationalise her uncanny experience. She'd then spent a restless night thinking about it, even the comfort of the farmer's large body next to hers in a bed that barely contained the pair of them not enough to stop her puzzling over what the five cards meant.

It was so clear, really there was nothing to puzzle about. Yet something inside Véronique resisted the obvious. Instead she sought other explanations. Other angles. But it all came back to the same two things.

The by-election. And her mother.

Frustrated by the battle waging within herself, she'd eased from the bed in the early hours, glad to leave Christian to whatever turbulent dreams he was having, his arms and legs twitching as though he too were fighting a war. Silently, she'd headed into the kitchen, made herself a hot chocolate and several hours later she was still sitting at the table, trying to come to terms with everything that had happened.

Should she stand in the election? Do her bit, as Serge would have said. A flare of anger coursed through her at the thought of local politics and what it had taken from her. Why should she give anything back? What did she owe the commune of Fogas and its people seeing as they had caused her father's early death?

And as for her mother . . . Véronique threw back her head and let a hiss of air escape from between clenched teeth. Maman. Theirs had never been an easy relationship. How could it have been when one was hiding a secret and the other was desperately trying to get behind the façade that secret had created. Somehow, it had survived the revelations the year before; now it was on the brink of collapse. Because, if the sudden loss of Serge had robbed Véronique of a future with him, she held her mother entirely culpable for the lack of a past.

But yet . . . There was always a yet. Images of Maman from childhood – a rough hand gently plastering a cut knee, a sharp nod of approval at a good report from school. And then last March, that act of madness when she'd revealed Véronique's parentage. She'd done it for her child. A reckless attempt to get a mourning Serge motivated and fighting to keep the post office open so that Véronique could retain her place in the community. The place she loved more than anything and the place where she had lost her heart.

Véronique glanced through the open door to the bedroom where Christian's tousled curls lay around his sleeping face. Would she be with him without Maman's intervention? After all, it was Maman's generous offer to Christian of the use of her farmland that had enabled the struggling famer to remain in the area. If Véronique's past had been lessened by her mother's actions, surely her future was brighter thanks to Maman's brave decisions?

She gave a quiet groan and dropped her head in her hands. Those bloody cards . . .

Afterwards she didn't remember what prompted it. She was sitting there in mental torment and then she was over at the dresser pulling open a drawer. It was still there. Neatly wrapped, untouched since the day of Serge's funeral.

She lifted it out, slipped a finger under a corner of tissue paper and carefully unwrapped it. Which was when the tears began to fall.

Eight fifteen. Christian surfaced bleary-eyed from a tangle of dreams which had seen him chasing Sarko the bull past a ruined tower and into a forest of swords, only to arrive at a tree with a noose swinging menacingly from it, the bull nowhere in sight. Unwilling to affix any relevance to it, the farmer dismissed his nightmare by cursing Stephanie and her tarot cards, and squinted at his watch, thinking there must be some mistake. But the halo of light seeping around the closed shutters told the truth.

Christ! He'd slept late. He rolled over, expecting to see Véronique but was greeted instead by the indent on a pillow and an empty space. Why hadn't she woken him?

Then the magnitude of the morning filtered through his cobwebbed mind. It was nomination day. The last chance for Véronique to change her mind.

Had she decided? Had the night before made any impact?

Suddenly galvanised, he threw back the duvet, stumbled into his clothes and entered the lounge, desperate to know. But fate was making him wait a bit longer. For Véronique was fast asleep on the couch, her body curled around a picture in a frame.

Curious, Christian leaned over for a better look. It was a photo taken up on the high pastures during the transhumance, flocks of sheep and cattle in the background, small against the peaks of the mountains. In the foreground, a man and a younger woman, arms around each other's shoulders. He was laughing, his broad forehead thrown back, face powerful, charisma emanating beyond the black-and-white print. And she was looking up at him, smiling unguardedly. If you didn't know, you'd presume they were lovers. Or would be.

Annie Estaque and Serge Papon. Taken sometime before Véronique was born.

Christian stood there awhile watching Véronique sleep and he felt his anxiety subside.

Ultimately, none of it was important. Fogas. The merger. Pascal Souquet. In the scheme of things, it was all transient.

But this. This wonderful woman asleep before him. She was what mattered. In the same way that the relationship between Annie and Serge had transcended everything, so Christian knew that his love for Véronique would overcome whatever she decided to do.

And in that moment, as he gazed down at the auburn hair framing the resting features of this amazing person who had somehow fallen into his life, Christian Dupuy knew she was the woman he wanted to spend the rest of his days with.

Head awash with emotion, he went into the kitchen and busied himself making coffee. It was easier than dealing with the fact that he'd just decided to get married.

'They're here!' René came barging in off the terrace, half-smoked cigarette still clinging to his lip. 'Christian and Véronique.'

It was like a bolt of electricity running through the place. Annie, Stephanie and Fabian came rushing in from the bar, breakfast coffees abandoned. Alain Rougé came hurrying forward from the newspaper rack, a gardening magazine still in his hand. Josette sat upright on her stool, closing her unfinished accounts once more. And Serge kicked awake a snoozing Jacques who'd taken a seat on the floor in the tinned goods aisle. At the back of the shop, Fatima Souquet stayed where she was, but she turned an ear to the door.

'Are they coming in?' asked Stephanie.

René nodded, stubbing out the cigarette and placing the butt behind his ear. 'Looks like it.'

Sure enough, the young couple were walking up the road, Véronique laughing gently at something Christian was saying.

'He's holding her hand,' mused Josette.

'So he is!' marvelled Stephanie.

'And?' asked René, not as au fait with romantic symbolism as the women.

'He never does that,' explained Fabian with precision. 'He doesn't like public demonstrations of affection.'

'Mon Dieu!' René tugged at his moustache, excitement rippling through his stout frame. 'It must mean she's said yes.'

'Or just that they had a good night together!' laughed Alain Rougé.

'Whateverrr it means,' said the sage voice of Annie, 'if she sees us all huddled up at the window like this, Vérrronique will suspect we've been up to something. So scatterrr!'

Which was why, when the door opened and Christian ushered Véronique ahead of him into the shop moments later, only Josette was at the till, as was normal at such a relatively early hour. Although an observant bystander would have noted the aisles of the small épicerie were somewhat busier than usual.

'Bonjour,' said Josette with an innocent smile. 'Isn't it a lovely morning?'

'Isn't it just,' beamed Christian and every head in the place turned to watch him, even the two ghostly ones that were hovering in the archway.

'And how are you this morning, Véronique?' continued Josette in a blithe manner that disguised the burning curiosity consuming her.

'Fine, thanks Josette. Ready for another day of selling stamps!' The postmistress stretched up onto tiptoe to kiss the farmer. 'I'll see you later,' she said with a wink as her hand stroked his cheek.

He blushed. To the very roots of his golden curls. 'Definitely.'

And he stood there, watching her walk off to her counter, a foolish smile on his face and his limbs turned to stone.

'So?' whispered René who had sidled up next to the petrified farmer.

'What?' asked Christian, gaze riveted on Véronique.

'Has she decided? Is she going to be on the list?'

'Oh!' Christian turned to face the plumber, hand to his forehead. 'Sorry. I forgot to ask.'

And René, feeling his heart stutter in his chest, feared that the death predicted by the tarot cards was going to be sooner than he'd thought.

'You didn't ask? What the hell was more important than this?' he hissed.

'Well?' Stephanie appeared on the other side of the farmer. 'Good news?'

René cursed. 'He didn't ask.'

'You didn't *ask*?' Josette had abandoned her till. 'What on earth have you been doing all morning?'

Christian blushed again. 'Look, I just didn't get round—'

'You haven't asked herrr?' Annie raised an incredulous eyebrow. 'What was the point of last night if you didn't ask herrr?'

'So we're still none the wiser?' asked Alain Rougé, appearing from behind a gardening magazine.

'Seems not,' growled René. 'Christian hasn't asked her.'

'Why does Christian have to ask her?' Fabian loomed over the plumber, genuine confusion on his face. 'Can't one of you?'

'Yeah! He's right. Why don't you ask her?' muttered Christian to the small huddle of people gathered around him.

'Ask who what?'

Véronique. She was standing right behind them.

'Nothing!' said Christian, kicking René who was about to open his mouth.

The postmistress let her gaze travel over the assembled faces. And then she dipped her head. And Serge, who'd been watching his daughter closely, on seeing that familiar movement – a gesture he remembered well from an unforgettable evening with Annie Estaque on the high pastures – grabbed hold of Jacques so tightly that the thinner man let out a squeal of pain. Which luckily no one else heard.

'By the way,' said Véronique to no one in particular. 'I don't know if the offer still stands. But I'd like to put my name forward for the by-election.'

Silence. And then René burst out yelping, throwing his beret in the air and pulling a startled Alain Rougé into a swing. Stephanie threw her arms around Fabian, Jacques was doing a jig with Serge, and Josette, her bad mood of earlier forgotten, was pulling Annie into an embrace, both women close to tears. Christian meanwhile, was standing there, his foolish smile reinstated, wondering at how perfect his life had suddenly become.

'Thank you,' he said, putting his arms around Véronique who seemed genuinely shocked by the reaction her decision had provoked.

'No, thank you,' she replied, linking her hands behind his neck and drawing his lips close to hers. 'Thanks for putting up with me over the last few weeks.'

She kissed him, and the small gathering in the épicerie went wild. While they clapped each other on the back and let excitement overcome them, from the rear of the shop, down behind the tins of cassoulet and boeuf bourguignon, Fatima Souquet watched on, forgotten about in the aftermath of the good news. She pulled out her mobile and made a call.

'You go in.'

'No, you go in.'

'I'm older than you, so you have to go first.'

'Do not. And you're only five minutes older anyway.'

'Chicken!'

'Coward!'

'Take that back.'

'Or what?'

'Or—'

'Shut up, both of you! Do you want us to get caught?' Chloé Morvan hissed at the bickering Rogalle twins who immediately fell silent.

After weeks of daring each other, the three of them had finally plucked up the courage to sneak around the back of Widow Loubet's house.

Half-term holidays, parents at work and only the Rogalle's grand-mère to keep an eye on them, they'd started the morning by playing in the twins' back garden, chasing each other in and out of Grand-mère Rogalle's voluminous dresses which were billowing on the washing line. When the foreseeable happened and Max, the older of the twins by the aforementioned five minutes, got entangled in one of the flowery outfits and ripped it to the ground, they'd fled before the heavyset figure of Grand-mère Rogalle could catch them.

Exiled to the square in the middle of the village, they'd played a half-hearted game of football around the old lime tree. But boredom had quickly set in, and so when Nicolas kicked the ball into Widow Loubet's garden, it seemed to be the perfect excuse. It was time, they'd decided, for a ghost hunt.

They'd been so brave, walking through the broken gate, collecting the ball and then scurrying around the side of the empty home. But once they rounded the corner into the back garden, things changed. The benign winter's morning, an egg-yolk sun shining down from a pastel-blue sky, had turned sinister, the light cut out by the looming trees, shapes and shadows shifting menacingly. And what had seemed like an enjoyable prank had developed an edgy undercurrent of genuine terror when the three of them faced the derelict building.

It leaned over them. Moss covered stones. Crazy wisteria reaching out twisted coils of wispy fingers. The rotten remnants of a shutter squeaking eerily on its hinges. And beyond the jagged teeth of broken glass in the window before them, the stale breath of damp and the forbidding dark of the interior. The place where Fabian had seen the ghost.

The idea had been for Max to enter the house first, being the oldest. Then Nicolas would follow with Chloé – she was a girl, after all – bringing up the rear. This decision, made under the branches of the lime tree ten minutes before, hadn't accounted for the terrifying reality, and once in situ, the bravado of the Rogalle twins had evaporated as fast as a summer mist over Mont Valier. Their terror had manifest itself as childish bickering. Which is when Chloé Morvan, accomplished acrobat and veteran of the high trapeze at the tender age of eleven and thus well used to conquering fear – as she reminded herself when she felt her heart start to thump – stepped forward.

'Here, Nicolas,' she commanded. 'Give me a leg up.'

She grabbed hold of the window frame, careful to keep her hands clear of the shards of glass, and with the aid of the younger twin, hauled herself up onto the sill.

'What can you see?' asked Max.

'Nothing,' replied Chloé, her eyes straining to define the shapes inside the part-shuttered house. 'I'm going to jump down.'

And with a bounce of black curls, she was gone.

The two boys looked at each other and, realising they had been outdone by a girl, raced to follow.

'Do you have a torch?' Chloé whispered as Nicolas dropped down beside her, his face no more than a blur.

'Max has one.'

'No I don't,' came a voice from the other side of her. 'You broke it last week.'

'No I didn't—'

'Quiet!' Chloé had already reached in her back pocket for her mobile, the phone providing a small glow of light. 'Here, we'll use this. Let's start upstairs first.'

And so the three intrepid explorers inched further into the haunted house, their proximity to each other increasing with each nervous step.

*

'Merde! Are you sure?' Pascal lowered his voice, held his mobile closer to his mouth and turned his chair away from the ever-alert Céline Laffont in the outer office of the town hall.

'Totally. I heard her say it with my own ears,' came the muted reply from Fatima down in La Rivière. 'Just thought you should know.'

The line went dead, leaving the interim mayor to stare out of the window at the slopes rising in the distance, his thoughts in turmoil.

'Merde!' he exclaimed, more forcefully this time as he slammed his mobile onto the desk.

'Everything all right?' Céline was standing in the doorway, a report in her hands. She crossed the room to place it before him, her words of concern belied by the delight in her eyes at witnessing his discomfort.

'Fine,' snapped Pascal, dismissing her with a flick of the wrist as the phone in reception began to ring. 'Close the door behind you.'

Which of course, she didn't. Instead she sashayed back to her seat to answer the phone. He didn't need to hear the conversation. The broad smile spreading across her face told him everything.

She knew, the jungle drums already carrying the news up and down the mountains . . . and across the river. Soon Henri Dedieu would know too. The thought brought a surge of bile up Pascal's throat, the sour taste of fear on his tongue.

Damn Véronique Estaque. And whoever had persuaded her to stand.

The interim mayor had no need for tarot cards to know that his rosy-looking future had just undergone a seismic shift.

*

'I can't see,' whined Max, as he edged his foot forward, trying to gauge the next step in near total dark. 'Perhaps we should go back?'

They'd crossed the first room – probably a kitchen, as they'd had to negotiate their way around a cobweb-covered table and chairs in the gloom – and had climbed the stairs three abreast, their breathing quick and shallow as they ascended into the dense dark of the upper storey. But halfway up, Chloe's mobile had died, plunging them into sightless panic.

'We're nearly there,' said Chloé, affecting nonchalance and feeling for the solid shape of Max to guide him up beside her. 'Where's your sense of adventure?'

She had just made contact with his arm when a banshee screech came from below.

'What was that?' Max yelped, grabbing hold of Chloé and almost knocking her down the stairs.

'It's the shutter, stupid,' muttered Chloé, heart racing despite her reassurances.

'And that?' Nicolas too had stopped, a warning hand gripping Chloé's shoulder. 'Up there?'

She turned her head to where Nicolas was pointing, his arm no more than an inky shadow before her face. There. A rustle of movement up above them. A soft sigh like wind through the trees. And then a reverberating rumble, the growl of a beast unleashed.

Chloé felt a prickle of terror run along her arms, up her neck and down her spine. Something was there and it wasn't far away from them.

'The ghost?' squeaked Max.

'It must be,' whimpered Nicolas.

And the two boys, joined by the magical connection of twinhood, wheeled around as one and fled down the stairs. Chloé, every fragment of her gypsy heritage alert and screaming danger, turned to follow and her outstretched hand, useless mobile still clutched within it, smacked into the wall, the phone falling to the floor with a clatter.

She froze, the harsh echo of metal on wood lingering in the empty house. Had it heard? Was it coming? One heart-beat. Two heartbeats. Nothing. The silence resettled heavily around her.

Legs trembling, she crouched down, blindly searching the stairs for the phone. She couldn't go home without it. Maman would kill her. Accompanied by the thump of blood pounding in her ears, she ran her hands over the bare wooden boards, feeling nothing but splinters and dust. Finally, several steps higher up, her hand connected with a familiar rectangular shape, still warm from her tight grasp.

Stretching up along the stairs, she closed her fingers around the mobile, her eyes inadvertently lifting to the landing as she did so. She blinked. A small mewling sound emerged from her throat as she stared. Tried to remember how it had been before. For it seemed as though the dark above her had changed. Become more solid. More black. And it was moving.

She pulled back her hand, forgot about her phone, and with a turn of speed that came from her acrobatics, flung herself carelessly down the stairs. Swinging around the newel post, she hurtled into the kitchen, crashing into the table in her scramble for the window and safety. But her escape route was too high. A chair. She needed a chair. She turned to pull one towards her and saw the doorway beyond.

She was too late. It was here. She tipped back her head to scream and the dark shadow pounced across the room and grabbed her.

13

The transition from winter to spring was well underway by the first Sunday in March, the day of the initial round of voting in the Fogas by-election. Thanks to the sunshine that had bathed the valleys throughout January and February, the cherry trees were already starting to show signs of buds and the daffodils outside the Auberge were in full flower. On the mountainsides, the changes were less dramatic but a faint bloom of green could now be seen softening the grey branches that had been scratching at the skyline for the last four months, and the music of birdsong was returning to the heavens above. There was even a rumour that the first cuckoo of the year had been heard in the trees behind the graveyard in La Rivière, which sent the more superstitious farmers into a panic, believing that snow would surely follow as local legend predicted.

But no snow came. Which surprised no one when it was revealed that it had been Bernard Mirouze who'd reportedly heard the herald of spring while out walking a recovering Serge the beagle in the company of Agnès Rogalle. After all, the man didn't know a cuckoo from a crow at the best of times and now that he was in love, his judgement was not to be trusted.

So, with conditions remaining fair, the farmers left their cows out in the low pastures, the trees continued to blossom – apart from the Christmas tree in La Rivière which had finally been dismantled, Véronique and Christian tackling it one afternoon shortly after the tarot night – and by this particular Sunday, it really did feel as though Spring had begun to dance her way through the Pyrenees.

Which was just as well, thought Christian, as he rounded the bend into Fogas where the early morning mist he'd driven up through had been ripped apart by the saw-toothed peaks of the mountains to reveal another glorious day. For with the fine weather, a large turnout for the election should be guaranteed. And with the opposition list looking the way it did, Paul and Véronique were going to need all the support they could get.

They'd canvassed hard over the intervening two and a half weeks since the nominations were declared, Véronique throwing herself into local politics with a passion which replicated that of her father before her. It was easy to see the reaction she caused amongst the older population who remembered not only Serge, but old Monsieur Papon too, a stalwart member of the Conseil Municipal in his time. For residents such as Widow Aubert, Véronique's surname was sufficient to get her elected.

But if that were the case for the postmistress, the same applied for Fatima. And even more so for Pascal's other nomination. For the last fortnight, Christian had tried not to think about Vincent Fauré, Gaston the shepherd's great-nephew. His name had emerged as Pascal's second candidate the day Véronique announced she would stand, and it cast a pall over the jubilation in Christian's camp at her decision. Because Vincent Fauré, although unknown to the majority of Fogas inhabitants, came from a legendary family: a family that could trace its Ariégeoise lineage back hundreds of years, that could count the famous composer Gabriel Fauré as a member (Gaston, the smelly shepherd, said to have been the spit of the musician if shaven and showered), and one that had no fewer than four heroes of La Résistance within its ranks.

Christian shook his head at the thought. Vincent Fauré's great grand-père, Gaston's father, had been a heroic figure during the war, renowned for his courageous treks over the Pyrenees, leading British airmen and Jewish refugees to the safety of Spanish soil. And if that weren't enough, his three sons, Gaston included, had helped him, their incomparable knowledge of the mountains acquired from generations of shepherding flocks on the high pastures. The three young men had also taken up arms within the local ranks of La Résistance, the eldest of the brothers killed in an ambush in the latter years of occupation. They were heroes indeed.

So, with a pedigree like that, young Vincent Fauré was a force to be reckoned with. Even if no one had known of his existence until two weeks ago. And when it had been revealed that the newcomer was a lawyer to boot, René had started predicting a catastrophe, it being well known that the inhabitants of the mountain valleys, whilst scornful of the *fonctionnaires* and politicians who ran the country, still maintained a sense of awe when it came to the legal profession. It was something that rankled the socialist Christian. After all, a law degree made a man no better than his neighbour in the farmer's opinion – just the opposite in fact, given some of the nefarious practices when it came to land sales that were related at the regular cattle marts and farmers' meetings he attended. But his neighbours didn't always see things the way he did, the concept of égalité their ancestors had died for failing to resonate with them in the way it did with him, and he knew the reverence with which they would treat this returning Fauré. Which meant Christian's chances of becoming mayor were looking very slim indeed. And the chances of Fogas surviving into the next decade were looking even more unlikely.

Particularly when Vincent Fauré's connections on his mother's side were taken into account.

It was Josette who'd remembered first. She'd mentioned it in passing as if of no consequence, an idle recollection thrown out for public amusement, but it had been enough to make Christian worried. Vincent Fauré's mother was Pierrette Dedieu, none other than Henri Dedieu's younger sister. To cut Josette's meandering reminiscences very short, Vincent's father, although born in Fogas, had been raised by an aunt in Sarrat following the death of his parents in a car crash when he was just an infant. He'd gone to school with Henri Dedieu and, in time, had married Pierrette and left the area to find work in Toulouse where his only son had been raised.

Was it merely coincidence? The return of this young man to his paternal homeland and his willingness to stand as a councillor just when things were on a knife edge? A situation precipitated by the very man's uncle. Christian couldn't be sure. But he knew what it meant for the vote. Because if Fatima Souquet had been considered formidable opposition for Christian's camp before – Paul Webster from the Auberge being no competition for her – the addition of the lawyer Fauré meant there was every possibility that Véronique, even with her incredible bloodline, might not win a seat. Which meant Christian would never be mayor. And Fogas would be no more.

Parking in front of the town hall in a plume of steam from the Panda's defunct radiator, Christian tried to look on the positive side of things. Perhaps the good people of Fogas would vote for what they knew and not be swayed by such inconsequential matters as the occupation or heroic background of the candidates. And perhaps his car would survive the repeated journeys up and down the mountain that today would necessitate. In which case, he promised to the God he didn't believe in, he would ask Véronique to marry him when the mayoral vote was over. And he would go down to the scrapyard in St Girons within the week and fix his blasted car.

With a hopeful heart, he walked towards the building where his fate, and that of his car, would be decided.

'Chloé? Are you up yet?'

Stephanie waited a second and then started up the stairs only to be met by Fabian at the top.

'She's gone,' he said, nodding over his shoulder to the open bedroom door. 'I saw her leaving as I came home from my ride. She said she was just popping over to the Rogalles' and would be back before we leave to vote.'

'Oh.' Stephanie looked at the empty bed and felt a pang of nostalgia for the Sunday mornings when a sleepy child used to come traipsing down the landing and into her room, wanting only to snuggle up beneath the duvet with her maman. Chloé had long outgrown such treats and would soon have outgrown this cottage. And perhaps even Fogas, her future seemingly destined for the world of acrobatics and the circus. A wave of nausea coursed through Stephanie at the thought.

'So it's just you and me for breakfast,' said Fabian, slipping an arm around his wife's waist. 'But we could always skip it . . .' he murmured, his lips nuzzling against her neck.

'I suppose we could . . .' said Stephanie, reaching a hand up to draw his face to hers. And then her stomach roiled and she was racing for the bathroom, bending double over the toilet, a concerned Fabian holding back her hair.

'It's okay,' he said, stroking her back softly while she heaved. 'It's okay.'

'God, I'm so sorry,' she finally managed, straightening to

reveal a pallor beyond her normal paleness. 'It must have been the pizza last night.'

Fabian nodded, taking in her tired face, her drawn features, and the hand resting on her stomach.

'Perhaps,' he said.

'Well, I can't think of anything else I've eaten that could have made me sick,' said Stephanie, leaning over the sink to rinse her mouth.

Fabian watched her bent figure and, for the man most people considered socially inept, he worked it out pretty quickly – much faster than his wife who, despite her gypsy heritage and future-telling prowess, was still casting aspersions on the innocent pizza.

'Neither can I,' he said with a smile. And he turned to head downstairs, reassessing the snug confines of the cottage as he did so.

They were going to need a bigger house, he concluded as he crossed the open living space to the corner kitchen and began to pour out his morning muesli. Seeing as there would soon be four of them.

'Your mother just texted you.'

In a room not far from the Rogalles' house where she was supposed to be, Chloé took the phone being offered to her and rolled her eyes. 'It's election day. I have to go.'

She stood, careful to lift her chair so no noise sounded as she placed it back under the rickety table. Secrecy, that was the key. He'd asked her to keep it all a secret – his presence here and the fact he owned the property – and without a moment's hesitation, she'd agreed.

It wasn't hard, the deception required. While the Rogalle twins had plied her with questions when she'd finally caught up with them the day they'd explored the haunted house, wanting to know what had kept her so long, she'd fobbed them off with a tale about leaping from the window and running home, being too scared to find them en route.

They'd swallowed it whole. Eyes fearful as they recalled the dark, the unusual sounds that had triggered their panic. And, as young males, they were happy to accept that Chloé had been even more scared than they had, that she had raced through the village without stopping, such had been her terror.

Although Chloé had to admit she had felt afraid, standing alone in the deserted kitchen. In that split second when his outline disentangled itself from the darkness behind. When he'd reached out and placed a large hand over her mouth, trapping the scream that was building in her throat. At that precise moment, Chloé had been shaking with dread. Then she'd realised, recognised his shape, the smell of the forest so peculiar to him. And her trembling had turned to exhilaration.

'Are you sure you don't need this?' A dark hand gestured at the mobile, which Chloé had returned to the table.

She shook her head and grinned. 'No. You can keep it. Just don't reply to Maman!'

A laugh greeted her words. 'Thanks Chloé. And thanks for this too.'

Another gesture, this time at the small bag of food that lay open between them. A couple of cereal variety packs – Miel Pops and something called Chocos, which promised maximum chocolate – a carton of milk, half a stale baguette, the tail end of a round of Rogallais cheese, and an old carrot.

She shrugged. 'It's not much. I didn't want Maman getting suspicious. But I'll try to bring more later. Is there anything else you need?'

'Not now I have this.' He placed the phone in his pocket. 'It should make it a lot easier to get Bernard's attention than whistling like a cuckoo at him. The man is not a born woodsman.'

Chloé giggled as her companion did a brilliant impression of the unfortunate *cantonnier* looking for a cuckoo in the trees. 'He's in love,' she said with another eye roll. 'It turns you stupid.'

'So I hear,' came the dry response. 'Now get going before your maman comes looking for you. And use the door, this time. No need to be climbing in that window.'

Chloé complied, heading out of the door that was being held open for her. She paused on the threshold and then spun round to hug the broad figure in the doorway.

'I'm glad you're back,' she whispered into the wool of his jumper. 'Fogas feels safer with you here.'

Arnaud Petit stared down at the young girl and only hoped she was right. Because he had a terrible feeling that Fogas wasn't safe at all.

Down in La Rivière, Véronique was sitting inside the bureau de vote. Which was the rather grandiose name that had been allocated to the storeroom on the ground floor of the old school. On account of the awkward geography of the small commune, it had been deemed necessary countless decades before to have two polling stations, so the residents of Picarets could be spared the long descent down into La Rivière followed by the steep climb up to the town hall in Fogas. At the time, the school on the valley floor had been a functioning part of the community and it had been relatively simple to set up the polling booth in the main room. But when the building had been converted into flats fifteen years ago, that was no longer an option. And so the cluttered storeroom below was commandeered for elections. Which meant a lot of clearing out in the days preceding.

This year had proved no exception, a group of locals having spent the best part of three days getting the space ready, moving boxes of bunting, the Christmas decorations, chairs with straw seats tattered and torn, a couple of antique desks from the school and several sets of broken shutters. They'd stacked all of it in the covered space that housed the snow-plough attachment and had then set to with mops and buckets and brooms until the room felt welcoming; a place befitting the seriousness of its duty.

Which was serious indeed. Three election officials – Véronique, Monique Sentenac and Fatima Souquet – were installed behind a long table; two neat stacks of the lists presenting the candidates were ready and waiting; a corner of the room had been curtained off, providing the privacy to vote; and there, sitting in front of Véronique, was the ballot box, its transparent sides showing it was completely empty.

Nine thirty and still no one had voted. The three women had been sitting there for over an hour and a half, their initial small talk soon dried up by the tension surrounding the day and Fatima's clear reluctance to engage in idle chatter. She'd very quickly thrust her sharp beak of a nose into a copy of the Code Électoral, preferring to pass the time reading the official guidelines for running an election than talking to her colleagues. Feeling awkward, Véronique and Monique had likewise fallen into silence and so now the quiet of the room was broken only by the regular click of Monique's knitting needles. It was going to be a long five-hour shift before they were relieved – especially if no one showed up to vote.

Fingers drumming a staccato of impatience on the abandoned book on her lap, Véronique stared out of the open door, which gave her a view of the épicerie and the bend where, following the river, the road twisted away from the hillside.

Not that busy at the shop either, judging by the lack of cars. And the garden centre gates hadn't even been unlocked yet.

Perhaps no one would vote? Maybe the people of Fogas had had a surfeit of politics, the last couple of years in the commune enough to try even Robespierre's love of state affairs.

Véronique dismissed the treacherous thought in an instant. This was Fogas. They would come, she told herself. But would they choose the right names on the ballot paper? Would they choose her?

After a fortnight campaigning, she was no more confident of her ability to win this vital seat than she had been before. She'd done her best, tried to appear animated and involved as she called in on her neighbours to ask for their support. And to some extent, she thought she'd succeeded. But all the time, the thin veil of darkness that had cloaked her days since the death of her father remained. No amount of electioneering had shifted it. Even the tension she was feeling today couldn't pierce it, the heaviness of her spirits lying damp across any other emotion.

Would she ever shake it off?

She stared again at the empty ballot box. If she won, perhaps then . . . ?

Her hand stole up to the empty hollow of her throat. Two months on and she still kept forgetting that her cross was no longer around her neck.

'What's the matter? Lost your appetite?'

An hour later, down the road from the storeroom where Véronique was marking the slow passage of time, Josette was indicating the golden curve of a croissant still on the plate in front of one of her customers.

'Something I ate,' said Stephanie, a hand moving gingerly

to cover her turbulent stomach. She'd been so looking forward to this election-day ritual – a leisurely breakfast in the bar where she lingered over an espresso and a croissant and Chloé gobbled up pain au chocolat, washed down with a hot chocolate. It was something she'd done since Chloé was very young, marking the importance of the day, marking the importance of the vote. Because it *was* important and Stephanie had been determined that her daughter should grow up appreciative of the electoral system and the freedoms it granted them. She'd been especially looking forward to this year, as it was the first one they would celebrate with Fabian.

But this morning, her unexpected indisposition had made them very late and the minute Josette had placed their usual order before them, Stephanie had felt sick. Really sick. It had taken all her effort not to race through the shop to the small toilet in the hallway. And it wasn't just the flaking croissant that had made her queasy. When she'd lifted her cup to her lips, the strong odour of coffee had made her gag.

Bloody takeaway pizza.

'I'll have it!' Chloé reached across the small table and grabbed the unwanted pastry.

'Nothing wrong with your appetite,' said Fabian with approval.

Which was true. Stephanie had noticed Chloé eating a lot more of late, the fridge seeming to empty a day after it was replenished. It must be a growth spurt, she mused, watching her daughter munch her way through the croissant with relish. Although Chloé didn't seem to be growing much, upwards or outwards. She was on the verge of adolescence and yet her body showed no sign of changing, the slight, boyish figure showing no signs of curves.

She'll be like her father, thought Stephanie. Small and lithe. The perfect acrobat.

'We should go and vote,' said Fabian, pushing aside his empty coffee cup and holding out a hand to help Stephanie down off her bar stool. 'And then get you home for a bit of rest.'

'Rest?' Stephanie shot him a glare. 'What do you think I am? An old lady? Besides, I intend to open the garden centre for a few hours.'

Josette laughed. 'Any excuse to hang around and see how the vote goes!'

Fabian shrugged, dropping a kiss on his wife's red curls. 'As you wish. Chloé, will you be all right here for a while?'

Chloé nodded, licking the last flakes of croissant from her fingers.

'We'll be fine, won't we, Chloé? In fact, why don't you go and have a look at the new magazines?' Josette nodded towards the épicerie. 'There's one on fashion you might like. I'll treat you if you like.'

'Thanks, Josette.' Chloé jumped down from her stool as Stephanie and Fabian left the bar. She watched them from the window, waiting for them to reach the old school before she turned towards the shop as though heading for the magazine rack.

Fashion! She shook her head in disgust. As if. She didn't have the least interest in it. But there was something in the épicerie she wanted. With a furtive check of the fireplace to make sure the two ghosts were fast asleep, Chloé passed the magazines without a second glance and edged further into the deserted shop.

'A voté!' Up in Fogas, René's clear tones rang out across the main room of the town hall and Pascal Souquet ground his teeth.

All morning. The idiot had been shouting all morning. When the plumber had offered to take the role of being in charge of the ballot box, Pascal hadn't foreseen five hours of torture due to René taking his official duties so seriously that, rather than uttering the obligatory 'a voté' in measured tones, instead he felt the need to let the people all the way down in La Rivière know that someone up the mountain had cast their vote. It was fraying Pascal's already tattered nerves into shreds.

The interim mayor glanced at his watch. Noon. Six more hours before the polling stations closed. Another hour before he would be relieved from this interminable chore. Sitting behind a long table, he'd had to endure the company of his fellow officials, René Piquemal and Lucien Biros, both incessant talkers, both imbeciles, a judgement Pascal had no qualms about making, even if the Toulousain Lucien was one of Pascal's staunchest supporters. And all the while, Pascal's stomach was churning with anxiety as the small mountain of blue envelopes in the ballot box continued to grow.

Who were they voting for, these peasants who were coming now in steady numbers? Beret clad, bare-headed, in Sunday best fresh from mass or in jeans fresh from the farm, they entered the town hall and they registered their opinion. Pascal had tried to read those faces but could see nothing more than broad foreheads, wizened cheeks, the dry skin of an outdoor life. He'd fared better with the second-home owners, recognising the self-importance of a school teacher, the arrogant swagger of an accountant. But those weren't the votes he needed to court. He already had them.

No, it was the older population he had to win over. The likes of the men who gathered daily around the *lavoir* at the entrance to the village – the very same men who had shifted their meeting place to the town hall car park today, ensuring that they were in the middle of everything, joking and bantering with the electorate as they came and went.

Would they vote for Vincent Fauré? Would the young

lawyer's name be enough to activate the atavistic ties that held communities like this together? The very same ties which, in Pascal's opinion, held communities like this back.

For once he was relying on that clannishness.

'A voté!' bellowed René again as another blue envelope fell into the box.

In six hours Pascal would find out what fate all those envelopes held. He just didn't know if his shattered nerves would last that long.

14

With the noon Angelus long sounded, Véronique was finally relieved from her polling duties. What had started off as a slow morning had morphed into a flood of voters as the church emptied and people dropped by before heading home. Feeling fatigued, the postmistress returned to her flat, intending to have a simple lunch of baguette and cheese, not sure her anxious state would tolerate anything more. But when she got there, Annie was waiting on the outside steps, a basket in her arms.

'It's what we always did on election day,' Annie blurted out before Véronique could refuse what was being offered. 'Papa would be on official duties so Maman and I would make a picnic and brrring it down to sharrre with him. I thought it might be nice . . .'

She faltered, the rare outpouring of words drying up under Véronique's frank gaze. And Véronique, in the weight of that moment, found herself thinking of the black-and-white photograph that was now on her dresser, and her final tarot card, the woman on a throne.

She opened the door and stood aside to let her mother enter.

She'd been caught.

All morning Chloé had hung around the épicerie and the terrace, pretending to read the fashion magazine Josette had insisted on giving her and trying to act like a normal bored kid, while waiting to seize her chance. At last, the late morning rush of voters and gossip seekers had died down as the lunch hour approached, and just after one she'd been able to make her move. The tin had been halfway up her jumper, joining the two already up there, when she'd felt the presence behind her. It was her gypsy heritage – as good as an alarm, telling her someone was there before she even saw them. Although in this case it had gone off a bit late and she'd been caught.

She turned, knowing what she'd see. Both of them, standing there watching her, hurt on one face, disapproval on the other.

'It's not what you think,' whispered Chloé, pulling her jumper down over her stash and zipping up her jacket.

Jacques shook his head mournfully while Serge wagged a finger at her, pointing at the spaces on the shelves where the tins had once been.

'I can't put them back,' she explained, one eye keeping watch for Josette. 'I need them.'

At this Jacques held out his hand, palm raised while Serge nodded furiously.

'But I don't have any money!' Chloé emptied her pockets, showing the ghosts her lack of funds.

Her plea fell on deaf ears, Serge crossing his arms and scowling at her while Jacques made gestures towards the bar. And Josette.

'No!' hissed Chloé. 'You mustn't tell Josette. This is important. Really important. You know I wouldn't be taking these if it weren't.'

Serge cupped a hand to his ear.

'I can't tell you,' said Chloé stubbornly. 'It's a secret.'

A furious conference ensued between the two men while Chloé wrestled with her conscience. She knew what it looked like. One tin of William Saurin Boeuf Bourguignon up her jumper and two lots of cassoulet . . . no wonder the ghosts thought she was stealing. But she wasn't. Or rather, she was, but only temporarily. They'd get paid back. Sometime.

In the meantime, they would have to trust her. Unless she told them . . . Should she? If she did, would it be breaking the secret that had been entrusted to her? Or were ghosts generally considered to be outside the realms of the laws that controlled confidences?

Her eleven-year-old mind was still trying to deal with the intricacies of this when Jacques and Serge broke off their discussion and, with one last disappointed look, Jacques started towards the bar.

Knowing the decision was out of her hands, Chloé sighed.

'Okay,' she muttered, her words making Jacques pause. 'I'll tell you. But you have to promise not to tell a soul.'

The two apparitions nodded solemnly.

'They're not for me,' said Chloé, pointing at the bulges beneath her jacket. 'They're for Arnaud Petit. He's back. And he needs our help.'

Two ghostly mouths dropped open. And then two broad smiles split the old faces before her.

Arnaud Petit had no idea that his return was being greeted with such delight down in La Rivière. As far as he was concerned, only one living soul knew he was back, which technically remained true.

He'd been torn out of a slumber when the kids disturbed him that day. Tired out from a night roaming the mountainside in search of the villain who was setting those evil traps, he'd collapsed on his camp bed and fallen fast asleep. Too fast asleep. He wasn't happy that the three youngsters had made it as far as the top of the stairs before he heard them. And then, it was only Chloé dropping her phone that woke him.

It was dangerous, letting his guard down like that. But a

month of night watch in the forests around Fogas had taken its toll. Luckily for him, it had been a friend who'd surprised him and not a foe. Even luckier, it was one of the few people in the commune he could trust to keep his arrival back here a secret.

Chloé Morvan. She hadn't grown much in the eight months that he'd been away yet she was noticeably older. When he'd crossed the kitchen to stifle the scream he could see building, it had only taken her a moment to realise what was happening, who he was. Then her eyes had widened and he'd felt a smile working its way onto her mouth beneath his hand.

She was a fantastic kid. And already she was proving invaluable, the mobile in his hand testimony to that. It was exactly what he needed.

Having returned to the area on a wave of emotion following the unexpected news of Serge Papon's death, he'd fully intended to put his plans into action. But in the days leading up to the funeral, hiding out in his house up in Picarets, he'd had time to reflect, and he'd come to the conclusion that the evidence he had was only circumstantial. A snippet of blurred video taken at night showing a hand and a signet ring, it would never stand up in court. No, if he was going to bring the person who'd murdered the bear the summer before to justice, he would need more. After all, he'd made his suspicions clear to his bosses back when he was employed as an investigator into the bear attacks and they had chosen to ignore him. Worse, they'd accused him of negligence.

So he'd decided that this time he was going to wait until he had everything in place to convict the man beyond doubt. Then he'd started discovering the illegal traps. He'd written to the relevant government department so warnings would be issued, thinking not only about the bear cubs soon to emerge but also about the danger for the likes of Chloé and the Rogalle twins as they played in the hills. He'd also taken it upon himself to try to track the hunter who was setting them. Many sleepless nights later, he still had no proof. But he had plenty of suspicions. His instinct, which was rarely wrong, was telling him that the same person who'd killed the bear was trying to kill even more of the creatures with these deadly devices.

Which was why he was sitting in Widow Loubet's kitchen – or to be more precise, *his* kitchen – on election day instead of joining the queue of voters down in the old school.

As the owner of a house in the commune of Fogas, Arnaud Petit had every right to vote. But registering would have revealed his presence here. And after the care he'd taken to conceal his identity when purchasing the widow's old home the previous autumn, he wasn't ready for that. Not when he had work to do.

For rather than helping Christian through the ballot box, Arnaud was going to help him in another way. He was going to bring down Henri Dedieu, the man with the boar's head signet ring. The man who was trying to destroy Fogas just as he wanted to destroy the bears. To do that, Arnaud needed to stay in the shadows. He also needed a favour.

Before he could have second thoughts, the tracker entered a number on Chloé's phone. Yet another person was about to find out he was in town. Arnaud only hoped he could be trusted.

'He's looking so much better!' Agnès Rogalle leaned over the couch and held out a hand, a wet nose pushing gratefully against her palm. 'Who'd have believed it?'

'All thanks to you,' mumbled Bernard, overcome with emotion at seeing his beagle and his beloved together. 'It was your quick thinking that saved his life.'

Agnès shrugged off the compliment. 'If it hadn't been for

my stupid advice, you wouldn't have been up on the Col d'Ayens in the first place.'

'And then we might never have got together,' added Bernard. 'So in a way, it all ended well.'

Agnès smiled, leaning over once more to give Serge another pat. It was meant to be, she thought, looking at the Butcher Burglar and grateful that her nemesis had survived. She hadn't told Bernard the truth about his freezer full of rabbits. She couldn't bear to ruin Serge's reputation as a first class hunter. Or hurt Bernard's pride.

The sound of a mobile split the companionable silence and Bernard reached for his phone.

'Chloé!' he said with surprise. 'Why is Chloé Morvan calling me?'

'Answer it and find out,' retorted Agnès.

So he did. And she watched his eyebrows shoot up into his hair, his eyes widening and a flush stealing across his face. Then he abruptly turned his back and left the room and Agnès felt a splinter of ice pierce the warm confines of her heart.

'Chloé Morvan, my backside!' she muttered to the dog. That was no child on the other end of the phone. It was a woman. Bernard was taking a call from another woman. Perhaps, wondered a worried Agnès Rogalle, she'd thrown herself into this relationship too quickly?

What had been a long day seemed to terminate rapidly. One moment Véronique was ticking off the minutes, watching the second hand on her watch crawl around. The next, Christian was declaring the polling booth in La Rivière closed and the three officials who had taken the last shift – Josette, Paul Webster and Philippe Galy – began the painstaking procedures that preceded counting.

'Remember, this is just the first round,' said Christian

quietly, giving Véronique's shoulder a squeeze before taking his place at the front of the room where the blue envelopes were being released from the ballot box.

Just the first round! While Véronique appreciated that the chance of any of the candidates getting an outright majority tonight was slim, thus necessitating a second round of voting in a week's time, she quailed at the thought of having to endure such tension all over again.

'I'd rather lose and be done with it,' she muttered to Christian's departing back.

'No you wouldn't. You'rrre a Papon, rrrememberrr!' Having elbowed her way through the crowd of onlookers that was forming at the rear, Annie had reached her daughter's side, triggering a surprising surge of gratitude in Véronique.

'Fatima Souquet,' announced Christian, reading out the first ballot paper. Annie's rough grasp enclosed Véronique's trembling hand. The counting had begun.

'Fatima Souquet!'

Pascal's voice rang out across the town hall, making René grind his teeth.

'Fatima bloody Souquet,' the plumber muttered, making a note on the list before him. He was one of three counters entrusted with keeping a tally of all the votes Pascal was reading out. And so far, it wasn't pleasant reading. Fatima was winning by a mile.

Glancing down the page, it was clear to see what was happening, even halfway through the counting process. Between them, Véronique and Vincent Fauré had split the vote. They were too alike – both with local roots, both of excellent pedigree. And while René would be aghast to be called sexist, he knew that for many in the community, the fundamental difference between them would give young Fauré the upper hand.

The consequence of this was that Fatima Souquet was running away with the election and there was every possibility that Vincent would be voted in alongside her, leaving the post-mistress a narrow loser and removing the need for a return to the polls the following Sunday. René chewed on the end of his pencil and prayed that the remaining piles of ballot papers would all go Véronique's way.

'Fatima Souquet.' Christian tried to keep the resignation out of his voice as he unfolded another paper and read out the all too familiar name. But it was hard. The wife of the interim mayor was clearly going to win.

He let his eyes drift across the now-crowded storeroom beneath the old school, locals, many of them equipped with pen and paper, standing at the back to witness the counting that was taking place in near silence. There she was, Véronique, Annie standing next to her in the trademark Estaque pose, chin up in defiance. But Véronique didn't look so confident. Her shoulders were drooped, her skin was grey and her eyes showed concern.

Perhaps this had been a bad idea all round, thought Christian as he took another ballot paper from Philippe who was in charge of opening envelopes. Perhaps they should have left her alone with her grief. Because with the way things were going, it didn't look like tonight was going to give her anything to be cheerful about.

He glanced at the paper in his hand and his heart plummeted.

'Vincent Fauré,' he said, wishing the evening was already over.

It was hard to say when the tide turned. Yves Degeilh, one of a swell of people standing anxiously at the back of the main room in the town hall, believed it was when the counting reached the bottom half of the ballot box. In his opinion, it was obvious. The majority of the locals still kept farm hours despite retirement. Whereas the second-home owners, he added with disdain, were more apt to take a leisurely approach to their Sunday. Ergo, he whispered to fellow Lavoir Gang member, Pierre Mené, who was earnestly marking each vote on his own notepad, it took a while for those early local votes to come into play. When Pierre pointed out that the ballot boxes had been tipped upside down on the table before counting commenced, thus discrediting his friend's theory, Yves lapsed into a sulk.

Others, like Widow Aubert, thought the sea change was merely the way of the Good Lord and not to be questioned. Although she personally could have done without all the added suffering.

René Piquemal, however, didn't give a damn about the causes of the swing in voting. He was too happy adding marks beneath the name of the woman he wanted to win.

'Véronique Estaque,' said Pascal Souquet in muted tones and René made another delighted stroke on the page in front of him.

She might just do it.

'Anotherrr one!' At the sound of her daughter's name being called from the front, Annie squeezed Véronique's hand so hard the postmistress doubted she'd be able to use her till for a week. But she didn't mind. For out of the desert that had been the first half of the counting, suddenly she had entered an oasis, her name appearing on ballot after ballot.

'You might just do this,' said Annie.

'I don't know,' murmured Véronique who'd been trying to keep a record of the votes herself but in her excitement, feared she might have missed one or two. 'It's so close. And don't forget, we've got to add in the numbers from the town hall yet and it's in Fogas that Vincent Fauré will probably get most support.'

'Trrrue. But this polling station coverrrs both La Rrrivièrrre and Picarrrets, which is about two thirrrds of the total population.'

Annie had a point. As Véronique turned her head to look at the crowd amassed behind her, she could easily believe all of that population was now standing in the old school's storeroom.

'Véronique Estaque,' called out Christian again and a murmur of excitement went around the room.

Serge Papon's daughter seemed to be as jammy as the old man himself.

Geographically the commune of Fogas was split asunder by the two valleys that defined it. But while this impediment of nature was often cursed by the postman and young children on bicycles riding to their friends' houses, all of whom had to trek up and down the intervening mountains to get from one side of the district to the other, surprisingly it had never proved to be an obstruction to the communication channels that flowed freely across the deep divides. The night of the election turned out to be no exception.

Faster than a crow can fly, word filtered down from Fogas, numerous text messages detailing the incredible reversal of fortunes for the postmistress pinging silently into muted mobile phones and setting up a low murmur of anticipation amongst those watching. Likewise, the news from La Rivière winged its way in the other direction, causing a ripple of noise to flutter through the gang of old men who had swapped their evening meeting point from the *lavoir* to the main hall of the town hall. It was enough to make Pascal stutter as he read out the final name.

'Véronique Estaque.'

The counting in the town hall was over. While René and his fellow clerks began the tedious job of cross referencing votes placed against votes counted using the tally sheets, the locals huddled together, comparing notepads. They had the result sorted long before Pascal was passed the official piece of paper. Before he even had a chance to read it out, the news was down in La Rivière.

At the back of the storeroom beneath what had once been the school, it was apt that mathematics had taken over the evening. Amongst those watching on, fingers, thumbs, toes, mobile phones, everything was being used to count up the votes, while the more numerically agile were busy working out percentages. For the results – unofficial, of course – were in from the town hall and with only a few unopened ballots left to be read out by Christian, everyone in La Rivière was frantically trying to calculate the margins.

'Eight-eight. She's got eight-eight percent—'

'But that doesn't add up—'

'Idiot! You divided it by a hundred instead of multiplying—'

'Here. Give me that calculator—'

Fifty-one, forty-seven, fifty-five, forty-nine…no one seemed to agree. But somehow, out of this morass of numbers, clarity suddenly came and a thrill of excitement charged the room.

'I think . . .' Véronique stared at her notepad again and then turned to Annie who'd been watching her daughter's fevered application of pencil to paper with tension. 'I think I might have . . .'

'Véronique!' It was Bernard, his soft shape appearing at her side. 'You've won! You've got a seat on the council.'

Annie threw back her head and laughed, her strong hand slapping Véronique on the back, while the newly elected councillor simply looked bemused, strangely unwilling to trust the grapevine of gossip that had so often provided her with all the news.

As for the *cantonnier*, who had canvassed hard on Véronique's behalf, adamant that the mayor's legacy should live on, the thought of a Papon taking the place of his beloved Serge, combined with his beagle being alive and his heart being filled with love – plus the other news he'd had on the phone earlier – all proved too much and fat tears of joy coursed down his cheeks.

'I've won?' breathed Véronique, turning to the front where the officials were still trying to tick all the boxes that French bureaucracy demanded of them. She caught Christian's eye across the mass of people and blew him a kiss.

And the farmer, having been restrained all evening as befitted his position, threw impartiality to the wind. He strode down through the throng of people to gather Véronique in his arms, making Bernard Mirouze cry even harder.

Only seconds later, down the road in the bar, a phone vibrated silently on the counter and the two men looked at each other.

'Go on then!' urged Jacques.

Serge swallowed hard, throat tight, blood pressure rocketing. Then he reached out a finger and swiped the screen. It was from Chloé using her mother's phone.

'Well?' demanded Jacques, peering at the screen.

'She won,' whispered a stunned Serge. 'We did it!'

Jacques grinned at his old friend. 'I told you we had power!'

Just as the news had flown so quickly up and down the mountainside, so too it traversed the river with the merest beating of wings and landed in a small workshop up in Sarrat.

'Merde!' Henri Dedieu gripped the mobile phone in anger, the boar's head signet ring cutting into his flesh. 'The imbecile!'

The voice on the other end carried on regardless, giving the mayor of Sarrat the gruesome figures. Forty-nine percent. His nephew had put up a good fight. In normal circumstances it would be enough to force a second round. But this was Fogas, as far from normal as you could get. And instead of a man with an impeccable heritage and a stellar future, they'd chosen two women: a postmistress and the wife of the interim mayor.

It was contrariness like that which made Fogas the place it was; a place ripe for being taken over. Only now, Henri Dedieu's Trojan horse had gone lame.

With more curses, he hung up, slamming the phone onto his workbench beside the open jaws of the trap he'd been working on. Pascal Souquet. He was a weak link. And from the look of things, he'd allowed his energies to be diverted to his wife's campaign, rather than the one that was the most important.

He needed to be dealt with. But first they had to get him elected as mayor.

Tethering his temper, Henri Dedieu reached for his mobile again.

Up in a raucous town hall, Pascal Souquet was going through the motions, overseeing the final procedures of the voting process while accepting the wave of congratulations that the result had generated with the best smile he could muster. In another corner of the large room, Fatima was basking in the praise which, to be truthful, no one could deny she'd earned.

Sixty-eight percent. A massive majority. She'd swept the opposition aside to take office with more votes than Pascal had ever garnered.

And in her wake, Véronique Estaque, limping home with a narrow margin, her fifty-five percent enough to ensure no second round was needed for either candidate.

But while the final figures had left his wife triumphant, Pascal's stomach was awash with bile. Two seats up for grabs and he'd secured only one of them, and even then, it wasn't as if he could trust Fatima. She'd made her views clear on the merger. But she was also ambitious. For her husband and herself. Would she go so far as to vote for Christian for mayor?

His mobile sounded in his pocket. He didn't even bother checking the screen. He knew who it was. And there was no way he was going to speak to him.

For anyone looking in the window of the bar later that evening, it would have been clear there was a celebration going on. The lights were ablaze, the place was packed and noisy and Josette and Fabian were busy serving drinks to a thirsty electorate. René was holding court, praising both Véronique and Paul for their efforts, and was just beginning to ruminate on the future of politics in a place that had elected two women when someone thankfully pulled out an accordion and started playing.

A space was cleared and an ecstatic Christian Dupuy, fuelled by love and victory and at least two beers, took to the improvised dance floor with Véronique Estaque – Councillor Estaque, as she primly reminded him.

The couple were soon joined by others, Bernard gently waltzing both Agnès and Serge the beagle, who was making great strides in his recovery, while Alain Rougé had his arms around his wife, and Paul and Lorna Webster were rocking their twin babies in time.

It was clearly a festive occasion. And no one was enjoying it more than the two ghostly figures who normally inhabited the inglenook. Light on their toes and grins in place, they danced a jig of victory around the small room, much to the delight of Chloé Morvan and the exasperation of Josette Servat.

But who could blame them? Véronique Estaque had been elected onto the Conseil Municipal and Arnaud Petit was back. Surely that would be enough to protect Fogas?

15

By the Wednesday following the election, for some in Fogas the euphoria of victory had yet to fade. Even the sullen clouds banking up behind the distinctive flat top of Mont Valier couldn't dampen the mood. Especially at the Dupuy farm on the far side of Picarets where three people were gathered around the large kitchen table.

'Married?' Josephine Dupuy leapt up from her chair and threw both hands over her face. 'Oh, Christian!'

'Hang on Maman, don't go getting too excited. I haven't asked her yet!'

'Can she cook?' André Dupuy was leaning over towards his son, the intensity of his question belied by the devilment in his eyes.

'Can she cook? Is that all you can say?' His wife clipped his ear affectionately. 'The last of our unwed children announces he's going to get married and all you can ask about is Véronique's cooking abilities?'

André grinned and stood to shake his son's hand. 'She's right, Christian. Talent in the kitchen isn't necessary for a good marriage. Your mother and I are living proof of that.' And he drew his now crying wife into an embrace.

'I take it you approve?' said Christian with a smile.

Josephine nodded and dried her tears. 'Véronique's a good woman. She'll cope with what life demands up here. When are you planning to ask her?'

'After the council meeting. I want to get politics out of the way first.'

'Wise move,' said André Dupuy. 'Do you think you've got enough to swing the vote?'

Christian shrugged. With only two days to go before the first meeting of the new Conseil Municipal, when Serge Papon's replacement as mayor would be elected by the now full council, he was feeling more and more confident with the passing hours.

'Logic says I should win. With Véronique taking that seat I can bank on five votes, as can Pascal. The deciding factor will be Monique Sentenac and I'm hopeful—'

'Oh, she'll not side with Pascal. Not now Fatima is on the council. She hates the woman.'

The conviction in Josephine's voice brought a smile to Christian's face. Having been a client at Monique's salon for decades, Maman knew her hairdresser as well as her hairdresser knew her.

'Well, this is Fogas,' he said, trying to temper his mother's certainty which carried more than a little maternal bias. 'No point in counting chickens. But when the vote is over, probably on Saturday, I'll ask Véronique to marry me.'

Silence fell in the kitchen, the importance of this moment lost on none of the Dupuys. And Christian felt a thrill of terror and anticipation as he thought about the days ahead.

'We'll have to move out!' said Josephine, turning to her husband who was already nodding.

'No, not at all!' protested Christian, gesturing towards the rambling farmhouse that contained them. 'There's plenty of space here.'

Josephine raised an eyebrow. 'And only one kitchen. It's a recipe for disaster. And besides, you'll be filling those rooms pretty quickly, I hope!'

Christian blushed. 'One thing at a time, Maman,' he muttered, making his father laugh.

'She's right, son, and you know it. It's time we moved on anyway. Put our feet up a bit more, perhaps.'

'But where would you go? You can't turf Stephanie and Fabian out of Grand-mère's place,' said Christian, in reference to the small cottage down the road at the entrance to Picarets which Josephine Dupuy had inherited from her mother and which Stephanie Morvan had been renting since she first arrived in the area nine years ago.

Josephine flicked a hand in the air. 'We've got lots of other options. After all, I hear your future wife owns several properties in the area! Either one would do us and they're close enough for your father to still lend a hand on the farm and for me to babysit.'

Christian laughed and shook his head. His mother had it all planned out as usual. She'd probably been plotting all this from the moment he'd got together with Véronique last November.

'If you're sure that's what you want,' he said, rising from his chair and gathering his car keys from the table. 'But remember, not a word of this until I've asked her. I'd hate for you to start packing for nothing!'

'Pah! No chance of that. What woman in her right mind would turn you down?'

Christian leaned over, kissed his mother on the cheek and headed for the door. He didn't tell her that with Véronique, there was every chance of that happening. Because despite winning the seat on the council, she was still far from in her right mind.

'Are you ready?' Véronique was standing outside the farm where she'd grown up, body turned sideways, her question addressed to the barn opposite rather than to Annie who had opened the door.

It was mid-morning, but for once the sun wasn't shining, hiding instead behind a mass of grey cloud that had gathered above the mountains leaving the air heavy with the threat of rain.

'Yes,' replied Annie, although it was far from the truth. She wasn't ready for this. She doubted she ever would be. But when Véronique had called and asked her along, she was too overjoyed at the rare contact with her daughter to say no.

They'd made progress since the tarot night, no mistake. The picnic they'd shared on election day had been the start, although they'd both found it awkward at times. But at least Véronique now had the photo of Serge on display in her flat. That had to be a good sign. And Sunday evening in the bar had been special, Véronique almost back to her old self, her display of happiness convincing most people. Annie however, knew her daughter and she could see the spectre of depression still lingering, the sadness that seemed to drape around her like a shroud.

Perhaps today would help. Although Annie didn't see how it could.

'Thanks,' murmured Véronique, head down. 'I tried doing it alone last time and it was just too much . . . So Christian suggested . . .'

Christian. The sense of optimism Annie had been harbouring waned a little. She should have known this was the farmer's doing. Trying to mend the fences the two women in his life had pulled down.

'Well, the soonerrr we starrrt . . .' said Annie, covering her upset with the pragmatism she was famous for.

Véronique nodded and they crossed to the car to begin the trek back down to La Rivière and then all the way up the other valley to Fogas, the clouds dark in the rear-view mirror as they drove off.

It was perfect. Well, not actually perfect right now, but it had amazing potential. Fabian stood at the end of the long garden and looked at the house once more, wondering why this brilliant idea hadn't occurred to him before.

Perhaps because there hadn't been a need to move before.

He reached for his mobile and began to make a list of all the work that would be needed to turn this place into a great family home.

First, where to fit a polytunnel? He knew his wife. If he was going to persuade her to move out of the small cottage they currently rented and buy a house nearby, her precious polytunnel was going to be her first concern.

Next, an extension to make the tiny kitchen bigger. And perhaps put in an en suite upstairs. After all, there would be four of them and Chloé was fast heading into her teenage years. Not that she showed any signs of becoming preoccupied with beauty regimes.

He grinned, glancing up from the screen to assess the garden in a new light. It was big – big enough to perform gymnastics in. Chloé would love it. Especially if they put in a small trapeze off a tree! There was room for a large workshop too; somewhere he could tinker with his bikes under cover.

He looked at the building once more, the familiar faded Dubonnet mural adorning the gable wall. The old Papon house, as it was affectionately known, had been his first home when he arrived in the area two years ago. Situated in the centre of the tiny village of Picarets, it had been built to give fantastic views out across the mountains – views which would be restored once the jungle of a garden was tamed. Luckily, the building itself was in great condition, unlike the half-derelict property next door.

Like he'd said. It was perfect. All he had to do now was persuade Véronique to sell it. But would she be prepared to relinquish ownership of the house where her father had been born? He'd call her later today and find out. Then he'd call an estate agent in Paris and put his ultra-modern apartment, which was currently rented out to an investment banker, on the market. After all, he had no plans to return to the capital. His home was here in Fogas where he was about to become a property owner. And a father.

Excited by his brainwave, he shoved his phone in his pocket and was walking towards the back door when he heard it. A stifled sound – like a squeak, or a giggle. A child's surreptitious giggle, that's what it sounded like – but from where?

He knew where. He just didn't want to acknowledge it. Even so, his feet took him towards the dense mass of briars and overgrown laurel hedge that formed the boundary.

There. Another sound . . . a low murmur . . . It was definitely coming from next door. From Old Widow Loubet's.

Recalling his last eerie encounter with that particular property, it was no wonder that Fabian's skin prickled with alarm as he crept towards it.

Bernard Mirouze felt his skin prickle with excitement as he lifted the storage box down off the shelf and onto his workbench. It had lain undisturbed for eight months, ever since Serge had asked him to hold onto it on the off chance that it was claimed someday. Had he known, that canny mayor? Had he predicted that Fogas would pull the owner of the box back?

He removed the lid and began lifting out the contents one by one until he found what was needed. Then he carefully, reverentially, placed everything back in the container and returned it to its shelf, label facing out, Serge's shaking hand forever identifying it.

Arnaud's Stuff.

Bernard grinned. The tracker was back in town. And he needed Bernard's help.

Gathering up the things he'd taken from the box, he shoved them into a bag and checked his watch. It was almost time, and with Agnès on her rounds and René having taken Serge for a walk, the coast was clear. The *cantonnier* was off on a secret mission.

'So, let's see if you've still got it, eh?' René Piquemal ran a hand over the small head nudging against his leg and slipped the lead off the eager hound who immediately began snuffling through the undergrowth.

'Not too far, mind,' cautioned René, wary of illegal traps that were rumoured to be further along the mountain in the forests above Picarets. And equally wary of Bernard's wrath should anything else happen to his beloved Serge.

It had taken some doing to convince Bernard to part with the dog for a while. At first he'd met René's suggestion – a walk in the hills to help with Serge's rehabilitation – with a flat *non*. But when he'd seen the enthusiasm the fully-recovered beagle had shown the minute René appeared in the back garden, he'd started to waver. As René pointed out, there was no denying that Serge had clearly missed their regular jaunts into the hills together, which had started the previous spring in an attempt to hone Serge's hunting skills. Besides, the plumber added when it seemed Bernard still wasn't about to relent, wouldn't Agnès be back soon having finished her deliveries? He'd nudged Bernard and given a roguish wink, suggesting that it wouldn't hurt to have the place all to themselves.

Still the *cantonnier* had seemed opposed to the idea. Then

he'd got a phone call, presumably from Agnès because when he walked back over to René in the garden there was a high colour to his cheeks and he'd had a change of mind. René got his way. But not without a long list of advice and warnings and several emergency telephone numbers, which Bernard made him add to his mobile. Finally, the plumber and the beagle were driving away from an apprehensive-looking Bernard, his face as dark as the troubled skies behind him.

Rehabilitation. If only Bernard knew. Up in the woods above the disused quarry, René watched the hound shuffling along, nose to the ground, tail wagging. He felt a flutter of excitement. Could the dog still do it?

It had all been uncovered by accident, this amazing skill of Serge's. Early last year, René had noticed the dog's penchant for foraging around on the ground, nose aquiver, and had decided to put it to the test up on the mountainside above Picarets – a specific part of the mountainside, a very particular place indeed. On a stretch of land which featured heavily in the Piquemal family legend, René had discovered that Serge did indeed have latent talent. And together, under the guise of getting the dog fit for the hunting season, they'd spent the rest of the year exercising it whenever René could find the time.

Today, it remained to be seen if Serge's incredible skill remained intact. Or had the brush with the pine processionary caterpillars damaged his sensitive sense of smell for good?

The dog trotted off, René jogging after him, deeper into the forest. Five minutes later, Serge was standing over a patch of ground that René had dug up only that morning. The dog barked sharply and scratched at the newly turned earth.

'Good boy!' exclaimed René, panting heavily as he caught up. 'Excellent doggie!'

He reached into his pocket and handed Serge a biscuit.

Then he scraped away the layer of top soil to reveal a small misshapen lump. He scooped it up and held it to the dog's nose, and then to his own. He inhaled deeply and happily.

There was nothing on earth like the heavenly smell of truffle.

Standing once more outside the home she'd inherited up in Fogas, Véronique braced herself to complete the task she'd left unfinished almost a month ago. It had proved so overwhelming that day, sorting through Serge's belongings. Would it be any easier now, some weeks on and in the company of her mother, the person she held responsible for the pain she was feeling?

She'd asked Christian to come with her, knowing she wouldn't be able to face it alone a second time. But he'd been adamant in his refusal, resisting her entreaties and urging her to ask her mother instead.

'It's only fitting,' he'd said when she'd protested. 'The two of you need to clear the air. Serge would be mortified to think you were at loggerheads because of him. Perhaps up in his house you might find the space you need to sort things out between you.'

It was the first time that he'd broached the subject of her relationship with Maman so openly. And it was the first time since they'd got together that she'd come across his stubborn streak. She'd yielded and had called her mother. And now, here they were.

Christian had better be right, Véronique thought as she stared at Serge's home, her right hand straying to her neck to touch the cross that was no longer there.

'Shall we?' asked Annie softly, gesturing towards the front door.

★

From her position behind the wheel of the butcher's van, Agnès Rogalle reckoned she got a pretty good measure of how the communities on her delivery route were faring. Traversing the countryside as she did, she noticed things. Like this morning up in Picarets, when she'd seen Christian Dupuy drive past, face lit up like a summer dawn, happiness oozing from him. Love or politics or both? It didn't matter. At least the man was happy.

Likewise, that thin Parisian, Fabian Servat. He'd walked by as she was taking down the side hatch on the van, her customers served for the day, and he'd had a jaunty way about him, an air of euphoria as though he were sharing a delicious secret. He'd been heading into the old Papon house, eyes flicking over it as he approached like a farmer at a cattle mart.

Rather him than me, she'd thought, as she pulled out of the small square. If she were looking to buy somewhere, it wouldn't be next to a crumbling, haunted premises, with no sign of an owner despite its recent sale.

With Picarets done, Agnès had driven down into the valley and up the other side to Fogas, aware of the gathering clouds, the darkening sky. She'd parked her van and was immediately besieged with customers, but not so busy that she couldn't note the arrival of the two Estaque women, tension vibrating around the pair of them. They stood for a few moments outside Serge Papon's house, the older woman finally putting her shoulders back resolutely before guiding her daughter inside.

There was a lot more sorting out to be done in there than merely going through a dead man's things, thought Agnès, as she passed Madame Degeilh her weekly ration of sausages. And she just had her cleaver raised to start cutting some lovely steaks for Monsieur Mené, whose ill-fitting dentures meant he had to have the tenderest of meat, when she saw Bernard driving past, wearing the same expression he'd had the other day after that mysterious call.

Animated. Flushed. Like a lover heading for a rendezvous.

With an almighty thud, the cleaver came crashing down, almost severing her left thumb. Sometimes, Agnès thought ruefully, staring at the mangled steak, she saw way more than she wanted to.

Voices. He was sure he could hear the low rumble of voices. But he couldn't see through the hedge. Nor could he see over it, offshoots having long been left to grow wild. There was only one option. He would have to climb through it.

Searching out a place where the vegetation looked less dense, Fabian thrust a leg through a narrow opening and started to crawl across into Widow Loubet's. With sharp branches tearing his skin and cobwebs clinging to his face, he wasn't entirely sure he wanted to be doing this, especially considering his hair-raising experience over there on the day of Serge's funeral. But despite living with a wife who dabbled in the mysterious, Fabian Servat remained tethered to the ground and a believer in logic.

Logic, which was telling him there was no such thing as ghosts. And a gut feeling which belied that rationality, telling him one of the voices he could hear was Chloé's. She was supposed to be with the Rogalle twins, a teachers' strike having granted them all a bonus day off school. But the other voice he could hear beyond the hedge didn't sound like a pre-adolescent boy. It sounded much older. And therefore, much more worrying.

Whether haunted or not, the prospect of his step-daughter being in that property with what sounded like a man was enough to force the Parisian through the hedge.

⋆

'Right, little one. It's time for you to go. I have to be somewhere.'

Chloé groaned. 'Can't I come with you?'

Arnaud's long mane of hair shook in response. 'Not this time. Perhaps we can walk up to see the cubs when they emerge in the spring?'

The dark cloud that had covered the girl's face lifted in an instant.

'That would be amazing! Do you promise?'

The tracker placed a hand across his heart. Even though he wasn't sure where he would be by the time the bears came out of hibernation.

'Do you need any more food?' she asked, stalling as she headed for the door.

'I think I have enough for now.' Arnaud eyed the stack of tins on the counter, not allowing himself to think about how she'd come by them.

'Are you sure? I mean I could—'

Arnaud was across the room in three silent strides, his hand firm across her mouth.

'Shush,' he whispered, head cocked to hear the slightest of sounds.

A footstep. Cautious. But not cautious enough as there was a faint crunch under a misplaced shoe. Someone was over by the broken window.

Gesturing at Chloé to stay where she was, Arnaud crept silently towards the noise, back against the wall, body pulled up flat, eyes focused on the opening with its jagged teeth of shattered glass.

Another step. Breathing. Ragged. Afraid. And then a shape, looming inside the window frame.

Arnaud lunged, both hands outstretched to grab a hold and give a mighty heave. But he miscalculated. Put far more effort in than was needed for the scrawny body he encountered and in a tangle of bony limbs, he fell to the kitchen floor, face to face with a human tree.

'Merde!' he leapt up, unsure of what he was beholding.

'Arnaud?' said the tree in some puzzlement.

'Fabian?' said the tracker, finally seeing beyond the bits of twigs and leaves covering the thin frame still on the floor. He held out a large hand and pulled the Parisian to his feet.

'What are you doing here?' asked Arnaud.

But Fabian's puzzled gaze was on Chloé. 'I was about to ask you both the same question.'

'He's here to help us,' said Chloé with a grin. 'He's come to save Fogas. But it's a secret!'

And Arnaud rolled his eyes. For if there was anything he'd learnt from his time in the commune, it was impossible to keep a secret in Fogas.

Down in the bar in La Rivière, Jacques and Serge were discussing the secret they had been made privy to, courtesy of Chloé. For two days they'd argued back and forth as to what was the best course and now, the third day after the election, they were no closer to a resolution.

'We should tell Arnaud. He needs to know about the report.'

Jacques threw his hands in the air. 'And how, exactly, are we supposed to tell him? He's not likely to pop in here any time soon to do some shopping and unless you've developed powers you haven't told me about, there's no way we can get up to Picarets.'

'Chloé!' Serge snapped. 'We use Chloé as a go-between.'

Jacques shot out of his seat. 'No! I've told you. We're not involving that child in this.'

'And I've told you, we have to. There's no other way. The contents of that report have to get to Arnaud so he knows what he's up against. You said yourself that he has incriminating video footage of Pascal collecting bear fur. If he was aware of the new report, the fact that his suspicions have been vindicated, he might take that evidence to the police.'

'What evidence? A grainy shot of someone up in the woods at night-time? It's hardly going to put Pascal away. And besides, Arnaud's not stupid. If he'd had enough to convict that weasel he would have been to the authorities before now.'

'So what are you suggesting we do?' seethed Serge, pacing up and down in front of the fireplace. 'Nothing?'

Jacques refused to react to Serge's irascibility. Instead he resumed his seat and motioned for his friend to do the same.

'We wait,' he said. 'We wait and see what happens on Friday.'

Serge glanced up at the clock where the minutes between now and the decisive council meeting would be slowly measured out. It was going to be a long wait.

Over the course of the morning, as the sky grew darker and the clouds became ever more ominous, the two Estaque women worked hard. They cleared the two bedrooms, the smaller room containing a wardrobe full of clothes belonging to Thérèse that Serge had obviously been reluctant to part with. In a decision the older woman sensed was her daughter's way of inflicting penance decades after the sin, Véronique gave Annie the task of bagging them all up, the lingering smell of Thérèse's perfume making Annie feel uncomfortable thirty-seven years on from her youthful indiscretion.

Meanwhile, Véronique cleared out the medicine cabinet in the bathroom and emptied the big closet on the landing of bedding, some of which dated back many decades, soft and threadbare from repeated washes. Much to Annie's chagrin, they didn't pause for a coffee before moving downstairs, Annie suspecting that Véronique didn't want to be in a situation where small talk might be called for. Instead, Véronique disappeared into the living room while Annie began work in the hallway. She started by bundling up Serge's coats and jackets from the pegs by the front door, checking the pockets as she went. She had to sit on the stairs for a few moments when she found a half-empty packet of confetti in his good coat, the sudden recollection of Stephanie and Fabian's wonderful Christmas wedding overpowering her and making her legs tremble; Serge waltzing her across the floor of the épicerie, his arms strong around her, his eyes dancing with a love of life. Less than ten weeks later and here she was helping her daughter – their daughter – put his life into bin bags and boxes.

'Are you okay?' Véronique was watching her from a doorway.

'Just needed a brrreatherrr. A coffee might have helped,' grumbled Annie, deflecting the concern and thrusting the coat into a bag.

'Why don't you make one and we'll take a rest?'

Annie didn't need to be asked twice. When she entered the living room with two coffees a few minutes later, she found Véronique on the floor in front of the fire, books piled around her and one open in her lap.

'Did you know about these?' she asked as Annie put the cups down on the hearth.

Annie nodded and picked up the nearest book, a beautifully bound copy of Zola's *Thérèse Raquin*, with an inscription on the flyleaf.

To my wonderful Thérèse on your thirty-fifth birthday. Love always, Serge.

'A classic. Everrry yearrr on herrr birrrthday.'

'Why? He wasn't a big reader. Not of fiction, anyhow.'

'Thérrrèse was. She came frrrom a differrrent worrrld to

most of us – a worrrld of literrraturrre and the arrrts. Wherrreas Serrrge worrrked in the mines when they met, the son of a farrrmerrr, and he was always conscious of theirrr opposing backgrrrounds. I suppose this was his way of trrrying to brrridge that gap.'

Véronique regarded the books afresh. Birthday presents. One a year for over forty years, Serge's writing getting progressively worse as his arthritis took hold, but the messages touching all the same.

'You should keep them,' said Annie, placing the Zola back on the floor.

Véronique looked up, a wry expression on her face. 'Do you think so? Love tokens from my father to his wife, the woman he cheated on and the same woman who wanted me aborted?'

Annie flinched. 'It's not that simple,' she said, sitting on the armchair closest to the fire. 'He loved herrr.'

'Well he had a funny way of showing it!'

'Do you know wherrre he gave Thérrrèse those?' Annie gestured at the piles of novels and Véronique shook her head.

'On the plateau above the épicerrrie. Serrrge made a picnic and even lugged up a table and chairrrs when she became ill. They neverrr missed a yearrr. I met them once as they werrre walking back down to Fogas. It was long beforrre you werrre borrrn, long beforrre . . .' She waved a hand to indicate the brief liaison that had resulted in Véronique. 'I was at the town hall dealing with some admin forrr the Conseil Municipal and decided to get some frrresh airrr. I bumped into the pairrr of them on the bend the farrr side of the village. Serrrge had his arrrm drrraped over Thérrrèse's shoulderrr, a picnic basket in the otherrr hand. And she . . . she was laughing at something he'd said, herrr face all flushed, theirrr eyes fixed on each otherrr.'

Annie paused to stare into the fire, the recollection so sharp she could hear the song of the cicadas and smell the freshly cut hay. And taste the bile that had risen in her throat.

'He was besotted with herrr. And I have neverrr felt morrre jealous in all my life.'

Véronique glanced sharply at her mother's sad face in profile. 'You loved him? Even before . . . ?'

Annie shrugged. 'I don't think I knew it then. I was so busy rrrunning the farrrm, trrrying to be the son Papa didn't have. I didn't have time to analyse feelings – mine orrr anyone else's. I don't think I even knew the evening we . . .' Another flick of the hand, to spare Véronique the details. 'It felt so naturrral. So unplanned, yet rrright.'

She turned her gaze onto her daughter. 'Who knows? Maybe I wanted it to happen. Maybe I wanted you to happen.' She reached out a hand to stroke Véronique's hair and felt a rush of relief when her daughter didn't pull away.

'I'm sorrry,' she said. 'I know you'rrre angrrry with me. And I'm sorrry.'

Véronique's grip on the book she was holding tightened and Annie's breath caught in her throat.

'That bloody secret, Maman. If only you hadn't agreed to that, I'd have had more time with him,' Véronique finally muttered.

Annie sighed. 'If you'd seen herrr . . . Thérrrèse Papon, this rrrefined woman, collapsed on the barrrn floorrr, sobbing . . .'

The images were as clear as if it had happened yesterday – Thérèse begging the newly pregnant Annie to travel to England to get rid of the baby; Annie reacting with an instinctive urge to protect her unborn child that she'd not wanted mere hours before; and then Thérèse thrusting money at her, desperate to remove the threat she believed would wreck her childless marriage.

'She was brrroken. Serrrge and I had brrrought the woman to herrr knees. And I couldn't live with that on my conscience. So I made the pact, prrromised neverrr to rrreveal who the fatherrr of my baby was in an attempt to sparrre Thérrrèse any morrre hearrrtache. Rrregardless of the consequences.'

She ran a finger down Véronique's cheek. 'You'd have done the same, love. We'rrre borrrn strrrong, us Estaques. It didn't feel like I was sacrrrificing much. But then you came along . . . You'rrre the only innocent perrson in all of this and the one who's been hurrrt the most. I just hope you can find it in your hearrrt to forrrgive me. To forrrgive the thrrree of us.'

Véronique dipped her head and swiped a hand across her face, her cheeks wet.

'So you think I should keep them?' she murmured, closing the novel on her lap and tracing a finger across the beautiful cover.

Annie swallowed hard and cupped the back of her daughter's head with her palm. 'I do,' she said. Then she pointed a finger at the book Véronique was holding. 'But perrrhaps starrrt on something else given yourrr mood lately.'

And Véronique let out a yelp of unexpected laughter, the sound rich and warm, as she read the title: *Bonjour Tristesse.*

'Oh Maman!' she said, shaking her head as the laughter continued, catching Annie in its wake and leaving the pair of them helpless.

Christian was as far from laughter as you could get. The good mood that had borne him down to St Girons on a wave of happiness had evaporated in the face of his futile search for a radiator for his Panda and he was on the verge of losing his temper. All morning he'd been trawling the scrapyard that sprawled across the edge of the town, looking for a part which the yard owner swore was out here somewhere.

But where?

There were acres of cars, stacked in rows, stacked on top of each other, some intact, others just shells. And in that giant haystack, he was looking for a tiny needle. To make matters worse, the storm that had been threatening in the distance was about to arrive, fat splashes of rain already falling and getting heavier.

'Another ten minutes,' he muttered, glancing at his watch and seeing it was almost lunchtime. 'And then I'm off.'

He paused at the end of one of the lanes of towering cars, which had created an automobile maze he thought he might never find his way out of. Should he go left or right? He glanced to his right and tried to remember if he'd already been down that aisle or not. He thought he would have remembered the black Peugeot with the doors ripped off. Then he saw something at the far end of the row.

A Panda. Orange. Just like the man in the office had said. Thinking he'd finally found what he was looking for, he made his way towards it. He had no idea that it would turn out to be the worst decision he ever made.

16

The rain was getting heavier, pitting the dusty ground of the yard and bouncing off the cars. Christian started to jog, head down, feet splashing in the puddles already forming. A quick look, that's all he needed, and then he was heading home, whether he'd accomplished his mission or not.

He was two strides away from the orange Panda when he heard the muffled curse on the other side of the row. It was enough to make him pause. Not because he recognised the voice, but because he recognised the subject.

Rain dripping down his shoulders, he crept closer to the tower of cars that shielded the speaker from view.

'Bloody Pascal Souquet. He's a liability.'

'So we get rid of him, then.'

'Let's not be too rash . . .' The speaker turned, his voice now muffled by the rain and the double thickness of car remains that separated him from Christian.

Intrigued, Christian pressed closer to the doorless Peugeot in front of him. Stepping carefully onto the sill, he gripped the wet metal of the roof and slowly pulled himself up. Weight balanced, aware of the cars looming over him, he leaned to his right, a small gap through the tangled vehicles affording him a glimpse of the back of a head. Nothing more. But at least he could hear.

'...remove him when the time is right.'

'You think he can still win on Friday?'

'Perhaps.' A brief pause and the strong scent of cigarette swirled across the sodden air. 'He'll do everything he can to make it happen. Don't forget there's a carrot dangling in front of him.' A harsh laugh and then the merest flicker of a hand visible, a cigarette butt dropping from it, a glint of gold on a finger. 'He thinks he'll be mayor of the new commune. That's enough to make him and that shrew-faced wife of his jump through fire to get their hands on the leadership of Fogas.'

The man stepped to the side, his partial profile appearing in the small aperture between the cars followed by the sound of a heel grinding gravel. Christian shouldn't have needed to see any more to identify him. The voice was enough. But he believed in the benefit of the doubt. So he stretched even further to his right trying to get a better look, calf muscles straining, arms shaking as he held himself in place, the rain running in rivulets under his jacket collar and down his back as he eavesdropped.

'When are you going to break the bad news?'

'Oh, he'll find out soon enough. Once he's got control of the council in that godforsaken place and handed it over to me, when Fogas is wiped off the map and Sarrat is reinstated to its proper position, then I'll tell him. Vincent Fauré will be taking my place as mayor when I resign.'

'And Pascal?'

Another venomous laugh. 'Ah, Pascal. I think perhaps . . .'

The man paused, as though contemplating the fate of the deputy mayor, then he turned towards the cars. Towards Christian. And for a split second, steel blue eyes stared straight at the farmer.

Christian couldn't help it. He jerked backwards, feeling exposed under that piercing gaze, and his left foot slipped on the wet sill. It was enough to break his fragile balance. His hands lost contact with the car roof and he tumbled backwards with a clatter.

'What was that?' The voice louder, closer.

The men were moving. Looking for the source of the noise.

Christian scrambled to his feet. He didn't want to get caught. Not with what he'd heard. So he ran. Back up the row of cars, his heavy strides carrying him quickly away from them. Hopefully quickly enough.

'There's someone there!' hissed Henri Dedieu, seeing a blur of movement through the mass of metal where the noise had come from. A blur of movement that was now heading up the row.

His companion gave chase, short legs pumping as he raced up the parallel aisle hoping to trap the person at the top. But Henri was a hunter. A brilliant hunter. He knew they had no chance of catching up – the man had too much of a head start. Far better to identify him. So he ran down past two cars and rounded the corner into the next row in time to see a lumbering shape take a fast left at the top.

Christian Dupuy. Blond hair flattened by the rain. Size unmistakable.

How long had he been there? What had he heard?

Calculating options. That was all successful hunting was about. Measuring the prey's next move in the curl of a trigger finger. Henri Dedieu was an expert at it. And he knew he couldn't risk Christian Dupuy running to Pascal Souquet with what he'd learned. It would ruin everything.

He pulled out his mobile and made a call, hoping luck was with him. Because no matter how good you were with a rifle, sometimes you needed the wind to blow in the right direction.

*

'You forgot to take lunch?'

Véronique nodded and laughed, the rare sound making Josette look up from the till.

'Maman wasn't pleased when she stopped at the Angelus bells and I suddenly realised I hadn't brought anything to eat!'

'I can imagine,' Josette chuckled, piling Véronique's purchases into a bag. 'Is there anything else you need?'

'Actually there is. Could I buy some of that decaf coffee Fabian uses for Maman's espressos? She's drinking it neat up there and I don't know which one of us will be killed by it first. Her of a heart attack or me from her incessant talking!'

Josette smiled. It was so lovely to see Véronique animated. Especially considering the subject matter at hand.

'Help yourself,' she said, pointing towards the bar.

The postmistress wandered through the archway, left her handbag on a stool, and went behind the counter to get the decaf coffee jar.

Back in the shop, the bell rang. And in that split second of coincidence, Christian Dupuy's fate was sealed.

He'd been driving down from Fogas, windscreen wipers slapping at the rain as he congratulated himself on a successful morning. With Fatima away visiting relatives overnight, he'd risen early and made the most of her absence by finally getting rid of the blasted report into the bear attacks that had been sitting in his safe like a primed bomb for the past couple of months.

Watching the smoke curl up the chimney from the smouldering pages, he'd felt empowered. Audacious even. Ready to burn more bridges. So he'd contacted a friend from Paris who was in town – a lawyer who specialised in divorce. Having arranged to meet over lunch in St Girons for a discreet conversation, he'd been running slightly late, thanks to Widow Aubert accosting him to complain about the town hall clock still not being fixed, and had just reached the Romanesque church that marked the beginning of La Rivière when his phone rang.

He'd glanced at the number and with a tremor in his hand, he'd answered.

Now he was outside the épicerie, tasked with an impossible undertaking. One that was definitely illegal.

He pushed open the door and felt a mixture of relief and panic. The post office was closed. Of course, it was Wednesday. She wouldn't be here.

'Can I help you?' Josette was looking at him.

'Véronique,' he blurted. 'I was looking for Véronique.'

And in that split second of coincidence, Josette jerked her thumb towards the archway, beyond which he could see the postmistress standing behind the bar, back towards him. Her bag was on a stool. Pascal Souquet stepped forward, thinking about the future and everything that was shining in the distance. Thinking too about what the hell he was going to say to distract her.

'I lost him.'

Henri Dedieu appraised the man before him. A fellow member of the hunting lodge, he was his apostle, his harbinger of violence. Only last autumn he'd unleashed him on Véronique Estaque, the woman Pascal Souquet had assured him was behind the blog SOS Fogas that had derailed the merger. The man had left the postmistress with a broken arm and lots of broken belongings. He was good.

But for this job? No. Better that he sort this one himself.

He shrugged as if the man's failings were no matter. 'Probably just a kid,' he said. 'But best we leave anyway. I'll be in touch.'

And with purposeful strides he made his way towards his car.

It was the finale. No more second chances. No more lieutenants. No more time. He was about to go hunting.

Christ! What the hell had just happened?

Christian was leaning up against a wall on the riverbank, heart thundering, sweat and rain running down his cheeks. He'd run as fast as he could up the row of cars, the sound of someone chasing him on the next aisle pushing him on. Tearing around a corner at the top, he'd then taken two switchbacks intending to throw off his pursuer. But he found himself facing a concrete wall. Not even taking time to weigh up the situation, he'd run at the wall and hauled himself over it. And landed on the riverbank amongst the trees.

They wouldn't look for him here. He slid to the wet ground, head pounding, lungs still gasping. The soft pattering of the easing rain seemed so incongruous, so innocent in the aftermath of that sudden violence.

As his heart began to slow, he assessed what he'd heard. What he'd seen. Then he made the connections, recalling events from as far back as last summer . . .

. . . Pascal Souquet. The image of him on the day the Tour de France came through La Rivière, caught by the helicopter camera as he loitered around the back of the hunting lodge, talking furtively to someone. His reluctance to reopen the post office in the épicerie after the original one burnt down. His quiet support of the merger, the opportunities it would bring.

Opportunities for him, mayor of the new commune: thirty fat pieces of silver for bringing Fogas to its knees. Only that wasn't going to happen. Christian had heard it from the mouth of Henri Dedieu himself. Pascal was nothing more than a patsy.

That's it! Christian slapped his forehead. How could he be

so slow? He'd been handed the means to deliver Fogas from this mess. He'd tell Pascal all he'd heard. Make the man realise that he'd got in bed with the devil and he stood to lose more than his soul. That way, no matter what happened at the council meeting on Friday, Fogas would be saved.

He stood, rejuvenated, thinking that the master of guile, Serge Papon, would be proud of him. Then he stopped dead. Because thinking of Serge made him think of the mayor's desk in the town hall. Of all it had contained. Or should have contained.

That bloody empty file in Serge's drawer.

Ever since it had been unearthed by Véronique, Christian had been expecting Pascal to use the damaging report into the bear attacks to destroy his opponent's campaign. But he hadn't. And that baffled Christian, especially now, having stumbled upon his fellow deputy's alliance with Henri Dedieu. Surely both Pascal and the mayor of Sarrat would have been eager to seize the political advantage the condemnatory report offered them? So why hadn't they?

Perhaps, thought Christian, he was looking at it the wrong way. Perhaps Pascal hadn't been sitting on the information, waiting for the perfect moment as Christian had suspected. What if he'd been hiding it? But that didn't make sense. Why would he—?

The bear attacks. They'd been the catalyst for a groundswell of opposition to Serge's tenure as mayor. If they had been staged, as the latest investigation suggested, then could they have been part of a more elaborate plan? A plan to remove a charismatic leader who would never condone a merger with the neighbouring commune?

Merde! Christian ran a hand through his curls. It was possible. Frighteningly so. And it would explain why the missing report had never surfaced. But if it was true, it could only mean one thing – Pascal Souquet had been involved in the fake bear attacks.

Perturbed by his discoveries, Christian began striding along the river towards the main road, barely noticing that the rain had stopped. He was halfway to his car when he made the final connection. Henri Dedieu. It was well known he'd been up in the forest with the hunters the day the bear had been caught in the fire and fallen to its death in the quarry. But while there was plenty of scepticism surrounding the accidental nature of the animal's death, no one had ever claimed it was anything more than a group of men with guns getting over zealous about protecting their livestock.

After what he'd just overheard, Christian had reason to believe otherwise. A dead bear. A commune almost torn apart. And two men who were prepared to use violence to get their way.

He needed to talk to Véronique. Urgently. He'd call her from the car. It wasn't a conversation he wanted to have in the open. Plus, if he was right, then it was a matter for the police. Because the way it was looking, there was every chance that the mayor of Sarrat was guilty of murder. And the interim mayor of Fogas too.

Jacques and Serge were at peace. Kind of. An uneasy truce had been called following their heated disagreement over involving Chloé in the business of the bear attack report. But while they had agreed to wait until Friday before deciding on any action, the sight of Pascal Souquet walking into the bar was enough to get Serge on his feet.

'Sit down!' urged Jacques. 'It's not worth getting stressed about. No wonder your heart gave out.'

Serge growled, in no mood to take orders, not even from a friend. Instead he strode up behind the man they believed had betrayed Fogas, fists curled in impotent fury as Pascal leaned casually on a bar stool.

'You two-faced bastard,' Serge hissed. 'You double-crossing piece of—'

'Bonjour Pascal.' Véronique had turned at the footsteps. 'Do you want a drink?'

'Yes . . . no . . . erm just a quick word actually. But take your time.' The interim mayor gestured towards the bag of coffee she was busy spooning into a small container. 'I can wait.'

'Thanks.' She turned away from him once more. And his hand dipped into her handbag.

'What the—?' Serge spun round to Jacques. 'He's stealing from her!'

'Can you stop him?'

Serge stretched out his arm, laid his arthritic fingers against the wiry forearm of the interim mayor and tried his hardest. But the angle was all wrong. He didn't have the height advantage he'd had over a sitting Véronique. And he felt Pascal pulling away despite his efforts.

'What's he taken?' shouted Serge as he finally let go and collapsed against a stool.

'Her phone.' Jacques was hopping from one foot to the other, face distraught. 'He's put her phone in his jacket. He's leaving. Stop him, Serge! Stop him!'

But Serge didn't have the power. All he could do was watch helplessly as Pascal Souquet slipped out of the door and walked quickly towards his car.

'Come back, you thief!' yelled Jacques, slamming his fists against the window to no avail. Quivering with rage, he swung back round and was appalled to see tears tracking down his friend's cheeks.

'I couldn't do it,' Serge whispered. 'I just couldn't do it.'

'Now then, Pascal, what can I help you with?' Véronique

turned to an empty room. No sign of the interim mayor. She shrugged, used to the man's whimsical ways, picked up the container of coffee and was almost at the archway when she remembered her bag. Laughing at her stupidity, she returned to the bar stool to retrieve it. She was oblivious to the two ghosts, one watching her through tear-filled eyes and the other doing everything he could to catch her attention. Which of course, didn't work.

Véronique Estaque waved goodbye to Josette, not knowing how much the sliver of timing that had placed her and Pascal Souquet in the same place on that afternoon was going to affect her future. And that of the entire commune.

He'd driven off in a panic, down the road, past the Auberge, around the corner and then he'd taken the sharp right over the bridge. He never took that turn. But today it had been an unconditioned reflex. He eased off the accelerator and pulled over into a lay-by that was tucked to one side, hidden from the main road a bit below.

This was Sarrat territory. He'd crossed the border. And only now did he feel safe to carry out the orders he'd been given.

Hands trembling, Pascal Souquet plucked Véronique's mobile from his jacket pocket and dropped it onto his lap as though the touch of it could burn him. He pulled out his own phone and copied, word for word, the text he had been sent. Scrolling through Véronique's contacts, he chose the designated recipient. Then he paused, finger above the screen.

What was he complicit in here? Why was he being asked to do this?

Stomach churning, he looked out of the window to a church sitting on a ridge beyond rolling fields of pasture, several houses, slate roofs gleaming after the rain – all of it immaculate. There was even a tennis court. What a stepping stone this would be. What heights he could scale from this place.

With no more thought for the consequences, his finger tapped the send button and he threw the phone onto the seat next to him, wiping his hands literally and metaphorically of the whole affair. It was done.

Christian was soaked through. He sat in the front seat of the Panda, feeling the moisture wick its way down his skin. Even his socks were sodden. But his mind was far from his physical discomfort.

Véronique. He had to call Véronique. He needed to talk this through and she was the best person to turn to. He reached inside his jacket and as he put his hand inside the damp pocket, his mobile vibrated beneath his fingers.

Someone was texting him.

He pulled out the phone to see a message from Véronique had arrived. He read it through, frowned, and then read it again. Then he typed a quick reply before turning the key in the ignition and thrusting the car into gear. With his frown still in place, he guided the Panda towards the mountains and home.

Although home wasn't where he was going. Not after reading that text. He pushed harder on the accelerator and prayed his car would be up to the journey.

A far-from-calm Pascal had resumed his interrupted journey to his meeting in St Girons and was driving down the twisting road that led to the roundabout at Kerkabanac when Véronique's mobile chirruped into life on the passenger seat, making him jump.

A text. A reply maybe? Should he read it?

Curiosity got the better of him. He reached over and

grabbed the phone, holding it with one hand, steering with the other. He swiped the screen and immediately wished he hadn't, the car swerving wildly as he jerked backwards in shock. For upon reading the fake, fairly cryptic message from Véronique saying she had 'discovered something about the elections' and they needed to talk, Christian Dupuy had responded with a revelation of his own. Only the farmer's was far from ambiguous.

Pascal possibly involved in death of bear! See you soon.

Christian knew! How? How had he found out?

Sweat beaded the interim mayor's forehead and any qualms he'd had about getting involved in Dedieu's latest scheme were quashed by the words in front of him. If Christian told anyone, it would be the end – Pascal knew that – and probably a long stint in jail.

Panic-stricken, he braked, wound down the passenger window and threw the phone into the gorge, the roar of the rain-swollen river below bouncing off the steep mountainside. He watched the mobile tumble through the air and disappear, and hoped with all his heart that Henri Dedieu had something similar lined up for Christian Dupuy. Then he turned the car around and headed back towards Fogas, abandoning his lunch appointment. He was too full of fear for his future to be planning a divorce.

Hunting. It all hinged on chance. You set your traps, built your hide, stalked your target, all the time taking bets on how it would move, where it would go to ground. If you understood your quarry, if you knew its habits, then you could swing the balance of luck in your favour.

Up in the collection of well-kept houses in Sarrat that had helped determine Pascal's actions, Henri Dedieu was very much aware of all that. He'd raced home from St Girons, conscious that the minute the text was sent, the clock would start ticking. He was already changed. Camouflage trousers and jacket. Rucksack. Strong boots. His hand automatically reached for the orange beret, customarily worn as a safety measure, but he pulled it back. No beret. Not today.

He had no way of knowing if his strategy would work, if the snare carefully laid would catch the one he wanted. But he knew his prey. And he was willing to stake everything on his ability to predict its actions. Plus he'd known exactly which bait to use.

Véronique Estaque. The woman who'd ruined his dreams last autumn. Well now she would be the unwitting architect of her own ruination.

Entering his workshop, he reached for his rifle, slinging it across his shoulder. Then he picked up the Unique pistol, tracing his thumb over the boar's head insignia. Making sure it was loaded, he slipped it into his inside jacket pocket and checked his watch.

That was another key to hunting. Timing. Being able to estimate the whereabouts of your prey at any particular moment. He had thirty minutes. That's what she'd said in the text. If he was going to get there and get in position, he had to leave now.

Hunting. How apt. He laughed as he drove down towards the small bridge and the main road, knowing not a soul would question seeing a man in camouflage with a rifle in the forests of the Ariège on a winter's Wednesday. Even without a beret.

Arnaud stopped to cast his eyes over the ground. But it was useless. No one could track in this. The deluge of rain had washed away any prints and left the earth an oozing mass of mud. Even he was finding it hard to walk silently, the saturated soil sucking at his boots.

Still. It had been a successful day so far. He'd had his rendezvous this morning, Bernard Mirouze doing his best to be covert for a man of his size. Arnaud smiled at the thought. The man was so eager to please. He'd brought the equipment Arnaud had asked him for. Had even offered to help set it up. But the tracker had turned him down. He worked best alone. And he wanted to make sure it was done right this time.

Because this time he was going to catch Henri Dedieu in the act.

He patted his pocket, feeling the hard lump of the remote camera. So small and yet so effective, if they could be used to film bears, the tracker reasoned, why not use them to capture someone trying to threaten the same creatures?

So he'd hiked up into the hills above Picarets and had set his own traps. Two installed so far, the final one to go. It was so difficult choosing where to put them in such vast terrain. But Arnaud was a skilled tracker. He knew his prey. Knew his preferences. And something told him Henri Dedieu would return to a place known to have housed bears before – the place where it all began.

Lengthening his stride, for there was still a lot of mountainside to cover before he reached his destination, Arnaud headed for the forests above the Dupuy farmhouse. He was on the most important trail of his life and he didn't intend to fail.

He was in place. Gun in hand, eyes watching the dense woodland beyond, ears alert for the smallest of sounds.

There – the splutter of an engine. Faint but sure.

He shifted position, eased his weight onto his back leg. Then he waited.

Why here?

Christian turned off the engine and sat for a moment,

staring at the forest encircling him. He was at the end of a relatively unused track that wound up from Picarets to the old quarry, not far above his own farm. He opened the door and got out. Her car wasn't there. Was she walking up from the village? It was a fair hike. Or perhaps she was just running late.

'Véronique?' he said, not wanting to call out too loudly. She had stressed the need for secrecy and after his experience this morning in the scrapyard, he felt she had a point.

Jesus! He ran a hand through his hair. It felt like Fogas was coming apart at the seams. Pascal involved in the bear attacks and probably the death of the bear. Henri Dedieu no doubt connected too. And now Véronique had found out something else. Another hidden file up at Serge's maybe? Her text had been vague – a brief message to say she needed to see him, with instructions as to where to meet and a stern warning not to call her as it wasn't safe. Whatever she'd discovered, it was too toxic to discuss in the bar or on the phone.

But up here?

He looked around, taking in the view down below of Picarets, nothing more than a huddle of houses in the far distance. And surrounding him, nothing but trees. And bears. Don't forget the bears.

With a grimace, he turned and began walking down the path as she had directed. He knew where he was going. Everyone knew this place. It was where the bear had been killed last summer.

Marvelling at the irony of it all, he headed further into the trap.

'That'll do for today,' said René, leaning down to rub the dog's belly.

So much for recuperating. The hound had more energy

than he did, running along, never tiring. But then he didn't smoke twenty a day and carry a spare tyre around his midriff, mused René mournfully, puffing on his habitual Gauloise.

Still, it had been a successful outing, even with the torrential downpour they'd had to shelter from. They'd established that Serge had retained the ability to unearth truffles. The next step would be to go back to the land on the other side of Picarets, to the mountainside above the Estaque farm where the truffles were rumoured to be.

Rumoured? It was a fact! His own great-grandfather had found one up there and the secret location had been handed down on the deathbed of each Piquemal generation to the oldest male of the next. Accordingly, René had inherited the map. And the headache of an endless search for an elusive treasure.

One day, he thought, patting the dog's head. One day he would find the source that had yielded the Piquemal truffle.

But until those bastards stopped lacing the hillsides over there with illegal traps, he couldn't risk taking Serge hunting. Instead they'd have to settle on training runs over here for now.

'Right, time to head home.' René finished his cigarette and, with the beagle scampering along beside him, started back through the forest towards the path that led to the quarry, René dreaming of lumpen fungi, Serge dreaming of rabbits.

'Véronique?' Christian was almost whispering. He felt unusually vulnerable. All these trees. The silence. The memory of the morning too, his adrenalin still pumping.

'Are you there?'

Nothing.

He walked on, the path soon emerging into a small clearing. To his left, the forest resumed, thick trunks holding back the light. To his right, visible through a thin scattering of trees, a vast expanse of charred stumps, twisted and black, marking the fire of the summer before. And in front of him, the disused quarry, a sudden laceration in the verdant landscape. Feeling his skin crawl in response to what had happened here, he picked up his pace, whistling softly as he emerged from the woods.

Last thing he wanted to do was surprise her.

Whistling. Getting louder. The hunter smiled. He'd made his decisions and they'd been the right ones. His prey had done exactly what he'd predicted.

And now he was going to die.

He raised his gun, the large figure of Christian Dupuy came into sight, and Henri Dedieu curled his finger around the trigger.

17

'Véronique? It's me. Christian.'

A breeze sighed through the tree tops, slapping wet branches against each other and sending a shower of delayed raindrops down below. Christian turned slowly in the centre of the clearing, scanning the edges of the forest. Expecting her to step forward.

'This is ridiculous,' he muttered as his eyes came to rest on the gash of quarry before him. He took out his phone, but his hand was stalled by a movement. Something emerging from the green tangle of woodland halfway between him and the path.

A smile of relief was already lifting his mouth.

'Véronique!'

'Not quite, I'm afraid.'

The farmer's smile faltered half-formed. Henri Dedieu was standing there, dressed in hunting gear, rifle slung across his camouflage jacket. And if Christian wasn't mistaken, what looked like a pistol in his hand. It was pointing straight at the big man's heart.

They were almost there. Which was just as well as René wasn't the only one getting tired.

'Idiot!' he muttered, berating himself. He'd allowed Serge's enthusiasm to lead them much further into the forest than he'd intended, which meant a long walk back to the quarry path from where they would pick up the track down to the village and his car. No wonder the poor dog was showing signs of fatigue.

Cursing himself for being so secretive in choosing to leave his car in Picarets rather than out in the open at the end of the track, René stopped, beagle at his heels, and checked his watch. Still plenty of daylight hours ahead. They could afford to take a short break.

'Here,' he said, reaching into his pocket before slipping the dog off his lead. 'Get this down you.'

Serge took the biscuit gratefully, accepted another one just as eagerly, and then flopped to the ground next to a fallen tree.

'Think I'll join you,' said René, taking a seat on the log. 'A couple of minutes, eh? Then we really must be off or Bernard will kill me.'

His hand automatically went back towards his pocket. His fingers were wrapped around the packet of Gauloises when he paused.

Perhaps he shouldn't. He'd had quite a few today already.

And with the sigh of the martyred, he let his hands fall back into his lap. He wasn't to know that he would never touch another cigarette in his life.

Christian felt the rapid thump of his heart as he stared the short distance across the clearing. He made no attempt to rationalise this. He knew. If the events that morning at the scrapyard hadn't warned him, one look at Henri Dedieu's eyes was enough.

Cold flints of blue, gaze unwavering, gun aimed steadily at the farmer's chest. This was no accident. No prank played out in the forest.

Which meant Christian had been seen. Somehow they'd

spotted him as he ran through the abandoned cars. And now this . . .

But a question was forming in the farmer's mind. How? How had Dedieu known where to find him? He tried to focus on the answer but it was difficult, the gun making his thoughts scatter on the wings of panic. And then another question shaped itself, rising logically out of the first, and Christian felt a darker fear than he had ever experienced take hold of his soul.

Véronique. Where the hell was Véronique?

Arnaud heard the clatter of branches overhead as the breeze picked up, drops of water falling onto his shoulders. The air smelled fresh, cutting through the dank heaviness of the earth, bringing with it the promise of spring. New life.

Not far now. He shifted the load on his back and continued striding towards the quarry, automatically scanning the terrain for evidence of recent activity. He saw it from quite a distance – an indentation on the wet mud, out of place. He paused, crouching down to run his ringers along the ridges.

A heel print. Overlaying a full print beneath. Someone had turned here. Up ahead he could see more prints. Coming and going. Someone not worried about leaving tracks. Then he saw another set of tracks. Different altogether. And something white, half-submerged in a twist of soil.

He picked it up and smelled it. It was faint, but unmistakable – the strong tang of Gauloises.

He grinned. René was up here. Judging by the smaller depressions next to the plumber's, he wasn't alone; Serge the beagle was with him.

They had at least twenty minutes head start, he judged. Even so, knowing the plumber's ambling pace, there was a chance Arnaud would overtake them before they reached the quarry path. It wasn't what he wanted. Although the thought of frightening the life out of René like he had last year was tempting.

Laughing softly, the big tracker resumed his journey, shortening his stride, eyes reading the tracks as he followed René and the beagle down the mountain. And into tragedy.

'If you've harmed Véronique . . .' The words ground out of Christian's dry throat and he felt his fear replaced by rage. 'What have you done with her?'

Dedieu said nothing. Simply flicked the gun, motioning for Christian to drop his mobile. It fell from the farmer's shaking hand.

'I mean it, Dedieu! If you've hurt her in any way . . .' Christian held his ground, watching the hunter approach.

'I'm sure you do. But it changes nothing. Put your hands above your head.'

The gun, significantly closer now, was steadfast. An ugly, snub-nosed handgun. It looked as deadly as the man wielding it. Christian complied.

'Now move.' A second flick of the pistol indicated the required direction.

Arms raised high, Christian took a step backwards. Then another. Then he glanced behind. The quarry. He was being forced ever nearer to the rim of the quarry, the stony ground below a dizzying depth away.

When he turned back to face Dedieu, the man was smiling.

'Worked it out have you, Christian? Just like you did this morning, no doubt. I hope you appreciate the symmetry of all this? This place.' He cast a hand at the burnt trees beyond.

'You're sick. All this over bloody local politics?'

Dedieu's smile morphed into a snarl. 'Tradition. It's about

tradition. Restoring what was taken illegally. Keeping things as they were.' His knuckles whitened, fingers curling around the trigger. 'And it would have all gone to plan but you couldn't help interfering – you and that stupid postmistress with her SOS Fogas blog. Well she got her rewards last winter. Now you're getting yours.'

'Last winter . . . ?' The question died on Christian's lips. The attack on Véronique. Her flat ransacked. Her arm broken in the fall as her attacker fled. 'You? You did that?'

'Enough!' spat the hunter, gesturing once again with the gun. 'Keep moving!'

'I won't do it,' Christian said, trying to inject confidence into his voice. 'I won't jump.'

Dedieu nodded. 'Then I will simply shoot you.' He shrugged, patting the rifle that hung across his chest. 'One more careless hunting accident. Fatal, unfortunately.'

Christian glanced behind once more, the plummeting land making his head spin. Could he survive? A fall down there? It had been enough to kill the bear last summer. But the alternative was certain death.

'What's it to be, Christian?'

'We should probably make a move.' René looked down at the beagle lying on his feet, reluctant to disturb the solid warmth of tired dog.

It was hard to tell in the depth of the forest but it felt like the temperature had dropped again. And the breeze had definitely picked up. It would be enough for old Annie Estaque to be predicting more rain. They needed to get home before they got soaked through, the shelter not as thick on the quarry path as it was here in the trees.

'Come on, Serge. How about I carry you for a bit?'

Brown eyes regarded him mournfully and René took that

for acceptance. With a grunt he bent down and scooped the dog into his arms, getting a lick on the chin as thanks.

'Christ,' he muttered, as he recommenced walking, slower now thanks to his surprisingly heavy burden. 'No more dog biscuits for you, my friend.'

'I said, what's it to be?' snapped Dedieu.

'Okay, okay . . .' Christian raised his hands higher, trying to pacify the man and wrestle a precious few seconds of thinking time. But his thoughts skittered beyond control, jittery on adrenalin and fear.

He looked over his right shoulder. The rim of the quarry was close. But so was the forest and that thick screen of trunks.

The trees. It was his only hope. If he could edge towards them . . .

The farmer took a step backwards, twisting his foot slightly to change his direction. He couldn't be too obvious. Couldn't risk looking over his shoulder again. Dedieu would suspect. But he had to get it right or he would run out of clearing and arrive at the lip of the quarry before he reached the forest.

He took another step, again shifting the direction almost imperceptibly. It was all about calculating the angles now. That was all that could keep him alive. Shuffling blindly backwards, he tried not to think about the precipitous drop that was getting ever nearer.

There! At last the quarry path beckoned ahead, a grey snake winding through the trees.

'Not far now, boy,' said René as they stepped out of the forest and onto the stones. 'Think you can walk the rest of the way?'

He lowered the dog gently to the floor and then stretched,

rubbing his aching back. He was going to need a long hot bath when he got home. And a beer. And at least five Gauloises.

'Come on then,' he coaxed the exhausted beagle. 'This way.'

Together they turned right. Away from the quarry, towards the track and the village. Leaving Christian Dupuy to die.

'Faster!' Dedieu growled. 'Pick your feet up, Dupuy!'

'Okay . . . okay . . .' Christian responded to the impatient flick of the gun by taking two quick steps and heard a soft crunch under his left foot. An acorn. The ground had altered subtly, the grass of the clearing becoming rougher, longer, threaded with dead leaves and protruding roots. The trees! They must be getting closer.

He risked a glance out of the corner of his right eye. There. The sanctuary of solid trunks, branches swaying in the wind. They were no more than a couple of strides away. He could do this.

He took another step, this time his right foot slithering on something soft, causing him to stumble. His arms flailed out to correct his balance and he twisted to the left. And was met with the dizzying sight of rocks far below.

Christian had run out of space. He was standing on the edge of the quarry with Henri Dedieu mere metres away. He'd failed.

'Any last requests?' A harsh laugh, Dedieu moving even closer. 'Or shall we just get this over with?'

Christian spoke through numb lips. 'Véronique. Don't harm her. She had nothing to do with SOS Fogas.'

Henri Dedieu's eyes narrowed. 'What do you mean?'

The farmer, sensing a chance to prolong his life, grabbed it with both hands. 'She wasn't behind it. I don't know who was. But it wasn't Véronique. I swear . . .'

And all the while, as the farmer gabbled away the seconds

he had remaining in this life, the crushed mound of fungus that bore the imprint of his right boot, the same fungus that had caused him to lose his footing, was releasing its spores, up, up into the forest. Carried on the breeze to where a very sensitive nose was waiting.

It was faint at first. But enough to make him pick up his weary head and sniff the air. He turned. There – stronger and distinctive. An earthy odour, musky, one he'd spent all day detecting.

Serge the beagle lifted his nose even higher. Just to make sure.

'—I swear Véronique had nothing to do with it.'

'Enough!' Henri Dedieu raised the gun, this time with a finality that Christian knew couldn't be sidetracked any longer. 'You have ten seconds to choose your fate, Dupuy. Then I will shoot you.'

One.

Two.

Three.

Christian couldn't help counting. Measuring out the last ticks of his life. Would it hurt? The shot. Because he knew there was no way he could jump. Not down there.

Four.

Five . . .

René didn't know what got into the hound. One minute he was dragging his paws along the ground like he was at death's door again. The next, he let out two sharp barks, the noise ringing around the forest. Then he was off.

He raced into the trees, in the opposite direction to the way they should be heading, René lumbering after him, lead dangling uselessly from his hand.

'Serge!' he shouted. 'Come back here, Serge.'

Those bloody biscuits, thought the plumber, as he ran through the undergrowth, brambles and branches pulling at his clothes, tearing at his face as he tried to follow the beagle. They must have caffeine in them! Vowing to have one himself if he ever caught the damn dog, René staggered on.

. . . Six.

Seven.

Eight.

Dedieu shrugged. 'Your choice.' And he centred the gun on Christian's heart.

The farmer closed his eyes. 'Véronique,' he murmured, trying to conjure her image so it would be the last thing he saw.

Then the discordant yap of a dog split the tension. Christian's eyes snapped open to see Henri Dedieu's head turning. A second bark – louder, closer. Dedieu's attention still wandering—

Move, you idiot!

For a man of his size he reacted quickly, springing across the short distance that separated him from his adversary, focus on the gun. Hands out, he lunged for it. But Dedieu was already twisting back, sensing the danger, stepping away. All the time his finger tightening on the trigger.

Slow. Time stretched out into nanoseconds, each beat funereal. Christian saw his hands connect with Dedieu's arms. Saw the two of them stumble, fall, the pistol pressed between them, the boar's head etched into the handgrip filling his vision.

Then he felt the gun shudder. The shot, a deafening roar followed by the rush of silence.

And then he saw her. Véronique. Standing at the edge of the clearing, cross glinting at her throat. She was waving, a summer breeze tugging at her skirt. Her bright smile lifted his heart. His poor heart, which was struggling. Stuttering. Dying.

René heard the shot. It carried through the forest, reverberating off the trees, making it difficult to place at first.

When he realised, he started running, proper running, head thrown back, knees high, arms pumping.

It had come from the quarry. Hunters. Right where Serge was heading. He knew what they were like. When the dog came hurtling out of the undergrowth, all fur and motion, they would shoot first and look later.

Serge wouldn't stand a chance.

'Come back!' he screamed. 'Serge, come back here!' But the beagle was already out of sight.

Lungs bursting, René Piquemal ran as fast as his short legs could carry him.

Arnaud halted at the sudden noise. Two clear barks from Serge the beagle, then a shot, further away, nearer the quarry.

Hunters? It was Wednesday after all.

But that particular area had never been a great favourite with the orange-beret-wearing brigade. He couldn't imagine it had become any more popular after the fire last summer.

He didn't even think it through. Instinct was taking over. That and staunch cynicism when it came to coincidences. The quarry was where he was hoping to trap Henri Dedieu. And that was where the shot had come from.

Long legs beginning to sprint, he tore through the forest.

Dark. The edges of his vision clouding. A cold stealing into his bones, making him shiver and shake. And that pain, spreading across his chest.

'Véronique,' he whispered. But she was fading too. In her

place, the damp ground beneath him, the soft smell of rain-soaked earth. He curled his fingers into the wet soil, filling his fist, trying to keep a grip on the life that was seeping from him, trying to stay in Fogas.

Lying at the edge of the clearing, Christian Dupuy was dying, all alone.

'Serge,' roared René, the dog fleetingly visible some way ahead. 'Come back here you stupid mutt!'

But the beagle raced on, the plumber struggling to increase his pace. Breathing reduced to short gasps, chest pounding, he ran, each step measured to the same incantation.

Please don't let them shoot him. Please don't let them shoot him.

He burst out of the forest and into the clearing, the dog already racing across the grass, barking frantically now as he approached the edge of the quarry. But what was he racing towards? Something on the ground . . .

René was still running. Eyes unable to focus that far and at this speed. He was almost upon it when comprehension came.

'Mon Dieu!' He fell to his knees, hand already pulling his mobile from his pocket and calling the number while his other hand felt for a pulse.

'Ambulance!' he screamed into the phone. 'Quickly. Up at the old quarry clearing above Picarets. Hurry. There's been a shooting accident.'

Phone pressed between shoulder and ear, he carefully turned over the body that lay before him. He didn't need to see the face. The blond curls, the huge frame, were enough.

'Christian,' he muttered, taking in the deep gash on the forehead and the much more worrying crimson bruise that was spreading across the broad torso. Doing his best to concentrate on what the dispatcher was saying to him, René pressed his hand against the chest wound, anxious to stop that precious blood from escaping between his fingers. But no matter how much pressure he applied, the blood kept coming.

'Please don't die,' he pleaded, 'please. Come on, Christian.'

The farmer's eyelids flickered, his lips moved, the sound the faintest of whispers stolen by the breeze.

'Christian, it's me, René. Hang on. Help is coming.'

The lips moved again, this time more resolutely. René leaned over the big man and caught the word he was so desperately trying to say.

'Bo . . . ar . . .'

Then he felt the body in his arms sag, the energy leaching into the soil around him in scarlet rivulets.

'No, Christian, stay with me. Christian!' René was sobbing now, tears rolling down his cheeks. 'Please!'

And in a prayer to the God he believed in, despite not being a regular in the Lord's house on a Sunday, René Piquemal made the only pact he could. He offered up his habit. The one he couldn't break.

'Let him live,' he cried to the darkening heavens, 'and I'll never touch another cigarette!'

But if God was listening, he didn't indicate it. For René could feel the pulse of life ebbing out of the man lying on the ground before him.

18

Whether or not God was listening to René, the emergency dispatcher certainly was. Both the volunteer fire brigade up the valley in Massat and the ambulance service down in St Girons were alerted. As chance would have it, the volunteers were already in the area, having been called out to a minor road accident just outside La Rivière. Having ascertained that neither their assistance, nor that of the doctor accompanying them, was needed as there were no casualties and the gendarmes were now on site, the young men turned their small fire engine around and headed for Picarets.

Sirens blaring, they raced through La Rivière, Josette following their progress around the river bend from the épicerie window.

'Wonder where they're off to in such a hurry?' she mused.

Fabian, who'd been trying to call Véronique all afternoon to ask about the possibility of buying the old Papon house, looked up from his mobile as the vehicle took the sharp turn up to Picarets.

'Heading up there? Hope it's nothing serious.'

'Is Chloé . . . ?' Josette raised an eyebrow, looking across the road to where Stephanie had just come out of the garden centre to stand in the road.

'She's with the Rogalles.' Nephew and aunt regarded each other, Chloé's ability to get into scrapes silently acknowledged between them. 'Perhaps I'd best check everything's okay,' Fabian finally said.

Josette nodded. While he made the call she watched until the fire engine disappeared up the road, noting that Serge and Jacques were equally transfixed at the bar window.

'Something's up.' Serge was frowning, eyes on the back of the fire engine as it passed by.

'Could be anything.'

Serge shook his head. 'I'm telling you, it's something serious.'

Jacques laid a hand on his old friend's shoulder. He'd been out of sorts since that bizarre incident with Pascal earlier in the day, which neither of them had been able to fathom.

Stealing a mobile, of all things. Why would the interim mayor risk everything over something so petty?

'Come on,' he said, trying to guide Serge away from the window. 'Let's put our feet up.'

But Serge shook off the well-meaning hand and continued to monitor the world beyond the glass. He was still there, staring into the distance, when the last notes of the siren faded and Jacques' head tipped back against the inglenook wall in a familiar pose.

Serge Papon might have been dead, but his sense of paternal responsibility for the commune of Fogas wasn't. And he could feel it in his bones that something was up.

Something was up. Stephanie followed the progress of the fire engine down the road, walking out of the garden centre to track it around the bend and down past the Auberge.

Chloé? She was at the Rogalles. At least that was where she was supposed to be. She turned, glancing over at the épicerie to see Fabian in the window, a phone to his ear. Obviously a step ahead of her, he caught her eye and raised a thumb, his lips forming a silent *okay*.

She smiled at him, a surge of love replacing her disquiet, and gave thanks yet again to the Fates for placing them on the same path. Then she returned to work. She was making wedding bouquets for a young couple from Massat who were getting married in two days' time. But the joy she normally took in such a pleasant task didn't manage to transcend the nagging sense of unease the passing fire engine had caused.

Cursing her sixth sense, she finally put the flowers aside and crossed the road to the bar. She'd put her feet up for a bit. Have a coffee and perhaps a bit of cake. She was feeling uncommonly tired.

Chloé was indeed with the Rogalles, the three of them in the square by the lime tree. They'd just finished a game of tag which had had to be abandoned because Nicolas was refusing to accept that Max's slap on his shoulder had actually touched him and the two boys were squaring up for a fight when the blast of sirens took their attention.

'A fire engine!' screeched Max.

'Where's the fire?' Nicolas demanded, wheeling around as though expecting to see flames shooting out of the surrounding houses.

'They're not stopping—'

'Let's follow them—'

'Race you—!'

The two boys ran off after the speeding vehicle, their young bodies hurtling through the village. But Chloé didn't move. She couldn't. She was caught in a grip of fear so strong her legs had turned to jelly.

Arnaud was up there, in the hills where the fire engine was heading. But that wasn't the cause for her concern.

'Christian . . .' she whispered to the wind, not sure why his name had come to mind.

The wind didn't reply, but merely blew against her face where tears were already forming in her eyes.

'A fire engine!' André Dupuy was out in the yard at the farm, tinkering with an old tractor that he'd been working on for three years and still hadn't fixed. He stood up to watch the progress of the red truck as it turned up the road towards the quarry.

'Must be a hunting accident,' said Josephine who was crossing the yard, tray in hands. 'It's almost the end of the season and you know how trigger-happy they get this time of year.'

But André's attention had already switched to what she was carrying.

'Cake!' he said, with glee, taking the tray from her and distributing the coffee and plates on the bonnet of the tractor. 'Shop-bought?'

Josephine laughed. 'Of course!'

'So what are we celebrating?'

'The good news,' she replied, slipping an arm around her husband's waist. 'Christian is finally getting married.'

André pulled her into an embrace, kissing her cheek. 'It is good news. Excellent news, in fact. And just think—'

'Grandchildren,' she whispered, sharing his thoughts with ease after years of marriage. 'This place will be filled with children again.'

They stood there, contentedly imagining the next generation running around the farm, not realising that up the mountain before them, their son was losing his battle for life.

Arnaud was almost there. He heard the siren, wailing, getting closer, and then abruptly stopping; the slam of doors; voices shouting. He ran faster, feet gliding over rocks and roots, sure-footed despite his haste.

'Over here! Hurry!' René's voice carried through the forest, accompanied by a frenzied bark.

The clearing. Arnaud shifted direction, still running, but easing up, wanting to assess the situation. It wasn't long before he slowed to a silent walk, able to see down now to the clearing. The expanse of grass, the blackened trees on the other side. And there, not far from him, René huddled over an inert form, shouting at the doctor and the volunteers who were running along the path.

'Hurry!' the plumber screamed. 'You have to hurry. He's dying.'

The doctor reached him first, the volunteers weighed down by the stretcher. Frantic moments passed, René openly sobbing as the doctor worked quickly. Then they were moving him, the man on the ground with the unmistakable blond curls, placing him gently on the stretcher, and hurrying for the path as fast as their load would let them.

Arnaud waited, hidden amongst the trees. There was nothing he could do. Not with them. His expertise didn't lie in medicine. Instead he watched as the group disappeared along the path, the beagle trotting after them. He waited still, until the sound of an engine cut the silence and the fire engine roared away.

Then he walked down to the clearing, his eyes scanning every inch of the ground.

He would find it – the clue. There was always a clue. And when he discovered who'd shot Christian Dupuy, he would take revenge. Because Christian was a good man, and Arnaud's friend – perhaps the only man ever to have held that title.

And friendship wasn't something the tracker took lightly.

*

'Can't you go any faster?' screamed René.

'We're nearly there,' said the fireman next to him as the fire engine emerged back onto the road that led to Picarets. 'The ambulance is meeting us in the village.'

'Thank God,' muttered the doctor, who'd done all he could to stem the blood loss but knew he was losing the battle.

Down in Picarets, the excited Rogalle twins were pestering the ambulance driver who'd parked next to the lime tree about what was happening.

'Someone got shot!' they shouted to Chloé who was hanging back, standing next to Grand-mère Rogalle. Woken from her afternoon nap by all the commotion, the old lady had just come to the front door.

Then the fire engine arrived and there was mayhem. René and Serge the beagle jumped out, followed by a doctor and several men lifting down a stretcher.

'Get out of the way, boys,' Grand-mère shouted at the twins and they moved reluctantly back as the stretcher was transferred to the ambulance.

'Chloé!' It was René, calling her. She ran over, feeling sick.

'Here,' he said, thrusting Serge the beagle in her arms. 'Look after him for me.'

'Is it Christian?' she asked, making him hesitate, his eyes wet with tears.

He nodded. 'Tell his parents.'

And then he was gone. The doors slammed shut, the ambulance screeching its way down the hill.

'Christian?' asked Nicolas, his elation fading as his eleven-year-old mind tried to process the shock. 'Christian Dupuy has been shot?'

'Is he going to die?' Max looked up at the only adult, expecting reassurance.

But Grand-mère Rogalle only made the sketch of a cross in the air, blessing the departing ambulance, before pulling the two boys into the house along with the dog. 'Go Chloé,' she said, nodding towards the farm. 'It's better they hear it in person.'

She rode, her bike flying up the hill. She could see them out by the old tractor, laughing, drinking coffee.

'Christian!' she screamed, jumping off the bike and throwing it to the ground to run crying over the yard. 'You need to go to the hospital. Christian has been shot.'

And the farm, which only moments before had been filled with the imaginary laughter of children, was now filled with the very real wails of Josephine Dupuy.

The news travelled fast. Grand-mère Rogalle had the presence of mind to call Josette, thinking Véronique would be down there. But she'd forgotten the post office was closed on Wednesdays. Josette, hand trembling, tried to call Véronique on her mobile, but there was no response. Fabian, having had as little success all afternoon in trying to raise the postmistress, suggested perhaps there was something wrong with her phone. There was of course. It was lying at the bottom of the river just beyond La Rivière.

Luckily, though, Stephanie was in the bar and had heard from Annie that the two Estaque women were going to be up at Serge's house all day. So Josette tried there. But the phone had been disconnected.

'Céline,' said Fabian. 'Call Céline and have her run down to them to break the news. It'll be quicker than us driving up there.'

So Josette called the town hall and Céline Laffont, in her shock, put down the phone and shared the news with the man standing in the doorway opposite her desk.

'Christian Dupuy,' she said, rising from her chair to slip on her coat. 'He's been shot.'

A crash of china smashing and the splash of coffee on the floor; Pascal Souquet didn't even react, his hand still held out as though the mug was contained within it.

'Shot?' he muttered, face pale.

Céline nodded, animosity buried in the face of this tragedy. 'It doesn't look good. I'm going down to tell Véronique.'

But the interim mayor didn't respond. He just stood there, staring at the shards of porcelain that littered the floor, trying to make sense of it all. And his role in it.

Considering it had been a day neither of them had been looking forward to, by mid-afternoon, both of the Estaque women would have agreed that it had been strangely enjoyable. More relaxed in each other's company as the day wore on, they'd cleared the living room of Thérèse's fussy knickknacks and ornaments – Véronique deciding to keep the curved walnut display case and the volumes of classics it housed – and had then moved on to the kitchen. As Annie started on the dresser, Véronique began working her way through the rest of the sideboard that she'd abandoned three weeks ago when she found the report on the bear attacks. She was more than halfway through when Annie let out a gasp.

'Look,' her mother said, holding up a small photograph.

Véronique stood up and crossed to where Annie was kneeling in front of the dresser, a white shoebox on her lap. She took the proffered photo, the edges torn, a large crease down the middle, and stared in wonder.

Four figures, lined up in the garden of the very house they were in. Christian Dupuy, in the early stages of adolescence, his body already filling out, was standing to one side with a broad grin. Next to him was the younger Fabian Servat, a thin and wary child, looking at the camera from swollen eyes, his trousers covered in mud. By contrast, Véronique seemed carefree, limbs dark from the summer sun, a reckless smile on her face, and a tie wrapped around her forehead holding back her auburn hair. Finally, there was Serge Papon, caught in mid-laugh, his head thrown back, his arm around Véronique and what could only be pride in his eyes.

'When was it taken?' asked Annie.

'The day Fabian fell down the shallow end of the quarry above Picarets. He tore his trousers and cried so much, Christian jumped down there with him while I ran to get help.' Véronique smiled at the memory. 'When I got back with Serge, he had to pull them both out with a rope!'

'And the photo . . . ?'

'Thérèse took it. Serge brought us back here and we had Orangina and pains au chocolat while Thérèse mended Fabian's trousers so his mother wouldn't go mad. Then we played war games in the garden . . .' She laughed softly. 'It was the summer *Rambo* was released, and Serge took off his tie and put it around my head. He said I was every bit as brave as Rambo. And then Thérèse took the photo . . . I can't believe Serge kept it.'

'He didn't.' Annie turned over the lid she'd taken off the box on her lap and showed her daughter the large letters written across the top.

Thérèse's Important Documents

'It was in this along with herrr birrrth cerrrtificate, wedding cerrrtificate, all the documents associated with the house, herrr drrriving licence . . .'

'You mean it was Thérèse . . . ?'

Annie looked up at Véronique. 'Like I said earrrlier, none of this is simple. As forrr Rrrambo,' she continued, taking hold of her daughter's shaking hand and trying to make light of the moment, 'I think you look morrre like Arrrnaud Petit! You'rrre so darrrk—'

A fist hammering at the door cut her off. 'Véronique! Open up! Hurry!'

'What on earrrth . . . ?' said Annie, getting to her feet and following her daughter as she hastened down the hallway. They opened the door to see the town hall secretary, ashen-faced before them.

'Véronique . . . Christian . . .' Céline stammered. 'It's Christian. He's been shot.'

The photograph fell from numb fingers and fluttered face down to the floor.

19

'Any news?'

'He's still critical. It's not looking good.'

'Christ. I can't believe it.'

Josette served a coffee to the latest arrival at the bar who was shaking the rain off his coat. She'd known this would happen. After a fraught evening and a sleepless night worrying about Christian, his parents and Véronique, she'd risen early and opened up, knowing they would come. The community. It always happened. Even in this age of mobiles and emails and instant messaging, everyone still congregated at the bar when trouble hit town.

And this was trouble. Which meant the bar was already full to overflowing on a wet Thursday morning, and it wasn't even nine o'clock.

'Have the gendarmes got any clue as to who it was?' Bernard Mirouze was looking over at Alain Rougé as though, being an ex-policeman, he'd have insider information.

Alain shook his head. 'Not that I've heard. They think it was a hunter who fled when he realised what he'd done.'

René nodded. 'I'm sure that's right. When I got there Christian was trying to speak and all he managed was the word "boar".'

'You think he saw one before he was shot?' asked Monique Sentenac.

'Possibly. Or he thought he'd been mistaken for one.'

Monique gave a disgusted snort. 'Same thing every year. Probably some bloke up there with a hip flask who'd taken one too many nips when poor Christian hove into view.'

'But what was Christian doing up there?' asked René. It was the question that had been plaguing him since he'd left the hospital and had a chance to digest what had happened. 'Why would he have been up at the quarry?'

'It doesn't make sense,' agreed Stephanie. 'Especially as he'd told his parents he was going to St Girons to get a radiator for the car.'

'How are they?' asked Monique.

Stephanie pulled a face. 'Not good. Josephine has fallen apart and poor old André is trying to comfort her but he's not exactly in a great place himself. Christian's sister is coming over today to look after them.'

'And Véronique?' Agnès Rogalle asked.

'Annie's down at the hospital with her. She won't leave Christian's side.'

'That's understandable,' murmured Fabian, placing a hand on his wife's shoulder as he walked past.

The place fell silent then, broken only by the patter of rain on the window and a whimper from the beagle who was sitting under the stool bearing the weight of his master.

'Here, Josette, give me another of those croissants,' said René gruffly. He took the proffered pastry and broke it into small bits.

'There you go,' he said, dropping it to the floor in front of the dog. 'That's the least you deserve,' he continued, stroking the silken ears as the beagle started eating. 'He should get a medal, Bernard. He saved Christian's life and that's for sure.'

Everyone looked down at the miracle dog, the hound that had wrestled with death and then possibly rescued someone else from it.

'How did he find him? That's what I want to know,' mused Bernard.

René shrugged. It puzzled him too. The way the beagle had sped off in the right direction before the shot had even been fired.

'No idea. But if Christian makes it, he owes you dog food for life.'

If Christian makes it . . . The words hung over the group like a black cloud and René's hand automatically reached for his top pocket. Which was empty.

'Merde!' he cursed.

'Fabian, fetch René a packet—'

'No, it's okay, Josette,' the plumber interrupted. 'I've given up. For good this time. I made a pact . . .' He shrugged, a tinge of red streaking his cheeks. 'You know, when I found Christian . . .'

And for once, despite years of watching René Piquemal fight and lose in his struggle with cigarettes, no one doubted him. There was a finality to the man's words that brooked no argument.

'Well, let's hope the man upstairs was listening,' said Josette, leaning across the bar to place a croissant in front of the plumber's twitching fingers.

'He'd better bloody have been,' grumbled the plumber as he bit into the pastry. 'I've got to go up to the town hall to see Pascal to discuss Friday's council meeting, with no nicotine in my system.'

'It can't be going ahead?' Monique asked. 'Not now.'

'There'll be a postponement, surely?' added Stephanie.

'I wouldn't bet on it.' René swallowed the last of his breakfast and rose to leave. 'Politics is politics and unfortunately we have to have a new mayor. And I'm sorry to say, with Christian out of the picture and our majority lost, it now looks like it will be Pascal Souquet. But you know, after yesterday, I don't think I care anymore.'

He paused, staring at the floor as though the explanation for everything that had befallen the commune in the last couple of months was written there. Then he sighed, bid farewell to the gathering and headed out to his car, his shoulders hunched against the rain, his heart weighed down by concern for his friend.

While the bar lapsed into a sombre silence in the wake of the plumber's departure, over by the inglenook, things were far from quiet.

'I told you!' fumed Serge, pacing back and forwards between the fire and the window. 'I knew something was up.'

'But you couldn't have known Christian was going to get shot!' retorted Jacques. 'It was an accident. Like René said, someone mistook him for a boar.'

Serge strode back across the floor and leaned in to his seated friend, face grim. 'You think so?'

Jacques blinked. 'You don't?'

Turning on his heel, Serge stared out of the rain-smeared window. He didn't know what to think. That incident with Pascal taking Véronique's phone. Then Christian being shot. And underlying it all, the knowledge that Pascal Souquet had been involved in the fake bear attacks last summer.

Had Christian put two and two together? He'd seen the report that had been hidden in the desk in the town hall and was astute enough to work it out. But how could that have precipitated him getting shot? And then there was the matter of Christian being up at the quarry. No one knew why he'd been up there, in that place of all places, with its gruesome connection to the summer before.

So many questions.

'If it was an accident,' said Serge, 'then we have to ask what Christian was doing up there. That's what's bothering me.'

Jacques shrugged. 'Maybe he was meeting someone?'

'Why there?'

'For privacy? You know what it's like round here.' Jacques tipped his head towards the throng of people around them, conversations resuming, the topic all the same but each opinion different. 'So he went up there to discuss something with someone.'

'What?' persisted Serge, prowling in front of Jacques like a lawyer with a witness.

'The meeting on Friday? He wanted to talk tactics?'

'But René was already on the hills. So who could it have been?'

'Véronique!' said Jacques, proud of his quick response. But as the name left his lips, he began to pale.

'Exactly,' said the former mayor. 'Which makes me ask, how did she know where to meet him—?'

'—when Pascal had stolen her phone?' Jacques was on his feet now. 'Mon Dieu. Do you think . . . ?'

Serge nodded. 'I do. I think Christian was enticed up there using Véronique's phone.'

'Which means . . .'

'This was no accident. Someone was trying to kill him.'

'But who? Pascal wouldn't be capable of that. Besides, he doesn't know one end of a gun from another.'

Serge stared across the river to the rolling fields of Sarrat, their borders blurred by the rain. He had a name in mind. A man who was more than capable of killing. A man whose footprints could be found in every bit of trouble that had beset Fogas in the last two years.

'Henri Dedieu,' he whispered. 'I'm sure of it.'

*

Crouched down, rain trickling over his collar, Arnaud looked at the footprint again. He'd taken a photograph with Chloé's phone yesterday but there was nothing like the real thing for giving you a feel for your prey. He ran his fingers over the ridges and indentations as though committing it to memory before it was washed away.

Once Christian had been rushed to hospital the day before, the tracker had remained on the mountainside up at the quarry. He'd had a clear half hour before the arrival of the gendarmes, who'd been delayed dealing with the car accident outside La Rivière. And he'd made good use of that time.

Scouting the area carefully, he'd found the shooter's escape route. Clever man, he hadn't made for the path but had run across the scorched terrain, the ground still covered in ash and debris, far less likely to yield a decent imprint than the rain-softened mud of the forest.

Brazen too, because he must have heard the bark, and René's shouting. Yet he had chosen the route with the least cover, calculating he had time to cross the burnt land and reach the trees beyond without being seen. All so he wouldn't leave tracks.

He was cunning – a true hunter. But he wasn't infallible. In his haste, tearing through the charred landscape, he'd left behind a trail of broken twigs and branches, the stark white of their torn ends as good as fluorescent paint for a man with Arnaud's talents. He'd tracked the hunter with ease and then, where the undergrowth had begun to grow back and the black gave way to green, he'd found the footprint.

Hunting boot, right foot, the heel worn away on the inside edge.

Confident he would have no difficulty resuming the pursuit when he had more time, Arnaud had taken a photo before hurrying back to the clearing to begin a systematic search. He'd started closest to the quarry, where the patch of ground had turned pink. Bending down, he saw the imprint of Christian's large body, the grass flattened by the impact. Something else had been flattened too. Bits of fungus – black, pungent.

A truffle, crushed by Christian's fall.

The tracker sat back on his heels, thinking about Serge the beagle, and that nose of his which René had been trying to train; the nose that had led the dog and René to the wounded farmer.

'Well, well, well,' murmured Arnaud with a soft laugh, remembering his encounter with René in the forests above the Estaque farm the year before when the plumber had divulged his family's secret. 'Who'd have thought it? The Piquemal legend is true after all.'

Then he'd gathered the fragments of truffle into his palm and, with a quiet apology to René and Serge the beagle, he'd straightened up and flung them into the quarry. He knew what would happen if word got out about Christian's inadvertent discovery and the last thing the delicate ecosystem of these mountains needed was hordes of truffle-hunters trampling over it in a mushroom-seeking frenzy. Especially when there were bears hibernating in the region.

Satisfied no evidence of the truffle remained, he'd turned back to the clearing and, across the grass, out of place in this setting, he'd seen the mobile. At the same time, he'd heard the whine of an approaching car. Moving swiftly, he'd picked up the phone in his sleeve-covered hand and melted back into the forest before the gendarmes arrived.

The phone. He pulled it out of his pocket, staring at it through the plastic bag that now protected it and any possible fingerprints. He should have given it to the police, along with the photograph of the footprint. But Arnaud Petit had no confidence in the officials in this area. Not after last summer.

Besides, what importance would they attach to Christian's phone? No one would be surprised to find it in the same area as the man it belonged to. And yet . . .

Arnaud touched the screen and looked once more at the message from Véronique, telling Christian to meet her here at the quarry.

It was curious. Almost as curious as Christian's reply hinting that he'd uncovered a link between Pascal Souquet and the killing of the bear the previous June, a link Arnaud had suspected for a while without being able to prove it.

But for the tracker, neither text was as intriguing as the fact that Christian's mobile had been some distance from the farmer when he fell – too far to have dropped from his hand as his body hit the ground. So what then?

Someone had made him drop it, and then manoeuvred him to the quarry edge? Which suggested this had been no hunting accident. Which also suggested Christian had been lured here.

Tucking the phone back in his pocket and turning up his collar against the rain, for the second time in two days, Arnaud began to follow the trail left by the fleeing shooter. He pushed through the undergrowth and arrived at the track that led down to Picarets. Which was where the trail went cold.

Knowing this careful hunter wouldn't have parked his car in the open where Christian would drive past it, Arnaud was presuming that he must have crossed the track and continued his journey through the forest opposite. Only, this sharp-witted man hadn't crossed directly, because, despite spending some time up here the day before after the gendarmes had finished their investigations, Arnaud had found no resumption of the trail on the other side. Instead, the hunter must have walked on the stony surface quite a distance, conscious he would leave no lasting prints, and then sought the sanctuary of the trees.

Today, Arnaud was hoping for better results. Eyes cast down on the ground, he walked along the far side of the track, hoping against hope that he would come upon something that would enable him to find the hunter.

Because with the news from Chloé this morning, it wasn't looking like Christian would be able to identify him. In fact, it wasn't looking good for Christian at all.

Shot. Christ. He'd been shot.

Pascal picked up his coffee and placed it straight back on the desk. His hand was shaking too much to negotiate it to his lips.

He should go home. But he couldn't. Not with Fatima there, her eyes boring into him, ferreting out his secrets. What would she say if she knew? How deep did her ambition lie?

He wasn't willing to find out. So he'd decided to come to the office, believing it would give him the semblance of normality. Of innocence.

Only he wasn't innocent – he was involved. That bloody phone! He'd lain awake all night, picturing it at the bottom of the gorge below the St Girons road. Picturing some pre-season fisherman stumbling upon it on the riverbank. Picking it up. Handing it in to the police. The last message still visible . . .

It had almost been enough to get him out of bed and down there in the depths of night, searching for the blasted thing. But he'd managed to reassure himself that it couldn't have survived. Not a fall of that distance with the river below. Which had in turn made him think about the bear the summer before, plunging over the edge of the quarry. Which had robbed him of any chance of sleep whatsoever.

Better to be here, then, in the town hall, pretending to be a shocked citizen just like the rest of them. Like Céline in there with her swollen eyes, tissues pressed to her mascara-streaked face.

Of course, he might be jumping to conclusions. The incident yesterday might have had nothing to do with the orders he'd received. Christian might have genuinely been shot by mistake.

The interim mayor allowed his feverish mind to settle on this sprig of hope. An accident. It had all been a fortuitous accident. Some buffoon up in the woods, IQ lower than the boar he was stalking, had pulled the trigger at the first sign of movement.

It happened all the time. So why not now?

It would explain the silence. No call from Henri Dedieu. Not even a text. Surely if the mayor of Sarrat had had a hand in this . . . ?

Telling himself he had no need to worry – in fact, considering what Christian had discovered, he should instead be relieved that the farmer was in no condition to talk – he stretched out his hand for his coffee once more. He barely managed to raise it off the desk before the jitters plaguing his arm set the whole thing shaking. Despite his rational explanation of events, it seemed his subconscious was refusing to succumb to such logic.

'René's here,' Céline announced from the outer office and Pascal looked up to see the sturdy figure of the plumber shamble into view, unshaven, face drawn.

'Bonjour, Pascal,' said René, hand held out in greeting.

'Bonjour. Terrible news about Christian.'

René nodded and took a seat. 'Awful. And so senseless.' He shook his head, eyes fixed on the floorboards as his fingers tapped out a nervous rhythm on his knee.

'It was good of you to come in,' continued Pascal. 'About the council meeting . . .'

'I understand.' René looked up. 'Rules are rules and we'll just have to make the most of it.'

Pascal nodded, heart beating rapidly. He hadn't expected such capitulation. But after all, it was in the Code Général, the rulebook that councils across France had to abide by. There could be no postponement. The commune had to have a mayor. And given the circumstances, the shooting accident had probably just ordained Pascal in that role.

'If there's anything I can do . . .' Pascal managed to squeeze the token gesture out between numb lips.

René sighed and reached for his pocket, stalled, and then cursed before standing. 'I don't know if you're a praying man, Pascal, but Christian needs all the intervention he can get right now. Miraculous or otherwise.'

With a brief handshake, the plumber departed, pausing to speak to Céline, his solid hand on her shoulder triggering another onset of weeping from the secretary.

Pascal clasped his trembling hands together, diminutive behind the massive desk within the grand proportions of the room. Looking to all accounts as though he were heeding the plumber's request, he bowed his head. But his prayers weren't for Christian. They were, as ever, for himself. For he knew that if the farmer recovered, his own chances of surviving the mess he found himself in were slim.

He needed Christian to die.

It looked like he was dying. Face cast from alabaster, tubes snaking across the bed, machines clicking and beeping, bandages swaddling his blond curls and his broad chest. That chest. She so wanted to lie her head on it and feel the gentle snag of his hands in her hair as he told her everything was going to be all right.

But it wasn't. He was unconscious. Dramatic loss of blood.

Shock. Concussion from the fall – to Véronique, struggling to understand, it seemed the doctors were throwing out opinions in the hope that one of them was right. Or perhaps all of them were. It made no difference. The end result was the same.

Christian Dupuy was fighting for his life.

'Come back to me, love,' Véronique whispered, her hand holding his unresponsive fingers. 'Please, come back to me.'

Nothing. The clatter of a trolley in the hall; a door opening and closing; voices. Normal life, continuing beyond the confines of this ward where everything that mattered to her had been put on hold. Again.

Only this time, she wasn't in a cocoon. Ripping through the layer of fog that had been suffocating her since Serge died, the news about Christian had flayed her right down to the nerves. She felt stripped bare. Raw. The very core of her uncovered. Like the victim of a lammergeier, the massive vulture that soared over the Pyrenees dropping its prey repeatedly from a height until bones shattered and marrow was exposed.

She stroked the back of his hand and then rested her fingers on its broad span, willing the energy that was coursing around her veins to cross over into him, to bring him back to life.

'How is he?' Annie appeared in the doorway, a basket in her hands.

Véronique shook her head. 'No improvement. Did you see André and Josephine on your way in?

'Yes. It's good they'rrre heading home. Josephine's in no state . . .' Annie nodded in the direction of Christian's inert form before focusing on her daughter. 'You should think about having a brrreak too, love.'

Véronique felt the heavy touch of a hand on her head, her eyes closing at the comfort she derived from it.

Almost twenty-four hours she'd been here. The journey from Fogas after hearing Céline's news had been interminable, the minutes dragging by as the car hurtled down the mountain towards St Girons, Annie in the passenger seat, muttering curses or invocations, Véronique couldn't tell which. Then in the hospital, a maze of corridors, the two of them hustling after the small nurse whose shoes squeaked across the lino, taking them to a waiting room.

They'd found the Dupuys and René Piquemal already in there, Josephine collapsing into Annie's arms, distraught, while André had taken hold of Véronique's hands and reassured her that Christian would pull through.

'He's strong,' the old man kept repeating, and Véronique sensed he was taking as much solace from his support as he was giving.

That had been the worst – the waiting. Hours. It couldn't have been but it seemed it. Sitting on hard chairs, listening to the muffled ticking of the clock on the wall, eyes staring vacantly at the dog-eared copies of *Paris Match* and *Le Point* abandoned on the coffee table. Nobody really talking apart from René, who kept blurting out odd things. Like how lucky Christian had been that the dog had found him.

Lucky? Véronique had had to bite her tongue, wondering how being on an operating table with a gunshot wound to the chest made someone lucky. Far luckier if Christian hadn't been up at the quarry in the first place.

She'd meant to ask René about that. Why either of them had been up there. But it had slipped into the dark corner of her mind and the effort to retrieve it had seemed too much. And then the nurse had been at the door, the same one with the squeaky shoes and the no-nonsense eyes whom Véronique now recognised as René's niece, Sophie Pujol.

Critical but stable. That's all Véronique heard.

'What does it mean?' she'd asked. But the answer had been vague. Christian had survived the operation. That was about all they could say. What was needed now was for him to wake up, to open those beautiful eyes of his and start living again.

They'd been ushered into his room where, faced with the tubes, the machines, the stark reality of the lifeless form in the bed, Josephine had broken down. When Christian's sister, Nathalie, had arrived from Perpignan, she'd persuaded her parents to return to the farm for the night, Véronique promising to contact them if there were any changes.

But there hadn't been. The world had turned dark outside the window, the hospital had fallen quiet, and Christian had continued to dwell in a place beyond Véronique's reach. She hadn't slept, resting only occasionally on the foldout bed a nurse had placed in the room. Mostly she just sat next to him, holding his hand, and whispering to him about the future – their future. The one she had been busy planning.

When the first thin needles of light had squeezed between the slats of the blinds, she'd finally fallen asleep in the chair, her head resting on the bed next to his inanimate hand. She'd woken to hushed voices, the scrape of a chair leg, the smell of coffee. The Dupuys and Maman had arrived. On the pretext of getting breakfast, the Estaque women had left the ward for thirty minutes, giving Josephine and André a chance to be alone with their son. But thirty minutes away from his side, long enough to consume a stale croissant and a lukewarm coffee, was all Véronique could endure before she anxiously resumed her vigil.

Now, mid-afternoon, she was still here. Hoping that he'd wake up.

'Herrre.' Annie was lifting a covered bowl out of the basket. 'If you won't go home, at least eat something. Lorrrna sent this forrr you.'

Véronique was forming the words to refuse when she noticed how weary Maman was looking. And old. So she took the bowl, removed the cover, and a bouquet of garlic and saucisson wafted up to her. Cassoulet.

'She said it's one of Chrrristian's favourrrites. She thought, you know, the smell . . .' Annie shrugged, not quite sure how a pungent aroma could bring someone back from the dead but willing to give it a try.

Véronique stared at the mound of beans and sausage, her throat constricting at the thought of having to eat. But under the concerned gaze of her mother, she did her best, taking a mouthful of food and washing it down with a glass of water.

'Everrryone sends theirrr love,' said Annie, taking a chair next to Véronique, 'and they'rrre all concerrrned about Chrrristian. I don't think the barrr has everrr known such business!'

Véronique managed a smile. Maman had arrived at the hospital early that morning along with the Dupuys but had taken the offer of a lift back to La Rivière from Christian's sister so that she could gather some things for Véronique from her flat. Typical that in even such a short time in the commune, the news could be picked up too.

'Have the gendarmes got anywhere with their investigation?'

Annie shook her head. 'They'rrre still worrrking on the accident theorrry. I suppose until something prrroves other-rrwise, they have to.'

'But why would you run away? I mean, if you shot someone by mistake, would you flee the scene?'

'Plenty would, Vérrronique. It's not uncommon.'

Véronique sighed and scooped another forkful of cassoulet into her mouth. It tasted of nothing. She wondered how much more she would have to endure before she could desist.

'Therrre was otherrr news,' Annie was watching the slow movement of fork to mouth. 'About the election of the new mayorrr.'

A shrug of disinterest. And another mouthful of food.

'Apparrrently the meeting is going ahead tomorrrrow, despite everrrything.'

Véronique paused, and then lowered her fork. 'I don't think I care, Maman. I won't be there. And I can't eat any more of this.'

She put the bowl to one side.

She had no appetite – for the wonderful cassoulet or for local politics. Nothing, not even concern for her mother, could change that.

20

Friday morning, the day of the mayoral election, brought another surly dawn, lumpen grey clouds smothering any efforts on the part of the sun to alleviate the gloom that had beset Fogas since the shooting incident two days before. High above the Estaque farm, in a particular part of the forest, a man was standing, looking at a map and breathing heavily.

'This must be the place,' he muttered with uncertainty, glancing from paper to trees to rocks in an effort to pinpoint his location.

Rotating the map to align it with his position, he traced a podgy finger over the contour lines, eyes lifting to take in the steep fall to his right where the woods gave way to a clearing down below. There – the large crevice that split the rock face at the back of the glade and above it, on the lip of the precipice, the twisted oak tree.

That was it. He refolded the map, stuffed it in his pocket and puffed and panted his way up the remaining few metres of climb, checking repeatedly to make sure he was alone.

His instructions had been precise. No one must know what he was doing. So he'd trekked cautiously up the mountain, employing every stealthy technique he'd learnt, watching his trail and keeping an eye behind him. Confident he'd succeeded in that part of his covert mission, he reached the gnarled tree and dropped his heavy rucksack to the ground, the noise loud in the dampened woodland.

Leave it here. That's what he'd been told. So that's what he would do. After he'd had a breather. He lowered himself onto a moss-covered log. Five minutes, and then he'd start back down.

He pulled a small bag from his pocket, took out the crushed croissant within it, and slowly began to eat.

It was early. But Josette flung open the shutters on the épicerie door and turned the sign hanging on the inside to declare the shop open.

Might as well. It wasn't as though she'd get much more sleep. Not with what was happening and what lay ahead.

Poor Christian. She'd popped into the hospital the evening before but hadn't stayed long, the farmer's ward crammed with family and friends. It had been such a shock to see him lying there, that vibrant man reduced to a bundle of bedclothes and bandages and those awful tubes. She'd felt the tears rising and had had to step outside to compose herself, not wanting Véronique to see her upset. The young woman had enough to contend with without having to comfort a stupid old lady who was supposed to be supporting her.

And if Christian's appearance had been distressing, Véronique's hadn't been much better. Hair hanging lank around her shoulders, skin taut over her cheekbones, she looked haggard. She needed a good feed and a good sleep but was refusing both, adamant that she wouldn't leave Christian's side until he came round.

God knew when that would be. Certainly not in time for tonight's meeting of the Conseil Municipal. Which, as René had casually mentioned at the hospital the night before, thanks to her status as the oldest serving council member, Josette would be in charge of.

Her, running the meeting that would most likely lead to

the demise of Fogas. It was enough to make her contemplate resigning. She'd have to sit there and read out the votes. She'd be the one to announce Pascal as the new mayor. Because that's what was going to happen. Christian was unable to participate. Véronique had stated she wouldn't be attending. Which left René, Bernard and Josette to fight Christian's corner. Against Pascal, Fatima, Lucien Biros, Geneviève Souquet and Philippe Galy. Whichever way Monique Sentenac had decided to cast her ballot was now an irrelevance.

Pascal Souquet was going to be the next leader of Fogas. And no sooner would the tricolour be draped across his chest, than he would be merging the commune with Sarrat. There was no way to stop it. Not now. Not without a miracle and Fogas had had its fair share of those over the last few years.

With a heavy heart, Josette Servat crossed through the archway to the bar where she was greeted by two solemn faces. Serge and Jacques were just as despondent about the future as she was.

'We have to tell Arnaud what we know. There's no other way,' hissed Serge.

For two days the old friends had sat in the inglenook and discussed every possible option open to them. The truth was, there weren't many options to discuss. And with the council meeting only hours away, they were running out of time.

'I don't know,' murmured Jacques. 'I'm just not comfortable . . .'

Serge gave a snort of exasperation. 'She's eleven years old, Jacques. And she's not exactly a wilting flower. Look what she's been through in the last couple of years.'

Jacques nodded, his eyes drawn across the road to the

battered blue van that was pulling up at the garden centre, the small figure in the passenger seat getting ready to hop out.

She was special. She'd survived a kidnapping attempt by jumping out of her bedroom window and running for help, saving her mother's life with her quick thinking. Then last summer, she'd rallied all the kids in the commune to support the bears, creating havoc. All of which she'd then topped by running away in the autumn to join the circus, somehow stumbling across her long-lost father in the process.

Chloé Morvan was truly unique. But she was still a child. Was it fair to use her in such adult matters?

'Quick, Jacques. Make up your mind.' Serge had one eye on the mother and daughter across the road, the girl twisting crossly out of her mother's embrace. 'This is your last chance to avert disaster.'

Jacques Servat joined his friend at the window and watched the girl begin to walk away, her face as dark as the clouds as she headed for the school bus stop in the lay-by opposite the Auberge.

Fogas. He was doing it for Fogas. Surely that made it okay?

'Chloé!' he shouted, hammering on the glass. 'Chloé! We need your help.'

The small figure hoisted her satchel higher on her back and continued walking, unable to hear the silent ghost.

It was Stephanie that was the catalyst. Well, not Stephanie exactly, but the tiny Servat inside her who she had yet to be aware of. Perhaps he – for it was a boy – was responding to the cries of his great-uncle in the bar. Perhaps he simply felt it was time he was acknowledged. Whatever the cause, he chose that moment to make his presence known. And he did so by making Stephanie feel sick.

She'd got as far as the gate of the garden centre, her

mind taken up with thoughts of Christian and the struggle she'd had with Chloé that morning, the child determined that school was no place for her when Christian was in hospital. The shooting accident had really affected the young girl. And when Stephanie had refused to yield to her pleas for an exemption from education for the day, a row had ensued.

So Stephanie wasn't surprised she was fatigued. She wasn't surprised that her energy levels had dropped lately. But when she got to the gate and her stomach heaved, making her double up with a yelp, through the waves of nausea, there came a sudden clarity.

She couldn't be…? She calculated back, still bent over, and heard the scurry of feet racing towards her.

Chloé was sure she hated Maman. How could she not? The woman was impossible. Making her go to school when Christian was lying in the hospital, possibly dying.

Her throat tightened at the thought. Big, strong Christian. How could he be dying?

She kicked at the stones that dared to line her path, shifted her satchel higher on her back as though the shell of it offered some protection from all her troubles, and wished with all her heart that Madame Rogalle was her mother.

Then she heard it – a sound halfway between a cry and a hiccup. She turned to see Maman leaning over, one hand holding onto the garden centre gate, the other clutched to her stomach.

Chloé forgot all about the argument that morning; Madame Rogalle's attractions as a mother faded from her mind. All she could see was Maman, red curls tumbling out of the pins that were supposed to restrain them. It looked like she was going to be sick.

'Maman!' she cried, racing back up the road. 'Maman, what's wrong?'

Fabian was making great time. He'd left the house on his bike before the two women in his life, had waved at Grand-mère Rogalle who was taking advantage of the dry morning by hanging out her washing, and had suffered the daily ritual of Stephanie and Chloé driving past and mocking him. He'd then watched with eyes half-closed as his wife careened down the mountain to La Rivière. She drove like a mad woman. Which was partly why he chose to cycle to work every morning. Plus he loved the solitude of it. Living in a commune where everyone seemed to know everything about him before he even knew it himself, he treasured the odd bit of peace and quiet.

He arrived at the T-junction opposite the Auberge, barely breaking a sweat after all the downhill, and swept smoothly out onto the main road, heading over the small bridge to the épicerie. He was almost at the bend when he saw two figures at the entrance to the garden centre. Stephanie, clutching her stomach. And Chloé, looking terrified.

Two quick pedal strokes and he was with them.

'What's the matter?' he asked, leaping from the bike and letting it fall as he ran towards his wife.

'It's Maman!' said Chloé. 'She's ill!'

Stephanie turned to him, face pale, a beautiful look of bemusement and joy spreading across it.

'I think . . .' she managed. 'I think . . .'

He grinned. Finally. It had taken an immense effort on his part the last few days not to blurt out the news.

'You knew?' she said, still stunned.

'Knew what?' asked Chloé, brushing angrily at tears which were beginning to form.

Fabian placed a hand on her head and pulled her towards him, his eyes asking his wife an unspoken question. Stephanie nodded, smiling now.

'Chloé,' said Fabian. 'Your mother has finally realised that she's expecting a baby!'

The young girl whirled round to stare at her mother. 'Really?' she squeaked.

'Really!' laughed Stephanie.

And Chloé, ever one to make the most of an opportunity, was quick to reply.

'You can't make me go to school *now*!'

They entered the épicerie in a clatter of noise. The three of them, a tight balloon of expectation carried between them. Josette took one look and knew something was up – something good finally, after all the bad news. She cried when they told her. Then got up to close the shop because this needed time to be digested. So the extended Servat family celebrated their happy tidings gathered around the fire drinking coffee and hot chocolate, and agreed that no one else should know. Not until Christian had recovered. After all, it didn't seem right to be joyous in the face of such misfortune.

And when the adults finally decided it was time to get back to work, young Chloé Morvan was granted her wish. She was allowed the day off school. Much to her mother's surprise, she elected to stay in the bar for a little while, content to read a fashion magazine Josette had given her. Thinking her daughter was growing into quite the young lady, Stephanie crossed the road to open up her garden centre. She glanced back to wave at Chloé, but the girl was absorbed, head down, reading about the clothes that were parading the catwalks of Paris and Milan.

*

'Do you think you could stop blubbering enough to tell Chloé what we need?' asked Serge, patting his friend on the back.

It had been a shock. A good one. Such amazing news after all that had happened. And for Serge, mayor still despite his inability to wear the sash of office any longer, his first thought was for the commune. The birth rate was finally heading in the right direction. Now all they had to do was make sure this new baby was born in Fogas and not in an annexe of Sarrat.

'Sorry,' muttered Jacques through a watery grin. 'I just wasn't expecting that. A baby Servat. The first one in decades.'

Serge sighed and pointed at the young girl who was watching them out of the corner of her eye, pretending, for the benefit of the living adults, to read a magazine.

'Come on. We haven't got long.'

With a shake of his shoulders, Jacques pulled himself together. Then he got the girl's attention and he began the routine of conversation, using mime and gestures to get his point across.

'Arnaud?' whispered Chloé, after a long couple of minutes. 'You need to get in contact with him?'

Jacques nodded, sagging with relief and the effort.

'He's not been home. Not in days. I don't know where he is.'

The two ghosts looked crestfallen.

'But you could tell me and I could call him . . .'

Serge's head snapped up. He held his hand to his face, thumb by his ear, little finger at his mouth, and raised his eyebrows.

Chloé nodded. 'Oh, yes. Arnaud has a phone. I gave him mine.'

When Josette popped into the bar a few minutes later, she took one look at Serge and Jacques twirling around the room in celebration and smiled.

'I guess they heard the amazing news,' she whispered to Chloé.

Chloé Morvan smiled back. The day had certainly been too good to spend at school.

She had him cornered. Backed up with nowhere to go. Agnès Rogalle wound down her window and leaned her broad arms on the steering wheel, fully prepared to wait. He'd be here soon, returning from whatever assignation he'd crept off to this morning, a note left on the bedside table asking her to mind Serge for the day.

Not that she minded looking after the dog. She glanced at the beagle sitting happily on the passenger seat, his belly full of Toulouse sausage.

'What's he up to, eh Serge?' she asked as she ran a hand over his soft ears, the dog stretching up to her touch. 'What's all this secretive business about?'

Not long now and she would find out. For before her, on a narrow track pretty much forgotten about by the residents of Picarets, whose village could be seen across the valley, was Bernard's car. And on the back seat was his lunch, the remnants of last night's magret de canard, which she'd made into a salad for him before going to bed.

It was already midday and Agnès knew her man. As regular as the tolling bell of the Angelus, Bernard's stomach would be sounding the lunch hour very soon. Which meant he would be coming back to his car. Which meant she would finally discover the cause of all his clandestine behaviour.

'Please, God,' she muttered to the heavy skies above. 'Don't let it be another woman.'

Her prayers were about to be answered.

'What should we say?' Jacques hovered anxiously at Serge's right shoulder, gaze flicking between the mobile on the counter and the archway through which he could hear his wife talking to Fatima Souquet.

'Let's keep it short,' said Serge, stubby fingers poised over the keypad on the phone's screen. 'Something that might get him thinking.'

'Fine. But hurry up. Josette could come in here any minute and then we'd have some explaining to do.'

'All right, all right. Give me a moment to think!'

While Serge's brow pulled into a frown of concentration, Jacques drifted towards the épicerie where he could now see Fatima, basket in hand, face filled with concern.

'So, no news, then?' she was asking.

Josette shook her head. 'He's still unconscious. The doctors have said they can't really assess his condition until he comes round. It could be days . . .'

Neither woman voiced the alternative – that Christian Dupuy might never come round.

Fatima pursed her lips, her voice unusually soft. 'I can't believe it. Such an awful accident. You will tell Véronique I was asking after her, won't you? And if there's anything I can do . . .'

Josette stretched out a hand and laid it on the other woman's arm. 'I'll tell her. And thanks, Fatima, for your concern.'

The interim mayor's wife nodded sharply, pulled her thin shoulders together as though gathering her armour around her once more to seal the crack that had just appeared, and retreated to the back of the shop.

'Concern my arse,' muttered a dry voice in Jacques' ear. 'She's probably in this whole thing up to her scrawny neck!'

Jacques was already shaking his head as he turned to Serge. 'I don't know. There's more to Fatima Souquet than meets the eye. Have you sent the text?'

Serge nodded.

'Well in that case, I need to tell you a story. About that website last autumn. SOS Fogas . . .'

And Jacques led Serge over to the inglenook, knowing that the story would require the former mayor to be seated. Because he was never going to believe who had helped divert the merger last year.

If only she could help them out this time.

Up in the hills, Arnaud Petit was in despair. The rain the past two days. The conditions. The trickery of his adversary. It all meant one thing. He had been unable to find any concrete evidence to confirm his theory that the accidental shooting of Christian Dupuy had in fact been attempted murder.

Hopefully attempted – although the news from Chloé hadn't been so good. She'd left him a hastily scrawled note at the house along with a couple of tins of chicken chasseur, a baguette and a half-eaten packet of Petit Écolier biscuits. It seemed Christian was still in a coma with no sign of waking up.

Which was bad news all round. Because without Christian's testimony, Arnaud couldn't prove his suspicions. And Henri Dedieu remained at large. At large but lying low, the cameras Arnaud had positioned in the woods redundant now the mayor of Sarrat had suspended his illicit trapping activities.

There was nothing for it, then, but to wait. However long it took the farmer to emerge from his protective cocoon, that was how long it would be before the truth could come out.

A small vibration in his pocket had Arnaud reaching for Chloé's phone. Bernard, he presumed. Texting to say he'd done what was required. The bumbling *cantonnier* had turned out to be an excellent choice of accomplice, telling no one about Arnaud's presence in the commune and carrying out orders without a question.

The tracker pulled out the mobile and felt a jolt of surprise when he saw he had a text from Josette Servat.

How the hell . . . ?

His astonishment at the omniscience of the Fogas grapevine was cut short when he read the message she'd sent him.

Pascal stole Véronique's phone just before Christian was shot. Could it be connected?

Pascal Souquet. The blurred image of him on the video up at the bear traps surfaced in the tracker's mind. Why would he have stolen Véronique's phone?

Arnaud reached into his pocket once more, this time taking out the mobile he'd found up at the quarry, Christian's phone. He scrolled through the texts to find the last one the farmer had received, the one that had placed him in danger – an urgent request to meet at the quarry, from Véronique. Purportedly.

Then the tracker looked at Christian's reply.

Pascal possibly involved in death of bear! See you soon.

Standing there, glancing from one text message to the other, Arnaud finally understood and all of his suspicions about the shooting being no accident felt suddenly very valid.

Christian had figured everything out. Perhaps he'd even found some evidence. Which had made him a liability, an obstacle that needed to be removed. Eradicated. And so, with the aid of the interim mayor of Fogas, he'd been lured to his death. Or, what would have been his death if it hadn't been for a beagle with a sensitive nose.

Arnaud cursed himself for having overlooked the ineffectual deputy, the man who was always in the shadows whenever Henri Dedieu was concerned. He checked his watch. The council was meeting that evening at six. And they would be electing the new mayor: Pascal Souquet – the man who had taken Véronique's phone. A man who by all accounts had helped kill a bear, and been an accomplice in the attempted murder of Christian Dupuy. A man, it seemed, who would do anything to bring Fogas to an end.

Arnaud Petit didn't have the evidence to stop the election of Pascal Souquet. But he knew a man who did. And it was time he was woken up.

Taking long strides, the tracker started jogging. He needed to get to St Girons in a hurry. But first he needed some extra clothes. Luckily, he knew where to get them.

21

He'd done it exactly as he'd been told. Considerably lighter without the rucksack, he'd made the return journey in good time and, with his stomach just beginning to rumble, Bernard Mirouze emerged from the forest feeling every bit like a ninja.

Until Agnès Rogalle spoke and nearly scared the life out of him.

'Well?' she said, standing beside his car, arms folded across her sizeable chest, Serge the beagle next to her, the pair united in disapproval.

Bernard stopped in his tracks, guilt stealing across his features.

'Who is she?' Agnès demanded. 'Just tell me that.'

'I don't . . . there isn't . . .' the *cantonnier* stuttered.

'Don't lie to me, Bernard. I can tell something's up.'

And in that moment he saw how it must look to her. The phone calls. The secret meetings. He also saw, with brutal clarity, that keeping the confidence he'd been sworn to could lose him the love of the woman in his life. The only woman he'd ever had in his life.

While Bernard Mirouze was a faithful servant, whose loyalty once earned could never be shaken off, he wasn't willing to jeopardise the brilliance that Agnès Rogalle had brought into his mediocre existence. Not for anything. Or anyone.

'Agnès,' he said, holding out a podgy hand. 'We need to talk. But first . . .'

Bernard's stomach rumbled loudly and his beagle yapped in response. Then Agnès reached down for the bag at her feet.

'How about we talk over a late lunch?' she said. 'I've got some fresh goat's cheese and a lovely bottle of Fronton which will go beautifully with the magret de canard.'

She placed her hand in his and Bernard knew he would never keep a secret from this wonderful woman ever again. Even if it meant he could no longer be a ninja.

Nurse Sophie Pujol had her eye on him. The big man with the flowing locks of black hair who was loitering – it was the only word for it – in the corridor. Clothes crumpled, face unshaven and, when she'd passed him a minute ago, a definite aroma of the woods about him, he should have had her worried. But there was something about him. Something vulnerable like a wild creature trapped in a zoo.

Smoothing her uniform over her young hips, she fixed her features into her sternest look and approached him from behind.

'Can I help you, Monsieur?'

She accompanied her words with a light tap on his lower back, his shoulder being ridiculously high up, and the man swung round, light on his feet despite his size. He looked down at her.

'I . . . erm . . . I'm here to see Christian Dupuy.'

Nurse Pujol didn't need to consult the computer. She knew this patient. He was her uncle René's friend, injured in some ridiculous shooting accident two days before.

'And you are?'

'A friend. Just a friend.'

She shook her head. 'Sorry, but it's family only. He's still in intensive care.'

The man's eyes flickered and she thought he would object,

at which point she probably would have relented, the definition of family for that particular patient having been stretched already. But he simply smiled, a dazzling white against the darkness of his skin, thanked her, and walked away.

She watched him all the way down the corridor, more because he was lovely to look at than anything else. Then she got on with her work.

Family only! Arnaud Petit could have kicked himself.

He'd arrived at the hospital aware of the valuable minutes ticking by, hitching a lift not the quickest means of getting into town. Then he'd wasted more time trying to figure out where to go. Struggling to interpret the medical terminology on the signposts at reception, he'd nearly jumped a mile when the small nurse had accosted him. And he'd made a basic mistake.

Of course visiting was restricted to family only. What a blunder. For a man who could track for days through the forests and never put a foot wrong, suddenly finding himself in a suburban environment in a hospital on the outskirts of St Girons seemed to have stripped him of his wits.

How the hell was he going to get in to see Christian now? The nurse had spoken to him, had fixed him with her ferocious but beautiful brown eyes. The same eyes he could still feel on his back as he retreated down the corridor. She'd notice if he went anywhere near Christian's ward.

Blend in. That's what he had to do. Become part of his environment. But how?

He turned the corner and saw what he needed. A surgeon. Not much smaller than him. He was pushing open the door to the gents.

Arnaud lengthened his stride and was through the door before it could close. It was time to disappear.

*

Véronique felt like the world had disappeared, shuffled off into oblivion, leaving her stranded here in this ward where the minutes passed like hours and nothing changed. Still the same machines blinking the same indecipherable messages. Still the same Christian, refusing to wake up.

She checked the time. Five o'clock. The Conseil Municipal would be meeting in an hour. René had called in earlier and had asked if she was going. She'd expected an outburst of reproach, a passionate remonstration at her demurral, but the plumber had simply nodded, cast one last sad look at his unconscious friend and had left, passing through the door and into the outside that had become so distant to Véronique.

Two days she'd been here, leaving the room only in brief stints to shower or to grab something to eat. She'd lost touch with life beyond the edges of the bed before her. It was hard to believe that, in the mountains she could see through the open slats of the window blind, everything in Fogas was carrying on as normal – as normal as it ever got up there.

And just like that, staring up at the horizontal strips of hillside to a place so familiar to her and yet rendered so remote by her current circumstances, she was felled by homesickness.

Fogas. It seemed an illusion, the life she'd been leading before this. The routine of the post office, the Sunday mornings in church . . . Even her depression had been reduced to a triviality by what had happened up at the quarry.

She was a fool! All those days she'd wasted, moping around instead of making the most of this wonderful man. The nights she'd banished him from her flat. She felt tears rising in her eyes as she squeezed his inert hand.

A squeak of hinges made her look round.

'I brrrought you a coffee.' Maman entered the room holding a flask. 'A prrroperrr one frrrom home!'

Annie Estaque never did know what she'd said to make her daughter, who until this moment had been stoical throughout, collapse in a flood of tears.

'Sorry, Maman. I don't know what brought that on.'

'No apologies needed, love.' Annie passed her daughter a cup of coffee. 'But perrrhaps you should take a brrreak? Go back to the flat forrr a bit?'

Véronique's hand strayed to her neck, fingers hitting bare skin. 'Maybe.' She checked her watch.

'Therrre's still plenty of time,' said Annie with a knowing smile. 'It doesn't starrrt until six.'

Véronique laughed softly. 'How did you guess what I was thinking?'

Annie shrugged. 'It's Fogas, love. And it's what Chrrristian would have wanted you to do. Fight to defend it. No matterrr what the odds arrre.'

Her daughter glanced back at the bed, the large body beneath the bedclothes, the regular breathing, the lack of awareness.

'But what if . . . ?'

'I'll stay herrre forrr now and Andrrré and Josephine arrre coming in at about seven. If anything happens, I'll call strrraight away.'

'I don't know. Do you think . . . ?'

'It's what he would want, Vérrronique. You know that.'

Again Véronique's fingers moved to her throat only to drop back into her lap.

'Herrre,' said Annie, leaving her purse on the table before reaching back into her bag to pull out a small white box which she passed across the bed. 'I bought this forrr you. I know it can't rrreplace the otherrr one but still . . .'

She watched her daughter's face as she opened the present.

'Oh, Maman!' Véronique's eyes flooded once more as she lifted up a silver chain with a small cross on it. 'It's . . . it's . . .'

'Let me put it on you,' Annie said brusquely, feeling her own eyes prickling.

But Véronique shook her head. 'Not yet.'

She leaned over the bed and draped the chain across the bedpost, the cross hanging down above Christian.

'I'll leave it with him tonight. He needs all the help he can get. Even if he doesn't believe in it.'

Then she turned to embrace her mother, the old lady hugging her back fiercely.

'Look after him, Maman,' she whispered. 'And if he wakes up, tell him I've gone to save Fogas.'

She slipped from the room, tissue to her eyes, nodding at a passing doctor as she headed for the outside world.

Fogas . . . Christian . . . The two were so interlinked, Véronique had this nagging sense that if she could rescue one, the other would surely follow.

Annie Estaque – he'd know that familiar figure anywhere, sitting by the bed like a guard dog. How was he going to get round her?

Dr Arnaud Petit, wearing surgical tunic and trousers, admittedly not as loose as they should be, hair tucked up beneath a cap and a mask across his face, peered into the ward. He looked the part, except for the carrier bag in his left hand. It had been ridiculously easy. A simple tap on the side of the neck and the surgeon had been out cold. He was going to wake up cold too, sitting on a toilet in his underpants, vest and socks with no recollection of how he got there.

It wasn't what Arnaud would have wanted, but it was unavoidable. There was too much at stake. And at least he could be confident of his disguise. Véronique had just walked past him without a second glance. He'd seen her tears though, and it had taken all of his self-control not to go after her. To put his arms around her.

He tethered his wayward thoughts. Christian. That's what he was here for. Christian and Fogas, the two so interlinked.

He could only save one with the other, so he needed Annie Estaque out of the way. But how? He glanced at the clock on the wall inside the ward. Time was racing. The meeting would shortly be underway. He had to make a move.

Then he saw a nurse at the far end of the corridor. Small. Brown eyes. Pretty. The nurse from reception. She was wheeling a trolley and it was exactly what he needed.

'I have to go now.' Josette kept her voice low, aware of Fabian in the épicerie. The two grave faces before her nodded. 'But I want you to know that I will do my best. For all of us.'

Jacques reached out a hand, his touch a vague sensation on her cheek.

'I'll let you know what happens as soon as I can.'

She turned to leave and then paused, reaching into her handbag.

'Here. You might as well take this. I think you already know the password.' She left her mobile on the counter, giving them both a stern look. 'To be used only in exceptional circumstances. And I'll get someone to text when I know what the outcome is. Although how I'll explain that one, I don't know!'

'Explain what, Tante Josette?'

Fabian was in the doorway and the two ghosts couldn't help but smile at her predicament.

'Explain the regulations for tonight, Fabian. Sorry, I must have been talking to myself. It's all this stress!'

She didn't have to act the part; she could feel the lines of worry deep across her brow. Fabian put an arm around her and kissed her on the cheek.

'You'll be brilliant. You know you will. As for the rest . . .' His thin shoulders heaved up and down in a shrug. 'It's up to the others to vote with their consciences.'

'Pah! That's exactly what I'm afraid of.' She pulled on her coat as an old blue van parked up outside. 'At least you'll have company while I'm gone,' she said, nodding towards Chloé and Stephanie who had got out of the van and were approaching the bar. Then, with one last look at Serge and Jacques, she blew a kiss in the vague direction of them all, and headed out of the door, a bitter wind biting at her the minute she got outside.

'Are you ready?' Véronique was sitting behind the wheel of her car.

'Yes,' said Josette, getting in beside her. 'And you have no idea how grateful I am that you're coming too.'

Véronique smiled and patted Josette on the leg before putting the car into gear. 'Let's see if we can't rescue Fogas,' she said as she pulled off, unaware of the two figures watching from the window, both pale faces fraught with concern.

'That's my girl,' muttered Serge Papon with pride.

'And mine too!' quipped Jacques.

They watched until the car's rear lights twisted around the bend, heading up towards the Romanesque church and the burnt-out post office. Then they settled impatiently in the inglenook. It was going to be a long evening.

'I'm sorry Madame, but I'm going to have to ask you to leave for a couple of minutes. Patient privacy and all that.'

Annie Estaque looked up at the tall doctor who'd just entered and was gesturing at the washbasin and sponge on the trolley he was pushing.

'No prrroblem. How long do you need?'

The question seemed to floor him, his eyes blinking above the mask.

'Erm . . . half an hour?'

Her eyebrows rose. Thirty minutes to wash a patient? Christian was big but he wasn't that big! And a doctor to do it, not a nurse? No wonder the health service was short of funds.

'Fine.' She picked up her bag, stroked Christian's cheek, and left. It was only when she was halfway down the corridor that something began to niggle her. That voice. Surely she knew it from somewhere?

Her thoughts were distracted by young Sophie Pujol who was standing further along the corridor in the doorway to a small ward, looking puzzled. René's niece, she'd turned into a fine woman and an even better nurse and Véronique had been relieved to see a familiar face taking care of Christian.

'Is everrrything all rrright, Sophie?' asked Annie.

'Yes, just going a bit mad. I left something here and now it's gone. Well, I think I left it here.' She laughed, a delightful sound after the sombre confines of Christian's room. 'It's been one of those days. How's my patient?'

'No change. He's being given a wash so I'm going to grrrab something to eat.'

'I can recommend the civet de porcelet. It's delicious. Bon appétit!'

Sophie disappeared back into the ward, scratching her head, while Annie wandered off towards the canteen, thinking that civet de porcelet sounded perfect, the anticipation of a good meal supplanting any notion of doctors with voices from the past.

'Christian, wake up!' Arnaud was leaning over the bed, a hand gently slapping his friend's pale face. 'Come on. You have to wake up.'

No response. Just the high-pitched accompaniment of the machines hooked up to the figure beneath the bedclothes and the muffled noise of conversation from the corridor.

He didn't have long. The nurse would go looking for the trolley that had mysteriously disappeared while she was in another ward. She was bound to find him. And the surgeon, if he had overcome his modesty at his state of undress, would be raising the alarm.

'Christian.' He spoke louder, mouth close to the farmer's ear. 'It's the council meeting tonight. Up in Fogas. If you care about your commune, you need to wake up.'

The monotonous pulse of the heart rate monitor didn't even vary. The man was beyond reach. Which meant that Fogas was beyond help.

'Merde!' Arnaud ripped off his mask in despair and shook the farmer gently by the shoulders. 'Come on! Wake up for God's sake.'

Christian didn't respond as the bed rocked under him, making the silver cross hanging from the bedpost twist and turn in the light.

Arnaud reached out to touch it. Véronique's. It had to be. She'd left it here to guard him. The tracker ran a dark finger over the tiny cross. Véronique. The woman who had turned him down. For Fogas. For Christian. And now she might lose both of them.

He grasped the cross in his hand and it came to him – the way to wake this slumbering giant.

'Christian,' he hissed, leaning down again. 'Are you listening? It's Arnaud Petit. I'm back. And if you don't wake up soon . . .' He bent even further, his lips close to the farmer's ear, making sure that his dire threats could be heard.

*

'If we're all here, we should make a start.' Pascal motioned for everyone to take a seat. He'd made the decision to hold the council session behind closed doors, decreeing that it would be faster that way and allow family and friends of Christian to resume their vigil at the hospital. So it was a small group of people who sat around the large table in the otherwise empty meeting room up in the town hall.

'Firstly, welcome to the new councillors.' He gestured towards Fatima and Véronique. 'And let it be noted in the minutes that our thoughts are with our absent deputy mayor, Christian Dupuy. We wish him a speedy recovery.'

'Amen,' said Josette while others leaned over to pass on their regards to Véronique.

'As you know, we've convened this evening to vote for the new mayor,' Pascal continued. 'And as the law stipulates, on such an occasion it is the oldest member of the council who must preside over events. So, Josette, you are our president for the duration of the vote. The floor is all yours.'

Josette cleared her throat and dropped her shaking hands onto her lap out of sight.

'Thanks, Pascal, for a dubious honour.'

The councillors laughed.

'Firstly, some regulations to remind you of.' Josette brandished a thick paperback, a copy of the Code Général, which laid out the rules that governing bodies across France had to adhere to, and she began to read. 'According to articles L2122-4 and L2122-7 of the Code Général, the ballot must be secret and the mayor must be elected by an absolute majority. If, after two rounds of voting, no candidate has obtained an absolute majority, then we will proceed to a final round whereby only a simple majority will be required to gain office. In the case that the election is tied after this third and final round, the oldest candidate will be declared mayor.'

Josette looked up from the book, giving the councillors a chance to digest the news. Especially those in Christian's camp. Because if the vote was still level at the end of the evening, Pascal, as the older of the two, would become mayor by default.

She caught Véronique's eye, the younger woman looking resolute, and then continued.

'So, I see no reason to delay this any longer. Bernard has distributed the papers and the envelopes. You will be called out one by one to bring your sealed envelope to the ballot box in front of me. Now, is everyone ready?'

Nine heads nodded.

'Right. In alphabetical order, Lucien Biros. Your vote please.'

Lucien stood and walked solemnly around the table to deliver his envelope.

'Christian Dupuy,' continued Josette, her voice stuttering slightly.

'Absent,' said Monique Sentenac, in her role as secretary.

'Véronique Estaque.'

Véronique stood, and with her back straight and her gaze fixed on Josette, she cast her vote, saying a silent prayer for Christian and for Fogas as it dropped into the box.

The first round of voting was underway.

Her purse. She'd left her purse on the table next to the bed. Foolish old woman. She'd got as far as the till with her tray of food and had been unable to pay.

Annoyed with herself beyond what was reasonable, Annie Estaque hurried back to the ward, and as she placed a hand on the door handle, through the glass she could see the doctor bent over his patient. The sponge and basin remained untouched on the trolley. Instead, he was dangling Véronique's cross from his hand as though trying to hypnotise an already comatose person. And he was no longer wearing his mask.

In fact, it was no doctor at all.

'Arrrnaud Petit!' she said on a gasp of surprise as she opened the door.

The big man glanced up at her, then quickly back down at the bed. And Annie had to grab hold of the chair next to her because it looked like . . . could it be? Christian Dupuy's eyelids were flickering.

The farmer was finally coming round.

22

'Christian!' Arnaud said, as the farmer's eyes slowly opened. 'That's it! Wake up!'

'You did it!' exclaimed Annie. 'We need to call the nurrrse and let herrr—'

'No!' Arnaud was across the room in two strides, closing the door behind a startled Annie. 'No doctors or nurses. We have to get him out of here.'

'What? Why—?'

'I don't have time to explain. You have to trust me, Annie. I'm doing this for Fogas.'

She looked up at him, the dark face so familiar, the intensity of his gaze no different. He was an incredible man. And he loved her daughter. Surely that meant he wouldn't do anything to hurt Véronique? Or Christian?

She glanced at the groggy figure in the bed, eyes unfocused, his mouth beginning to shape sounds that couldn't be heard.

'They'll neverrr let you take him out of herrre.'

Arnaud reached for the bag he'd been carrying and emptied it onto the bed, a strong scent of washing powder and mothballs rising from the contents. And Annie began to chuckle.

'Are all the votes in?' asked Josette.

Monique Sentenac nodded and passed the ballot box to Josette who upended it, spilling the envelopes onto the desk.

She picked one out, opened it and read aloud the name on the paper inside.

'Pascal Souquet.'

Monique made a mark on the notepad in front of her as Josette reached for another envelope.

'Christian Dupuy.'

Monique's pen moved again, this time to a different column.

'Pascal Souquet,' said Josette, already opening the next one. 'And Christian Dupuy.'

'We'll be here all night at this rate,' grumbled Geneviève Souquet, earning her a glare from René Piquemal.

'Christian Dupuy,' continued Josette, trying to keep her voice neutral.

Down at the other end of the table, Véronique was making no such effort. With every announcement of Christian's name, a smile ripped across her face. Only to be quashed the next moment.

'Pascal Souquet.'

'It's neck and neck,' muttered René, fingers tapping on the table. 'God, I could do with a cigarette.'

'Pascal Souquet.' A rustle of paper. 'Pascal Souquet.'

Véronique dug her nails into her palm. Five votes for Pascal. With only ten people voting, he needed just one more to have the majority. She glanced around the table: Bernard, René, Josette, herself. She knew there were four votes for Christian. But what about Monique Sentenac? Leaning towards the merger for economic reasons but a lifelong friend of the big farmer. How would she vote?

'Christian Dupuy. And the last one . . .'

Silence as Josette tore open the envelope. And then grinned in a very unpresidential way.

'Christian Dupuy. The ballot is tied. We will proceed to a second round.'

Véronique felt the air escape from her lungs. Monique had voted with them. But her joy was short-lived. For without a major change in the voting pattern, the office of mayor would be Pascal's at the end of the night, simply because of his age. It looked like Fogas would be lost on a technicality.

'Wherrre in God's name did you find this?' asked Annie, holding up an oversized dress in a garish material that she vaguely recognised.

Arnaud grinned. 'Let's just say I liberated it.'

'And that?' Annie's nose wrinkled as she pointed at a floppy hat reeking of camphor.

'Widow Loubet's wardrobe.'

With an appreciative cackle, Annie began pulling the dress down across Christian's body, the sharp smell of detergent as good as a dose of smelling salts for the befuddled farmer.

'Where am I?' he muttered, as he was manhandled into the outfit.

'In hospital,' said Annie. 'But we'rrre leaving soon. Do you feel up to that?'

She cast a worried eye over the farmer. Arnaud had convinced her that removing the various tubes and drips that had been tethering the patient to the bed wouldn't do any harm, but she wasn't totally convinced. Christian however, seemed to be getting sharper by the minute.

'Arnaud? You're back?' He focused on the large shape of the tracker who was busy unfolding something in the corner of the room.

'I'm back,' Arnaud said, placing a wheelchair by the bed and glancing up at the clock.

Christian ran a hand through his hair and encountered the bandage. 'What . . . ? I don't . . .'

'You were shot,' said Arnaud, leaning in to hold out an arm

and guide Christian into the wheelchair. 'That happened when you fell. Do you remember any of it?'

The farmer shook his head and instantly regretted it, pain skittering across his skull. 'No . . . Wait . . .' He frowned, hand dropping to his chest which was now covered in gaudy flowers. 'The quarry . . .' he whispered, eyes darting to the tracker. 'I was at the quarry . . .' Then a flash of concern lit his face. 'Véronique . . . Is she safe?'

Arnaud nodded, and gestured for Annie to check the corridor.

'She's up at the town hall for the council meeting. That's where we're going. So it's vital you remember what happened. In the meantime, I'm sorry my friend but until we're clear of the hospital, you have to pretend you're a woman.'

He placed the hat on the farmer's head, pulled his surgical mask back into place and turned to Annie.

'What do you think? Will we pass?'

Annie looked at the large lady in the chair and the concerned doctor standing behind her.

'If he keeps his chin down, maybe. Although Widow Loubet did have a bit of stubble I seem to rrrememberrr!'

Arnaud laughed, Christian groaned and Annie opened the door. They were heading for Fogas.

'Any news?' Jacques peered over Serge's shoulder at the silent mobile.

'Not a whisper.' The former mayor looked at the clock. 'They must be having a second round. Which has to be a good thing.'

'Mon Dieu, but this waiting is hard!'

Serge nodded.

The trill of the landline behind the bar startled the pair of them.

'News?' asked Jacques as Fabian stood from the table where

he'd been having his evening meal with Stephanie and Chloé and strode past the two ghosts to pick up the phone.

'Annie?' the Parisian said. 'Annie, slow down. I can't . . . You need what?'

A pause, the sound of rapid-fire speech from the other end and Fabian's eyebrows shot up.

'You're mad!' he exclaimed. 'But I'll be there as soon as I can. Just don't get into trouble.'

And he slammed down the phone.

'What's going on?' asked Stephanie.

'I need the keys to the van,' said Fabian.

'For what?'

'I can't explain. But I have to get to St Girons in a hurry.'

Stephanie was already standing, eyes on her husband, knowing this was serious.

'I'll drive,' she said, slipping on her coat.

'And I'm coming too!' said Chloé, running for the door.

'No!' Fabian's voice was firm. 'You both have to stay here. Haring around on dark roads is no place for a child or a woman in your condition.'

Stephanie and Chloé wheeled round, hands on hips, chins raised, and Serge chuckled. The Parisian had just made a fatal mistake.

'I'm pregnant, Fabian. Not sick.'

'And I'm not a child,' added Chloé.

'Besides,' continued Stephanie, eyes flashing. 'You drive like a girl!'

'Maman! That's sexist.'

'Sorry, Chloé, you're right.' Stephanie grinned. 'He drives like an old man!'

Chloé frowned, not sure this was any less sexist but at least it wasn't denigrating her so she let it pass.

'So,' continued Stephanie, dangling the car keys from her

fingers. 'Shall we get going? You can tell us what's happening on the way.'

She turned on her heel, Chloé following, and the two Morvan women hurried for the door. Fabian brought up the rear, muttering prayers that the next person to join his family would be male. Just to even things up.

Minutes later, Stephanie's van was roaring down the road. Lights still blazing, the bar and its ghostly occupants were abandoned.

'Whatever was all that about?' demanded Jacques as he watched the van disappear in the distance beyond the street light outside the Auberge.

Serge grinned, rubbing his hands together. 'I don't know,' he said. 'But something tells me things are about to get interesting.'

'Well,' said Jacques, watching the steady sweep of the second hand on the clock. 'Let's just hope it's in time.'

'He's on his way,' said Annie, putting her phone away.

'Good.' Arnaud readjusted Christian's hat which had fallen back, revealing too much of the farmer's face. 'Now for stage two.'

They'd made the first leg of the journey, getting down the corridor unseen, but as they reached the corner, Annie had spotted Nurse Pujol and the three fugitives had had to take refuge in the ladies' toilets.

Which is when they'd realised that they needed transport back up to the town hall.

'Fabian is coming for us?' asked a still-woozy Christian.

Arnaud nodded. 'But never you mind about that. Just concentrate on the quarry. On what happened up there. Okay?'

Christian frowned. 'It's so hazy. Apart from . . .'

'What? Come on, Christian, try.'

'A boar's head,' said the farmer, looking up at the tracker with bemusement. 'I remember seeing a boar's head.'

'You saw a boarrr?' asked Annie. 'Beforrre you werrre shot?'

'No. Not a boar, just the head. It was right in front of me . . . It was . . . on the gun!' Christian snapped upright in the wheelchair, the hat tipping off him again. 'The gun,' he breathed. 'I can remember the gun. A pistol, ugly little thing, with a boar's head on the handle.'

Arnaud's lips formed a thin line.

'Does that mean anything to you?' asked Annie, as she placed the hat back on the farmer.

'Oh yes,' said Arnaud. 'That means a lot. Keep it up, Christian. You're doing well. Now, let's get out of here.'

'So the results for the second round of voting . . .'

Josette stretched for the pile of envelopes once more and Véronique clasped her hands under the table.

'Please God,' the postmistress murmured.

'Pascal Souquet,' started Josette. 'Christian Dupuy.'

And Véronique had a terrible feeling of déjà vu.

'Clear?'

Annie nodded and waved them out of the ladies, the doctor and his rather large female patient with the floppy hat obscuring her face.

'Not much furrrtherrr,' Annie muttered as they caught up with her in the corridor. 'Two morrre corrrnerrrs and we'll be at the exit.'

'Good,' said Arnaud. 'And where have you asked Fabian to pick us up?'

'At the farrr end of the carrr parrrk. It's darrrkerrr. I thought that was best.'

Arnaud nodded. 'We just have to get there—' He stopped abruptly, letting out a smothered curse.

Nurse Sophie Pujol had just turned the corner and was coming towards them.

'So who are we going to rescue?' asked Stephanie, as she threw the van around a bend, taking the liberty of crossing the white line as she did so.

'Christian,' muttered Fabian, peeking through his fingers, which were clamped across his terrified eyes.

'Christian?' Chloé squeaked. 'He's awake?'

'Seems so. Arnaud is with him.'

'Arnaud Petit?' Stephanie took her eyes off the road to give her husband an incredulous look and the van swerved across the tarmac towards the river before its course was hastily corrected. Fabian closed the gaps between his fingers, deciding he preferred not to see his death coming.

'He's back,' said Chloé, unperturbed by her mother's driving. 'He's come home to save Fogas.'

'You knew he was here?' This time Stephanie's gaze went to the rear seats where Chloé was sitting, taking the van towards the rock face on the other side. 'And you didn't tell me?'

Fabian groaned, restraining himself from reaching out to rectify the weaving path of the van. He'd done that once before and the reaction from the driver hadn't been great.

'Stephanie, please,' he begged, uncovering his face so she could see the green tinge she was inflicting on him. 'Just drive. We can talk about this when we get there.'

And with a flounce of red curls, Stephanie pressed her foot further on the accelerator, propelling the van into the darkness. Fabian shielded his eyes once more.

*

'So, with five votes each and one absentee, the second round is also tied.'

A suppressed groan could be heard from the far end of the table at Josette's formal announcement. Perhaps Geneviève Souquet had got it right, thought Véronique. They were going to be here all night.

'Which means, we have a third and final ballot. And remember, a simple majority now would be sufficient to obtain office. I must also remind you that a third tie will result in the oldest nominee being elected mayor.'

Josette's words hung like a sword over those in the camp of Christian Dupuy. The farmer was going to lose thanks to a difference in years. Fogas would be merged simply because Christian was born too late.

'May I interrupt?' René's hand was raised in the air.

'Of course, René. What is it?'

'A break. I need a bloody break. And if anyone has a drink on them, I'll kiss them.'

Bernard produced a hip flask from his back pocket and puckered his lips and the tension in the room was broken by laughter.

'A break sounds like a good idea,' said Josette with a smile. 'Let's take fifteen minutes. But I must ask that you respect the confidential nature of this meeting which has yet to conclude by refraining from contacting anyone outside this council.'

With a scrape of chairs, the councillors headed for the door.

'Annie! How was the civet de porcelet?' Nurse Sophie Pujol was advancing on them with a smile.

Annie tried to calm her thudding heart, marshalling her lips to speak without a stutter.

'Verrry tasty,' she said, keeping her eyes on the young

nurse in the hopes of holding her attention and allowing Arnaud to sneak past with Christian. But Sophie was too sharp for that.

'And who's the lucky lady getting assistance from this lovely doctor?' asked the nurse, bending towards the slumped figure in the wheelchair and getting a blast of camphor and savon de Marseille from the folds of the flowery material.

'Solange Loubet,' replied Annie without a pause, sticking as close to the truth as possible. 'Frrrom Picarrrets.'

It was enough to make Sophie look up at her and away from the wheelchair. 'Old Widow Loubet?' she whispered, eyes puzzled. 'The mother of the man who used to own the Auberge in La Rivière? I thought she was . . . dead?'

Annie shook her head firmly while Arnaud shot her daggers over the nurse's head.

'Not a bit of it. She's verrry much alive as you can see. But she's drrreadfully deaf. And a bit blind. She's been in to see Chrrristian.'

'Oh!' The nurse nodded, her attention back on the slouched form in the hideous dress. 'Bonsoir, Madame Loubet,' she called out loudly, not bending too close thanks to the old lady's unique perfume.

A muffled response came from beneath the floppy hat.

'And bonsoir, doctor,' added Sophie with a flirtatious smile, hand held out. 'I don't think we've met.'

A streak of red stole above the doctor's mask as he reluctantly took the nurse's hand in his.

'Bonsoir,' he murmured. 'I'm new. From . . . Spain.'

'Spain? I didn't know we had a doctor from Spain.' Sophie frowned and then grinned, before launching into rapid fire Spanish. And the doctor's Adam's apple bobbed frantically up and down his throat.

'Sorrrry Sophie,' said Annie, cutting across the young girl

in mid-linguistic flow. 'We have to go. I need to get Solange home. She gets unbearrrable if she goes past herrr mealtime.'

'Oh, okay. Are you coming back later to see Christian?'

It was Annie's time to falter. 'Errr . . . prrrobably . . . I'll see. Au rrrevoirrr.'

'*Adiós*!' said Sophie with a smile just for the doctor.

And the three of them scuttled off, Arnaud pushing the wheelchair so fast that Annie had to half-jog to keep up, the weight of Sophie Pujol's stare on her back all the way.

'Solange Loubet!' hissed Arnaud as they turned the corner and saw the exit ahead of them. 'You told her we were taking home a dead woman?'

'It was all I could think of!' retorted Annie. 'And at least I didn't claim to be frrrom a countrrry whose language I don't even speak!'

Arnaud growled. 'It's where I was before here and I can speak enough to get by. But how should I know the bloody nurse was fluent?'

'Herrr surrrname might have been a clue!' shot back Annie.

'Oh really? Does that mean you're a fluent Spanish speaker too, Madame *Estaque*?'

Annie opened her mouth to retort but was cut off by a large hand flying up from beneath the folds of floral fabric.

'Quiet, both of you!' Christian Dupuy sat upright in the chair and pushed back his hat. 'I think I know who shot me!'

Across the dark ribbon of river from the épicerie, up over the silent fields washed silver in the moonlight, in one of the cluster of houses that formed the heart of Sarrat, Henri Dedieu was busy cleaning his guns.

He should throw it away, he thought, rubbing a rag over the pistol, the boar's head resting comfortably in the palm of his hand. It was traceable. Stupidly so.

He hadn't meant to fire it. It had merely been a prop – a touch of theatre, easy to wield and a tribute to his ancestors. The rifle had been the real weapon, a hunting gun which wouldn't raise eyebrows if it were involved in an accident in the forest. Instead that buffoon had lunged at him and forced his hand, the pistol going off as they struggled.

If only it had put a bullet through Christian Dupuy's heart and killed the man as had been intended.

How long did he have? No doubt the gendarmes would eventually get round to some forensics and while they didn't have the cartridge case, thanks to his presence of mind in picking it up as he fled, they would have the bullet. From a handgun. That would set them thinking.

What they also had, should Christian Dupuy emerge from his coma, was a witness.

Henri Dedieu laid down the rag and began reassembling the pistol. He clicked the fully loaded magazine back into place, gave the gun one last wipe with a cloth, and laid it gently on the table, his fingers tracing the snarling boar on the handgrip.

Tomorrow he would decide its fate. Once he knew the outcome of this evening's mayoral election up in Fogas. It would break his heart to get rid of a family heirloom but if it meant securing the future of a reunited Sarrat, then it would be worth the sacrifice. It had already served its purpose.

His mobile sounded and he glanced at the screen: a text from Pascal Souquet. After two ties, the vote was going to a third round.

Henri Dedieu sat back in his chair and smiled. Fogas was as good as his. Finally. And perhaps his inherited pistol might have one last task to fulfil. Because, when the merger was formalised in a month's time, the soon-to-be-elected mayor of the commune across the river would be superfluous to requirements.

And Henri Dedieu had no time for anything that had outlived its usefulness.

23

'We're here!' Stephanie jerked the van left into the hospital grounds, pools of light cast across the tarmac by sporadic street lamps. 'Can you see Annie?'

Fabian peeled his fingers from his eyes and scanned the darkened car park. 'There, under that tree.' He pointed through the gloom at two people sheltering under a broad oak some distance from the hospital entrance, a slumped figure in a wheelchair between them.

'And that's Arnaud,' shouted Chloé as they got closer. 'Why's he dressed like a doctor?'

'I've no idea,' muttered Stephanie, parking alongside the threesome. 'And who the hell is the old lady in the hat?'

The side door screeched open and a familiar face appeared, teeth white against brown skin.

'Bonsoir!' said Arnaud, helping Annie into the back. 'Fabian, can you give me a hand?'

But Fabian was already out of the van, peering at the person in the wheelchair and holding his nose against the odour of mothballs that was assailing him.

'Christian?' he asked. 'Why are you wearing a dress?'

'It's Grand-mère Rogalle's dress!' shrieked Chloé in delight, recognising a regular feature on the Rogalle washing line.

Fabian looked even more disconcerted.

'Just help me up,' Christian growled. 'We can talk on the way.'

And with two firm sets of hands on his backside, Christian

was shoved onto the front seat, losing his hat in the process. Arnaud jumped up next to him, leaving Fabian to hop in the back with the folded-up wheelchair. The Parisian barely had the door closed before Stephanie was wheeling the van around and screeching away, the one-way system taking her past the front door of the hospital in a roar of tired exhaust.

Nurse Sophie Pujol was taking a sneaky cigarette break round the side of the building. She was smoking a Gauloise, not her normal brand, but thanks to Oncle René's recent sudden abstention from the habit, she had acquired three of the familiar blue packets and had decided to give them a try.

She inhaled and almost coughed her tonsils out. Strong, so strong. She took another drag, her eyes on the ex-police van that was racing towards her in a cacophony of splutters and rattles. Through an exhalation of smoke, she spotted the handsome Spanish doctor sitting on the front seat, mask off. He looked vaguely familiar now she could see his face. And next to him, Old Widow Loubet, only, without her hat, and in the yellow glow of the street light, she looked strangely like . . .

'Merde!' Sophie threw the cigarette to the ground unfinished and ran for the hospital door. She had a sneaking suspicion that one of her patients had just absconded.

Standing on the steps of the town hall, the night sky above him, Pascal Souquet should have been feeling victorious. He was going to win the vote. Two tied rounds already, no one looking likely to change sides, and age, for once, a benefit. Fogas was his.

Funny, he thought, as he stared at the silent mobile in his hand, how all he felt was afraid. There was so much in the balance while Christian Dupuy remained alive. And now Henri Dedieu was ignoring him, his text eliciting no response.

'Disobeying the rules, Pascal?' Fatima was next to him, pointing at the mobile with a taunting smile. 'Or are you more afraid of *him* than Josette?'

'No . . . I wasn't . . . it's not like that . . .'

She leaned in, her eyes savagely bright in the light streaming out of the open town hall doors. 'Don't lie to me,' she hissed. 'I'm about to get you elected mayor. Remember that.'

Pascal swallowed. 'I was checking the weather . . . for tomorrow. I thought we might go somewhere, take a picnic maybe . . . celebrate.'

Fatima's eyes narrowed to slits, her cheeks no more than hollows in the shadows, and a wave of revulsion passed over the interim mayor. 'That would be nice,' she said, studying his face, looking for the deception.

'I'm glad you think so, Madame Mayor.'

A feral smile appeared and she laughed. 'I like the sound of that!'

'We're reconvening.' Monique Sentenac was at the top of the steps, calling them in.

'Come on. Let's go get you elected.' Fatima started towards the town hall.

She doesn't have a clue, Pascal thought, as he followed his wife towards his destiny. She had no idea what he'd sacrificed for Fogas – for his future. And she had no perception of just how dangerous a man the mayor of Sarrat was.

Pascal had chosen sides the moment he'd stolen Véronique's phone. It was too late now to change.

Wondering how soon he could call his lawyers in St Girons and have them draw up divorce papers, he took his seat back at the table. In less than twenty minutes it would all be over. His marriage along with it.

*

'*Henri Dedieu* shot you?' Stephanie stared at the pale form of Christian Dupuy sitting next to her, the van veering across the road in response.

'Please,' begged Fabian from the rear, one hand covering his eyes, the other clutching his stomach which was threatening to revolt thanks to the violent twisting and turning and the reek of savon de Marseille and camphor. 'Can you save the storytelling until we get there?'

'*If* we get therrre,' muttered Annie, sandwiched between the Parisian and Chloé.

'On purpose?' Stephanie had her focus back on the way ahead, flinging the van around the roundabout at Kerkabanac and onto the road that led to La Rivière.

Christian nodded weakly. 'Definitely.'

'Why?' asked Chloé.

'Because—'

'Enough!' interrupted Arnaud. 'Let the man rest. He's just woken up from a coma and he's going to have a lot of talking to do when we get to the town hall. If the meeting is still going on, that is.' He looked pointedly at the driver. 'Can this clapped out piece of rust go any faster?'

Stephanie threw the tracker an evil look at the disrespect and then stomped her foot on the accelerator.

'Oh God,' moaned Fabian as he was thrown to the side on the bend, Annie's elbows digging into his ribs. 'That's done it.'

The van roared up the road. Still a long way from Fogas . . .

They heard it coming up the valley – the engine straining, the screech of tyres down at the bend before the Auberge.

'It's them!' said Jacques, pointing at the dark shape passing under the distant street lamps.

'And? Who's with them?' Serge had his face pressed against the cold glass of the window.

'I don't know. Can you see?'

'Stephanie's driving. I can tell that much.'

'But who's next to her?'

The vehicle lumbered over the small bridge and, without any indication, took the sharp turn that led up to Fogas, allowing the light on the corner to fleetingly unmask the occupants of the ex-police van.

'Arnaud,' said Jacques, excitedly. 'Arnaud Petit is with them.'

But Serge was concentrating on the other front seat passenger. 'Christian,' he murmured, a smile lighting his face. 'Christian Dupuy.'

Jacques was shaking his head. 'You're mistaken. It was a woman. I'd stake my life on it.'

A rumble of laughter prefaced the reply. 'It's a good job you don't have one to stake, my old friend,' said Serge as he thumped Jacques on the back. 'Because I'd know that face anywhere. Christian Dupuy is heading to the meeting.'

'But . . . but . . .' spluttered Jacques. 'Why was he wearing a dress?'

'Christian Dupuy.'

'Absent.'

'Véronique Estaque.'

Véronique rose slowly and walked towards Josette, envelope in hand. How she wanted to prolong this moment, to stall the third and final round in the vain hope of changing the inevitable outcome. Which was ludicrous. There was no way of stopping this now. Tears flooding her eyes, she dropped the envelope into the ballot box and glanced at Josette.

'We tried,' murmured the older woman with a wan smile.

It was no consolation.

'Philippe Galy.'

As the beekeeper strode forward to cast his vote with confidence in the future, Véronique took her seat and briefly found herself thinking the unthinkable. That perhaps it would be better if Christian never awoke from his coma. Because the prospect of telling him the fate that had befallen Fogas in his absence was just too awful to contemplate.

'Bernard Mirouze.'

Another futile blue envelope fluttered into the box, leaving six to go. And then that would be it. Fogas would be no more.

'Would it help if we all got out and pushed?' muttered Arnaud caustically as the blue van struggled and strained on the steepest part of the incline up to Fogas.

Stephanie didn't even look at him. She was concentrating too hard on keeping the tarmac under the tyres on each bend as the road twisted up to the mountain village.

'Come on,' murmured Annie from the back, eyes on her watch. 'Come on.' A small hand slipped through hers, squeezing it reassuringly.

'We'll make it,' said Chloé with the confidence of youth.

The five adults around her were not so sure.

'Fatima Souquet.'

Véronique rested her head on her arms, aware she was signalling defeat. But there was no purpose in pretending otherwise. She knew the content of the ballot box. If only they could stop it now. Because with seven votes in, Christian would be leading by five votes to two, all of his contingent having had their say. But, with the final three votes going to Fatima, Geneviève and Pascal, the Souquets were about to even the score and give Pascal the victory, thanks to a quirk in the law.

'Geneviève Souquet.'

Pascal's cousin from Toulouse flounced forwards, provoking

a groan from René Piquemal, and it was all Véronique could do not to walk out of there, to leave the town hall and Fogas and never look back.

She'd let it down. Let her father down. And she wasn't sure she could stay here once Pascal was in charge.

'Go go go!' Annie was shouting from the back as Chloé slid the door open and tumbled out into the car park, short legs already racing for the town hall steps. 'Stop them, Chloé!'

Stephanie was close behind her, long legs covering the ground quickly, red hair whipping around her face while Fabian and Arnaud helped Christian into the wheelchair.

'Come on!' yelled Annie, already at the door as the two men pushed the farmer at a running pace, Christian hanging onto the sides of the chair, his dress blowing up in a most unlady-like manner.

But Chloé was ahead of them all, skidding across the tiled hallway and racing for the closed double doors, her heart thumping. She slammed both hands against the wood and flung the doors open.

'Pascal Souquet.' A small sigh escaped Josette's lips on the last syllable but she was beyond impartiality. She knew that no prolonged soak in a bathtub would ever make her feel clean again after the role she had been forced to play in tonight's fiasco.

She'd been the one to oversee the demise of their commune.

Jacques would never survive this. Nor Serge. In fact, life in the bar and épicerie would become unbearable.

She fixed her eyes on the slim figure of the interim mayor as he advanced towards her, a smirk already playing on his lips.

'The last one, I believe, Josette,' he said, pausing dramatically before placing his envelope in the box. And as Pascal Souquet's vote fell softly onto the others, the doors at the end of the room crashed open and Chloé Morvan came running in.

'Christian's here!' she screamed. 'He's come to vote!'

Mayhem. Véronique shot out of her chair. René Piquemal made a dive for the ballot box. As did Pascal Souquet, the two of them wrestling over it. And ten voices started shouting.

'He can't vote, it's too late—'

'Of course he can vote—'

'But he's been listed as absent—'

'That's irrelevant—'

'Hurry, hurry,' yelled Chloé back down the corridor and Stephanie, Annie, Fabian and Arnaud Petit burst into the room pushing a wheelchair. Sitting in the wheelchair, face grey and head bandaged, was Christian Dupuy. And he was wearing a dress.

It was enough to bring some sort of order to the chaos.

'Christian!' Véronique covered the floor in a matter of seconds, her hands holding his face, her lips kissing him. 'Oh, Christian.'

'God, it's good to see you,' murmured Christian, kissing her back.

Arnaud coughed gently and tapped his watch.

'Yes, sorry. I need to vote,' said the farmer, gently untangling himself from Véronique's embrace.

'You can't vote,' said Pascal Souquet, arms still locked around the ballot box and part of René Piquemal, and his voice squeaking with apprehension. 'You've already been declared absent.'

Arnaud growled and took a step towards the interim mayor but Christian held him back.

'I think, Pascal, when everyone hears what I have to say, they will want me to vote, don't you?'

The hard edge to the normally placid farmer's voice sent a current of tension through the room and Pascal's grip on his future slipped, René staggering back under the sudden transfer of weight.

'What do you mean, Christian?' Fatima had moved to the front of the straggle of bemused councillors, a disbelieving look on her face. 'You've already been declared absent. What on earth could you have to say that would persuade us to override the regulations of the Code Général and grant you a vote?'

Christian eased up out of the wheelchair, resting an arm on Véronique as he walked towards his co-councillors. 'For a start, I think Philippe would be interested to know that there's new information surrounding the bear attack on his beehives,' he said, glancing over at the beekeeper. 'Information from a report which suggests it was fabricated.'

'You mean someone . . . ?' Philippe shook his head, refusing to believe it.

'That's exactly what I mean. Someone destroyed your hives on purpose. The same someone who tried to cover his tracks by stealing the original report into the attack, not knowing that Serge had made a copy. Someone,' continued Christian, switching his gaze onto Pascal Souquet, 'in this very room.'

'Pascal? You can't be serious . . . ?' Fatima stalled and turned to her husband who was now as grey-faced as the farmer. 'Pascal?'

'I've no idea what he's talking about,' said the interim mayor.

Christian's eyes narrowed. 'Are you denying involvement in the incidents last summer? Even though we have video footage of you taking bear fur from a trap in the forest? Fur which was then used to simulate attacks here and in Sarrat.'

A gasp from Fatima and a murmur of disquiet rumbled through the room.

'I don't believe you,' hissed Pascal. 'This is all conjecture.'

'That's hardly a robust denial,' said Christian.

'But why would he do that?' asked Lucien Biros, still trying to defend his former leader. 'What possible motive would he have?'

Christian smiled. 'Greed. Ambition.' He shrugged, the ideas alien to him. 'He'd been promised the world by someone. And all he had to do was one simple thing.'

'What?'

'Deliver Fogas to them.'

A buzz of reaction rose from the group.

'Are you saying . . . ?' Philippe broke off and stared at Pascal while Christian nodded.

'Yes, Philippe. The bear attacks were staged. The bear at the quarry was deliberately killed. And chaos was brought upon all of us, including the brutal robbery at Véronique's flat last winter which left her with a broken arm, just so Fogas would be merged with Sarrat. As for the reward for this treachery?' Christian turned to Pascal. 'Perhaps you'd like to tell them?'

But he didn't get the chance. Fatima rounded on her husband.

'You believed him? You really believed that bastard Henri Dedieu would make you mayor of a reunified Sarrat?'

'He would have!' shouted Pascal, finger pointing at the group before him. 'You're all so behind the times. You can't prevent the changes that are coming. Henri Dedieu saw that. So did I. And if it hadn't been for you—' He glared at Fatima. 'You and your bloody SOS Fogas. You ruined everything!'

Fatima reeled back as though slapped. 'You knew?' she whispered.

'Oh yes,' sneered Pascal. 'But I let Dedieu think it was her!' He pointed at Véronique.

'You mean . . .' Véronique was working it out. 'I was burgled and ended up with a broken arm because . . . ?' She glanced over at Fatima who was staring at her husband, mouth agape.

'That's not all,' said Christian. 'Pascal is also possibly guilty of attempted murder. Am I right?'

Pascal didn't reply, the remaining colour drained from his face.

'You see,' continued Christian, 'I overheard something I shouldn't have. A conversation involving Henri Dedieu in which he was planning the future. One in a new-look Sarrat, a much bigger Sarrat. One where Fogas didn't exist. Only thing was, it didn't include you, Pascal. He was happy to embroil you in his sordid schemes but he had no intention of making you mayor.'

'You're lying!' hissed Pascal.

Christian shook his head. 'If I were lying, why would Henri Dedieu have shot me?'

The words fell into a pool of silence. And then everyone started talking and commotion ensued.

Making the most of the uproar, Pascal made a lunge for the door, knocking René over in the process. The plumber fell heavily, smashing the ballot box, and in a tangle of arms and legs, took out Philippe Galy and Fabian Servat. Amongst the shouts and cries and writhing bodies, Pascal leapt over the empty chairs and was at the exit, swinging a door closed behind him as he fled. All the while, Arnaud Petit watched events from the side with a satisfied smile.

'Pascal!' shrieked Chloé at the passive tracker. 'He's running away. Get after him!'

'Don't worry,' said Arnaud, resting a hand on the panicked child's head. 'He won't get far.' And after a quick conversation with Bernard Mirouze during which a key exchanged hands, the tracker slipped out of the door and merged with the shadows, leaving the room in chaos behind him.

'Order, order,' Josette shouted, standing on a chair so she could see everyone as she tried to bring the meeting back under control. 'Quiet please!'

A hush descended as those knocked over in the dramatic escape picked themselves up off the floor.

'In light of Christian's revelations,' she continued, 'we need to decide what we do next,'

'Call the gendarmes?' suggested Fabian, ever the pragmatist.

But his aunt, embracing her role as president of the council session, wasn't about to let the mayoral election be derailed by such trivialities as the police.

'Yes, yes, all in good time. First we need to sort the matter of the vote.' Josette directed her gaze at the nine elected councillors before letting it rest on Fatima Souquet. 'As far as I see it, we can either adhere to the official regulations and count the votes already cast.' She pointed at the envelopes littering the floor. 'Or, we can allow Christian to have his say.' She held up a blank ballot paper.

The councillors looked at each other. Everyone knew the situation as it stood. Those ten envelopes on the floor would deliver Pascal as the mayor of Fogas thanks to his seniority. With one more vote, however . . .

'Christian should vote,' said Philippe Galy.

'Agreed,' said Lucien Biros.

'I don't care either way,' snapped Geneviève Souquet, picking up her coat and handbag and stalking towards the exit. 'I'm resigning.'

René shrugged, watching her go, then turned to Pascal's wife who, for the first time in Fogas memory, looked fragile. 'What about you, Fatima?' he asked gently. 'What do you think we should do?'

Fatima blinked, shook her head as though clearing it, and then looked at Christian, her face resolute once more. 'There's a time and place for the Code Général. I don't think this is one of them. Go ahead and vote.'

And with a trembling hand, Christian took the ballot paper Josette was holding out, put a mark next to his name, and elected himself mayor to the applause of all those present.

'Seriously,' said Fabian, cutting through the poignancy of the moment as Fogas began a new era. 'It's about time we called the police.'

Run. Where to? Someone would have called the police. They might even be at his house already. Taking his chances, Pascal pelted along the road, down the hill and in through his front door. Up the stairs two at a time, he reached the bedroom and started flinging clothes in a bag, fear gnawing at his guts.

Run. His only option. They had a copy of the report. That bloody report which would see him sent to prison. Damn Serge Papon! Even from the grave the former mayor had managed to defeat him.

Run. Down the stairs, stumbling, tripping, bag banging against his leg. Car keys. He spun round, back up to the bedroom and grabbed the key ring from the bedside table. With no thought as to where he was heading, Pascal Souquet was running for his life.

He slipped the key into the lock and turned it quietly.

'Is that you, Bernard?' A woman's voice. The tracker smiled. He hadn't been expecting that.

'Bernard?' This time the question was accompanied by a familiar bark, the patter of paws and then Serge the beagle had his nose pressed into the tracker's hand.

'Good boy,' he said softly as he ruffled the floppy ears.

When he lifted his gaze, a robust woman with a fearsome

expression was standing in front of him, a large cleaver in her right hand.

'Who the hell are you?' she asked.

The tracker took a step back and raised his hands. 'Arnaud Petit,' he said, watching the knife. 'I'm a friend of Bernard's. I've come to collect something.'

Agnès lowered her weapon, her face relaxing into a smile. 'Ah, the mysterious Arnaud Petit. I've heard all about you.'

She stood aside and gestured him into the kitchen, watching the silken movement of his body as he passed. So this was the man, the one who had her Bernard running all over the place doing odd errands. She let her eyes follow him as far as the back door, revelling in the muscles, the long hair, the bronzed skin. Then he turned, catching her in his dark gaze, and she understood.

This was a man to be followed. And he'd chosen her Bernard as his deputy. Flushed with pride, she showed him out to the shed where Bernard had left everything ready.

'So, wait a minute,' René was saying. 'Fatima was SOS Fogas?'

'And that's why my flat was burgled!' stated Véronique.

'And Henri Dedieu and Pascal destroyed my hives!' said Philippe Galy.

'And where the hell are the police?' asked Fabian.

'Mon Dieu, I can't put all this in the minutes,' muttered Monique Sentenac whose hand was flying across the paper as she tried to keep up with the outburst of conversation following Christian's election. The farmer was surrounded by well-wishers and was being faced with a barrage of questions as the councillors of Fogas tried to make sense of what had happened.

'Please,' said the newly elected mayor, shuddering under the enthusiastic back slaps, his energy slipping by the second. 'Please. I need to say something while I still can.'

The room fell quiet and he turned to them all. 'Seeing as we've dispensed with bureaucratic conventions for the time being, instead of holding a formal vote, I would like to propose René as my first deputy.'

'Seconded,' said Philippe Galy and a loud shout of agreement met his words.

'And as my second deputy, Fatima Souquet.' Christian paused to allow his suggestion to sink in. 'I think, after all we've learned tonight, she is the ideal choice. Without her brilliant website and her constant undermining of the opposition, Fogas would have been merged last year.'

'Seconded,' said René Piquemal to unanimous approval, a pale Fatima accepting her unexpected appointment with a sharp tilt of her head.

'And finally,' Christian turned to face Véronique and then with some difficulty and a lot of wincing, got down on one knee before her, his dress billowing out around him.

'Véronique Estaque,' he said, gazing up at the woman he loved, whose fingers were fidgeting with the bare skin of her neck. 'You know how much you mean to me. You're my entire life. But you also know I take my council responsibilities seriously. And as mayor, I have a duty to look out for this commune. So . . .' he fixed her with a roguish grin from beneath his bandages. 'How would you like to help me increase the population of Fogas?'

Véronique blinked. 'You mean . . . ?'

'I'm asking you to be my wife.'

Véronique's hands flew to her mouth, Annie let out a cry, Chloé started jumping up and down and René was beaming. It was only Josette who noticed the farmer, eyes closing, head swaying.

'Christian, are you okay?' she asked.

But it was too late. Without hearing his true love's answer,

Christian Dupuy slumped to the floor in a graceful flutter of floral fabric.

His car. He hadn't noticed it when he'd run past and into the house. But now he could see. Two of the tyres had been slashed.

In the distance he could hear sirens. The police? He had no choice. He would have to run.

Crossing the road, he headed down the alleyway towards the orchards and the path that led across the valley to Picarets. From there he could drop down to the main road, hitch a lift into St Girons and be on the bus out of the town by the morning. After that . . .

He refused to dwell on the answer, lurching into the orchards instead, a faint smell of blossom greeting him, the trees ethereal in the moonlight. Beneath them, however, the path plunged into night. Heels clicking on stones, Pascal Souquet hurried along into the dark. He didn't notice the tree trunk beside him morphing into a more human shape. He didn't hear the light swish of air as the dart was released. And when it hit him, he cursed the mosquitoes, not thinking it was way too early. Then his knees buckled, his limbs betrayed him and the former interim mayor sank to the damp earth.

'Jesus,' muttered the figure standing over him as a second, more rotund, shape emerged panting from the direction of the road. 'How much tranquiliser did you put in this?'

A shrug of rounded shoulders. 'I wanted to make sure he didn't get away.'

White teeth flashed and a soft laugh disturbed the silence. Then a muscular arm slapped the smaller man on the back. 'You did well. I couldn't have done this without you.'

And Bernard Mirouze thought his heart would burst with joy.

*

'Where's Arnaud?' asked Véronique, kneeling down beside the comatose farmer. 'We need to get Christian back to hospital.'

'He left.' Chloé pointed at the open door.

'We'll just have to go without him,' said Annie, beckoning René and Philippe forward to help.

'Where's bloody Bernard when you need him?' muttered the plumber, placing one of Christian's arms around his shoulders. 'Always shirking, that one.'

'On three,' said Véronique. 'And be gentle! One, two, three . . .'

With grunts and groans, the mayor of Fogas was lifted back into his wheelchair.

'Sorry, Josette,' said Véronique, already hurrying Christian towards the door. 'I won't be able to drop you home.'

'I can give her a lift,' Stephanie volunteered before turning to Josette. 'As long as you don't mind a bit of a wait. The gendarmes have just arrived and seeing as Fabian called them . . .' She threw an affectionate look at her husband who was in the doorway, his face lit up by the flash of blue lights.

'I'm in no rush,' said Josette. 'It's not as if anyone's sitting up for me—'

And that's when she remembered. The two men who *were* sitting up. Waiting for news.

As the Estaque women wheeled the newly-elected but unconscious mayor out of the town hall and two gendarmes came rushing in, Josette approached her nephew.

'Oh, Fabian,' she said, placing a hand on his arm and doing her best to look bewildered. 'Can I borrow your phone? I seem to have mislaid mine.'

Fabian rolled his eyes and handed over his mobile to his scatty aunt. Caught up in official police business, it was some hours before he thought to check what she'd sent. When he did and saw that she had texted herself, it did nothing to restore his faith in her sanity.

'It's beeping!' Jacques jumped off his bar stool and pointed at the phone.

'A text,' said Serge, leaning in over the screen.

'Well . . . ?'

Serge looked up, eyes misted over, and Jacques grinned.

'He did it?'

'Yes. Christian is our new mayor. And . . .' Serge stuttered, his throat suddenly constricted, a hand wiping at his eyes. 'He proposed. He asked Véronique to marry him!'

Jacques collapsed back on his stool, an inane smile on his face. It was almost too much to take in – the new baby on the way, a marriage coming up, and Fogas finally safe.

'This place is amazing,' he said as his friend sat next to him, the two of them happily staring out of the window into the dark. 'I never want to live anywhere else.'

And Serge Papon nodded his agreement.

24

Nurse Sophie Pujol had worked a double shift, a late followed by an early. Despite the added nicotine kick of Oncle René's Gauloises, she was bone tired and irritable. But even so, as she approached the ward at the far end of the corridor as dawn began to break, she could feel her lips curving into a smile.

What a carry on. A patient smuggled out of hospital so he could vote in an election that made him mayor and bring to justice the man who had shot him. The *Gazette Ariégeoise* would fill three weeks' papers with the story. And she'd been part of it, albeit unwittingly.

She paused at the door, peering in through the glass to see the postmistress of Fogas asleep in her chair, head leaning on the bed. While the mayor of Fogas was lying in the bed, his eyes just beginning to open.

Sophie Pujol turned away. She'd give them a few moments and then check how he was. From what she'd heard, they had a lot to talk about.

'Bonjour!' Christian whispered, running a hand through Véronique's hair, which was splayed across the bedclothes. 'I believe this is yours.'

Her eyelids fluttered open and she focused on the silver cross he was holding. Then she sat up, awake in an instant. 'Did you mean it?' she asked.

He knew straight away what she meant. 'Yes. Of course. I'm sorry I didn't hang around for the answer. Did you accept?'

Véronique smiled, dimples creasing her cheeks. 'I've asked First Deputy René Piquemal to post the banns today. We get married in ten days' time.'

And he pulled her to him, the pain beneath the bandages around his chest far outweighed by the lightness in his heart.

Dawn. It streaked across the mountaintops, laying fingers of pink on the stony crags and sprinkling the fields with dew.

It was cold. Perhaps that was what woke him. Or maybe it was the loud snort from nearby.

He came to slowly, head groggy, limbs heavy. What . . . where . . . ?

He became aware of the damp that had seeped into his clothes, the tickle of grass on his nose. He opened an eye. A field. Green, stretching before him, a neat fence at the far end and beyond that, the Pyrenean peaks, looking magnificent in the first rays of sun.

Moving gingerly, he lifted his head, the dull ache making him feel nauseous. Then he pulled his legs under him, preparing to stand. Like a newborn calf, he rose to his feet, tottering slightly as he gained his balance.

Where was he?

He turned his head and heard once again that snorting sound. And caught on the breeze an odour so strong, so animalistic, that he knew at once where he was.

'Sarko!' he squeaked as he pirouetted round to see Christian Dupuy's Limousin bull standing some distance away, head down, pawing at the ground. No fence between them, just shivering strands of grass.

He was in a field with Sarko the bull. Pascal Souquet was in trouble.

'Help!' he shouted, patting his pockets for his mobile phone. 'Help!'

But his pockets were empty and no one replied. Not even the two men crouched in the trees close by.

'How long should I give him?' asked the shorter of the two, who was wearing an orange hunting beret.

The larger man shrugged. 'Long enough so he'll be happy to talk.'

'And you're recording it?'

The other man grinned. 'I'm not. Sarko the bull is. Straight onto the internet.'

When Nurse Sophie Pujol called back in on her favourite patient much later in the morning, she saw, with a tut of disapproval, that his ward was crowded, his 'family' having grown considerably since the day before. Spotting her uncle amongst the gathering, and it being the end of her shift, she decided not to reprimand them. It was with some disappointment, though, as she pushed open the door, that she noticed the gorgeous fake doctor wasn't there.

'So,' she said, strolling into the room to take Christian's chart. 'How is Widow Loubet this morning?'

A burst of laughter met her greeting.

Christian had never felt better. Which was bizarre as it was only three days ago that he'd been shot in the chest at close range.

'Widow Loubet indeed!' said Véronique, sitting next to her fiancé, his hand in hers as Nurse Pujol checked his chart. 'I can't believe you took him out of the hospital, Maman. You could have killed him!'

'Pah!' Annie dismissed the accusation with a grin. 'It did him good. He became mayorrr and he had enough enerrrgy left to prrropose!'

'Not enough to stay awake for the answer though,' quipped René.

More laughter and Christian blushed.

'Ten days. It's not much time to get a wedding sorted,' said Josephine Dupuy as the nurse left the room. 'Still, it's not as if I'm catering for it!'

'Thank God,' muttered André Dupuy with a grin.

'I suppose we need to start packing,' continued Josephine. 'Though I don't know where we'll move to.'

'There's no hurry, Maman,' said Christian.

'No, none at all,' agreed Véronique. 'My flat will do us for now.'

'As long as we can get a bigger bed!'

It was Véronique's turn to blush.

'We might be able to help you,' said Stephanie to Josephine Dupuy, her landlady of nine years. 'We're hoping to move so you could live in the cottage.'

'No!' Annie looked shocked, her eyes going to Chloé who was sitting on the end of the bed, a smile dancing on her lips. 'You'rrre leaving Fogas?'

Stephanie shook her head. 'Not if we can help it.'

'Actually, it's Véronique who can help,' corrected Fabian. 'We were wondering,' he continued, turning to the postmistress, 'if you would be willing to sell the old Papon house up in Picarets?'

Véronique didn't hesitate. 'To you? Of course. I've been thinking about selling it but I didn't want second-home owners moving in. You'd be perfect.'

'But what's wrong with the cottage?' asked Christian.

'Nothing,' said Stephanie. 'It's just—'

'Maman's expecting a baby!' blurted Chloé, no longer able to tolerate the diplomacy of adults. 'And I'm getting a trapeze.'

Congratulations rained down on the newlyweds and on the

budding acrobat who was about to become a big sister. In the midst of the noise, René heard his phone sounding.

An email. From Arnaud Petit. Simply entitled 'Urgent' and containing an internet link.

He clicked on it and the sound of an enraged animal filled the ward.

'Sarko!' said Christian, sitting up and wincing at the effort. 'What's happening?'

'It's the Sarko cam,' said René. He held out his phone so everyone could see the blurred images being projected from the camera around the bull's neck, a person visible in the foreground. 'Someone is in the field with him.'

'Oh God,' groaned the famer, struggling to get out of the bed. 'Bloody idiot tourists, they'll get killed. We need to get up there.'

'No, wait!' René increased the volume and suddenly they could hear him – Pascal Souquet, sobbing, pleading.

'Please,' came the disembodied voice. 'Please help me.'

Then another voice. 'Tell the truth, Pascal, and I'll call him off.'

'That's Bernard,' exclaimed Christian, peering at the screen where two blurred figures could now be seen, one a lot closer than the other. Too close given Sarko's temperament.

'It was Henri Dedieu. All of it,' gabbled Pascal Souquet, his face clear enough now to show his abject terror. 'It was all his idea . . .'

The people in the ward watched in awe as Pascal Souquet told them and the entire universe about Henri Dedieu – about the way they'd faked the attacks, about the death of the bear, about the raid on Véronique's flat, and about stealing Véronique's phone and setting up Christian at the quarry.

'I've told you everything,' he finally said, his sobs almost drowned out by the snorting of the bull. 'Please, Bernard. He's going to kill me.'

'Jesus, Bernard,' swore Christian to the unheeding camera. 'You're never going to get him out of there.'

But Bernard Mirouze knew a thing or two about Sarko the bull. As the sun hit the field with dazzling force and the bull lowered his head for a fatal charge, the *cantonnier*, satisfied he had got a full confession, whipped off his orange beret and with a flick of his wrist, sent it sailing across the field, the material turned vibrant in the sunshine.

Sarko should have known better. He was a wily creature and he'd had this trick played on him before. But he couldn't resist the burning disk as it flew over his head. And with a snort, he was off, chasing the elusive beret down the far end of the field.

The camera of course went with him.

'Did Pascal get out?' asked René, as the image focused on an orange circle of material, hooves and horns tearing it to shreds.

'Shame if he did,' muttered Annie.

'Mon Dieu!' said Christian, slumping back weakly into the bed. 'I don't think I can take much more of this.'

'But at least we have a confession now,' said René. 'All we need next is for Henri Dedieu to be caught.'

'Has there been any sign of him?' asked Josephine Dupuy.

René shook his head. 'The gendarmes called up there this morning after they took Christian's statement, but he was gone. Hunting apparently. There was no sign of the pistol he used to shoot Christian. The one with the boar's head on it you dug up last summer, Fabian, remember?'

They all remembered. The fun of the treasure hunt wedding proposal that had backfired and unearthed a war relic and scared the potential bride-to-be.

Stephanie shuddered, recalling the feeling she'd had when she'd touched the old weapon. 'That gun. I said it would bring trouble.'

'Yeah,' muttered Christian. 'You did. You told me you couldn't read my tarot cards too . . .'

Stephanie flinched. 'Sorry, Christian. It was so vague. All I saw was turmoil and violence. I didn't know what to say.'

'I'm not sure I'd have believed you anyway,' said Christian with a smile.

'So, what's happening with the council in Sarrat?' asked André Dupuy. 'Are they going to keep Dedieu as mayor?'

René grinned. 'Not a chance! The Conseil Municipal has already petitioned to have him removed. I think a few of the councillors might take this opportunity to retire too . . .'

'Huh!' Annie snorted. 'Rrrats and sinking ships!'

'Well, at least it will mean no more talk of a merger,' said Christian. 'I can't see any of them having the appetite to resurrect that idea after all this. Not when the gendarmes are chasing the last man who proposed it.'

'Are they out looking for him, then?' Josephine asked.

'Yes. And they'll find him too,' said René.

'Not unless Arnaud finds him first,' retorted Chloé with conviction.

The room fell silent as they digested what the youngster had said. And without exception, all of them were betting on the tracker.

It was the endgame. He knew it. The authorities were involved. They'd been to his house. Luckily he still had enough contacts in the area that he'd got a tip off and he'd made for the hills, telling his wife he was going hunting. The gendarmes would have found nothing incriminating. Nothing to back up the ludicrous story that Christian Dupuy would be telling.

Henri Dedieu was confident he could brazen this out. There was just one minor detail; one insignificant fact that needed to be dealt with.

Pausing, he took his bearings, shifting the rifle that hung across his shoulder as he surveyed the landscape. Forest, buds beginning to appear on the trees, and through the trunks and down below, the Estaque farm on its lonely ridge.

Another twenty minutes and he'd be at the rendezvous. Though why Pascal Souquet had chosen such a remote place to meet confounded him. It wasn't like the man was a natural woodsman – just the reverse. He must be panicked to have made it all the way up here.

Henri Dedieu had got the text message that morning. Brief in content, it had still managed to convey the man's loss of control, the threat of exposure if help wasn't imminent.

Fortunately for the failed interim mayor of Fogas, he wouldn't have to worry about how he would get back down the mountain. Henri Dedieu and his family heirloom would see to that.

He followed him with ease, footsteps light across the forest floor as he tracked his prey. This was the one. The one he'd been waiting for. For the second time that morning, he took the trail above the Estaque farm, knowing that everything was in place. The time for revenge had finally come.

Arnaud Petit, hair pulled back in a ponytail, face fierce as he moved panther-like through the woods, wasn't going to let this one go.

Bernard Mirouze had never had a morning like it. Having extracted a confession from the spineless Pascal Souquet, who was now in the custody of the gendarmes, he'd driven up to the track on the opposite side of Picarets; the very place where Agnès had discovered him the day before.

Agnès! She'd woken him when the alarm went off before dawn and handed him a packed breakfast and a flask, along with food for Serge the beagle. She'd asked no questions, knowing the mission was covert. But she was proud of her boys. He could see it in her eyes. She'd sent him off with a kiss on the cheek and Serge with a pat on the head, and told them to be safe.

It wasn't them who had to worry.

Bernard glanced at the clock on the dashboard. It was time to go.

Donning his spare orange beret – the one he'd put on this morning now no more than strips of fabric in Christian's field – he picked up his rifle and got out of the car. Reaching for the snoozing beagle on the passenger seat, he was almost reluctant to involve him. It could be dangerous after all. But he was part of Bernard's cover and so the *cantonnier* gently lifted him onto the ground.

'Come on, Serge,' he said, clipping a lead onto the dog's collar. 'We've got to go hunting.'

He was standing on a small path, the trees thinning as the land dropped away to a clearing down below. An enclave ringed by ash and oak, rocks strewn across the grass. In the dappled sunlight of a March morning, it was paradise.

It was also bear country.

He slipped his hand in his pocket, fingers curling around the familiar handgrip. Pascal should be further along the path to the left, standing above the large creviced rock, awaiting help.

Henri Dedieu was going to make sure he got it.

The man in front was cautious, moving more quietly now, sneaking up on his rendezvous, his right hand in his pocket.

The tracker didn't need to guess what was in there.

Ah well. Two birds with one stone.

He hung back, moving sideways to circle his prey and get ahead of him, making for the twisted oak tree above the creviced rock. It was time to lure him in. He didn't rush, feet placed carefully as he crossed the rough terrain. No point in spooking him now. It wasn't as if he was going to be getting away. Not this time. Not ever again.

'Pascal?' Henri Dedieu whispered. Then he caught the rustle of careless footsteps and a subdued cough from up ahead on the narrow path where a twisted oak marked the edge of the precipice. He fixed a smile on his face as his hand discreetly pulled the gun from his pocket.

'Pascal? I'm here. How can I help, my friend?'

If he'd stayed where he was, had the patience of a true hunter and let the prey come to him, he would have been fine. But the proximity of his target set his heart pacing, dulled his instincts. And so he took a step forward, gun raised, preparing to shoot on sight. He didn't notice the slightly different shade of the earth beneath his feet, the uniform covering of leaves.

One last fatal step and then the ground exploded, dirt and forest debris flung into the air as two ferocious steel jaws sprang up and bit deeply into his left leg. He was aware of losing his balance, his leg collapsing, tipping him backwards, the gun flying from his hand. He heard the bones shattering, felt the tendons sliced through, saw a shard of white protruding jaggedly out of his skin. Then he heard a hideous noise, a high-pitched cry so primeval it felt trapped inside his head.

The mayor of Sarrat's scream echoed around the enclosure, tearing through the leafless trees and shredding the solitude of the forest.

*

It was a raw brutal sound. Harsh. Discordant. Suffering in its purest form. It set the tracker running. A couple of long strides and he saw him, lying on the ground, screaming, blood covering his leg, his hands reaching down, clawing uselessly at the steel trap that held him.

His own trap.

Arnaud Petit watched the man without remorse. Then he turned and walked away.

Bernard had made good time. So when the horrific noise tore through the woods, he wasn't far away. Serge cowered as the scream rippled past; Bernard slipped the rifle off his shoulder and into his hands.

The man would be trapped. He would be desperate. But Bernard wasn't afraid. He knew what he had to do. This was justice.

The scream ricocheted around the enclave down below. It bounced off the rocks and thundered back from the trees. It was loud enough to disturb even sleeping creatures. Deep in the crevice of the largest rock, Miel, the brown bear who had been the focus of so much chaos in the commune of Fogas the summer before, was roused from her hibernation by the noise.

She lumbered half-asleep over to the opening in the rock and placed her nose in the air.

Spring. It was here. And beyond the smell of early flowers, something else . . . The heavy scent of humans. Then she heard it again – a wail from an animal in distress. She stood on her hind feet and lifted herself up, letting out a low moan in response.

The emergency call from a Monsieur Mirouze was sent to both Massat and St Girons. A man was caught in an illegal trap in the woods above the Estaque farm. Annie, recently returned from the hospital, saw the ambulance go haring past, the gendarmes and fire brigade after it, and said a silent prayer that it wouldn't be someone she knew.

The Rogalle twins and Chloé, playing in the front garden of the old Papon house, which was no longer out of bounds seeing as Chloé would soon be living there, stopped their games to watch the vehicles race past. And Agnès Rogalle, who'd juggled her delivery schedule to make sure she was in Picarets that morning, paused in serving her distant cousin, Grand-mère Rogalle – a lady whose feathers were still ruffled over the unauthorised requisition of her favourite dress – to stare after the flashing lights and send a fervent wish to the God above that her two boys, Bernard and Serge, would be okay. In an afterthought, she added Arnaud Petit into her devotions. The man was too good a specimen to be lost.

'So you stumbled upon him while out hunting?' The young gendarme was watching Bernard intently.

'Yes,' said Bernard, convincingly pale from shock.

'Just like you came across Pascal Souquet in a field with a bull this morning?' asked the older gendarme lightly.

Bernard shrugged, the gesture making his belly wobble. 'I'd rather have come across a boar. Something I can take home to the missus!'

The older gendarme smiled. 'Well, it was lucky for both men that you were around.'

Luck had had nothing to do with it, but the *cantonnier* of Fogas wasn't about to admit that. 'Will he . . . I mean . . . Henri Dedieu . . . is he going to survive?'

'I can't say. The paramedics got here in good time. But he lost a lot of blood. And when he regains consciousness, we've got a lot of questions we need to ask him. Particularly about the distinctive handgun we found next to him.' The gendarme shook his head, looking back at the patch of forest floor covered in blood, the dismantled trap still lying there. 'He's wanted for the attempted murder of Christian Dupuy. And now this. He gets caught in one of his own traps while setting it. Who would have thought it? The mayor of Sarrat, of all people. And the deputy mayor of Fogas under arrest too.'

The younger gendarme didn't share his colleague's shock. 'Pah! Politicians. They're the worst of the lot. But I don't think those two will be at liberty anytime soon. As for you, Monsieur Mirouze, we'll need you to call in to the office in Massat to make a formal statement later today if that's okay?'

Bernard nodded, feeling suddenly tired. He'd followed his instructions to the letter and everything had turned out as it was supposed to. Now he just wanted to see Agnès. He picked up his dog before speaking.

'If it's all right with you, I'd like to go home first. It's been a long morning.'

The two gendarmes stood aside and Bernard made his way wearily down the mountain towards his car. His day of hunting was over. In fact, after what he'd just witnessed, he thought all his hunting days might be over.

'Sorry, Serge,' he said as he laid the dog back on the passenger seat. 'I think you've just been retired. You can stick with catching rabbits from now on.'

The dog pushed his head into Bernard's hand and let out a sharp bark. And in the bright light of the morning, the pair of them set off home.

25

On the first day of spring in the Pyrenees, high in the mountains not far from where the border of France touches that of Spain and Andorra, in the small village of La Rivière in the commune of Fogas, bells were ringing. Long joyful peals spilled from the arching tower of the Romanesque church, tumbling over the graveyard below, stretching over the river and across the fields bathed in sunlight. And under that exultant canopy of sound, the people of the commune were gathered.

'He looks good considering—'

'Not as good as he did in Grand-mère Rogalle's dress—!'

'And nowhere near as good as the bride—'

'Someone pass me a tissue—'

At the front of the church, being given the final blessing for their new life together, Christian Dupuy and Véronique Estaque stood staring at each other.

'I love you,' he murmured as he reached down to kiss his wife.

'And I love you too,' she replied, stretching up to return his embrace.

The gentle sound of sobbing could be heard from both front rows, the groom's party being no less prone to tearful celebration than the bride's. And then, hands clasped firmly together, the recently crowned mayor of Fogas and his beautiful mayoress walked down the aisle and out into the spring sunshine. A hail of petals and rice met them, raining down along with shouts of congratulations and wishes for the future.

With Chloé Morvan having taken charge of the route that would bring the newlyweds to their reception at the Auberge, the couple were guided by fluttering silk ribbons tied along the way, not down past the burnt-out post office as would be expected, but up the road to a small path. Followed by their guests, they picked their way along the uneven ground which led behind the épicerie gardens, the wall Christian had once scaled in a snowstorm down below. Then, at the handmade signpost being held by one of the Rogalle twins, they veered left, in through a gate at the back of what had once been an abandoned orchard that lay between the épicerie and the old school. Today, the fruit trees which Stephanie had been lovingly tending were covered in soft blossom, pink and white flowers providing an archway of spring for the bride and groom, and blue and yellow crocuses a soft carpet underfoot.

'It's beautiful,' breathed Véronique, tears in her eyes.

Christian nodded, unable to speak, the memories of childhood and adulthood and the potential of the new life that stretched before him overcoming him completely.

When they reached the road, they turned left at the other Rogalle twin's direction, and came along the front of the bar where two familiar but invisible faces were waiting for them.

'They're here!' shouted Jacques Servat even though Serge Papon was standing right next to him.

And they were. True to her word, Chloé Morvan had brought the bride and groom to where the two ghosts could see them. Christian Dupuy, resplendent in a suit which hung a little on his thinner frame following his accident, walking slowly, his left hand leaning on a walking stick with a carved stag's head. And on his right, Véronique, formerly known as Estaque, but as of ten minutes before, now a Dupuy. Auburn hair twisted through with small red roses, silver cross sparkling at her neck, in a simple dress of lace and satin, the bride looked exquisite. And happy.

'She's beautiful,' said Jacques, slapping his friend on the back.

'She looks just like Maman,' said Serge, his eyes filling with tears of joy and of regret. Then he cleared his throat, straightened his back and turned to Jacques. 'How do I look?'

Jacques inspected the former mayor, leaning forward to flatten an errant strand of hair. 'Like the father of the bride,' he said.

And the pair of them stood up on the chairs Josette had left beneath the window.

'Stop! Stop!' A voice was shouting from the long line of guests outside and Chloé came racing up. 'We need to take a photo.'

'Herrre?' asked Annie, looking questioningly at the backdrop of the bar window.

Chloé nodded firmly. 'Yes, here.' And she made the wedding party line up on the terrace, including a few extras like René and Bernard and Serge the beagle and, after much persuasion, the best man, Arnaud Petit. Then, handing her mobile to Alain Rougé, she ran across to join them.

'Smile!' said Alain.

And they did – Christian and Véronique and Stephanie and Fabian and Annie and Josette and Chloé and all the rest. And behind them, peering over their heads, Serge Papon, father of the bride, and his best friend, Jacques, grinning from ear to ear.

'Can we go and eat now?' grumbled René as Alain signalled they could step down from the terrace. 'This marrying business makes me hungry.'

'Of course,' said Christian, placing an arm around his deputy who, earlier that morning, had officiated over the civil wedding up in the town hall, the chimes of the repaired clock commemorating the occasion. 'And thanks, René.'

'For what?' asked the plumber.

'For saving my life. Without you, I wouldn't be here today.'

'And without you,' said René gruffly, 'I'd be enjoying a cigarette right now!'

On a wave of laughter, they carried on, down towards the Auberge at the end of the village, where, what seemed so long ago, it had all begun.

'Arnaud's staying, you know,' said Véronique to Christian as she caught sight of the tall, dark figure, his black hair long across his shoulders, his movements lithe as he bent to talk to Annie. 'He's going to open an outdoor centre up in Picarets. Offering courses in tracking and the like.'

Christian smiled. It was good news. The man had become a close friend. And as mayor, Christian couldn't help but think of the extra income such a business would generate for the commune. Likewise, the venture Bernard and Agnès were setting up, a butcher's shop here in La Rivière, would be vital for the community.

'We owe him a lot,' continued Véronique. 'After all, Arnaud was the one who brought you out of the coma.' She glanced at her husband. 'You never did tell me what he said to make you wake up.'

Christian shrugged. 'I don't recall his words,' he lied. 'I think I was coming round anyway. But yes, Fogas owes him a lot.'

If Véronique doubted his answer, she never said. But there was no way, wedding day or not, Christian would tell her the truth. Because he remembered. And in remembering he held his wife's hand even tighter. For the farmer had been torn from his comatose state by the direst of threats, the voice of Arnaud Petit penetrating his subconscious to tell him that if he didn't wake up soon, he, Arnaud Petit, would marry Véronique in Christian's absence.

It was a threat Christian had taken seriously.

'One last photo!' said Alain Rougé, as they reached the bridge just up from the Auberge, Paul and Lorna Webster coming out to join them, their twins in their arms.

'Do we have to?' groaned René, his stomach grumbling at the scent of roast lamb filling the air. 'Can't we go in and eat?'

'Come on,' said Josette. 'It won't hurt. Everyone in this time.'

And so Alain Rougé set up a camera on the wall of the bridge, shouting and gesturing until his audience could all be seen.

'Where's Chloé?' asked Fabian, stretching his long neck to see over the heads around him.

'Therrre,' said Annie, pointing back along the road.

'Chloé!' called Stephanie. 'Come on. We're taking a photo.'

Up at the bar, Chloé Morvan was sharing the day with the two ghosts inside, holding her phone up to the window and scrolling through the photos she'd taken of the happy couple.

She hated to leave them, these guardians of Fogas who watched over everyone yet missed out on all the fun. But Maman was calling her from the bridge.

'I have to go,' she mouthed at Jacques.

His white head nodded.

Then she waved and was gone, running down the road in a manner that suggested she had already forgotten she was wearing a dress.

'That's Fogas, right there,' said Serge proudly, watching the people on the bridge laughing and joking in the warm sunshine as Chloé was welcomed into their midst, Tomate the Auberge cat in her arms. 'That's what we've been fighting for.'

'And Christian is going to make a wonderful mayor,' said Jacques with equal pride, the blond curls of the man he'd always considered a surrogate son standing out from the crowd.

'That's as may be,' said Serge, arms folding across his chest. 'But Véronique will make a better one.'

'Véronique . . . ?' Jacques turned round ready to argue and then saw the twinkle in his old friend's eyes. 'Oh, Serge,' he said, laughing, an arm around the other man's shoulders. 'I think we've finally left Fogas in a safe set of hands.'

Acknowledgements

As with the previous Fogas Chronicles, the shaping of this final volume has benefited from a rich and varied input, all of which was gratefully received – if not always adhered to! Consequently, any errors, should they arise, must be placed firmly at my door. Or Bernard Mirouze's. For their advice, belief and endless encouragement, I owe the following a miniature-Sarko toy and a pastis:

Sally Roe, Ariège neighbour, friend and ICU nurse – I pulled the tubes out, Mrs Roe!; Pauline Green, for advice on all things Tarot and for being so open to someone asking crazy questions; the *Association des Maires Ruraux de France*, which never tires of my enquiries and whose circular emails reinforce my belief that there are many communes like Fogas in France; Jacqueline Brown, for invaluable behind-the-scenes insight into the voting process in French local elections and for setting a brilliant example of participating in politics by becoming a *conseiller* – Serge Papon would approve!; Jean-Michel Motte, a Frenchman who has settled in my hometown and willingly responds to my sporadic demands for help with his native language; Jane Marshall, for dragging me away from my desk and onto my bike when I need it most; Ellen McMaster and Claire Jones, first readers and wonderful sisters whose support and honest input is always vital and always (nearly always!) right; Brenda Stickland for reading first drafts and loving Fogas so much; my parents, Mícheál and Ellen Stagg

– see what happens when you make a kid tell stories?; the amazing team at Hodder who yet again have produced a wonderful cover and worked so hard on my behalf – thanks especially to Francesca, who is everything an editor should be; the mighty Oli, for keeping everything ticking and for always looking to the future; and to Mark, who believed long before I did – Fogas owes a lot to you, *mon amour*! Finally, to the people of the Couserans district of the Ariège: for the inspiration that led to the chronicles and for safeguarding such a special area – *mille fois merci*!

The chronicles of Fogas continue with

Julia Stagg

THE PARISIAN'S RETURN

Cri de coeur

When Stephanie brains an intruder with a stale baguette, she doesn't realise she has assaulted the new owner of the *épicerie*. Fabian's welcome goes from bad to worse as his attempts to drag the shop into the modern age are met with a resounding *non!* by the residents of the small commune of Fogas in the French Pyrenees. He is on the verge of admitting defeat when he's hit by a *coup de foudre* and falls in love.

Stephanie herself is too busy for *l'amour*. Working at *l'Auberge* and getting her garden centre off the ground is taking all her energy. She doesn't even notice that her daughter Chloé has something on her mind. Troubled by a sinister stranger she has seen loitering in the village, Chloé has no one to turn to. Her only hope is that someone hears her cries for help before it's all too late.

In a *chanson d'amour* with more twists than a mountain road, the unexpected is just around the corner.

Out now in paperback and ebook

The third chronicle of Fogas

Julia Stagg

THE FRENCH POSTMISTRESS

Zut Alors!

When her post office burns down, postmistress Véronique starts lobbying for its replacement. But her fellow residents of the small commune of Fogas in the French Pyrenees are too preoccupied to rally to her cause.

Mayor Serge Papon, overwhelmed by grief at the death of his wife, has lost his *joie de vivre* and all taste for village politics (and croissants) and it seems as though deputy mayor Christian (whose *tendresse* for Véronique makes him her usual champion) will soon be saying *au revoir* to the mountain community. And to Sarko the bull.

Add to this a controversial government initiative to reintroduce bears to the area and soon the inhabitants are at loggerheads, threatening the progress of the sacred *Tour de France* and the very existence of Fogas itself.

Out now in paperback and ebook

A Fogas novella

Julia Stagg

A CHRISTMAS WEDDING

It's six days before Christmas, and preparations are well underway in the little French village of Fogas for Stephanie and Fabian's wedding on Christmas Eve.

Their best-laid plans are scuppered, however, when the caterers and the venue both call to cancel. And on top of that, Fabian wants to know what love is . . . He has last-minute jitters which everyone, bar Stephanie, is well aware of.

With only days to go, the Pyrenean mountain community must pull together if the festive nuptials are to go ahead. It's all set to be a Christmas they'll never forget . . .

Out now in ebook only

Do you wish this wasn't the end?

Join us at www.hodder.co.uk, or follow us on Twitter @hodderbooks to be a part of our community of people who love the very best in books and reading.

Whether you want to discover more about a book or an author, watch trailers and interviews, have the chance to win early limited editions, or simply browse our expert readers' selection of the very best books, we think you'll find what you're looking for.

And if you don't,
that's the place to tell us what's missing.

We love what we do, and we'd love you to be part of it.